MU
IN
THE FOLLY

by Margaret Addison

A Rose Simpson Mystery

Rose Simpson Mysteries (in order)

Murder at Ashgrove House
Murder at Dareswick Hall
Murder at Sedgwick Court
Murder at Renard's
Murder in the Servants' Hall
Murder on Bonfire Night
Murder in the Folly

Chapter One

Cordelia Quail sat back heavily in the sturdy garden chair. The wood gave a momentary groan as it received her ample frame, clothed in generous amounts of silk satin. The woman in question, however, appeared quite oblivious to the potential collapse of her seat and the subsequent threat to her dignity. Her attention, instead, was drawn to the spectacle in front of her. Patting the back of her silk velvet turban in rather a distracted fashion, she surveyed the scene with an appraising eye, her position on the grass lawn affording her an excellent view.

From her vantage point on the sloping lawn, which descended gently from the makeshift stage and ran down to the lake behind her, she could see one or two small groups of amateur thespians huddled together gossiping, or going through lines. It was not this, however, that swelled Cordelia's heart and made her stop for a moment in her contemplations to take a breath. Rather, it was the stage itself. A folly or eye-catcher, it was an imposing building of smooth grey stone. Rectangular in shape, it resembled an Ancient Greek temple with a portico of six fluted columns, constructed in the Corinthian style. Topped by a triangulated roof, the great pillars appeared to loom up out of the very earth itself, dominating the immediate landscape. This perception of scale was further heightened by the positioning of the folly on the top of a grass mound, which acted as a plinth of sorts, displaying the edifice to perfection.

'Magnificent,' said Cordelia to herself in a voice that carried, for she rarely spoke quietly. Certainly, one or two of the actors looked up sharply, and not a little nervously, for Cordelia Quail had a formidable reputation among the Sedgwick Players as a director not to be trifled with. Only vaguely aware of the fear that she generated in the hearts of the younger thespians in particular, Cordelia gave a contented sigh, the action making her chair wobble in a most precarious manner. Yes, the folly was undoubtedly an ideal setting for Shakespeare's longest play. For the temple lent itself most readily to represent the castle of Elsinore. The acting might be found wanting, but the set could not be criticised. She congratulated herself heartily for her own initiative. For hadn't it been she who had suggested to Hilda Best, the Player's honorary secretary, that the woman write to inquire in to the possibility of staging a play in the grounds of Sedgwick Court?

A frown creased Cordelia's forehead for a moment and she sniffed contemptuously. Of course, Algernon would insist that it had all been his idea, but then he would. He was like that. It was very small-minded of him, but there it was and there was very little one could do about it. She cleared her throat and dealt with her frustration by glaring surreptitiously at the man in question, who was playing Claudius, trying to find fault in the way he was conducting himself among the younger actors and actresses. Certainly, he was preening himself, as if he considered himself an object to be admired. No doubt he was regaling his attentive audience with tales of the many plays in which he had performed or directed. Though she was too far away to catch his words, Cordelia could well imagine that he was telling them of the rapacious receptions he had received, the standing ovations as the audience demanded that he remain on stage to receive their adoration.

Cordelia bit her lip and, in spite of herself, admitted rather grudgingly that there was something about Algernon Cuffe that set him apart from the common man. It was predominantly his manner, she supposed, though his height and bearing made him appear regal, which was particularly suited to his present role as King of Denmark. He might have a slight tendency to fat, but clad in ermine and velvet, he certainly looked the part of usurper to Old Hamlet's throne. Very quickly on the heels of this notion came the thought that she really must remember to congratulate Mrs Simpson on the costumes. What a find she had been for the company. She had done a simply marvellous job of clothing the Sedgwick Players for their parts. By turning her head, Cordelia spared a glance at the woman in question. She was standing at the edge of the lake, holding up a length of shimmering satin, which Cordelia presumed she was considering for Ophelia.

Somewhat reluctantly, Cordelia returned to her study of Algernon. Inwardly she cursed herself for noticing that his hair was still a fine shade of auburn, the colour it had been when first she had made his acquaintance some seven years ago. Only now, if one looked very closely, could one glimpse the first signs of grey, highlighting the hair like drops of ice on a frosty day. Algernon had grown a full beard to play his character which, in contrast, was a most striking shade of red. The thought idly crossed Cordelia's mind that he would make a very fine King Henry the Eighth, should he ever be required to play the role.

Cordelia was brought up with a start. Unintentionally, she had caught the eye of the actress playing Gertrude. Quickly she looked away. Trust Ursula Stapleton to be watching her. Had she seen the way she had been staring at Algernon, Cordelia wondered? Mooning, that's what the young people called it, and she felt her cheeks grow crimson. Ursula, though rather advanced in years like herself, would no doubt delight in her discomfort. Cordelia saw Ursula lean forward and whisper something in Miriam's ear. The younger woman, her hair tangled and in disarray following her mad scene as Ophelia, turned and stared at her. Even the awful Prentice twins standing beside them were giggling as if at the same shared joke.

For one awful moment, Cordelia saw herself in their eyes. They would consider her little more than a belligerent director, a plain aging woman indulging in foolish fancies. Flustered and embarrassed, she clutched at the sides of her chair and averted her gaze, staring instead down at the lawn, marvelling, in spite of herself, at how green the grass was in the late afternoon sunshine. She caught the sound of laughter and her cheeks, still flushed, turned a deeper shade of red. She lifted her head and sought out the identity of the person mocking her. However, no one appeared to be staring at her, or affording her any attention. Perhaps she had imagined it, or it had not been directed at her. She gave herself a stern talking to. It really didn't matter much either way, though she still found herself clapping her hands loudly and bringing the break to a close rather sooner than she had intended.

Out of the corner of her eye she noticed that Algernon was staring at her in surprise and even the Prentice twins looked taken aback, as if they had been planning to play some odious trick before the rehearsals resumed and realised that they had been denied their fun. None of this troubled Cordelia, however, who noted with something akin to delight that she had now regained control of the situation. For it was to her that the face of every thespian was turned, as they waited on her command.

Cordelia rose abruptly from her seat, and it was only due to the sudden intervention of an attentive footman that her chair did not topple over.

Pulling back her shoulders and drawing herself up to her full height, she spoke to the cast in a voice that carried over the air to the folly.

'Places please, ladies and gentlemen, and that includes you Freddie and Gerald,' Cordelia said, looking pointedly at the Prentice twins, who looked half minded to saunter down to the lake probably to skim pebbles across its tranquil surface. 'We'll do the final scene now, I think. Let me see …' She broke off and looked down at the script in her hand. 'Yes … I don't see why we shouldn't start at the very beginning of the scene with the entrance of Hamlet and Horatio and proceed on to the end of the play.'

There was a series of groans and mutterings among the cast, which Cordelia was swift to dismiss with a wave of her hand.

'It is all very well to rehearse this scene in two parts as we usually do, but on the night of the performance itself we shall have to perform it as one continuous scene.' Cordelia smiled at them encouragingly. 'And do remember that this is the dramatic ending for which the audience has been waiting. There needs to be passion and a sense of urgency. I want the audience to hold its breath with excitement until the final curtain falls.'

'I didn't think we were having a curtain as such,' said Freddie Prentice.

Cordelia ignored him and threw her arms up in the air in a dramatic gesture. 'A magnificent sword fight fought between two young men avenging their fathers' deaths. A fencing match –'

'If you please, Miss Quail,' interrupted Gerald Prentice, a little more tentatively than his brother, 'Freddie and I are not in this scene.'

'No,' agreed Freddie. 'We're supposed to be on our way to England to suffer our miserable fate. Or are we actually dead by this stage in the play? I can't remember, but whichever it is, it's not very sporting of Hamlet, is it? Arranging that his old school chums be killed in his place, I mean. It's not their fault if they're buffoons.'

'They're not the full shilling,' concurred Gerald, with increased confidence. 'But dead or riding the ocean waves, we're quite definitely not in this scene, Miss Quail.'

'Today, you are,' Cordelia said firmly, glaring at the twins. Really, she couldn't count the number of times she had despaired of the young men. Why would they not take their parts seriously? She could, however, blame no one but herself and she admonished herself severely. How clever she thought she had been to cast monozygotic twins as Rosencrantz and

Guildenstern. It hadn't occurred to her then to consider the boys' characters. After all, everyone knew they had both been sent down from Oxford for playing some foolish prank.

'You will both play the parts of courtiers and attendants and Freddie, as you appear to have so much to say in the matter, you will also read the part of the lord and … ah, Walter, there you are,' Cordelia added as she spied a man, small in stature and of middle years, lurking unobtrusively behind one of the middle columns, looking for all the world as if he wished to be invisible. 'Now, remember, Walter, you have thrown off the mantle of Polonius. You are now playing Osric, a far more outlandish version of the Lord Chamberlain.'

'Yes, Cordelia,' Walter mumbled, with some reluctance. He made to move to the edge of the stage and hesitated for a moment before turning to face the director. 'You don't think it will confuse the audience, do you, if I play both parts?' There was a forlorn note of hope in his voice that was not lost on Cordelia. 'I mean to say, will they realise I am playing another character? Won't they think me Polonius in disguise?'

'Polonius is dead,' said Cordelia.

'Aren't we all?' said Freddie, supposedly in a whisper, though Cordelia heard him quite clearly.

'The audience witness him being murdered,' said Cordelia coldly, glaring at the twins. 'They also see Hamlet drag his body off the stage. I think we can, therefore, safely assume the audience will be left in little doubt that he is dead.' She turned her back on them before anyone was tempted to prolong the discussion. 'And besides, Walter,' she added, as an afterthought, 'you will be dressed in a different costume, to say nothing of the fact that you will be wearing a wig.'

'If you say so,' Walter muttered in a resigned fashion.

'I do. Now … oh …' Cordelia broke off from what she was saying, aware of a sudden presence at her shoulder. Turning around, she found herself staring up in to the face of Miriam Belmore, with all its stony beauty. Cordelia gave an involuntary start for, not having seen the girl descend from the temple, she had thought her still on the stage with the other players.

'Oh Miriam, my dear, don't creep up on me like that; really, you did give me the most awful fright.'

There was no softening of the young woman's features, no sympathetic look. Instead, her eyes flashed black and she said rather impatiently: 'Do you require me anymore, Miss Quail? Like Freddie and Gerald, I'm not in this scene; long drowned and all that. And Mrs Simpson does keep beckoning to me. I think she's found a piece of material that she thinks will be more suitable for my dress. I mean to say, anything would be better than this old rag.' She looked down disparagingly at her gown and held out the skirt. 'Coarse cream cotton and it isn't a bit fitted. Really, Miss Quail, what were you thinking?'

'Now, now my dear,' said Cordelia in conciliatory tones, 'remember you are mentally deranged in your last scene. I want the audience to be shocked by your transformation from palace beauty to a mad young woman. Wearing something that resembles a sack will help the audience to realise something is very wrong with you.'

'I'd prefer to wear Mrs Simpson's pale blue satin,' Miriam said mulishly. 'We could tear the hem and make it look quite ragged.'

'We'll see, my dear,' said Cordelia, unwilling to be drawn. Really, the girl could be quite trying when she set her mind to it and Cordelia could not quell a feeling of resentment that was welling up inside her. She had been inclined to let Miriam have her own way as far as her costume was concerned because the girl was very prone to sulking, such a very unattractive trait in a young woman, she thought. This time, however, she was reluctant to give way. Perhaps it was the memory of the way Miriam had looked at her in that rude and insolent manner, when Ursula had whispered in her ear. Whatever it was, it made her say: 'Well, run along to Mrs Simpson now while Hamlet and Horatio are conversing, but I should like you to be on the stage for the fencing scene to play a member of the court. I shall need to know how many courtiers and attendants we shall require to fill the stage.' As much to put an end to the discussion as anything else, Cordelia turned and regarded the stage. 'Of course, I shan't want them to get in the way of the fighting ...'

When she looked back a moment or two later, Miriam had disappeared. Cordelia sighed and looked at her wristwatch. A frown appeared on that part of her forehead not concealed by her turban. Was it really a quarter to four? She had been intending that they go through the scene at least twice. Henry required as much practice as possible, unless he had miraculously managed to improve his swordsmanship, which was hardly likely given his performance at the last rehearsal when he had very nearly taken out poor Laertes' eye.

She was about to clap her hands again when Hamlet and Horatio appeared on the now empty stage and launched into verse.

'So much for this, sir; now let me see the other ...'

Cordelia smiled to herself tentatively. Henry had begun well. He was speaking loudly and with a sense of purpose, not mumbling or shuffling his feet. It was so very necessary in this scene that his character should appear confident, she thought. For was this not the part in the play when at last the prince fulfilled his promise to the ghost?

The scene progressed. Cordelia clenched her hands and bit her lip. Much to her surprise, Henry was playing the part very well indeed. She had cast Henry Rewe as Hamlet with some misgivings, but today he really was frightfully good, quite a joy to behold. She permitted herself to relax a little, and sat down slowly in the garden chair, arranging her Chinese, silk-embroidered kimono about her, her eyes not leaving the stage. A few minutes later and she was leaning forward in her chair, watching the scene unfold before her. Freddie entered to deliver the lord's lines, and though he stumbled over the unfamiliar words, she realised with a sudden thrill that she was caught up in the drama. It was almost as if she had never seen the play before, never winced or cringed during a succession of bad rehearsals. With almost bated breath, she looked forward immensely to the theatrical climax of Shakespeare's play.

Lady Belvedere proceeded along the earthen path that rose above the lake and wound its way between the firs, pines and weeping willows, which overhung the bank, casting shadows on the ground and reflections off the water. Centuries had flattened the earth so that underfoot the track was as smooth and regular as a man-made road. Only in a few places did the roots of trees protrude, causing an unwary visitor to stumble. The countess, however, did not lose her footing for she was familiar with the path.

As she approached the folly, the path, bordered by laurels and similar shrubs, followed a sharp incline, which forced the track to weave and twist its way between the rich undergrowth. The branches of the trees above seemed to extend towards her in something of a menacing fashion, their twigs like witches' fingers trying to claw and pull at her face and clothes. The young woman quickened her pace and darted expertly between the various obstacles. Though the path ahead of her was partially obscured by the rich canopy of trees, she knew that when she turned the corner the side of the folly, which had until that moment been concealed, would emerge, springing up out of its thick veil of leaves in majestic fashion. And though she was fully expecting to see it appear, and for the dappled grey stone to contrast sharply with the greenness of the leaves that framed it, she was still a little taken aback when she spied the temple. Not for the first time did she consider it remarkable that so large a structure could remain hidden from view until the very last minute. Had she approached the temple from the lake instead of the path, as the landscape architect had intended, she knew the temple would have been in constant view, drawing her eye and compelling her to come ashore and explore its depths.

As she had set off from the house rather later than she had intended due to an unexpected telephone call, she had half worried that she would discover the rehearsal had finished and that the Sedgwick Players had departed from the folly. Now, however, as she stood with her outstretched arm leaning against the cold wall of the temple, having stopped a moment to catch her breath, she caught the welcome sound of voices. Keeping to the wall, she edged her way forward, her fingers brushing over the smooth stone surface as she walked. The wall ended abruptly. Before her lay the temple's open portico with its six fluted columns, and beyond that Cordelia Quail perched on her chair on the lawn below. If she turned the corner, she would join the actors on the stage. Instead, Lady Belvedere crept away from the folly and descended the grassy bank. She walked slowly and quietly so as not to distract the actors on the stage, grateful for the grass underfoot which deadened the sound of her footsteps.

'The king and queen and all are coming down,' announced Freddie to his fellow actors on the stage.

Lady Belvedere breathed a sigh of relief. She had not missed the fencing match after all, and it was this event that had drawn her to the folly that afternoon. She made her way quickly across the grass to where her mother stood inspecting the costumes, a long trestle table in front of her covered in various yards of material, some of which shimmered in the late afternoon sun.

As she joined Mrs Simpson, she realised that, for all her care, her sudden appearance by the side of the folly had not gone unnoticed. It was evident that Cordelia Quail had caught a movement out of the corner of her eye for she turned to glare at her. On determining the identity of the newcomer, the frown had quickly been replaced by a strained smile. Lady Belvedere, however, was left with the distinct impression that she had intruded upon a private performance and that her presence was unwelcome.

'Oh, there you are, Rose,' said her mother, encroaching on her daughter's thoughts. 'I was afraid you wouldn't come. Now, tell me what you think of my using this bit of fabric for Horatio.'

Before Rose could comment, both women were distracted from their conversation by the arrival of a footman, who was bearing two Victorian cranberry-coloured wine glasses on a silver tray. This was not unusual in itself, but it was evident that the servant had been hurrying, for he was clearly out of breath. Rather unceremoniously, Cordelia snatched the tray from his hands and marched up on to the stage.

'Ursula Stapleton was making the most frightful fuss because there was no water in her glass,' Mrs Simpson explained to her daughter in a lowered voice. 'She demanded that her glass be filled because she has to drink from it in this final scene.'

'Couldn't she pretend to drink?' asked Rose.

'Apparently not,' answered her mother, with a faint note of contempt. 'It appears that her acting skills do not extend as far as that.'

'Poor Miss Quail,' murmured Rose. 'I expect she has far more important things to think about than check whether the glasses have water in them.'

It was only later that she wished she had kept the wine glasses in sight, had followed their progress across the stage, through the doorway at the back, and into the circular room beyond where the props were stored, and where the troupe rested until they were required on stage.

Chapter Two

Rose marvelled at the assortment of clothes and material that covered the trestle table. Rich velvets were draped over luxurious furs, delicate lace caressed pastel silk satins, and leather belts, with brass or celluloid buckles, straddled brightly-patterned cottons and rayon. It all made for rather a dazzling display, the overall effect being one of colour and texture.

'I consider myself very fortunate,' Mrs Simpson was saying, following her daughter's gaze, 'to have such a choice of fabric, I mean.' She lowered her voice a little before continuing, though it was hardly necessary for the director was some distance away. 'I must admit that when Miss Quail first asked me if I would consider helping out with the costumes, I was awfully afraid that I would be given some old moth-eaten rags to work with.'

'I believe Mrs Farrier donated quite a few clothes from Sedgwick Court,' said Rose, referring to her housekeeper. She paused a moment to pick up a pair of faded green corduroy trousers. 'Yes, these were Cedric's. He tore them on some brambles; look, here is the tear just below the knee.'

'Well, they will make a very fine pair of breeches for Horatio,' said her mother, taking the trousers from her daughter, and draping them over the arm of a chair.

'Have you many more costumes to make?' Rose asked. It was only four weeks until the performance, and she thought her mother looked tired.

'No, only Horatio's. I've finished all the other costumes, except for adding the odd bit of trimming or embellishment, if I have time.' Mrs Simpson gathered up some of the material and clothes and sighed. 'Fortunately, I have not been required to make the courtiers' outfits. Mrs Dobson and a few of the women from the village are making those. There will be quite a lot of them.' Looking up, she caught a glimpse of Miriam, who was heading towards the stage. 'Oh, and Ophelia, of course; I quite forgot about her. I intend to make her another costume for her final scene. If Miss Quail is agreeable, that is. The dress she is wearing is not at all suitable. I have my heart set on a full-length gown of pale blue satin coupled with a headdress of wild flowers and leaves.'

The sound of a fanfare of sorts from a trumpet, blown rather inexpertly by Miss Quail, brought the women's conversation to an abrupt end. Instinctively, they both moved forward to obtain a better view of what was happening on the stage. Hamlet and Horatio, the latter looking rather out of place in a mixture of Elizabethan and contemporary attire, had walked to one end of the stage and stood before the outer column, fixedly regarding the door at the back of the temple, which led to the circular room.

The king and queen were the first to emerge from the doorway in all their finery, Algernon Cuffe in his ermine and velvet, and Ursula Stapleton in a Tudor style gown of gold and burgundy embroidered taffeta. They were quickly followed by the man playing Laertes, and also by Walter Drury, in his guise as Osric, who carried a small wooden table. On their heels followed what was obviously intended to represent a small band of courtiers, but was, in fact, no more than the girl playing Ophelia, looking rather petulant, and the Prentice twins, dressed in matching black and red striped doublets and breeches. One of the twins was struggling to carry several foils and gauntlets, and the other was clutching the tray with the two Victorian cranberry-coloured wine glasses.

'Hold the foils by their hilts,' cried Cordelia, dashing up from her seat. 'Don't carry them in your arms like that, you'll be like –' The rest of her sentence was drowned out by a loud crash as the foils clattered on to the old stone floor. 'Pick them up,' cried the director, quite beside herself. 'Walter, for pity's sake, help the boy.'

Walter Drury put down the table and came forward to help. Together with the offending Prentice twin, he knelt and gathered up the weapons. The other twin deposited the tray and glasses none too carefully on the wooden table and positioned himself behind it, grinning rather unkindly at his brother's mishap. The foils restored, the play progressed in rather a slow and halting fashion as the table was repositioned between two of the inner pillars and the king and queen and makeshift courtiers circled the two young swordsmen, who had ventured forward and were now standing in the porch area in front of the great columns.

Against this backdrop of cool grey stone, the costumes of the players showed as a vivid burst of colour, drawing the eye. Rose, who, until her elevation in society, had worked in a dress shop, marvelled at her mother's skill as a dressmaker and seamstress to create such a visual spectacle.

'To the sides, courtiers, or stand behind the pillars,' instructed the director. 'Otherwise the audience will not be able to see the fight. Now …' Cordelia paused in what she was saying, aware suddenly that the countess and her mother were no longer positioned behind the trestle table immersed in fabrics. Instead, they were a few feet from her, and she beckoned to them hurriedly to stand beside her. It seemed, in her eyes, that her cast now had a proper audience.

'Ah, Lady Belvedere, how good of you to join us,' she said, when Rose was by her elbow. 'I know that I speak for the Sedgwick Players when I say what a great honour it is –'

'Not at all,' said Rose quickly, thinking it was nothing of the sort. 'In fact, I do hope you won't consider it to be a nuisance, my being here. I'm just fascinated by the idea of seeing the fencing match. Cedric … Lord Belvedere, has spoken of it a great deal.'

'I am sure he has,' replied Cordelia, giving her rather an indulgent smile. She leaned her head towards Rose and lowered her voice. 'Of course, I shouldn't really say this, your ladyship, but he is awfully good in the role.'

Rose smiled and blushed, and returned her gaze to the stage. Amid the mass of rich fabrics and brightly coloured costumes, the man playing Hamlet was conspicuous. Dressed entirely in black from doublet to hose, there was something of a melancholy air about him, in keeping with his character on stage. In addition, she noticed, he was looking rather pale and holding the hilt of his foil awkwardly and with obvious reluctance, which surprised her.

'Poor Henry,' muttered Cordelia, following Rose's gaze. 'He's frightfully good at reciting the soliloquies, but he does so hate the sword fighting.' She sighed. 'Of course, Laertes is supposed to be the better swordsman, but it is Hamlet who scores the first hit.' She moved forward a step or two and raised her voice. 'Henry, you must at least pretend to fight. If you could chase Laertes around the stage a bit, that should do. Remember, Osric needs an opportunity to say his line about a palpable hit.'

Henry mumbled something under his breath and moved a step or two towards the man playing Laertes, who darted behind one column, only to spring out from behind another and thrust his foil within inches of the poor man's chest. Henry flinched visibly, and all but dropped his foil. Fortunately, however, Cordelia Quail's attention had been drawn elsewhere, for another actor now held her notice.

'Algernon, did you hold up the pearl for the audience to see?'

'Yes,' replied the king rather grumpily. 'I made quite a good show of it too. You were obviously not watching, Cordelia; too busy shouting at the twins, I shouldn't wonder.'

Cordelia glared at him, and opened her mouth as if to make a suitable retort, but thought better of it.

'A hit, a very palpable hit,' cried Walter, amid the tension, though the excited note in his voice sounded rather false. It occurred to Rose that he spoke as much to calm the situation as for anything else, for, as far as she had seen, there had been no actual hit. Certainly, the man playing Hamlet had not appeared to go anywhere near his opponent's body, let alone touch it with the tip of his foil. If anything, he had recoiled from his adversary and was now clinging to one of the inner columns beside the table.

'Stay, give me drink,' demanded the king.

With that, Algernon marched towards the table and, in something of an exaggerated manner, picked up one of the crimson wine glasses. In his other hand, he held out the pearl as if for inspection. 'Hamlet, this pearl is thine. Here's to thy health,' he said, vaguely in the direction of the cowering Hamlet. Cordelia, caught slightly off guard, blew the trumpet rather belatedly and Algernon threw the pearl carelessly into the wine glass. 'Give him the cup,' he snarled, waving the wine glass wildly in the air. Walter leapt forward and took the glass, before the contents spilt on to the stage, and stood nursing it as if it was his own.

'I'll play this bout first,' said Hamlet, somewhat reluctantly. 'Set it by awhile.'

Walter looked about him for the queen, who was standing some distance from him. He tried to catch her eye, but she was fiddling with her hair, a strand of which had become tangled in one of the faux jewels embroidered on her elaborate collar. She should have been standing beside him, not fussing over her costume. He felt himself begin to yield to panic. He would not be able to cross the stage in time for Ursula to drink to Hamlet's fortune. It was only a few lines away and Ursula, without the will or talent to improvise drinking without a glass, was sure to create a scene. That would then infuriate Cordelia, who would more than likely insist that they do the scene again from the very beginning until they got it right. And that would mean ...

Perhaps the distress was evident in his eyes, or possibly others on the stage were keeping abreast of the script and foresaw the difficulty, and had no desire to prolong the rehearsal any more than he did. Whichever it was, he felt the wine glass being snatched roughly from his hand. Instinctively, for one brief moment, he tightened his grip on the stem.

'Let go, Walter, there's a dear,' said Miriam in a sharp whisper in his ear.

Obligingly, he released his hold and watched as she carried the wine glass to the queen in time for Ursula to say: 'The queen carouses to thy fortune, Hamlet.'

'Good madam,' mumbled Henry over his shoulder, his attention fixed on parrying desperately as his opponent lunged enthusiastically.

Ursula raised the wine glass to her lips.

'Gertrude, do not drink,' cried Algernon, in so loud a voice that all the cast, including Henry, stopped what they were doing and turned to stare at him. Ursula appeared a little taken aback, and hesitated a moment before delivering her next line: 'I will, my lord; I pray you, pardon me.' With that, she glared at Algernon and drank heavily from her glass.

'Ursula, don't look at Algernon like that,' protested Cordelia. 'He is the king and you are defying his command. And don't make a face when you drink from the glass. It is not until later that you realise the wine has been poisoned.'

Ursula scowled, but made no comment. Meanwhile, Algernon was holding his head in his hand and muttering dejectedly and aside to one of the columns: 'It is the poison'd cup; it is too late.'

'Very good,' murmured Cordelia from the audience. 'You said that line with great feeling, Algernon.'

Meanwhile, Rose's attention was drawn again to Hamlet.

'I dare not drink yet, madam; by and by,' said Henry, as he made some rather feeble attempt to pursue Laertes.

'Come, let me wipe thy face,' said Ursula, lowering herself gingerly into a gaudy, gold-painted chair that was intended to represent a throne.

Henry lowered his foil and ran gladly to the voice, falling on his knees before the queen, and resting his head in her lap.

'I think,' said Cordelia, quickly, 'that on reflection it might be better if you remain standing, Ursula.'

It was possible, Rose thought, that Ursula did not hear her. Certainly, she made no effort to rise from her chair. Instead, with one hand she dabbed absentmindedly at Henry's face with a cotton handkerchief, and with the other touched her own forehead, as if she felt some dizziness. Henry was looking up in to the woman's eyes, a flash of something akin to concern or puzzlement revealing itself in his face. Rose stared at the queen more closely. Was Ursula not supposed to be stroking the young man's hair or patting his cheek? She thought such gestures likely, but instead, the woman appeared distracted. She had removed her hand from her forehead and was clutching the arm of her chair tightly. Her other hand that held the handkerchief made a fist, crumpling the white cotton within its grasp. Instinctively, Rose felt that something was amiss. The woman seemed flushed, her complexion a rosy pink. Of course, it was possible that she was only a little warm encased as she was in her yards of taffeta and three-hooped underskirt, but Rose was of the distinct opinion that the queen looked unwell.

It was while she was wondering whether she ought to say something to that effect to the director that Cordelia said rather loudly in her ear, but in what was obviously intended to be a whisper: 'There's no need to worry, dear Lady Belvedere. It is quite all right. Ursula ... Mrs Stapleton, considers this her dramatic scene.' She sighed. 'And I'm afraid today she is rather overdoing it, even for her.'

'Her performance is very convincing,' Rose said, and yet still she felt uneasy.

'Oh, do you think so?' replied Cordelia, sounding surprised and not a little annoyed. 'I have played the role of Queen Gertrude and I must say I played it rather differently. I pride myself in –'

'Look to the queen there, ho!' cried Walter. Seemingly on cue, Ursula began to swoon, sliding down in her seat a little.

'No! No!' cried Cordelia, stepping forward. 'Ursula, dab at your forehead with your handkerchief if you must, but do not faint until Hamlet's next line.'

Ursula's response to this command was to put both hands to her throat and gasp as if for air. Her frame, attired in the splendour of its Elizabethan gown, shuddered violently. Henry jumped up with a startled cry. To those who looked on, it was as if some ferocious seizure or convulsion had taken hold of the actress, causing her to shake frenziedly and for her muscles to contract involuntarily.

'Ursula!' cried Cordelia, quite beside herself. 'What are you doing? Are you intentionally ruining this scene?'

'Miss Quail,' Rose said, aware of the note of urgency in her own voice. 'I do believe Mrs Stapleton really is ill.'

'Nonsense,' cried Cordelia, almost sobbing. 'She is trying to spoil the rehearsal, that is all. She's a ...'

But she did not finish her sentence. Instead, the words faltered on her lips; for Ursula had stopped shaking and for a minute, after the frantic, wild movements of her body, looked strangely tranquil and composed. But before the watchers could take a collective sigh of relief, Ursula fell forward abruptly in her seat. It was then that gravity seemed to pull at her, tearing her from her stately throne. With a sickening crack, her head hit the stone floor, and the rest of her body came tumbling down after her, until it lay collapsed in a heap on the ground.

For several seconds, no one moved or made a sound. It was as if all those present were trying to comprehend and digest inwardly what they had just witnessed. Was it a remarkable piece of acting? Or was it something else, something sinister and altogether more appalling? For there had appeared nothing feigned or pretend about the performance. Utterly confused, they felt compelled now only to stare helplessly at Ursula's sprawled body, not quite knowing what to do.

It was the man playing Laertes who was the first to gather his wits. He threw down his foil and ran to the body, crouching down beside it and feeling for a pulse. Ursula's limp wrist did not oblige. He stared into the glazed eyes that did not blink, hung his head for a moment and then looked up, searching out his wife's face on the lawn below.

'Cedric ...' Rose began, but she was immediately interrupted by a shriek from Cordelia, something more akin to an animal cry than a noise made by a woman in distress. A strange gurgling sound came from her throat, and Rose turned and looked at the director in alarm. But the woman was merely sobbing, huge tears of anguish pouring down her rouged cheeks. Her turban had become dishevelled and was perched at an unbecoming angle on her head, her hair escaping from its folds.

Before Rose could decide how best to comfort her, her mother had stepped forward and was busy putting an arm around the woman's shaking shoulders, drawing her away. Rose tore her gaze from Cordelia and looked back at her husband, who remained kneeling beside the actress. He shook his head, his face ashen. Slowly he got to his feet and with emotion in his voice spoke the words they had all been dreading: 'I'm afraid she's dead.'

Chapter Three

For a few unbearable seconds, there was nothing but silence; quickly on the heels of which followed a series of horrified gasps. Cordelia herself wailed and flailed her arms about in a wild and undignified manner, seemingly oblivious to all else. Whether her distress was due to the fate of her leading actress or the impact of the woman's unfortunate death on her production, was not quite clear. Whatever the cause, she allowed herself to be taken firmly by the arm and led whimpering from the scene. She was only vaguely aware that it was Mrs Simpson who guided her steps and spoke to her in soothing and encouraging tones, much as she would have ministered to a distressed child.

Half walking, half stumbling, Cordelia went, her black silk kimono, on which was embroidered a tangle of cream leaves, flapping about her in the light summer breeze very like the sail on a rudderless boat. It was only when she reached the very edge of the lake that she faltered. Indeed, to those who looked on, there was a fear that she might slump to the ground. However, instead, with considerable effort, the director seemed to gather herself, turning her head to take one last, agonising look at the still figure in the distance, lying spread-eagled on the cold stone stage.

The Earl of Belvedere, after some deliberation, got slowly, and rather shakily, to his feet and addressed the man who had been playing Horatio.

'Kettering, would you mind awfully running back to the house and telling Manning what has happened, there's a good chap?' While there was a forced lightness to the earl's words, his voice shook.

Giles Kettering, looking solemn and ashen, nodded and mumbled: 'Of course not, my lord.'

'Ask him to ring for the doctor,' continued Cedric, 'though heaven knows there's nothing he can do for the poor woman now, more's the pity.'

'Ursula told me she had a dicky heart,' volunteered Algernon, a forlorn look upon his face. 'I suppose it was that –'

'And tell him to telephone for the police,' continued Cedric curtly, as if the thespian had not spoken.

'The police?' queried Algernon, paling significantly. 'I say, do you think it absolutely necessary to involve them?'

It was not lost on any of those present that he sounded anxious. Indeed, almost without exception, each and every one of them exchanged worried and furtive looks as if the death had taken on a more sinister air. Certainly, the man who had played Horatio looked surprised.

'Surely,' said Giles Kettering, 'you don't think, my lord, that –'

'No, of course not, Kettering,' said Cedric hurriedly, aware of the growing tension and cursing himself inwardly for contributing to it by his choice of words. 'It's just routine. An unexplained death and all that.'

'I see,' said Giles, though he sounded far from convinced, 'Well, if you say so.'

'I do.' There was a certain finality to the words that could not be ignored.

Giles glanced briefly at Algernon Cuff, and then set off down the lawn at a brisk trot. The others gazed after him, as if they were half minded to follow, anything but stay on the stage and stare down at the lifeless body that had once been Ursula Stapleton.

'Poor old Ursula,' muttered Algernon, shaking his head slowly, all the while putting a hand to his head to steady his faux gold crown, which looked hideously gaudy in the circumstances. He lifted his head abruptly as if a sudden thought had just occurred to him. 'I say, my lord, oughtn't we to cover her face with a cloak or –'

'No,' said Cedric, rather brusquely, and perhaps a little louder than was strictly necessary. 'We shouldn't touch anything, that's to say not until after the police have arrived.'

Algernon made to protest, but obviously thought better of it. Meanwhile, the earl caught his wife's eye. Rose had initially run a few steps forward when Ursula had collapsed, but then she had halted transfixed, watching the scene play out before her on the stage. It had not been idle curiosity that had stayed her steps but a growing realisation that what happened next might be of the utmost importance and should be observed closely. For, unlike the others, Rose had not missed the expression on her husband's face as he had risen from examining Ursula Stapleton, nor had she overlooked his obvious unwillingness to disturb the body after Algernon's quite reasonable suggestion to do so. A certain look passed between husband and wife but, before either could do or say anything, they were interrupted by another Sedgwick Player.

'I say, I feel … I feel rather sick,' said Henry, his complexion going a ghastly shade of grey, which oddly complemented his funereal attire. 'I think I had better sit down.' He looked about him for a suitable seat on the stage and, much to his dismay, discovered there was none, other than the throne. For one awful moment, the image of Ursula's last few minutes of life seated on the golden chair was conjured up vividly before his eyes. He recollected all too well how she had clutched at its arms and then slipped slowly down its cushioned velvet seat, until she had fallen to her final resting place on the floor with a sickening thud. Henry shuddered violently, rejecting the throne. He might conceivably have retreated to the circular room beyond the temple, which boasted several hard-backed chairs, but instead he made do with remaining where he was and sitting cross-legged upon the floor, leaning his back against one of the grand stone columns. With a heartfelt sigh, he closed his eyes and took great gulps of air in an attempt to steady his breathing.

Ophelia, no doubt, under such circumstances, would have attended to Hamlet with gentle compassion; Miriam Belmore, however, frowned at the ailing Henry with a look of ill-concealed disdain and sniffed. 'Well, speaking for myself, I never much liked the poor old biddy,' she said, her words uttered with remarkably little feeling. 'But even I wouldn't have wished the poor old thing dead. And fancy her dying on stage like that. How very melodramatic of her. Trust Ursula to do something like that.'

There was a sharp intake of breath, and Rose realised it was her own.

'Oh, do be quiet, Miriam,' said Walter Drury, with barely concealed fury, who, until this outburst, had been standing a little way off from the others with his head bowed, his large felt, courtier hat, with its ridiculous feather, clutched tightly in his hand. 'Don't try and be flippant, it doesn't become you. If you cannot say anything appropriate, I suggest you say nothing at all.'

'That's put you in your place, Miriam, darling,' said Freddie with a sneer. 'Haven't you heard the saying that it is better to keep quiet and be thought stupid than to open your mouth and remove all doubt? And there you were pretending you didn't care a jot when all the time –'

'Oh, do shut up, Freddie,' cried his brother, giving him a sharp poke in the ribs. In contrast to his twin, he, like Walter, was visibly shaken by what had occurred and looked very close to tears.

'I think,' Rose said quickly, fearing the situation was about to deteriorate further into bitter recriminations, 'that everyone should wait in the drawing room until the doctor and the police arrive. They will no doubt wish to speak to everyone who was present when Mrs Stapleton was ... was taken ill.'

'Jolly good idea,' Cedric said, rallying a little and nodding enthusiastically. There were various mutterings among the cast, though none appeared inclined to object. 'We've all had the most dreadful shock,' he continued. 'Hot, sweet tea with a dash of brandy in it; that's what's called for.' He turned to face the actors and the sole actress, who were now standing around rather awkwardly on the stage, not quite knowing where to look, or what to do with their hands. 'If everyone wouldn't mind going back to the house,' said the earl. 'No, not you, darling,' he added quietly, looking pointedly at his wife. 'If you wouldn't mind coming here for a moment ...' He stopped in mid-sentence for he had caught sight of the twins, who were now staring down at the corpse with a morbid fascination. 'Hurry up boys. Off you go, and don't touch anything.'

As the others departed with the odd backward glance, Rose hastened to the stage to join her husband. Together, they watched the Sedgwick Players scurrying away in their odd assortment of brightly-coloured Elizabethan costumes, rather like frightened rabbits in fancy dress. By common accord, Lord and Lady Belvedere did not speak until the cast was out of earshot. Though the troupe made good progress across the lawn, it seemed to the earl and countess an age before they could speak openly, confident in the knowledge that their words would not be overheard. All the while, as she waited, Rose studied her husband closely; to her well-trained eye, he appeared preoccupied, and every so often she noticed that he looked down at the body, stretched out before him, and shook his head. When at last she deemed it safe to do so, she said: 'What is it, darling? Is something wrong? Other than poor Mrs Stapleton being dead, I mean.'

'I don't know.' Cedric crouched down beside the body again and, somewhat to his wife's surprise, gingerly leant forward until his head was not far from Ursula's face. He sniffed. 'It was an impression I had. I daresay I was wrong but I thought I detected ... but perhaps it was only my imagination.' He looked up and hesitated a moment before proceeding. 'Darling, I hardly dare ask you to do this; it seems so ghastly, but can you tell me if you can smell anything?'

'On Mrs Stapleton's lips, do you mean?' Rose asked, rather shocked.

'Yes.'

With some great effort, Rose willed herself to kneel down beside the dead actress' body and placed her own head near Ursula's. Despite having had considerable experience of violent death, she had never squatted on the ground in such a manner beside a corpse. She tried not to look at the terrible vacant eyes or the contorted expression on the dead woman's face. Taking a deep breath, she focused her attention instead on sniffing tentatively, as she had been instructed, half afraid that some dreadful stench would reach her nostrils.

'Can you smell anything, anything at all, however faint?' asked Cedric, crouching down beside her, a note of urgency in his voice, as if much depended on her answer.

Rose shook her head. For a moment, she had all but forgotten that he was there, so engrossed had she been in her task. She closed her eyes, gritted her teeth, and sniffed again. While thus engaged, she tried desperately not to recall to mind the living, breathing Ursula Stapleton, whose very presence had commanded the stage. Much as she tried, however, she could not rid her mind of the thought of decay which seemed to muddle her senses. She opened her eyes and was greeted by an eager expression on her husband's face. It was, therefore, with a sense of frustration that she said, 'No … no, I don't think so.'

Cedric stifled a frown while Rose, relieved that her ordeal was now over, scrambled to her feet. To her annoyance, she discovered that she was shaking. Noting his wife's condition, her husband quickly put an arm around her shoulders and pulled her towards him. Despite the intimate gesture, she knew he was disappointed with her answer, though he was attempting to hide the fact.

'Not at all? Not a very faint smell of anything?' Cedric persisted gently after a few seconds had elapsed. Rose sighed and leant her head against her husband's shoulder. The warmth from his body was beginning to revive her.

'No. I'm sorry. I couldn't smell a thing.'

'Not to worry. I should be grateful and yet …' Cedric left his sentence unfinished and for a moment looked thoughtful. Then he shrugged, looked down at his wife and gave a half smile. Had she answered him with a similar expression, it is quite possible that they would have abandoned their investigation into the cause of Ursula's death and returned to the house with the others to await the arrival of the local police. Rose, however, found herself oddly reluctant to depart the scene until Cedric had voiced his concerns regarding the actress' death. She was familiar enough with her husband's moods to know that he was greatly agitated, an occurrence that was far from frequent. Something had undoubtedly aroused his suspicions.

'You are convinced you smelt something, aren't you?' Rose said. Though she put it as a question, in truth, she spoke aloud to herself in an attempt to gather her own thoughts. 'You think something is not quite right ...' The words had hardly escaped her lips before she was filled with apprehension. She knew then that had Cedric made as if to set off for the house, she would have detained him. But instead, he met her gaze and said quietly: 'I thought I did, yes. But of course, it's quite possible I was mistaken.' He gave a half-hearted laugh. 'After all, we have had more than our fair share of suspicious deaths. Perhaps it clouds the mind and makes one see crimes where there are none.'

'I see,' Rose said, not returning his smile. Instead, a look of dawning astonishment appeared on her face. 'You believe Mrs Stapleton was poisoned, don't you?'

'The thought had crossed my mind,' Cedric admitted rather sheepishly, 'though when one puts it into words like that it sounds dreadfully far-fetched.' He laughed. 'There's probably a far more reasonable explanation for her death. I daresay we'll discover it was some trouble or other with her heart. Didn't Algernon Cuffe mention something to that effect? I'm probably making the most terrible fuss about nothing.'

'No,' said Rose slowly, 'I don't think you are. The more I think about it, the more I think you may be right. Tell me, what made you think of poison? Was it the wine glass? If I recall correctly, she died only a few minutes after drinking from it.'

'It wasn't the wine glass, no,' answered her husband. 'What actually put me in mind of poison was the faint smell of bitter almonds.'

'Bitter almonds?'

'Yes. It's a sign of cyanide poisoning, don't you know.' Cedric uttered a sharp cry and struck his head with the palm of his hand. 'I say, what a damned fool I've been. All this time we should have been looking for the wine glass, not bending over the body. Where is it? It would serve me jolly well right if it had disappeared.'

'I didn't happen to see any of the cast taking it away with them,' said Rose, looking about her. 'Though,' she added as an afterthought, 'I suppose they might have stuffed it into a pocket or hidden it under a cloak without my noticing.'

'Yes, or carried it inside one of those blasted hats with a feather. I say, confound those costumes!' At a raised eyebrow from his wife, Cedric added hastily: 'Nothing against your mother's sewing, of course. They're jolly fine costumes and all that. It's just a pity that each garment comprises yards and yards of material in which to hide things ... Oh, I say, there it is!'

In one stride, Cedric was beside the table, which had been placed at the back of the stage, a little distance from the throne. On the top of it was the silver tray, and on that a Victorian cranberry-coloured wine glass.

'It was here all the time,' said Cedric, sounding relieved. 'Well, I –'

'Wait,' said Rose. 'There should be two glasses, not one.' She picked up the wine glass and studied it carefully. 'Yes, I was right. This glass has not had any liquid in it; it's quite clean. Ursula Stapleton didn't drink from this glass; she must have drunk from the other one.'

'I say, are you quite sure?' enquired her husband, peering over her shoulder at the offending glass.

'Yes. I was there when the footman brought the tray and I remember quite distinctly that there were two wine glasses on it, not one. There was quite a to do about it, as it happens, because Cordelia had forgotten to arrange for Ursula's glass to be filled with water.'

'You're quite right,' said Cedric, 'she did make a fuss now I come to think of it. I was in the circular room at the time and didn't pay it much attention, though I do remember Cordelia hurrying into the room with the tray.' He took the glass from his wife and stared at it. 'Ursula was always most insistent during rehearsals that her glass be filled with water. She said that it helped her to immerse herself in the part, though why she didn't just pretend to drink from the glass as anyone else would have done, I really don't know.'

'I wish I could remember what Ursula did with her wine glass after she had drunk from it,' said Rose. 'She was sitting on the throne as I remember.'

'That's right,' agreed her husband. 'And Miriam handed her the glass, which now I come to think of it was rather odd in itself. Walter Drury usually hands it to her, you see.'

'Ursula Stapleton takes the glass from Miriam and drinks from it,' Rose said, miming the action. 'Now, what did she do with it then, I wonder?'

'It seems to me quite reasonable to suppose that she handed it back to Miriam,' said her husband. 'That's what I would have done, and Miriam would no doubt have put it back on the table. But, for some reason, it isn't there now.'

'Ursula might have dropped the glass,' suggested Rose. 'She became ill almost immediately after drinking from it.' She looked about her. 'In which case, it would most probably have rolled under the throne.'

'Well, it's not there now,' said Cedric, lifting up the curtain of velvet that was draped over the seat of the throne, and which fell to the ground concealing the chair legs. He got down on his hands and knees and peered under the chair to make quite sure.

'I suppose it might have rolled off the stage completely,' suggested Rose. 'Or possibly someone might inadvertently have kicked it on to the grass while it was lying on the floor. Why, you might have done so yourself, darling, while you were fighting your duel.'

'If it was rolling about on the floor, I'm somewhat surprised poor old Henry didn't trip over it. It is the sort of thing he'd do, poor chap. However, if that had been the case there would undoubtedly have been some pieces of broken glass on the floor.'

To be quite sure, they undertook a thorough search of both the stage and the area of lawn directly beneath the folly, on the off chance that the wine glass had rolled off the stage and was lying concealed somewhere in the grass. As Rose crouched down and studied the floor for shards of broken glass, Cedric busied himself with exploring the lawn. All the while, Rose found her eyes involuntarily drawn to Ursula's remains. She tiptoed quietly around the body, careful not to disturb it, conscious of the irrational feeling that she was trespassing, and aware that she felt a certain sympathy with Algernon's view that the body be covered.

Ten minutes elapsed during which there was frantic activity on the part of the two searchers; every inch of the stage floor was carefully explored and every blade of grass in the immediate vicinity of the folly closely examined. Yet, despite their efforts, no trace was found of the missing wine glass. It was almost as if it had vanished into thin air. Not to be discouraged, however, they turned their attention next to an extensive study of the circular room, behind the stage, picking up props as they went and rummaging through the piles of discarded costumes and everyday attire, looking for some hiding place or other where a wine glass might successfully be concealed.

'Well, it isn't here,' remarked Cedric, abandoning the search. 'We've looked everywhere and it's nowhere to be found.' He looked despondent, as if he felt they had wasted a great deal of time in their fruitless search of the scene. It was obvious, however, to the most casual observer that this emotion was not shared by his wife.

'You do realise what this means, don't you, darling?' she said. The note of uneasiness in his wife's voice caused the earl to glance at her sharply. 'If Mrs Stapleton's death was from natural causes,' Rose continued, conscious that she had his full attention, 'the wine glass, or at the very least the remains of it, should be here. The fact it is not means that someone quite deliberately and intentionally removed it from the scene.'

'And the only reason for anyone to do that,' said her husband, continuing on from his wife's line of reasoning, 'was that it contained incriminating evidence relating to Ursula's death.'

'Yes,' agreed Rose. 'I am awfully afraid there is very little doubt that Ursula Stapleton was murdered.'

Chapter Four

The word 'murdered' hung in the air, its ghastly echo seeming to reverberate within the confines of the stone folly itself, resounding across the lawn to the lake below. They had spoken readily enough of poison as some theoretical thing, but it was the first time since Ursula Stapleton's death that either of them had alluded to the wilful and premeditated act of murder. Rose gave an involuntary shudder. Cedric, meanwhile, his face ashen and his head bowed, leaned against one of the stone pillars and gave a heartfelt sigh. Though he did not give voice to his thoughts, Rose guessed he was wondering how it was possible that another murder had occurred in the grounds of Sedgwick Court. The thought overwhelmed them both, rendering each temporarily speechless.

In the end, it was Cedric who broke the silence. 'First the maze,' he said, speaking barely above a whisper, though loud enough for his wife to catch the note of bitterness in his voice, 'and then here.' He swung his arm about him in a desperate, sweeping gesture, which encompassed the Greek temple, the circular room beyond and the lake below.

'Yes,' said Rose, nodding sadly, though the word seemed inadequate even to her own ears. She moved forward and took her husband's hand in hers. 'It doesn't bear thinking of, and yet,' she said tentatively, 'I suppose we must.'

'But another murder here at Sedgwick Court; our home,' exclaimed her husband, shaking his head in disbelief. He looked up at her despairingly. Then his mood seemed to alter for the better and his manner became more cheerful. 'I say, do you think it possible we've got it all wrong?' His face relaxed a little, as if he saw the first glimmers of hope beyond the gloom. 'Perhaps there is a perfectly logical explanation for why we can't find that wine glass.'

'Maybe,' said Rose slowly, though she spoke with little conviction. 'I suppose it is possible that someone might have noticed the glass rolling about by their feet and picked it up, afraid someone might fall over it. They might then have stuffed it into their pocket quite innocently.'

'Well, there you are,' said Cedric, with obvious relief. 'Perhaps nothing untoward took place today after all. I can't tell you the fun we were all having, acting and the like; giving voice to Shakespeare's words ...' His sentence trailed off, as he gave a furtive glance at the corpse. It was quite possible that he thought his words had been disrespectful in the presence of death. Certainly, he moved a step or two away and averted his eyes to take in the lawns and the lake below. In a more melancholy voice, he said: 'I couldn't believe my luck when Miss Quail cast me as Laertes. I mean to say, I have so little experience of acting. And it was for a good cause too. All the proceeds from the performance were to go to a deserving charity, and now ... why, it's all ruined.'

'Not necessarily,' Rose said quickly. 'If Ursula Stapleton died of natural causes, perhaps the production need only be postponed.'

'Yes, there's a thought,' said Cedric, brightening considerably. It was not long, however, before the expression on his face darkened again, reminiscent of a storm cloud. 'But if it is as we first feared –'

'If Ursula Stapleton was murdered,' said Rose slowly, 'then the sooner we can identify the murderer, the better.'

As she spoke, she felt the weight of responsibility upon her shoulders. Not for the first time did it occur to her that her very presence seemed to attract death. Had she not decided to attend the rehearsal would the actress still be alive, laughing with the rest of the cast and sipping carelessly from her glass of water without consequence? It was an irrational thought, she knew. If Ursula Stapleton had indeed been poisoned, it had been a carefully planned affair, intended to mirror the very action of Shakespeare's play itself, and nothing to do with her chance attendance at the rehearsal.

Though she reproached herself severely for her illogical sense of guilt for what had happened, the feeling resolutely remained with her. She could not rid herself fully of the ridiculous notion that she was in some way accountable for what had happened. This, in itself, did not alarm her unduly. On other such occasions, she had found herself overcome with the same melancholy, similarly considering herself to be in part to blame for the tragedy that had enfolded. Then, she had put such sombre emotions to good purpose. For it had proved the impetus she had needed to strengthen her resolve and help her on her quest to solve the murder. And even while she was thinking these very thoughts, it was almost as if her husband could read her mind, for he turned towards her, an imploring look upon his face. 'You will investigate this death, won't you? If it proves to be murder, I mean?'

Overcome suddenly with emotion, Rose found that she could say nothing. Instead, she nodded her head slowly, all too conscious of her husband's unwavering faith, as always, in her detecting abilities. Perhaps, though, there was something about his optimism that was infectious, for as some of the colour returned to Cedric's cheeks, she felt a sudden unexpected wave of optimism lift her spirits. There was no reason to suppose after all that what lay before her was beyond her capabilities. She had helped solve crimes before which, on initial examination had appeared, as this one did, without obvious motive. Thus resolved, she gathered her thoughts about her quickly.

'We must return to the house at once,' she said. She consulted her wristwatch. 'Our absence will be commented upon if we remain here any longer.'

'You mean the others might suspect we have suspicions regarding Ursula's death?'

'They may even believe we have found some evidence to suggest that she was murdered.'

'Other than my vague belief that I smelt bitter almonds on her breath?'

'There is also the missing wine glass, though that, in itself, isn't really evidence at all. Unless one thinks of it as negative evidence, that is; it should be here on the stage, and the fact that it is not, is suspicious.'

'I see.'

'Do you?' She looked up at him earnestly. 'We must do everything in our power to allay their fears, make them believe Ursula Stapleton's death was from natural causes.' She laughed at the puzzled look that crossed her husband's face. 'You know as well as I do, darling, what people are like when they realise a murder has been committed and they are a potential suspect.'

'They wail and sob like poor old Cordelia,' replied her husband, 'or else they retreat within themselves and won't look at anyone?'

'Yes. But, more importantly, they won't reveal anything. They tend to think before they open their mouths, and their natural inclination is to say nothing which might incriminate themselves or another.'

'Well, I'm not so sure of that,' said Cedric. 'I think there is nothing more that Freddie Prentice would like to do than accuse poor Miriam of poisoning Ursula; you saw the way he behaved towards her just now. If Walter Drury hadn't intervened ... ah, splendid,' he added, as a gardener came into view. 'I didn't feel we ought to leave the body unattended.'

'Begging your pardon, m'lord,' said the servant respectfully, as he approached them, doffing his cap. 'Mr Manning told me how I was to come and guard the ... the body.' In something of a guileful fashion, he tried to look beyond them to the stage and catch a glimpse of the corpse. Meanwhile, the earl and countess descended the stone steps and went forward to meet him. Under the collective gaze of his employers, the gardener shifted his feet uncomfortably, conscious of his dirt-stained hands and face. He clutched his cap so tightly in his hands that Rose feared for the fabric. 'I was in the servants' hall having a cup of tea when Mr Manning came in and asks if any of us be minded to go to this here folly,' he mumbled. 'Stand over the body of one of them poor thespians, he said. The maids, they were frightened something shocking, and the younger men, they didn't want to volunteer even if they thought they ought to, like. One or two of 'em have never seen a dead body. But me, I've done my bit for King and Country in the Great War; seen more than my fair share of bodies in all sorts of sorry states, I have, more's the pity.'

It was only when the man had referred to the war that Rose realised that she had been vaguely conscious all the time that, as he walked towards them, he had a slight limp.

'Well, I'm very much obliged to you,' Cedric was saying. 'Hawkins, isn't it?'

'Yes, m'lord,' replied the servant, obviously flattered that the earl knew his name. He drew himself up to his full height. 'I'm the new under-gardener, come to replace young Smith. Been here two months, I have.'

'Very good. Well, the body's over there, in the folly.' Cedric gestured towards the Greek temple behind them. 'Be careful not to touch anything.'

Leaving the gardener to watch over the corpse, the earl and countess set off at a brisk pace in the direction of the house. As they came to the lake, Rose spared a moment to glance back at the folly and saw that the gardener was standing over the body, his cap still in his hands and his head bowed. Remembering how the Prentice twins and Miriam Belmore had squabbled in so disgraceful a fashion moments after the actress' death, it struck her that the gardener, of all of them, had shown most respect towards the dead woman, a person who was no more than a stranger to him. Rose sighed. Perhaps she was being a little unfair on the others. Algernon Cuff had expressed regret at Ursula's death and Walter Drury had shown genuine grief. It was only the Prentice twins and Miriam who had appeared quite heartless and flippant, and most probably that had merely been an act to disguise the horror they had felt at what had happened. And she must not forget the violent way that Cordelia Quail had responded to the death, though how sincere her display of emotion had been, and how much had been affected, she could not say.

Their progress back to the grand Georgian mansion, which for years had been the Sedgwick family's ancestral home, was relatively slow. For the lawn in front of the Greek temple was as nothing compared with the vast gardens and parkland that comprised the estate itself. To return to the house, they were obliged to follow long, winding paths and navigate sunken ha-ha fences before they reached the formal gardens and terrace. During their journey, other eye-catchers vied for their attention, most notable among them a castle ruin and a venetian bridge, both of which served no useful purpose other than as decoration; however, preoccupied with more serious matters, Rose and Cedric were oblivious to these distractions.

It was not, however, the sprawling estate alone that made their journey back to Cedric's childhood home a prolonged affair. For quite often they stopped to peer over a box hedge, or to inspect a bush or a clump of trees, anywhere, in fact, where a wine glass might easily be disposed of.

'Suspecting what we do now, I wish I had returned with the others to the house,' said Rose. 'I feel quite sure I would have noticed if anyone had run on ahead, or held back and waited for everyone else to go on.'

'In order that they could get rid of the wine glass without being seen, do you mean?' asked Cedric, looking about him. 'I shouldn't think they would have wandered too far from the path in case they aroused suspicion. It is the sort of thing that would have been commented upon.'

'Yes,' agreed his wife. 'And unless they happened to be wearing gloves, they would have needed to spend a little time wiping their fingerprints from the glass.'

By this process of elimination, their search of the gardens was narrowed so that they deviated very little from following the established paths. Cedric had somehow acquired a sturdy piece of tree branch along the way, which he used with great enthusiasm to prod the undergrowth, all the while listening for the sound of broken glass. Rose contented herself with looking in the hedges and stone urns; she searched the fountains and peered behind the marble statues which adorned the gardens. But their various activities were all to no avail. There was no sign of the crimson wine glass, either whole or broken, not even a shard of glass among the shrubberies.

'Of course,' said Rose, 'we don't know for certain that they returned to the house by this route. There are other paths they might have taken. And it's quite possible that they didn't keep to the paths at all, but ran across the grass instead.'

'Quite likely, I'd say,' replied her husband. 'They'd have been in a great hurry to reach the house.' In an act of frustration, he threw his branch on to the ground. 'Dash it all, they might have hidden it anywhere. It will take an age to search these grounds properly. And the more I think on it, the more I'm certain that, if I were the murderer, I would have smashed the glass in to as many pieces as possible. It would have been too great a risk to leave it intact.'

'Because there would have been traces of the poison at the bottom of the glass?' said Rose. She did not pause to give her husband the opportunity to answer, but went on. 'Though it's quite possible of course that there was no time for the murderer to smash the glass without being spotted.'

'Or perhaps there was, but he was afraid it would make too much noise,' said Cedric, following his wife's line of reasoning. 'The sound of glass smashing and breaking is quite distinctive, you know.'

'In which case,' declared Rose, 'it seems to me that there are three possibilities.'

'Three?' Cedric looked surprised.

'Yes. The first one is that the murderer hid the wine glass quickly, with the intention of picking it up when he left, and disposing of it elsewhere.'

'That would seem the most logical thing for him to do,' agreed Cedric, 'and if you're right, a proper search should uncover it readily enough.'

'Yes. But it does mean, of course, that we must ensure that he doesn't have an opportunity to leave the house until after a thorough search of the grounds has been made.'

'What's your second scenario?'

'That the murderer has disposed of the glass in the house.'

'What?' cried Cedric. 'But, if he did that, it would be discovered at once. You know as well as I do, darling, how thoroughly the housemaids clean the house. A stray wine glass would look out of place at once.'

'Not if it was hidden behind an ornament or a curtain. And remember, all the formal rooms are cleaned in the morning,' his wife reminded him. 'It would not be until tomorrow morning at the earliest that the wine glass would be discovered.'

'By which time our murderer would be holed up safely in his own dwelling?'

'Yes.'

'And the last possibility?' Cedric asked curiously. 'You said there were three.' A thought struck him and he looked incredulous. 'Surely you don't think –'

'Yes,' said Rose, laughing at the look of disbelief on her husband's face. 'He might still have the glass upon his person.'

'Surely, he wouldn't take such a risk?' protested Cedric.

'He might. You see, he may consider it hardly a risk at all. Think, darling,' Rose continued earnestly. 'We are the only ones who believe that Ursula Stapleton was murdered. Everyone else is of the opinion that her death was from natural causes. Our murderer believes he is safe; as far as he is concerned, no one suspects Mrs Stapleton was poisoned, or has noticed the wine glass is missing.'

'I say, you're quite right.'

'That might be turned to our advantage,' said Rose.

'Do you mean because we can lull our murderer into believing that we do not suspect foul play?'

'Yes, and he might give himself away.'

'And the others?'

'They will speak more freely if they believe there is nothing suspicious about Ursula Stapleton's death.' She quickened her pace. 'Now, we really must join the others. While we're waiting for the police to arrive, I shall casually make mention of the missing wine glass, as if in passing. I won't connect it with Ursula Stapleton's death, of course. It is just possible someone noticed something.'

'Very good. Meanwhile, do you suggest I telephone to the chief constable? I could tell him that we suspect a murder may have been committed and suggest that he organise an extensive search of the grounds.'

'I think it would be better to speak to the constable, first,' said Rose, 'the one who will undoubtedly arrive in summons to Manning's telephone call. You could take him aside and tell him of our suspicions. No one will think it very odd if you speak to him first.'

Thus resolved, they hastened to the house to follow their plan of action. As they made their way along the paths, the lawns stretched out before them invitingly. Rose was conscious all of a sudden that the folly and the violent death that it harboured like some sepulchral chamber, seemed strangely very far away. It had consumed their thoughts and actions but now, as they negotiated the paths and stone steps leading from one ground level to another, and watched as the lakes glistened and sparkled in the late afternoon sunshine, she was reminded only of being in the most idyllic of settings on a brilliant summer's day. She knew also that if she were to turn her head now, she would discover that the great pillars of the Greek temple were concealed from view by the trees. How very odd it felt, this contrast between light and dark, the sudden lifting of the spirits compared with the heartfelt sorrow. If she were of a fanciful nature, she might almost believe that the death was no more than a dream or a piece of play-acting.

Rose quickened her pace. It would do no good to think what a wonderful day it might have been had death not so cruelly intervened. Too well could she imagine Cedric talking enthusiastically about the fencing match, and asking her whether she was not a little impressed that he had remembered all his lines without a prompt. Try as she might, the joyous scene sprang up stubbornly before her mind's eye, the laughter and the chatter, the applause, her complimenting the other thespians on the quality of their acting, and congratulating Miss Quail on the performance …

They were just approaching the house when a noise roused Rose abruptly from her musing. At first she felt bewilderment, for she could see nothing out of place which might have caused the sound. The building looked as it always did, a colossal palace of a place with its smooth, plain alabaster-coloured exterior; its corner towers topped by pyramidal roofs; and its great Corinthian columns flanking the entrance porch, bringing to mind the folly. Yet, amid all this splendour and tranquillity, Rose was convinced that something had startled her. She caught her husband's eye. From his expression, it was evident that he too had heard something. Before she had an opportunity to open her mouth to speak, however, Cedric was running towards the house. She did her best to follow him.

As they crossed the terrace, there was a commotion, the sound of two men shouting now clearly reaching their ears. However, Rose did not have time to try to listen to what was being said. Her attention was drawn instead to the strange and somewhat unexpected spectacle of two of the servants hurrying towards them, almost running, while attempting rather unsuccessfully to maintain a dignified appearance. The sense of foreboding that filled the air, and made Rose take a sharp intake of breath as she prepared herself for some awful revelation, was not helped by the servants' attire of black trousers, waistcoats, and tailcoats, which added something of a funereal air to the proceedings.

'What is it, Manning?' cried Cedric, rather sharply. He was addressing the butler, who was one of the hurrying servants. 'What is the matter?' It was evident from his brusque manner that he felt himself to be on edge, eager to be informed of the worst and be done with it.

'Begging your pardon, m'lord,' gasped Manning, between breaths. 'There's an awful to-do in the drawing room. Charlie and me,' he indicated the footman, who was the other servant that had accompanied him, 'we've done our best to quieten the two young gentlemen and bring them to their senses, as has Mr Cuffe and Mr Drury to give them their due, but there's no reasoning with them; the young men, I mean. Going at it hammer and tongs, they are.'

In spite of herself, Rose was forced to conceal a smile, wondering whether Torridge, the Sedgwicks' former head-butler, a rather formidable old fellow, would have put the matter quite so eloquently as his successor.

'To whom do you refer?' said Cedric, looking slightly irritated.

'Why, the young Prentice gentlemen, m'lord. Fighting, they are! Almost upset a table they did, and a pot of tea. I fear for the china, I do.'

'Good lord!' exclaimed Cedric, looking appalled. This was not the usual behaviour of his house guests.

'And that's not all, m'lord,' said the butler, beginning to enjoy himself. 'One of them has punched the other in the face. Blood pouring out of his nose … begging your pardon, m'lady. Can't say which one 'as done it, looking so alike as they do that no one can tell one from t'other but their own mother.'

At that moment, the sound of a startled cry floated to their ears.

'Quick, m'lord,' implored Manning. 'You'd better hurry, before one of 'em does the other a serious injury.'

Chapter Five

A strange sight indeed met Lord and Lady Belvedere's eyes as they entered the drawing room of Sedgwick Court. In his agitated state, the butler had thrown open the door somewhat noisily. The room's occupants, considerably alarmed by the act, had been arrested in their various activities, their movements frozen for a moment as if they were subjects in a photograph. In consequence, the earl and countess found themselves greeted with an odd tableau of sorts. The impression of a staged scene was further heightened by the fact that the characters were still dressed in Elizabethan costume. And it was also only now that Rose realised that greasepaint had been smeared rather crudely on the faces of one or two of the older thespians, a fact that had not been apparent outside in the bright afternoon sunlight. Here, in the drawing room, however, it was very obvious, its garishness contrasting sharply as it did with the exquisite ornaments, rich furnishings and ornate decoration of the room.

The scene itself focused on the Prentice twins. It was evident that some attempt had been made to keep the two young men apart. This endeavour had been met with only limited success, as evidenced by the bloody nose that adorned the face of one of the twins; it was difficult to tell which one, being as they were so alike in appearance and dressed identically in their black and red striped doublets and breeches. While undoubtedly, they had at some point been entangled, as evidenced by the injury, they had subsequently been separated, and now occupied opposite sides of the room. Algernon Cuffe was standing resolutely in front of one of the twins forming an impenetrable barrier, a restraining hand placed on the young man's chest, while poor Walter Drury clung doggedly to the arm of the other, a rather feeble shackle, it must be said. Fortunately, the twin in question was at that moment giving little thought to retaliation, content instead to nurse his bloody nose. He was whimpering slightly, his eyes full of unshed tears. His brother, meanwhile, was glaring at him with barely concealed anger, his face flushed and crimson, a wild look in his eyes.

'Good lord!' exclaimed Cedric, echoing the words he had uttered to his butler a few minutes before when first hearing of the skirmish. Though he himself was dressed in Tudor breeches, his face was innocent of any grease paint and revealed clearly an expression of amazement. Indeed, it took the young earl a moment or two to fully digest the scene before him. When he spoke again, there was a note of anger mingled with bewilderment in his voice.

'What is the meaning of this?' he demanded. He might have added: 'How dare you behave in such a disgraceful manner in my house?' but did not. The look he gave, however, conveyed the thought as effectively as if he had uttered the words.

Both the Prentice twins had the grace to look shamefaced, though it was not clear whether this was because they regretted their conduct, or were simply embarrassed at being spoken to in such a manner by a member of the aristocracy. Certainly, one of the young men began to mumble a series of apologies, while the other bowed his head and remained silent.

'Look here, this won't do,' said Cedric sighing, and adopting a more paternal approach, though in truth he was only a few years older than the twins. 'We have all had the most awful fright and I daresay it has affected us differently. But that is no excuse to start fighting in this ludicrous fashion. Now, will one of you two boys tell me what you were arguing about for this to happen?' He pointed to the injured twin's bloodied nose and looked expectantly from one to the other. Both the Prentice brothers, however, were strangely reticent, remaining resolutely silent. Cedric frowned and looked enquiringly at both Algernon and Walter, who merely shook their heads and shrugged their shoulders as if they were as equally perplexed as himself. Next, Lord Belvedere cast a surreptitious glance at Miriam, who he noticed was standing apart from the others and looking out of the window as if uninterested in what was happening in the room. It occurred to him to wonder whether her air of indifference was assumed. Had she really been such a disinterested party to the recent proceedings? Why, surely, he reasoned, it would have been quite a spectacle?

The same thought had occurred to Rose, who was standing a step or two behind her husband. She took the opportunity, while he was speaking, to survey the room. It was quite likely, she thought, that Miriam had been the cause of the disagreement between the brothers and, for chivalrous reasons, Algernon and Walter had decided to pretend ignorance. She stole a glance at Henry Rewe who, crouched on a footstool, was regarding the twins rather nervously, twisting his hands together in a timorous fashion. It was quite possible that, if pressed, he might reveal what he knew of the argument. However, Rose had not the heart to approach him at that moment for the poor boy looked as if he would be quite sick, given any little encouragement. As it was, he was clutching at his stomach while taking sips of water from a glass.

She looked about her to ascertain if there was anyone else they might approach. Giles Kettering, whom she considered would have made an admirable witness, she noted with regret was absent from the room. However, this in itself was not of particular note, for when he was not donning the robes of Horatio, he was employed as her husband's secretary. It was quite probable, therefore, that, on delivering his message to the butler, he had retired to his own quarters to change into his usual attire of blue serge suit, to await the arrival of the doctor and the police.

The only other occupant of the room was the director, Cordelia Quail. It was with some relief that Rose noticed the woman was calm now, though there remained about her the air of someone who had been through a painful experience. Most noticeably, her face showed signs of a handkerchief having been dabbed in rather a tardy fashion around her eyes and face, for her make-up was rubbed and smeared in places. The rouge that she had daubed on her cheeks mingled with her blue eye shadow, and her lips, until recently a deep crimson shade, were now bare of colour and looked oddly naked in the light of the drawing room. It was no good, Rose thought, to interrogate Cordelia on what had caused the fight between the Prentice twins, for she seemed absorbed in her own little world, far removed from the drawing room at Sedgwick Court. Looking at the expression on the woman's face, it was as if Shakespeare's play was still proceeding before her eyes much as it had been performed that afternoon, a living breathing thing, the final scene unfolding ...

Rose was roused from her musings by the appearance of Mrs Simpson. With a start, she realised that she had quite forgotten that her mother had been present when Ursula Stapleton's death had occurred, so preoccupied had she been in focusing her attention on the Sedgwick Players. Mrs Simpson entered the room clutching a shawl in her hands, which she proceeded to drape around Cordelia's shoulders.

Meanwhile, it was evident from his manner that Cedric had quite abandoned his attempts to ascertain the cause of the disagreement between the brothers. The twins themselves, recollecting where they were and conscious of the fact they had caused an unsavoury spectacle, had composed themselves sufficiently to make some gestures of atonement. The twin who had thrown the punch was now patting the arm of the other in a conciliatory manner, while mumbling something under his breath. Walter Drury, once he had satisfied himself there was no threat of further violence, had released his grip on the sleeve of the injured twin and was instead dabbing at the boy's nose with a clean cloth, which he dipped in a basin of hot water.

Liberated of the need to form an obstruction, and finding himself at something of a loss, Algernon Cuffe stepped forward, tall and magnificent in all his regal finery. He cast a fleeting glance at Cordelia, as if he expected that she, as director, might wish to address his lordship, to apologise for the disgusting behaviour demonstrated by some of their party of thespians. One glimpse, however, was sufficient to inform him that Cordelia had not recovered her equanimity; it was quite possible that she was oblivious of both her surroundings and even that a fight had occurred among her cast.

Algernon, aware that the eyes of the Sedgwick Players now rested firmly on his person, and conscious of the responsibility that he carried on his shoulders as a founding member of the group of thespians, cleared his throat, and began to speak in a rich, full-bodied baritone voice, the same voice that had thrilled provincial audiences.

'I really must apologise, my lord, on behalf of us all. Quite frightful behaviour, what.' He paused, as if waiting for a reply of sorts, but Cedric, watching him closely, made no comment. 'I am sure you can appreciate that we are all rather shaken up over what has happened,' Algernon began again in more appeasing tones. 'By Ursula's death I mean. I know I am, I don't mind telling you. And these two,' he made a vague gesture towards the Prentice twins, 'why, they are little more than boys and quite clearly on edge. Shameful behaviour, I know, but best forgotten, what?'

Cedric frowned and looked thoughtful. He opened his mouth to speak, but obviously thought better of it. Instead, he sighed and then summoned a footman to bring some brandy. Advancing further into the room he said:

'I do wish one of you would tell me what caused the fight.'

'It was nothing, your lordship,' said the twin with the bloody nose.

'I'm afraid I was being rather flippant about poor Mrs Stapleton's death that's all and Freddie very properly took exception. Served me right, of course, but I'm awfully sorry we caused a scene in your house … and in front of your servants, too,' he added as an afterthought.

'You won't tell Mother, will you?' mumbled the other brother. 'She's awfully strict about that sort of thing.'

'Yes. She hasn't forgiven us yet for being sent down from Oxford.'

Rose was of the view that Gerald Prentice's explanation for the disturbance lacked truth, yet his words were spoken with an odd conviction, and were accompanied by an imploring look. However, there appeared little to be gained in pursuing the matter any further.

The next few minutes were employed by members of the Sedgwick Players helping themselves to brandy. Certainly, both Algernon and Walter each poured themselves a generous glass, and Mrs Simpson added a few drops of the liquid to Cordelia's cup of tea.

Walter edged his way over to Lord Belvedere, lowering his voice to a whisper and speaking in rather a delicate manner. 'The body, my lord … Mrs Stapleton …?'

'She is quite safe,' said Cedric quickly, taking a gulp of brandy. 'One of the servants is keeping watch over her until the doctor and the police arrive.'

Though both men had taken efforts to speak quietly, their words had evidently been heard by Algernon, who crossed the room to address the earl.

'Poor woman,' he said. 'I suppose it was her heart?' He did not wait for Cedric to reply, but continued. 'As it happens, I inquired about her health only the other day. I thought she looked a little peaky at the last rehearsal. She told me she had suffered dreadfully from ill-heath all her life. But she wasn't one to complain, was she, Mr Drury?'

'I would have said, myself,' said Walter Drury rather tersely, 'that the woman did very little else.'

'Walter!' Algernon Cuffe looked appalled.

'She certainly made my life a misery,' sniffed Henry Rewe from his place on the stool. His voice, which had a rather unpleasant whine to it, made everyone start, for they had almost forgotten that he was there.

'Henry –' cried Algernon, his face now as red as his beard.

'It's no use pretending, Algernon, that she was anything but a thoroughly unpleasant woman,' objected Walter. 'The poor boy is only speaking the truth. You saw the way she spoke to him.'

'Well, I must say, you've certainly changed your tune a bit,' retorted Algernon angrily, adjusting the position of his crown, which shone majestically. 'You were quite unpleasant to Miriam earlier, accusing her of being flippant.'

Walter glared, but said nothing. Instead, he turned his back and made a great show of looking about him at the paintings on the wall. A still life painting hanging in an alcove in the far corner of the room appeared to attract his particular attention, and he walked over to study it more closely. Algernon, meanwhile, snorted and made a face. He then seemed suddenly to recollect where he was. He turned to Cedric again in preparation for bestowing another apology for the troupe's unpardonable behaviour.

Fortunately, Cedric was spared this ordeal. At the very moment he was preparing mentally to grit his teeth and don an outward smile, Giles Kettering appeared to announce the arrival of both the doctor and the village constable. The earl quickly made his excuses and bade a hasty retreat, catching his wife's eye as he left the room.

'What ghastly people,' whispered a voice in the countess' ear. Rose gave a start, for she had been so fully engrossed in listening to the arguments being played out before her in the room that she had been quite oblivious to all else. It was with a sense of relief that she found that it was her mother standing beside her, and not Miriam Belmore, as she had first feared, mocking her fellow thespians. She gave her mother a brief smile and then glanced idly over at Cordelia Quail. The director appeared to have recovered a little. Certainly, Mrs Simpson appeared to be of the view that the woman no longer required her ministrations.

'How does poor Cedric put up with them?' Mrs Simpson continued, shaking her head.

Rose laughed in spite of herself. 'I don't expect they usually behave like this. In fact, I know quite well they don't. Cedric speaks of them quite warmly.' She sighed. 'It is the shock, I suppose. People behave in different ways when they are faced with sudden death.'

'As you know to your cost from bitter experience,' said Mrs Simpson, with feeling. The sour note in her voice was not lost on her daughter, who frowned inwardly. Rose knew only too well how heartily her mother disapproved of her sleuthing activities.

'There is no reason to suppose that this is anything but a death from natural causes, is there?' said Mrs Simpson rather anxiously, having made her point.

'No,' Rose said quickly, conscious that her mother was no longer whispering. She looked about her and noticed with dismay that one or two of the Sedgwick Players had turned to stare at them with undisguised curiosity. Even Cordelia Quail had looked up from her cup of tea and appeared to be regarding them with interest. 'I believe Mrs Stapleton had a weak heart,' Rose added, speaking rather louder than was absolutely necessary. 'There is no doubt in our minds that it contributed to her death. It is very sad of course …' She gave a forlorn smile and allowed her sentence to drift, fervently hoping that it was not obvious to her watchers that she did not believe a word she was saying.

Her mother proved an unexpected ally in this respect. For she nodded and murmured: 'Yes, most unfortunate', in a voice that carried. It seemed to reinforce Rose's statement that Ursula Stapleton had died from natural causes. To Rose herself, it indicated equally Mrs Simpson's sense of relief that her daughter was not inclined to view Ursula's death as suspicious. The overall effect on the listeners however was the same; they had nothing to fear.

Rose glanced at her wristwatch. Ten minutes had elapsed since Giles had appeared in the doorway and Cedric had followed him out into the hall. She assumed that her husband had gone to his study to talk with the doctor and the constable before they examined Ursula's body. A thought suddenly occurred to her. Perhaps Cedric was speaking only with the policeman. For was it not possible that even now the doctor was making his way to the folly? She could imagine him hurrying, clutching at the vain hope that they had been mistaken, that Ursula Stapleton, though unconscious and very ill, was still alive. Her thoughts returned to the study and the village constable. How would he react, she wondered, when her husband informed him of their fears that the actress had been murdered? Would he stand there with his mouth open, his expression incredulous?

She was brought to her senses by William, the footman, inquiring whether he should arrange for another pot of tea and some more refreshments; some plates of sandwiches, perhaps, or Cook's chicken soup? He understood it was very good for shock. Rose nodded, barely listening, reminded only that the events of the day had bestowed upon her the role of hostess. So far, she had neglected her duties dismally. She had not mingled with her guests and inquired how they were bearing up. Instead, she had observed them quietly and surreptitiously, waiting for one of them to make some fatal mistake.

Closely on the heels of this thought came the realisation that she had wasted time. She should have been commencing her investigation in earnest, while her suspects were still ignorant of the fact that Ursula Stapleton had been murdered, not dithering and prevaricating as she had been. Time was marching on and at any moment the constable might appear and announce the awful truth concerning the actress' death. Then, any advantage of ignorance or surprise that she had possessed over her audience would be lost.

It was with this thought in mind that Rose took a deep breath and walked over to Cordelia, conscious all the while that her mother was staring at her thoughtfully.

Chapter Six

It was all very well to decide to do a task, thought Rose, but putting it in to practice was quite a different matter. For one thing, she was very aware that Cordelia Quail was in something of an agitated state, and she did not wish to upset her unduly. And then of course there was the fact that the other Sedgwick Players were watching her every movement closely. Algernon Cuffe was staring at her quite blatantly, as if it were a sign of deference, and Walter Drury did so furtively, as if he feared being caught in the act. One of the Prentice twins was scowling at the other, while also covertly stealing a glance at Rose every few moments, the other, with a handkerchief clutched to his wounded nose, was watching her nervously, his lip trembling. Rose was quite sure that even Miriam, who was very pointedly ignoring everyone, was nevertheless conscious of her presence. It was almost, Rose thought, yielding to a brief flight of fancy, as if she were herself an actress on the stage and they were her audience, so closely did they monitor her every step.

She wondered idly whether they would have been half as fascinated by the activities of Rose Simpson, shop assistant, as they were by Rose, Countess of Belvedere. On reflection, however, she thought that her social position probably had very little to do with their interest in her. It was her reputation as an amateur detective which no doubt intrigued them the most. This fact reminded her that she must tread carefully if she were not to arouse their suspicions. As far as the Sedgwick Players were concerned, they had witnessed the sad and untimely death of one of their members from natural causes.

She could almost imagine the thoughts racing through their minds. It was most unfortunate and regrettable, and perhaps, if they were not feeling very charitable, a little inconvenient to be detained like this. For weren't there more pressing matters to attend to? They weren't paid after all to perform; they gave up their own time graciously for the enjoyment and advancement of others. That being said, how wonderful it was to have the opportunity to look around Sedgwick Court. The grand and sweeping oak staircase was just as it should be, the exquisitely decorated drawing room was even finer than they had envisaged. Really, one was almost afraid to sit down for fear of leaving traces of the gardens, a grass stain here perhaps, or there a bit of mud caught on the heel of a shoe. And what an array of servants, when everyone knew how difficult good servants were to find these days since the war …

'Miss Quail,' said Rose. 'How are you feeling? Would you like me to ring for some more tea? No, please don't get up,' she added hurriedly, as Cordelia made as if to scramble to her feet, in her haste large strands of hair falling from under her scarlet turban. 'I'll just sit down beside you, if I may?'

Rose did not wait for a reply before perching herself on the edge of a Queen Anne chair and smiling kindly at Cordelia. The woman blinked rapidly, opened her mouth once or twice, as if to speak, though no words came out, and dabbed at her face rather vigorously with her handkerchief. Rose felt a stab of something akin to guilt. It seemed an act of meanness to disturb her. The woman was evidently distressed by what had happened and the sudden appearance of the countess had done nothing to alleviate this; if anything, Cordelia was more flustered now than before, pulling her black silk kimono about her so that she seemed to disappear into its folds as if it were a blanket.

'Oh, dear Lady Belvedere, what must you think of me?' Cordelia Quail said at last, all too aware, rather belatedly, that she must look a frightful sight with her red-rimmed eyes and runny nose. 'And your kind hospitality … it is very gracious of you.' She stifled a sob. 'It was the shock of course, that made me behave in such a way. Utterly disgraceful of course. Oh dear, I shouldn't like you to think that I am *that* type of woman.' She paused to make a face, which involved screwing up her nose as if some unpleasant smell had drifted into the room. 'Not one of those timid, frail little creatures that wouldn't say boo to a goose. Oh no, dear Lady Belvedere, I shouldn't like you to think me one of them.'

'Certainly not,' said Rose politely, while trying to reconcile in her mind the woman who had barked orders to the actors on the stage with the one who had been led wailing from the folly.

'I have always been of the belief that women are much stronger than men,' confided Cordelia, lowering her voice a little. She leant forward in her seat so that her head was not far from the countess'; Rose could feel the woman's breath on her skin. 'Emotionally, I mean, not physically, of course,' clarified Cordelia. 'Particularly spinster women. We have no one to depend upon but ourselves.'

Rose opened her mouth with the intention of saying something to the effect that she was quite sure Cordelia had a great many friends on whom she might depend, but changed her mind. For it was clear to her that Cordelia Quail was still in rather a distracted mood and likely to go off at a tangent given any little encouragement. And Rose was all too conscious of the fact that time was against her; she must get to the point of her interview. Inwardly she sighed. If only the woman could be persuaded to rally a little. How welcome the return of the formidable lady director would be, a woman who would answer her questions in a candid and forthright fashion. But it could not be helped. Cordelia Quail might well be a shadow of the woman she had been an hour ago, but Rose could not give way to compassion and sentimentality. She must interview the poor woman while she had the opportunity to do so. It would be a dereliction of her duty not to. And above all else, she must raise the matter of the missing wine glass.

She pictured the crimson wine glass as she had last seen it in the folly. Indeed, a vision of it appeared before her eyes as vividly as if it had been suspended in the air in front of her, a glittering, tangible object catching the last rays of the late afternoon sun. She imagined that, if she stretched out her hand, she would feel the delicate glass as she traced her finger around its rim ... It was in that moment a possible opening occurred to her.

'I'm sorry we rather took our time; returning to the house, I mean,' Rose began cautiously, hoping that her voice did not carry across the room. 'We didn't feel we ought to leave Mrs Stapleton quite alone. And then of course we were worried about the wine glasses ...'

She had been watching her companion closely. There was no more than a flicker of a reaction from Cordelia at the mention of the glasses. Certainly, the woman did not start or take a sharp intake of breath.

'We were worried that they might be trodden underfoot. Quite unintentionally of course ...' Rose continued, stealing another glance at Cordelia. It was difficult to ascertain what the woman was thinking from the expression on her face. It was quite possible that, distracted though the woman was, she would think it a little strange that Lady Belvedere, when confronted with the death of a woman in her grounds, should be preoccupied with the fate of some glassware.

'Wine glasses?' murmured Cordelia rather dully, a faint echo of the words uttered by her hostess.

'Yes,' said Rose. 'The beautiful crimson ones that were used on stage. I believe they are yours, aren't they? Victorian, if I'm not mistaken?'

'Yes.' said Cordelia, recovering her senses a little. 'Cranberry.' After a moment, she looked at Rose sharply. 'What were you saying about the glasses, your ladyship?'

'We found one of the wine glasses on the tray on the little table. But unfortunately, we couldn't find the other one.' Rose leant forward in her chair. 'There were two, weren't there?'

'Yes,' said Cordelia, and this time she frowned. 'There were six in the set originally, but only two are left. You found only one, you say? I do hope the other one isn't broken. They belonged to my grandmother, you know. She was quite a remarkable woman …' She gave a heartfelt sigh. 'I knew I shouldn't have used them in the play, but Ursula … Mrs Stapleton would insist on our having proper wine glasses instead of goblets. Silver goblets really would have looked so much better, don't you think?' She did not wait for Rose's reply, but continued, a sudden outpouring of words as if she had been keeping it all bottled up inside her. 'And dear Lord Belvedere told me he had a couple of goblets that he could lend us, but Ursula made such a fuss about it. Said the silver would make the water taste odd, or something equally foolish. Of course, I tried to reason with her, but once Mrs Stapleton had set her mind on something …'

'I suppose she had a point,' said Rose, thinking she ought to say something, while wondering how she might turn the conversation back to the missing wine glass.

'But it made things awfully difficult,' complained Cordelia, 'Because of course a plain, transparent glass would have been no good. It wouldn't have shown up on the stage, not in brilliant sunshine. The audience would not have been able to see it at all from where they were sitting. That's what made me think of my grandmother's wine glasses; such a very vivid shade of red.' Cordelia paused a moment, as if she too were picturing the glass in front of her. 'When Claudius holds the glass up to the audience and later when he drops the pearl in to it, it makes quite a nice spectacle. He always makes a great show of it, you see.'

'I am sure your glass is quite safe,' said Rose, fearful that the conversation was digressing. 'Perhaps Mrs Stapleton dropped it on to the ground when she became … ill, and someone else picked it up fearing it would be broken if it was left where it was.'

'Do you think so?' Cordelia said. 'I suppose it might have happened as you say, but why didn't they put it back on the tray?'

'Perhaps they weren't standing near the table at the time,' said Rose. 'In which case, they may have picked up the glass with the intention of placing it on the table at the end of the scene.'

'Then, why didn't they?' demanded Cordelia, sounding rather vexed. 'Why didn't they put it on the table? Where is it now? That's what I should like to know.' Rose looked about her hurriedly, conscious that the woman's voice had risen with her indignation.

'Perhaps they put it in their pocket and forgot about it,' Rose said hurriedly. 'It's the sort of thing I might do.'

Cordelia pursed her lips and looked to be about to say something. Rose imagined the words that she had in mind were something along the lines of 'rubbish' or 'nonsense'. But on reflection Cordelia appeared to change her mind, for the words did not escape her lips.

Rose realised too late that she had allowed herself to relax a little, certain in the belief that danger had been averted. Indeed, she was on the point of breathing a sigh of relief when Cordelia sprung suddenly to her feet, pulling her kimono about her as she went, and straightening her turban. With dismay in her heart and a feeling of abject helplessness, Rose waited for Cordelia to speak. The woman opened her mouth, and when she spoke it was in a loud voice, which seemed to fill every corner of the room, spilling out into the hall beyond. This, in itself, would not have been so bad had everyone else not been huddled together in twos or threes, speaking in hushed tones. Cordelia's voice penetrated through these snatched conversations as easily as a knife cutting through butter, for she spoke in the booming voice of the director issuing commands to the actors on the stage. Certainly, the effect was to cease all idle chatter. All eyes turned to her, the thespians regarding her with mouths slightly open as if they had been disturbed in mid-sentence, their hands twisting nervously with the fabric of their costumes. Even Miriam, aloof and in splendid isolation by the window, turned her gaze from looking out at the garden, and Gerald Prentice lowered his handkerchief from his swollen face and sniffed.

'Which one of you took my wine glass?' demanded Cordelia. 'Where is it?'

Her words were met with a somewhat surprised and awkward silence. There was the sound of a sharp intake of breath and Rose realised it was her own. What a mess she had made of it all. She had tried to lead up to the subject of the missing wine glass gradually, so as not to show undue interest and arouse suspicion. But in this she had failed miserably. Cordelia was now accusing the whole gathering of theft, glaring at each and every one of them, as if they were all guilty. And all the while, the woman was trembling with righteous indignation. It would have been amusing, comic even, if the situation was not so very awful.

Rose held her breath, trying desperately to think what she could do for the best. Thoughts, however, evaded her and she could only glance around quickly at those assembled, trying to gauge their individual reactions. In this she was rather late, for the first flickers of unguarded emotion had disappeared from the faces of most by the time she had overcome her own shock at what had happened. Now only surprise at Cordelia's outburst featured in their expressions in equal measure, but not fear. She cursed herself severely for her own stupidity. The murderer had been forewarned and would now be on his guard.

It was while these depressing thoughts were whirling through her mind that Rose caught a vague glimpse of something out of the corner of her eye. It had been a slight movement, so fleeting that she almost convinced herself that she had imagined it. But it left a distinct impression upon her. There had been an exchange of looks between two of the Sedgwick Players. They had glanced at each other merely for a brief second but with such a fierce intensity that it had struck Rose as strange, particularly as now they appeared to be staring at anything but each other. Perhaps she would not have considered this, in itself, so very odd had there not been something furtive in their manner. She wondered also why each had been drawn to regard the other, for she did not think they were on particularly friendly terms. Certainly, the way they had behaved towards one another in the folly had suggested otherwise.

Algernon Cuffe was the first to recover from the director's outburst. 'Cordelia,' he said, advancing forward, and taking her firmly, but kindly, by the arm. 'Don't go to pieces, there's a dear. We have more to concern ourselves with than the fate of your wine glass.' He patted the woman's arm affectionately and steered her back towards the chair she had so recently vacated, talking all the while in soothing tones.

It surprised Rose greatly that Cordelia, in her current belligerent mood, had allowed herself to be manoeuvred in such a fashion, for she was led away by the thespian without demur. The wild look of anger disappeared from the woman's eyes to be replaced by something else; Rose could not quite put her finger on what exactly. It might have been relief, or an odd sense of contentment. Whatever it was, it had the effect of subduing Cordelia sufficiently for her to sit quietly, clinging to Algernon's arm. Rose noticed that the director gave him the occasional imploring look, as if she sought the answer to some question in his face. Algernon, meanwhile, continued to speak softly. At length, he said:

'I don't suppose Lord and Lady Belvedere undertook a very thorough search.' He was at that moment half kneeling, half crouching on the floor beside the director's chair. His back was towards Rose so she could not see the expression on his face. She saw Cordelia's, however; the woman responded to Algernon with a smile. He turned and looked up inquiringly at Rose, repeating his sentence.

'No, not at all,' Rose muttered. 'A cursory look at best.'

This statement was so far removed from the truth that she was obliged to turn her face away to conceal the fact that she was blushing. However, in that moment she was conscious not only of her crimson cheeks, but also of the possibility that perhaps all was not lost as she had first feared. If she allowed a few minutes for the dust to settle the situation might be salvaged. And if it were, then it was due to the unwitting actions of the actor king. She found herself feeling benevolent towards him. A quick glance at Cordelia revealed that the woman was almost recovered to her usual self. Relief was showing itself visibly on the faces and in the actions of the others. Rose began to plot her next move. She imagined that she might be able to pass from one small group of thespians to another, alluding softly to the missing wine glass, remarking how wonderful it would be if they could find it and present it to Cordelia. Perhaps someone had noticed where it had been left …?

'There they go!'

Rose awoke abruptly to reality at the sound of Freddie Prentice's voice, for the young man had almost shouted the words. But his attitude, she noticed with relief, was not that of one consumed with horror. Indeed, there was something of a gleeful nature in the way he bounded across the room. Together with his brother, he scrambled over to the window for a better look. 'Out of the way, Miriam, there's a dear,' he cried, 'don't hog the window. There they are; I told you so.' This latter remark seemed to be directed to his twin, who merely nodded. 'I don't think I've ever seen Constable Bright walk so quickly, have you? Why, he's almost trotting. I suppose he has to, with those short little legs of his, just to keep up with the other two. Though I must say, if he'd kept up that pace when we pinched his helmet ... '

'There's the doctor,' mumbled his brother, who did not appear to be viewing the scene with such youthful exuberance.

'And Lord Belvedere leading the way,' said Freddie.

Rose edged forward until she could see out of the window. It appeared to her that the men were hurrying, certainly, but a sense of delicacy prevented them from actually running. And besides, there was no need, she thought. There was nothing they could do for poor Ursula Stapleton now save catch her murderer.

It was with a heavy heart, therefore, that she regarded the three-man procession as it made its way in a dignified fashion to the folly. Contributing to her sense of melancholy was the knowledge that the advantage that Algernon had unknowingly won for her regarding the wine glass had now been lost. For how could she speak to the actors of such seemingly trivial matters now? It would appear very odd.

It was only later that she realised that she had been so absorbed in her own thoughts that she had missed something very obvious, something that had such a bearing on the case, that she admonished herself afterwards for having been quite oblivious to it at the time.

Chapter Seven

The twins' fervour appeared to be contagious for, with much ado, the Sedgwick Players crowded round the window and craned their necks. It was almost as if they imagined that some fascinating scene would be played out before them on a distant stage, such was their enthusiasm. Certainly, there was considerable whispering and fidgeting, and jostling for space, with the taller of the actors gazing over the shoulders of the shorter, amid much grumbling. In the midst of it all, Rose was conscious that they kept a respectful distance from her. Only her mother came to stand beside her, peering rather short-sightedly through the glass, as she stared out at the view below.

They all stood there watching the progress of the three men as they made their way along the terraces and the paths. They trudged across the well-tended lawns down to the cool lake, and out to the stone folly beyond, hidden from their view by a veil of leaves.

The little procession made something of an amusing sight. It might almost have been said to be comical, had it not been for the bitter circumstances that had brought the three men together. Varying considerably in age, height and build, as they did, they brought to mind a set of Russian dolls. Rose herself was reminded of Shakespeare's seven ages of man, of whom the three men could be said to represent three. First, there was Cedric. Tall and fair and youthful, to her somewhat biased mind, he was the lover sighing like a furnace. After him, and struggling to keep up with the earl, came the village constable, a short and portly fellow, breathing heavily from his exertions; he was Shakespeare's justice, then, in fair round belly. Finally, bringing up the rear, was the sixth age of man, the old village doctor rather shrivelled and stooped in posture, and bent over a walking stick, his *pince-nez* perched at a precarious angle on the top of his nose.

Very often, the three men disappeared momentarily from sight, obscured by the hedges, bushes, and trees in leaf, that lined the route, only to appear again a little nearer to their grim destination. An odd silence had sudden befallen the group in the house. As if one, they stared avidly out of the window as the little procession wound its way to the Greek temple.

Even the footman, who had entered the room, seemed to incline his head in order that he might catch a peek at what was happening in the grounds.

If nothing else, it relieved the tension and boredom that pervaded the room in equal measure. For the three-man spectacle gave them something to occupy their minds and focus their attention as the minutes dragged on endlessly. The drawing room, which the troupe had so admired on first view, had something of a cloying, claustrophobic feel to it now, like a beautiful gilt cage from which they could not escape.

After a short while, the watchers grew bored with looking at the spectacle. Sighing and shrugging their shoulders, they turned away from the window at intervals. Even the twins began to show signs of being weary of the sight that had drawn them to the casement, forsaking their places at length to join the others in the room.

And so it was that only Rose remained looking out, ostensibly watching, but actually in deep contemplation. It was only afterwards that she regretted having been so deep in thought as to be quite oblivious to what was happening behind her in the room. It was a little while before she woke from her reverie and realised that she alone stood at the window. The Sedgwick Players had returned to the body of the room and were either drinking tea, which was now rather lukewarm, or else sipping brandy from lead crystal glasses. Some had wandered around the room in an aimless manner, from time to time stopping to regard an ornament or stare at paintings in which they were not the least bit interested.

During her musings, Rose had concluded that it would do no good to pursue the matter of the missing wine glass any further. For the moment at least this subject, though not fully exhausted, was likely to prove unpalatable for discussion. She had lost her chance and must focus her attention instead on something else. And on reflection, it seemed to her that her next priority was to determine the approximate route the party had taken to arrive at the house. If she could discover this it would considerably narrow the area to be searched.

The question that occupied her mind uppermost was who she should approach to find out this information. The twins, she noticed, were huddled together in a corner whispering to each other furiously. Cordelia had returned to her chair and appeared to have relapsed into her own little world again, oblivious to all else. She was being tended to by the ever diligent Mrs Simpson. It naturally occurred to Rose that she might speak to her mother, though as soon as the thought crossed her mind she dismissed it, for she remembered that Mrs Simpson and Cordelia had set off for the house before the others. It was unlikely, therefore, that their paths had crossed.

Algernon Cuffe and Walter Drury were standing beside one another, both looking a little awkward and ill at ease. Frowns creased their foreheads and Walter appeared worried. The object of their concern was Henry Rewe, the young man playing Hamlet, who was still looking rather ill. The two older men were gazing down at him as he drooped on his stool and rested his elbows on a convenient occasional table. They were making rather clumsy attempts to comfort him by patting his arm and offering him a glass of water. The gestures, kindly meant as they undoubtedly were, appeared, however, futile. For Henry had turned purposefully away from them and buried his head in his hands so that his face was all but hidden. It was almost as if he were in character; Hamlet, spurning the advances of friendship offered by Claudius and Polonius, suspicious of their true motives.

Despite the appearance given by Henry of a person not wishing to be disturbed, Rose was very tempted to approach him anyway. For she wanted to speak to him on a matter that had been preoccupying her mind for a while. If only she could have fathomed a way to prise him away from the others, she might have done so, but she could not and she did not wish their conversation to be overheard. She also wanted Henry to speak freely, which she thought unlikely if he had an audience. It was with some reluctance, therefore, that she acknowledged that she would have to wait for another opportunity.

This left only Miriam, who was standing by herself a little way from the others, apparently regarding the scene about her with something akin to bored amusement, her lips pouting in a sullen fashion, as if it were all somehow beneath her. The look she bestowed on the room in general seemed to say that Ursula Stapleton's death was little more than an annoying inconvenience, and the responses of the others to the tragedy were exaggerated and overdramatic. Rose wondered idly how the young woman would react when she learned that Ursula Stapleton's death had not been from natural causes, that she had in fact been murdered. Would Miriam still assume her look of weary indifference? Rose contemplated the girl who aroused her curiosity. There was something very detached about Miriam, as if she were standing in the room alone. Certainly, there was a certain arrogance about her posture which seemed to deter the other Sedgwick Players from approaching her. Only Algernon Cuffe, Rose noticed, appeared to be making any attempt to catch her eye. Every so often he stared at her anxiously, as if he feared she was concealing a wealth of emotions beneath her cool facade. Miriam, on her part, appeared to be equally at pains to ignore him, pointedly averting her gaze whenever she felt his eyes upon her.

Rose hesitated a moment, wondering whether there was anyone else to whom she might speak. It was not merely the young woman's cold aloofness that discouraged her from approaching Miriam. Rather, it was the distinct impression she had that any attempt to engage her in meaningful conversation would be pointless. There appeared, however, no other course of action which she might follow. It was with some trepidation, therefore, that Rose advanced on the girl playing Ophelia.

Miriam was still in her loose, unflattering costume, her black hair tangled and unruly, and festooned with flowers which, on closer inspection, revealed themselves to be made of silk rather than of real vegetation. Rose was struck by the thought that the girl's outward appearance of a wild, unkempt creature contrasted sharply, not only with the girl's own cool composure and sense of superiority, which emanated from her like an aura, but also with the heavily brocaded and richly coloured garments worn by the other thespians.

Miriam, on her part, watched Rose's approach with a mild curiosity, her mouth turning up slightly at one corner in what may have been a half smile, but which could just as easily have been something resembling a sneer. Whichever it was, Rose was not sure it boded well for the interview that was to follow.

'Miss Belmore, won't you have another cup of tea?' she began tentatively.

'No, thank you, your … ladyship.'

The words were polite enough, yet they were said in such a manner as to suggest insolence or, if not that exactly, at least that the girl was mocking her listener. Certainly, there had been a slight pause before the word 'ladyship', as if the speaker did not consider her companion deserved to be addressed as such, that it was nothing more than a mock title to cause amusement. Instinctively, Rose felt her own cheeks flush crimson and cursed inwardly for allowing herself to be intimidated by the likes of Miriam Belmore. She reminded herself sternly that she was no longer an assistant in a dress shop, and Miriam was not a customer to be served and pandered to. Rather, she, Rose, was a countess, if only by marriage, and as such the girl's social superior. And what was more, the palatial palace in which they were standing, and which had so impressed the Sedgwick Players when they had first laid eyes upon it, was her home. In ordinary circumstances, Miriam Belmore would never have set foot across the threshold of Sedgwick Court.

It was with renewed confidence that Rose set about her self-appointed task.

'Did it take you very long to get back to the house, Miss Belmore?' Miriam looked at her quizzically and Rose continued hurriedly. 'It has only just occurred to me that you might not have known the way. Back to the house, I mean. I do hope that you didn't get lost. Did you take the lower path or the upper one? Or perhaps you ran across the lawns? That is the most direct route, and is the one I should most probably have taken myself …'

Rose faltered, conscious that she was rambling. To make matters worse, a sullen expression had come into Miriam's face; the girl looked almost resentful, a feature which did little to enhance her good looks. It was only then that it struck Rose that Miriam was not quite as young as she had first supposed. A handful of tiny lines were etched at the corners of the girl's eyes, and at close quarters it was apparent that her fresh, unsullied complexion owed more to lotions than to nature. On reflection, Rose placed the woman as being in her late twenties, rather than in her very early twenties, as she had first supposed.

'We kept to the paths, your ladyship. We didn't trample on your flowerbeds if that is what you were afraid of.' The impertinence of Miriam's words was blatant now, softened only by being uttered in a voice that was rather musical and artificially bright, so that it might be supposed by a casual auditor that her intention had been only to amuse. The words were accompanied by a smile and a little high-pitched laugh. Both appeared a trifle forced, and revealed teeth that were small and even, and very white.

'The thought never occurred to me, I assure you,' said Rose, smiling, rather taken aback. She had difficulty mirroring Miriam's light-hearted tone. Indeed, she found herself speaking more sharply than she had intended, for she felt quite certain that the girl's real purpose had been to cause offense. Certainly, Miriam's smile had not reached her eyes, which remained cold and rather calculating, as if she were regarding an object of which she was distrustful. To Rose, who studied her closely, the girl was clearly agitated, even if she was putting on a very good show of being otherwise.

Inwardly, Rose sighed. It was difficult to know what to say next. How was she to engage with a woman who so very obviously did not wish to speak to her? If only she could penetrate the girl's icy shell. She could not rid herself of the feeling that she had made a complete hash of things. She felt as if her newly elevated position in society had removed her from those of a lower station, who had formerly been her peers or equals, or even her superiors. There was a great distance between her and the others in the room; they spoke to one another as if she were not there and, when she came upon them, they eyed her shyly, the words frozen on their lips, as if they feared they might be speaking out of turn. Miriam didn't act like that, of course, but Rose's social status still placed a barrier between them. The girl could not snub her or be blatantly rude to her as she might have wished.

If only, Rose thought, she had approached matters differently. Then, she might have acquired some valuable information. Instead, her endeavours to locate the whereabouts of the missing wine glass had been sadly thwarted, if only temporarily, by the sudden appearance of the doctor and the policeman in the grounds, which had drawn everyone's attention to the window. Her initial attempts to discover the route taken by the troupe to arrive at the house had not fared much better, for she admitted to herself now that she had been careless and blundering in the way she had tackled Miriam. Even to her own ears, she had sounded too eager and inquisitive.

To make matters worse, it was obvious to her that Miriam Belmore had quite taken against her. In the silence that followed, a wall of hostility and suspicion seemed to have sprung up between them. The slightly mocking smile of her companion had quite disappeared and the girl's eyes now flashed at her angrily. As Rose watched transfixed, Miriam tossed her head back and drew herself up tall, rather as if she were a stallion preparing for a fight. The movement dislodged the silk flowers, which caught in the tangles of her hair before they could fall to the ground. It was all rather theatrical and Rose wondered how much of it was real and how much done for effect. Certainly, she had a sense of how Miriam might play the unfortunate Ophelia, driven mad by her father's untimely death.

It was then that it occurred to Rose that she really had very little left to lose. There was no reason now why she need beat about the bush when talking to Miriam. She might say anything she wished; it would not make the girl feel the slightest bit differently towards her. With this realisation, came a lightening of her spirits. She would not pass the time of day with this rude and ignorant girl. Instead, she would assume the mantle of the amateur sleuth she aspired to be, the one who had been involved in six murder investigations and had earned the admiration, if rather grudgingly, of both the provincial police and of Scotland Yard.

'I should like you to tell me the route you took through the grounds when you returned to the house,' said Rose slowly and quietly, as if she were addressing a stubborn child.

It was apparent to anyone who wished to observe that Rose's solemn tone startled Miriam. The girl blinked rapidly a couple of times, and opened her mouth to speak before thinking better of it. Fearing the girl would remain mute, Rose took a step forward, the effect of which was to force a word to escape from the girl's lips.

'Why?' The word was spoken in a whisper.

'I should like to know,' said Rose firmly. 'Surely it is not too much to ask that you tell me such a very simple thing?'

An emotion akin to fear appeared on Miriam's face. Her eyes seemed to dart about the room until they settled on the little trio of actors comprising Algernon, Walter and the ailing Henry. Rose followed the girl's gaze and Miriam, suddenly aware that she had made some fatal error, grabbed at Rose's sleeve, so that she might have the countess' full attention.

'Is it true what they say about you?'

'What do they say?' inquired Rose, wondering if she really wanted to know. She could only imagine what the village gossip was about her.

Certainly, she thought it likely that many of them thought Cedric had married beneath him, for an assistant in a dress shop was not the obvious choice of bride for an earl. No doubt they thought she gave herself airs and graces and considered herself better than she was ...

'That you're an amateur detective?'

'Yes,' answered Rose, somewhat relieved that she was not about to hear some spiteful village gossip regarding her character.

'They say you've been involved with murder cases,' said Miriam. 'That business last year on Bonfire Night ...' She faltered.

'It is true that I have been in a position in the past to help the police with their inquiries,' said Rose carefully.

'You think Ursula Stapleton was murdered, don't you? That's why you and his lordship took an age to return to the house, isn't it? We were all wondering where you were.' Miriam's tone was challenging now. She looked vexed, as if she thought some frightful trick had been played upon them.

Rose looked about her anxiously, aware that Miriam's voice had risen with her growing indignation. She hoped fervently that the others were still engrossed in their own activities and had not heard Miriam mention the word 'murder'.

As she gazed about the room, her eyes caught sight of something perched on the top of a bookcase that she had not remembered being there before. The object was half hidden behind a vase of flowers and, had she not been standing where she was, she might not have noticed it at all. As it was, she could only see the smallest bit of it, and she might well have ignored it, had it not been for its colour, which had drawn her attention to it.

Quickly, she made her excuses to a somewhat bewildered Miriam and, aware that her heart was beating rather fast, crossed the room until she was abreast with the bookcase. In case she was being watched, she made a show of rearranging the flowers in the vase, though her attention was focused elsewhere, in fact on what had been pushed behind the vase itself. She gave a sharp intake of breath; she had not been mistaken. It was definitely red and made of glass. Rather gingerly, Rose moved aside the vase, conscious that she should not touch the object itself. She kept her back to the room in an attempt to hide her discovery from the prying eyes of the others. Certainly, she did not wish them to see the expression on her face. For, reflecting back at her, and looking strangely innocent and fragile, was a Victorian cranberry-coloured wine glass, twinkling in the light from the chandelier.

Chapter Eight

For a moment, all Rose's senses seemed to have left her. She could do nothing but stare dumbfounded at the object in front of her, which seemed to glisten and shine in the light, even as she watched it, like some malevolent deity. She fancied that she could even see traces of the poison that had polluted it at the bottom of the glass. Certainly, the red glass seemed to mesmerise her like some malignant force.

It was with some effort, therefore, that she tore her eyes from the wine glass and took measures to regain her composure. It was fortunate, she thought, that she had her back to the room. There was no one to witness the expression on her face, or ask her if she were unwell, for she was quite sure that she must look a ghastly shade of white, such was the shock she had experienced.

She recalled vaguely that she had voiced the possibility to Cedric that the murderer would decide to rid himself of the wine glass in the house. She had surmised that he might consider it his best course of action. For there would be a strong possibility that it would not be discovered until the next day, and then only by some exhausted housemaid who might not be aware of the significance of her discovery. Rose realised now, however, as she stared at the offending object, that she had never given the idea much credence. For one thing, it would require the murderer to take an awful risk; the likelihood of being spotted disposing of the glass by someone in the room was great.

Rose took a deep breath and, with trembling hands, positioned the vase so that the offending wine glass was hidden behind it, obscured from view from all but the most astute observer. Slowly, she turned and surveyed the room apprehensively. However, somewhat to her relief, it appeared that the others were too engrossed in what they were doing to be interested in her own activities. Certainly, no one seemed to eye her surreptitiously; there was no furtive glance cast in her direction and conversely no one appeared determined not to meet her gaze, aware of what she had unearthed behind the vase.

Quickly she looked about her and spied one of the footmen standing beside the table of refreshments. Summoning the servant to her, she gave him strict instructions to stand in front of the bookcase and, on no account, to forsake his post.

'And, Charlie, don't, whatever you do, let anyone pick up the wine glass,' Rose said quietly.

The footman nodded and gave his mistress a respectful look. If he was surprised by his mistress' strange instructions, or alarmed by the note of urgency in her voice, he did not betray the fact by his expression. Neither did he show any surprise at discovering the sudden appearance in the drawing room of one of the wine glasses he had earlier filled with water and taken to the folly. It was all distinctly odd, as he would remark later to Edna, Rose's lady's maid, in the safety of the servants' hall; but in the drawing room he merely muttered: 'Yes, your ladyship,' as if such requests and happenings were commonplace.

Satisfied that she had put measures in place to ensure that the wine glass would neither be handled, nor vanish into thin air the moment her back was turned, Rose hastened out of the room in search of pen and paper. It was with something akin to relief, therefore, that she found the butler, Manning, patrolling the hall outside rather like a sentry. On discovering what his employer sought, the upper servant hastily produced a pencil from one of his pockets and tore a page from his own notebook. Rose hurriedly scrawled a note to her husband.

'Manning, please see that Lord Belvedere receives this note at once. I suppose he is still at the folly with the constable and the doctor?'

'I believe so, m'lady. I'll take the note to his lordship myself.'

With that, the butler disappeared and Rose was left to imagine him scurrying across the grounds to the Greek temple. It reminded her of another occasion when Manning, then under butler, had hurried towards her and Cedric in the grounds, when they had been admiring the follies and parkland. Then, Manning had been almost running in his haste, while all the time trying rather unsuccessfully to maintain a dignified appearance. This had not been helped, she remembered, by his attire of black trousers, waistcoat and tailcoat, which had rather given him the appearance of a waddling penguin.

Rose hesitated for a moment in the hall. Etiquette dictated that she should return to the drawing room and entertain her guests, or at the very least keep them company while they awaited the arrival of the constable and the doctor. However, she found herself reluctant to return to the room with its stifling atmosphere of apprehension and its strange assortment of characters. Instead, she chose to linger a little longer in the hall, to breathe deeply and take stock of the situation in which she found herself. She basked in the welcome solitude the hall offered her for, now that the butler had departed on his errand, there was not even a servant present to observe her. For a moment, she might have been plain Rose Simpson again, instead of Lady Belvedere, for all the interest the world took in her as she stood in the black and white tiled hall, staring up at the great oak staircase that loomed above her like some huge monument.

A noise startled Rose, rousing her from her reverie as effectively as if someone had splashed cold water upon her face. It took a moment for her to realise that what she had heard was a commotion of sorts emanating from the outer hall, which itself opened out on to the terrace. It was consistent with the sound of the three men returning to the house after their visit to the folly. Instinctively, she moved towards them, to be there to greet them when they entered the main hall. As she approached, she recognised the sound of Cedric's long strides crossing the tiles even before she caught a glimpse of him, or heard his voice, which was strangely muted and lacking in enthusiasm. This surprised her greatly, for she had expected her husband to be excited, to come bounding into the house and rush up the stairs, taking them two at a time in his eagerness to see the wine glass in its hiding place. Instead, when she saw him, he looked oddly deflated, like a small boy who had broken his favourite toy.

Before she could ask him what was wrong, he spied her in the hall and came marching over to her. As he walked towards her, she noticed that he raked his hair with the fingers of one hand in an irritated fashion. His face was a mixture of emotions.

'Confound the man!' said her husband angrily, his forehead now deeply furrowed with frustration. He spoke the words in something akin to a rough and harried whisper, as if he did not wish those following him to hear what he was saying yet sought a release for his anger.

'Whatever's the matter?'

'That damned doctor. That's what. And Constable Bright too, of course. I say, did you know the man lacks a backbone? The police constable I mean, not the doctor.'

The earl did not wait for his wife to reply but hurried on, as if he feared at any moment the imminent arrival of his colleagues in the main hall. Certainly, the sounds coming from the outer hall had ceased.

'Our good constable,' he continued, lowering his voice after pausing for a moment to glance furtively over his shoulder, 'doesn't want to contradict the eminent doctor. Neither does he wish to ruffle my feathers. I think the aristocracy might have taken precedence over the medical profession if the old man had not helped deliver our constable's wife of a healthy baby boy.' Cedric scowled. He took a deep breath and some of his anger seemed to disappear with it. 'Poor old Constable Bright. I suppose it's not the poor fellow's fault if he's a trifle lily-livered. But he knows as well as I do what his duty is; to fully investigate a potential crime, that's what. Still, I suppose he's used to dealing with petty theft and damage and drunken louts, not –'

'What *are* you talking about, darling?' Rose asked, interrupting, rather taken aback by the ferocity of her husband's tirade. For it was seldom, if ever, that she had heard him speak in such a manner of his social inferiors. Ludicrous as it seemed, given the circumstances, she had a sudden urge to giggle. Instead she bit her lip and, as she did so, sudden comprehension came to her as clearly as if it had been written before her on a page. 'Surely you're not saying that –'

'Yes, I am. Of all the ridiculous things. The doctor doesn't believe Mrs Stapleton was poisoned!' Cedric threw his hands up in the air in a gesture of exclamation mingled with disgust. 'Well, perhaps I am being a little unfair,' he added, making a face. 'What the old fellow actually said was that the body's appearance was not inconsistent with that of a person who had died from some heart disease or other. You know, the rosy complexion and all that.' He sighed. 'Still, I suppose I should be thankful for small mercies. By that I mean the old chap didn't set about issuing a death certificate. Fortunately, it appears that Ursula was not his patient, otherwise I wouldn't have put it past him.' Cedric shook his head. 'To tell you the truth, I suppose I am most angry with myself.'

'Oh?' Rose put her hand on her husband's arm and he looked down at her and smiled.

'If I am to be quite honest, it's all my fault. No use apportioning blame or, if I do, I should look no further than myself.'

'What do you mean?' Rose looked at him quizzically and wondered whether it was possible that they had both made rather a mess of things regarding furthering their inquiries in to the actress' death.

'Well, I was fool enough to remark on Ursula having had a weak heart. Sheer stupidity on my part because it put the notion in the doctor's head. I doubt he would have considered it if I hadn't blurted it out. Do you remember Algernon Cuffe mentioned it? The heart business, I mean, not my stupidity.'

'Yes, I do. We were in the folly, weren't we?'

'Yes. But really, it's too absurd to believe that Ursula died from natural causes.'

Cedric grinned at his wife half sheepishly, as if he were suddenly conscious he had overdramatised the situation. He stretched out a weary arm towards her, and she, sharing in his sudden fatigue of everything that had happened, moved towards him and rested her head on his shoulder. Rose was aware only of a sense of peace and contentment. They might have been alone at Sedgwick Court for all the notice they gave to their surroundings. It was as if the house was quite empty of servants, and the Sedgwick Players were still in the folly, treading the boards of the makeshift stage.

A couple of minutes elapsed, and it was with obvious reluctance that they tore themselves apart and faced the awful reality of the situation in which they found themselves. Death had once more come to Sedgwick Court and they must deal with it as best they could.

'Not that I suppose it matters,' said Cedric, clearly resigned to what was to follow. 'They'll determine the cause of death soon enough when they do the post-mortem. But it is all rather galling. It appears, darling, that it is only me who can detect the smell of almonds on the poor woman.'

'You must have a remarkable sense of smell,' remarked his wife. If the circumstances had been different, Rose might have laughed. As it was, her thoughts were elsewhere for it had occurred to her suddenly that Cedric had made no mention of the missing wine glass.

'Did Manning find you?'

'Manning? No, should he have done?' Cedric looked at her with interest, for the eager note in his wife's voice was not lost on him.

'I sent him after you.' Rose took a step forward and lowered her voice to a whisper. 'I've found the missing wine glass. It was in the drawing room half hidden behind a vase on the bookcase.'

'Have you, by Jove!' exclaimed Cedric, his eyes wide. 'Why, that's capital.'

'Ssh!' said Rose hurriedly, for Cedric's voice had risen in his excitement. She gave a furtive glance at the door of the drawing room, praying it was firmly closed and not just ajar. For she had no wish for the troupe to overhear the news.

'They'll have to believe it was murder now, won't they?' continued Cedric in a lowered voice. 'I mean to say, why else would anyone wish to hide the wine glass?'

Before Rose had a chance to reply, the constable and the doctor appeared in the hall, the latter carrying a rather battered old Gladstone bag which he placed on a convenient console table.

'Ah, your ladyship,' muttered the old doctor, peering at Rose from behind his *pince-nez*. It was evident that the lenses were particularly strong, for the doctor's eyes were magnified in rather a grotesque fashion so as to give the appearance of being rather too large for his head. Certainly, Rose could see clearly that the eyes themselves were rather red rimmed and watered profusely. She also observed that the doctor was obliged to screw them up in order to focus them upon her, and she wondered idly whether she resembled anything more to him than a dim, shadowy form.

'Very pleased to make your acquaintance, my dear,' croaked the old doctor, before coughing nervously as if he feared he might have spoken out of turn. He shuffled a step or two backwards with the aid of his walking stick, as fast as his stiff, old legs would permit, while muttering: 'Begging your pardon, your ladyship.'

'Not at all,' replied Rose kindly. 'How do you do, Dr Henchard? I am very pleased to meet you, though I should have preferred it to have been under less unfortunate circumstances. And Constable Bright, how do you do?' she added, addressing the plump little policeman, whom she had met previously, and who was evidently somewhat out of breath due to his exertions round the grounds.

Constable Bright went crimson, mumbled something, the only words of which Rose could decipher being 'your ladyship', and proceeded to remove his helmet and mop at his forehead with an extremely large white handkerchief.

'I should like you gentlemen to come to my study,' said Cedric briskly, as soon as the pleasantries had been exchanged. 'My wife has something of importance to tell you.'

The earl's companions followed him into the room in question without demur. Cedric closed the door firmly behind them and remained standing. The others seated themselves around the large, walnut estate desk, the doctor taking Cedric's buttoned-velvet captain's chair.

'Look here,' began Cedric, 'Lady Belvedere has found the missing wine glass, the one with the poison in it. It was hidden behind a vase in the drawing room. I say, darling,' he added, almost as an aside to his wife, 'it is quite safe, isn't it? That's to say, our murderer won't be able to get his hands on it?'

'It's quite safe,' replied Rose. 'Charlie is guarding it, though ...' She allowed her sentence to falter as an idea came into her head.

Her husband looked at her inquiringly. He was, however, impatient to make his point and, when Rose did not appear inclined to say anything further on the matter, continued with his argument. 'You see, gentlemen, it just goes to prove that I was right. Mrs Stapleton was murdered. I'll wager that if you have that glass analysed, Constable, you'll find traces of poison in the dregs.'

'Because it was deliberately brought from the folly to the house, you mean, my lord?' asked the constable, scratching his head. He fumbled in his breast pocket and produced a pencil stub and a rather dog-eared looking notebook, the pages of which he flipped through rapidly until he found one on which nothing was scribbled.

'Well, there is that, of course,' agreed Cedric, somewhat impatiently. 'Why would anyone want to bring the wine glass to the house unless they wished to dispose of it?'

'They might have been afraid it would be broken if it was left in the folly, my lord, or perhaps they picked it up, absentminded like,' suggested the policeman somewhat nervously.

'The point I was trying to make, Constable, was that they saw fit to hide it,' said Cedric, trying to keep his temper in check. 'Why would anyone want to do that unless it contained something incriminating?'

'I'm afraid that I may be to blame,' admitted Rose rather sheepishly. 'That's to say, if there is an innocent explanation for Mrs Stapleton's death.'

Cedric looked quite taken aback by his wife's statement, as if the wind had momentarily been taken out of his sails. The constable, seeing that this was a moment when he might assert the authority of the law, cleared his throat rather noisily, clutched his pencil and rather ostentatiously smoothed with his hand the page in his notebook.

'What do you mean by that, your ladyship? That you might be to blame?'

'I should perhaps say, Constable, that I don't believe for one moment that Mrs Stapleton's death was from natural causes.'

'But, if that was to prove to be the case, are you saying as how you might be to blame for the wine glass having been hidden as it were?'

'Yes.'

'Why, his lordship is just after telling me how careful you've been not to arouse any suspicion that Mrs Stapleton's death was anything but natural,' said the constable looking confused. 'Not that the doctor is saying it isn't,' he added hurriedly, giving a quick glance at the doctor, who was sitting quietly, his walking stick clutched between gnarled hands.

'Well, you see, I think I may have given Miss Quail the impression that someone had stolen one of her wine glasses,' said Rose quietly, aware that all eyes were on her. 'I didn't mean to, of course. I was only trying to discover what had happened to the wine glass, and it occurred to me that Miss Quail might have seen someone pick it up. My intention was to question everyone on the matter.'

Constable Bright coughed and looked slightly uncomfortable, as if he wished to say something but thought better of it. Not for the first time, Rose thought that, had she still been plain Rose Simpson, he would most probably have criticised her actions.

'Unfortunately, Miss Quail became a little hysterical,' Rose continued. She bit her lip and added rather miserably: 'To tell you the truth, she made a frightful scene.'

'A scene, you say?' said Constable Bright, looking up from his notebook. 'What kind of a scene?'

'She raised her voice, Constable. She addressed the whole room and demanded that the glass be returned to her at once. It was all rather dreadful. The wine glasses belonged to her, you see,' Rose explained. 'They were part of a set and I believe she rather treasured them.' She glanced apologetically at Cedric, 'I'm afraid she made such a fuss that I am not a bit surprised that no one owned up to having taken it.'

'So, what you are saying, your ladyship, if I understand you correctly, is that only a fool who didn't mind a good lashing from Miss Quail's tongue would have admitted to having it on their person.'

'Exactly, Constable.'

'I was in one of her plays, once,' the constable remarked, making a face. 'Second villager from the left, I was. Frightened me half to death, she did. Not the sort of lady you'd want to cross by not knowing your lines or where you had to stand on the stage, I can tell you.' He started abruptly, as if he recollected where he was. 'So what we are saying is that there might be quite an innocent explanation for why someone took the wine glass from the folly and hid it in your drawing room?'

'Yes.'

'Or there might not be,' said Cedric, rather sulkily. 'I say, Constable, surely you are still intending to interview everyone?'

'There doesn't seem much point in that, my lord, if what you mean is speak to them separate like. A waste of time if you ask me, seeing as now we don't know if a murder has been committed or not and likely as not it hasn't. That's the opinion of the good doctor here, isn't it? And he should know. He's of the opinion that the poor woman died from natural causes. Isn't that right, Dr Henchard?' The constable had raised his voice slightly and jerked his head in the direction of the aged doctor, who nodded his head sagely and mumbled: 'Quite right, Constable.'

'Now, look here, Constable –'

'Begging your pardon, your lordship, but there is not much we can do for now, not until we know what's happened.'

There was a stubborn note to the constable's voice, and it occurred to Rose that the policeman was a little frightened. While he would naturally be nervous of incurring the earl's wrath, he was also wary of launching a murder investigation, particularly if it was likely to prove unfounded.

The constable raised a hand as Cedric made to object again.

'I'll speak to everyone in the drawing room and advise them as we may need to speak to them at a later date. I'll take the glass with me and telephone the police station at Bichester, ask them to arrange for its contents to be analysed. That's the best I can do. And of course, it goes without saying that we'll know more after the post-mortem.'

'Very well,' said Cedric rather bitterly, 'if you don't mind losing some vital clue or other. I only wish, Dr Henchard,' he said, turning to the doctor, 'that you suspected foul play.'

'Well, I for one think the constable's proposal is a very good one,' said Rose cheerfully.

'Do you?' Cedric stared at her in surprise.

'Yes, I do,' said Rose. Her voice was filled with such quiet conviction that her husband eyed her curiously and made no further protest.

'If you will excuse me, Constable,' continued Rose, 'I should like a word with our butler. Darling,' she added, addressing her husband, and giving him something of a meaningful look, 'why don't you give Constable Bright a detailed description of the events leading up to Mrs Stapleton's death? I am sure he will need to make some report or other.'

Before either gentleman had an opportunity to comment on her suggestion, Rose had opened the door and fled the room. She crossed the hall, thinking rapidly. She was all too aware that there was very little time to put her plan into action.

Chapter Nine

She was roused from her thoughts by the arrival of Manning, who entered the hall slightly panting, as if he had been running.

'Begging your pardon, m'lady,' began the butler between breaths, 'but I can't find his lordship. Perhaps he has returned to the house?'

'Yes, he has,' said Rose. She looked at the servant somewhat apologetically. 'I'm afraid I shall require you to return to the folly.' Her next words to him were uttered in a hurried whisper, as she proceeded to give Manning detailed instructions. The butler listened intently and did his utmost to hide a look of surprise from appearing on his face.

'Quickly as you can, Manning, we haven't much time.'

'Yes, m'lady.'

Rose stood for a moment watching the butler's retreating back. It was then that she wondered if she were not being a little foolish. Should she confide her plan to the constable? But no, on reflection, she would not do that. For she remembered the sceptical way he had dealt with Cedric, dismissing his suspicions with a wave of his hand or, perhaps more accurately, with a rustle of the pages in his notebook. It would be far better, she decided, to leave the policeman in ignorance until the deed was done. Her thoughts then turned to her husband. How she wished she had an opportunity to whisper in Cedric's ear. Yet, if he too were oblivious of her plot, did it not mean that there was more chance of it succeeding? Still, she hesitated. She should return to the study, and yet she was disinclined to do so. She wanted to wait for Manning to return and yet to do so would only draw attention …

It was with some reluctance, therefore, that she retraced her steps and opened the door to the study. Cedric's words floated across the room to her. 'Collapsed in a heap, Constable,' he was saying, evidently drawing his narrative to a close. 'It all happened so jolly quickly. It took us a few minutes to realise she was dead.'

'Would you care for a cup of tea?' inquired Rose, addressing both the constable and the doctor. She bestowed on them a smile which seemed to suggest that there was nothing in the world that she would like more than to pour each of them a cup of the fortifying liquid. It certainly conjured up in the minds of both gentlemen a rather pleasing image of a fine bone china tea service; they could almost hear the tinkle of teaspoons on delicate saucers.

The party of four were still seated in Cedric's study, though some time had elapsed since Rose had returned to the room from the hall. The countess, rather unnecessarily in her husband's opinion, had insisted on providing the constable with a most detailed account of her own observations during the period immediately prior to Ursula Stapleton's death. Rose herself was conscious that Constable Bright had done his utmost not to look bored, though her tale was one he had heard before, for it largely mirrored her husband's rendition. She had added a few little embellishments and flourishes to her narrative to make it a rather long-winded account; even the old doctor, comfortably seated in Cedric's chair, had experienced some difficulty in stifling a yawn.

'That's very kind of you, I'm sure, your ladyship,' began Constable Bright, consulting his pocket watch, 'but –'

'Oh, it wouldn't be any trouble at all, Constable, I assure you,' replied Rose rather breezily, casting a furtive glance at the clock on the mantelpiece. She wondered desperately if the butler had returned to the house or whether he was still making his way back from the folly. If she were to pull the bell rope she might …

Someone coughed, and her thoughts returned to the room. The constable was beginning to fidget. No doubt he was impatient to speak to the thespians and be gone. Rose looked at his flushed face and the way that he clutched his pencil and notepad. He did not hold these articles as if they were symbols of authority, instead as if they were a crutch or a screen, behind which he might hide. She felt, in that instant, that she had the measure of the man. He was comfortable dealing with the petty crimes of a village like Sedgwick, where every person was known to him. He had grown up with most of the lads, and was as familiar with their history and misdeeds as he was with his own. The goings on in the 'big house', as he referred to Sedgwick Court, were quite a different kettle of fish. They were as foreign to him as if they had occurred in some distant land. The inhabitants too were unusual, with their elegant clothes, posh voices and privileged backgrounds. 'Never done a proper day's work in their lives the lot of them', he might have said to his wife in the sanctuary of their own home, had he not heard something of Rose's past that made him view that young lady particularly warily.

Rose thought rapidly. 'The library,' she said.

'The library?' inquired the constable, raising a startled eyebrow.

'Yes,' said Rose. 'I thought you might wish to interview everyone in the library. It's more formal than the drawing room. That's to say, it makes a more fitting interview room. And besides,' she added, 'I expect they could all do with a change of scene, don't you? They have been rather cooped up in the drawing room for simply hours, poor things,' she exaggerated.

Rose held her breath. She observed the workings of the constable's mind as clearly as if they had been set out before her on a sheet of paper. And it was with a sense of relief that she saw that he was minded to concur with her request. The library really was more suitable for such an activity, and the drawing room … well, if truth be told, he would find it rather daunting. All those precious ornaments, which he might inadvertently knock off the shelves given how clumsy he was; least, that was what his wife was always telling him. Richly upholstered furniture … and exquisite Persian rugs … really, he wouldn't know where to put his feet for fear of ruining the carpets with his police-issue boots. No, far better that they should be seated in the library with only a few shelves of dusty old books.

'Darling, will you be a dear and arrange for a cup of tea to be sent to the library for the constable?' Rose asked her husband, doing her best not to catch his eye; she could only imagine what was passing through Cedric's mind and how his thoughts might be reflected in his expression. 'I'd better get back to my guests.' She returned her attention to the policeman. 'I'll inform them, Constable, that you wish to see them in the library.'

Rose bustled out of the room before anyone could stop her. She half feared that Cedric would come running after her demanding to know what she was up to. It was with something akin to relief, therefore, to discover that no one had seen fit to follow her. There was no unwelcome sound of footsteps behind her, and no one called out to her. Yet, quickly on the heels of this sense of deliverance came a feeling of apprehension. It was caused, she knew, by the certain knowledge that she was about to do something of which the constable, at least, would wholeheartedly disapprove.

She crossed the hall and, taking a deep breath, opened the door to the drawing room, trying to compose her face into something that resembled a smile. All the while, her heart was beating rapidly in her chest.

She was greeted at once by half a dozen or so anxious faces. It was obvious that, as if one, they had turned to confront the door as soon as they had heard it open. Also evident was the fact that they had been expecting to see the constable. For, on identifying the newcomer as the countess, they had relaxed visibly; mouths that were gaping open closed, hands that were clutched were let go, and foreheads that had been furrowed became smooth. Rose noticed all these little outwards signs of relief and felt a stab of something akin to guilt.

'Lady Belvedere,' said Algernon Cuffe, being one of the first to recover his composure and step forward. 'Is there any news? I am sure I speak for everyone when I say we have been kept here for an awfully long time. Not that we aren't very grateful for your hospitality, of course,' he added quickly, as if he were afraid that his remarks might have caused offence. He gave her a hopeful smile. 'Are you come to tell us that we are free to leave?'

'Yes and no, Mr Cuffe,' replied Rose, matching his smile. 'The constable would like a word with you all in the library and then you may leave. If you would all follow me.' She turned towards the door and added over her shoulder, almost as if it were an afterthought: 'You may leave all your things here and collect them when you leave.' She glanced back at Walter Drury. 'You won't want to carry your hat into the library, Mr Drury, will you? It is far too cumbersome. And that goes for all of you. I daresay you'll want to leave your cloaks and shawls here, to say nothing of your swords and daggers.'

There was a collective mumbling of assent as the troupe rid themselves of their various trappings and properties.

'Why should the constable wish to see us?' enquired the director rather nervously.

'It is merely a formality, Cordelia,' said Algernon, taking off his crown and propping it rather precariously on the edge of a table. 'There is nothing to worry about.'

'I am afraid that is not quite true, Mr Cuffe,' said Rose quietly. She turned around, aware that she now had their full attention.

'Oh?' enquired Walter, his hand poised in unfastening his cloak.

'Yes,' replied Rose. 'I'm afraid it is all rather ghastly. You see, the constable is dreadfully afraid that Mrs Stapleton was murdered.'

She was vaguely aware of a cup slipping from the hand of Cordelia Quail and its contents spilling on to the floor. Rose stared transfixed at the damp patch that the liquid had made, reluctant to meet the eyes of those gathered, conscious that her cheeks flushed with her lie. The tea, she noticed, appeared to be spreading with every passing second. At the same time, she wondered what the constable's reaction would have been had he been there to hear her utter her last sentence. Her thoughts became tangled. A ludicrous image was conjured up in her mind of the red-faced constable on his hands and knees rubbing vigorously at the rug, trying to rid it of the tea stain.

Rose had stood and watched while the Sedgwick Players had divested themselves of their outer garments and paraphernalia, their movements and actions oddly slow and stilted as they had digested her words, expressions of shock and bewilderment showing on their faces. Even Miriam, who had raised the question of murder and who, Rose observed closely, was quiet and withdrawn, her hand discernibly shaking as she tore at the silk flowers in her hair until they were strewn tattered and abandoned on the floor. If she had had a hairbrush on her person, she might very possibly have been tempted to use it. As it was, her hair remained tangled and wild. Running a hand awkwardly through her curls in the manner of a comb, the young woman clutched at her shapeless gown, wrapping it around her like a cloak.

Mrs Simpson appeared at Rose's shoulder, a look of reproach on her face.

'Really, Rose, I don't know what has come over you; I really don't. How could you speak as you did? To be so flippant about murder when you know very well that Ursula Stapleton was a friend of theirs. It was a mean thing to do.'

Mrs Simpson glared at her daughter, and Rose was reminded of how she had felt as a child when she had done some naughty deed and been admonished for it by her mother. She opened her mouth to speak, and then thought better of it. Instead, she bit her lip and lowered her eyes.

'Oh, I daresay you had some reason or other for saying what you did and causing them distress,' said Mrs Simpson sighing. 'But really, Rose, did you have to be so unkind? I thought I had brought you up differently.'

Her mother's words stung her to the quick, and Rose felt herself reeling from them, almost as if she had received a physical blow. Perhaps she did see violent death where there was none. It was quite possible, she thought, that she and Cedric would be proved wrong in their assertion that Ursula Stapleton had been murdered. For it might well transpire that the woman's death had been from natural causes after all.

Ready at last, the Sedgwick Players filed out of the drawing room. A more forlorn, nervous group of people it would have been hard to imagine. Even Algernon Cuffe appeared to have lost some of his air of authority and bluster, though Rose was conscious that his eyes darted from one to the other of them, and that he alone seemed to take note of their surroundings.

Rose led the way across the hall and into the library. There, they found the constable awaiting them, seated behind a carved oak, octagonal library table with a cup of tea in front of him. The earl was leaning against the mantelpiece in something of a nonchalant manner. There was no sign of the old doctor, who had evidently taken his leave.

On their entrance, the constable coughed rather self-consciously and rose to his feet. He proceeded to bid the troupe to be seated on the various chairs that were scattered about the room, while he himself remained standing. It was a moment or two before he spoke, for he desired that they take in their impressive surroundings, which had so overawed him when he had first entered the room. If nothing else, they appeared to him to add an air of authority to the proceedings. For, from floor to ceiling, rows upon rows of books were arranged in great Georgian mahogany bookcases giving the room something of an ornate formality. Certainly, for a minute or two the Sedgwick Players appeared speechless, the atmosphere thick with their fear and anxiety, which mingled uncomfortably with the dust from the old volumes.

The constable cleared his throat noisily and began to talk, though what he said was immediately lost on his audience. For a voice, considerable louder than his own, had chosen that very same moment to speak.

'I say, Constable,' said Algernon. 'Is it true? Do you believe Mrs Stapleton was murdered?'

Constable Bright, taken somewhat unawares by the abruptness of the question, commenced to stutter a vague sort of response. 'Well, I wouldn't …' he began, and then decided to stop and take a gulp of tea in order that he might formulate in his mind a suitable response.

'Lady Belvedere said you did,' said Miriam in an accusing tone.

The constable went very red in the face and began to splutter. There was a very strong possibility that he would either choke on his drink or else cover those present with a smattering of tea. Even Cedric, from his position by the mantelpiece, looked somewhat taken aback by Miriam's statement. Rose herself blushed crimson and looked resolutely ahead. She had expected just such an eventuality and yet … She gave herself a good talking to. It could not be helped; she must deal with it the best she could. In the meantime, she would try not to catch the constable's eye, for she could only imagine the look he was giving her. She stole a quick glance at her husband, who was looking at her curiously, his eyebrows raised.

After such an eventful start, the conversation that followed was somewhat tedious and dull. For the constable emphasised at every opportunity that the cause of Mrs Stapleton's death was not yet known. They would have to await the results of the post-mortem just like everyone else and it did no good to speculate. As he had stressed this latter point, he had seen fit to glance up from his notebook and give Rose a meaningful stare. The constable had then asked for a brief account of the events leading up to Ursula's death. Algernon Cuffe, who appeared to have elected himself as the thespians' foreman, did most of the talking, accompanied by the odd nod of a head or muttering by some other of the Sedgwick Players as the individuals saw fit.

At last Constable Bright closed his notebook and rose from his seat. The others took this as a sign that they had been dismissed and all but leapt from their own chairs and fled from the room, eager to gather their belongings from the drawing room and depart. Cedric and Rose followed slowly in their wake. In the hall, Cedric made as if to follow them into the drawing room, but Rose tugged at his sleeve and requested that he remain where he was. Together they waited in the hall and bid each of the thespians farewell as they came out of the drawing room clutching their effects. The earl and countess watched their retreating backs as the actors departed. Mrs Simpson, who was obviously still annoyed with her daughter, showed little inclination to linger, and followed the Sedgwick Players out of the front door and down the steps.

'Right,' said Cedric. 'Now the coast is clear, let's see this wine glass you've found.' He bounded into the drawing room. 'Hello? Where's Charlie? I thought you said he was guarding the said glass.'

Rose joined her husband in the drawing room. Other than themselves, there was no one else present in the room. Certainly, there was no sign of the footman.

'Where did you say it was hidden?' Cedric asked, a note of anxiety in his voice.

'Over there on the bookcase, behind the vase of flowers,' said Rose, pointing to the spot.

Cedric ran to the bookcase in question, picked up the vase and all but flung it from him. Rose remained where she was, all too aware that something had stopped Cedric in his tracks, for he was standing there still clutching the vase, staring where it had been positioned on the bookcase. Slowly, he turned around to face her, a look of horror on his face. Rose knew what he was about to say even before he opened his mouth to speak.

'It's gone,' Cedric said. 'The wine glass; it's gone. Someone has taken it!'

Chapter Ten

Husband and wife stood for a moment staring at the empty space on the bookcase, which seemed strangely magnified. Such was the intensity of their gaze, it might almost be supposed that they imagined the cranberry-coloured wine glass would magically materialise of its own volition. Looking at the void, Rose recalled how, only half an hour earlier, the glass had glistened in the light like some malign and vindictive presence.

'Are you quite sure it was there?' asked Cedric, at length. Rose nodded, a slow, deliberate movement, for she hardly dared breathe. 'Of course, I'm not suggesting that you imagined seeing it,' Cedric added quickly, 'only that perhaps you glimpsed it on another piece of furniture or ...' he broke off from what he was saying to walk to the other end of the room. 'This bookcase, perhaps. It might be here behind this ornament.' He picked up the object in question and glanced behind it, a hopeful look upon his face, which quickly faded.

'No,' said Rose, 'it was definitely behind that vase on that bookcase. I spotted it when I was standing here.' She moved further into the room and regarded the place where the vase had stood, concealing its deadly treasure.

'Then it's disappeared,' said Cedric rather forlornly, replacing the ornament on the bookcase. 'Someone's taken it,' he reiterated, somewhat unnecessarily.

'Yes,' said Rose.

Had her husband studied her more closely, he would have seen that there was a certain gleam in her eye. However, at that very moment, Cedric's attention was drawn to a sudden movement behind one of the curtains.

'Hello? I say, who's there?' He marched over to the window just as a figure emerged from behind the drape of silk brocade. 'Good lord!' exclaimed Cedric. 'Charlie! I say, you did give me a fright. Why on earth are you skulking about there of all places?' His face clouded, and a note of annoyance entered his voice. 'Lady Belvedere asked you to stand guard in front of the bookcase. Why did you leave your post?'

'Because I asked him to,' said Rose quickly, coming to the servant's aid. For the poor footman, she noted, was looking distinctly nervous at incurring his master's wrath. 'Charlie was following my instructions.' She addressed the servant. 'Did you see who took the wine glass, Charlie?'

'Yes, I did, m'lady,' said the footman eager to redeem himself in his master's eyes. 'It was –'

'But it was evidence,' protested Cedric, not permitting the poor man to finish his sentence. Instead, he gave his wife an incredulous look. 'It was the only evidence we had in our possession that proved Ursula was poisoned. If we are right, the cyanide was administered to her in that wine glass. And there should still be traces of it in the glass. But now it is gone, we will never know whether we were right or not.'

Before Rose could reply, she found herself distracted by the sudden appearance of Constable Bright, who was hovering in the doorway of the room.

'Ah, there you are, your lordship, your ladyship.' The policeman half bowed his head to each in turn, as if he had just arrived at Sedgwick Court. He hesitated for a moment before he entered the drawing room, treading with the utmost care. 'I've come to take the wine glass, the one what you say's got poison in it. On the bookcase, did you say it is?'

'It was,' said Cedric, a touch of bitterness in his voice. 'But it isn't there now, Constable.' He paused to look rather despairingly at his wife. 'I'm afraid the murderer has seen fit to take it with him.'

'Has he indeed?' The constable looked visibly shocked.

'No, he hasn't,' said Rose lightly. 'It's in the study. I think you'll find it's on the desk. At least, that's where I asked Manning to put it.'

'What?' cried Cedric. 'But Charlie said he saw someone take it from the bookcase.'

'Charlie did see someone take a wine glass from the bookcase,' agreed Rose. 'But it wasn't the glass that contained the poison; it was the other one.'

'What other one?' demanded her husband, looking distinctly confused. 'Darling, you told me the murderer had hidden the missing wine glass on the bookcase. That was the one that had contained the poison, wasn't it?' Rose nodded. 'Then how –'

'I think it would be best if I explain,' she said quickly.

'I wish you would, your ladyship,' said Constable Bright, evidently having some difficulty in following the conversation.

'Here, here,' agreed Cedric, his usual good humour restored now that it appeared a disaster had in fact been averted. The murderer had not made off with a crucial piece of evidence as he had at first supposed.

'It was an idea that came to me when you told me Dr Henchard wasn't of the opinion that Mrs Stapleton had been poisoned.' Rose might well have added that it had actually been the constable's decision not to launch an investigation into the woman's death that had persuaded her to devise her own plan. 'It seemed so very simple. Really, I can hardly believe that it worked. I hoped it would, of course, but I couldn't be certain.'

The constable looked a little mystified, as if he thought Rose was talking in riddles. He had somewhat reluctantly produced his notebook and pencil from his breast pocket. Now, he looked as if he were rather tempted to return them.

'It struck me that I could use the fact that there were two wine glasses to my advantage,' continued Rose quickly. 'If you remember, two glasses were carried on to the stage on a tray in the final scene. Ursula Stapleton drank water from only one of them, the one that we think contained the poison. The other glass was empty. But in appearance, the wine glasses were identical. They came from the same set and were most distinctive, the bowls being rather a marvellous cranberry colour,' Rose raised a hand as the policeman made to protest. 'Yes, I know, Constable, it is quite possible that Lord Belvedere and I are just being fanciful in assuming poor Mrs Stapleton was murdered. But for the purposes of my story I would be grateful if you would humour me.'

The constable nodded, though he looked a little ill at ease. It was possible that he now regretted his rather hasty decision to arrange for the body to be removed before it had been photographed in situ. He said rather gruffly: 'Very well, your ladyship. If you say so and given as how we're in your house and not at the police station.'

'Thank you, Constable. As I was saying, the wine glass was taken from the folly and an effort had been made to hide it in this drawing room,' continued Rose. 'The attempt might quite well have been successful had I not discovered it purely by chance. If I hadn't been standing on that very spot …' She paused to indicate an area of the rug. 'Well, I wouldn't have noticed it at all.'

'Ah!' cried Cedric, enlightenment having suddenly come to him. 'You swapped the glasses. I say, how did you do that?'

'While you were giving the constable your account of the events leading up to Mrs Stapleton's death, I asked Manning to get the other wine glass from the folly. I instructed him to substitute it for the glass in the drawing room as soon as the coast was clear.'

'I see,' said Cedric. 'That's why you suggested that the constable interview the thespians in the library? It was an opportunity to get them to leave the drawing room for a few minutes. I thought it a little odd at the time.'

'Yes. Manning needed an opportunity to swap the wine glasses.'

'And Charlie here,' said Cedric, indicating the footman, who all the while had been standing behind his shoulder, 'needed a chance to hide behind the curtain without anyone noticing so that he could see who took the wine glass from the bookshelf when they all returned to the drawing room.'

'Yes. That's why I asked them to leave all their belongings in the drawing room and collect them when they left,' said Rose. 'Because I didn't want the murderer to take the wine glass that contained the poison before we had swapped it with the other one.'

'I say, he'd have been taking an awful risk if he had done,' objected Cedric. 'Charlie would still have been standing in front of the bookcase, wouldn't he? Our murderer would have had to ask him to stand aside so that he could get to the glass.'

'Yes,' agreed Rose. 'It would have meant drawing attention to both himself and the wine glass. I think that, on reflection, he would have decided that his best option was to leave the glass where it was. After all, the chances were that the domestic staff would just wash it up and return it to Miss Quail. You see, as far as our murderer was aware, no one suspected foul play.'

'Ah,' cried Cedric, as further enlightenment dawned. 'That's why you announced that Constable Bright was of the opinion that Ursula had been murdered.'

'Did you indeed, your ladyship?' began Constable Bright in rather sombre tones, drawing himself up to his full height, which was not very considerable. 'Well, I must say that –'

'You wanted to be certain that the murderer would take the glass when he returned to the drawing room,' Cedric continued in his excitement, rather rudely interrupting the poor constable, who was looking somewhat deflated by the fact that he was being ignored. 'Otherwise he most probably would have left it where it was.'

'Yes. But if foul play was suspected,' agreed Rose, 'he couldn't take the risk of leaving the glass on the bookcase where it would be discovered and sent to be analysed.'

'Well, that leaves only one question to be answered,' said Constable Bright, determined to have his penny's worth, and feeling it was high time that a representative of the law took charge of the conversation. He turned his attention to the footman and gave him a particularly fierce look. 'Now, young man. Out with it. Who took the wine glass?'

Charlie, finding all eyes turned on him, went a deep crimson and began to splutter.

'Come on, lad,' said the constable more kindly. 'There's nothing to be frightened of. Did you see who took the glass from the bookcase, or didn't you?'

'I did,' said Charlie. 'It was … it was Mr Rewe.'

There was the sound of a sharp intake of breath. 'What?' cried Cedric, considerably taken aback. 'Henry? I say, are you absolutely certain it was him?'

The footman nodded rather tentatively. When he had been requested to spy on the troupe, it had not occurred to him that he was being asked to observe a murderer stealing incriminating evidence. The realisation had come to him swift and sharp while listening in a discreet fashion to the conversation of the others. It had been with a degree of excitement that he had kept this knowledge of the murderer's identity to himself. Indeed, he was almost fit to burst with the thrill of it all, longing for the moment when he might return to the servants' hall and divulge what he knew. For he alone knew who the murderer was! Until the words escaped his lips, the others were left in ignorance.

However, now he had uttered the name, he felt rather deflated, for the reception to his news had not been what he had envisaged. Instead of his master clasping him warmly by the hand and congratulating him for a job well done, the earl was staring at him with a look of disbelief.

Rose herself shared something of her husband's scepticism. It was only then that she realised she must subconsciously have imagined the murderer to be someone else. For, had the footman mentioned Algernon Cuffe or Walter Drury, she did not think she would have felt as she felt now. There was an awful sinking sensation in the pit of her stomach. Surely the servant had been mistaken or else her plan had gone awry.

'Mr Rewe?' she queried dully.

'Yes, m'lady,' replied Charlie eagerly. 'The man that's playing Hamlet, least I think he is. Dressed in black breeches, he is, and 'as a black shirt that has ruffles on it and is laced at the neck.'

Rose saw Cedric nod his head and murmur something to the effect that it was the outfit Henry wore in the final scene of the play when he discarded his black velvet doublet to fight the duel.

Encouraged, the footman saw fit to add to his description. 'Little fellow, thin as a rake,' he said.

The image was conjured up before Rose's eyes of Henry, as she had seen him first, pale and nervous, holding the hilt of his foil awkwardly as if it were some foreign object. She remembered how he had mumbled and flinched visibly when Cedric, in the guise of Laertes, had thrust forward with his foil, the smaller man all but dropping his own weapon. She played the final scene of the play over in her mind, recalling how Henry had jumped up with a startled cry as soon as Ursula had begun to choke. Indeed, he had seemed quite overcome by her death. His complexion had gone a ghastly shade of grey and he had been required to sit down lest he collapse. Had it all been an act, she wondered, or had he felt a horror or remorse at what he had done? Was it really possible that he poisoned Ursula in so callous a fashion? Had he knelt by her side and watched as she took her final breath? And what of afterwards, when he had half lain crouched on the footstool in such a dejected and pathetic fashion, attended to by the dutiful Algernon Cuffe and Walter Drury, who had regarded him with such obvious concern and apprehension?

The constable coughed, startling Rose and rousing her from her reverie. She had been so deep in thought that she had all but forgotten Constable Bright, who stood there before her, regarding Cedric and herself with something akin to a veiled amusement. It was obvious from his expression that he thought her elaborate plan had come to nothing, that she and Cedric had been playing some strange game to enliven lives that had little purpose, or else that she were playing at being detective when she had neither the necessary skills nor training to do the job well. His next words seemed to confirm as much.

'Well, I'd better be going, your lordship, you ladyship.' He noted the looks of disappointment on their faces and seemed to take pity on them. 'I'm not saying it isn't a little strange that the young man saw fit to take Miss Quail's wine glass, but I don't think it signifies what you're suggesting. No, not at all. In my experience, folk do many a queer thing and it don't mean nothing; nothing bad any roads. I'm not saying I won't have a quiet word with him tomorrow, like, and ask him to replace the glass and no harm done.'

'I take it you will arrange for the wine glass in the study to be analysed, Constable?' demanded Cedric rather coldly. 'I will think it a great dereliction of your duty if you don't. I ought to warn you that I mean to say as much to the chief constable.'

The constable paled significantly at such a threat. In truth, he had been half minded to leave the wine glass where it was. He didn't hold with the gentry dabbling in things that didn't concern them, adding two and two and making five. The good doctor had said that the poor woman had died due to a complication with her heart, and that was good enough for him. But if the young earl was going to …

'Of course, Constable Bright was intending to take the glass with him,' Rose said, coming to the policeman's aid, and bestowing on him a kindly smile. 'You have been most thorough, Constable. I don't believe there is anything more to be done until we know whether Mrs Stapleton's death was from natural causes or the result of foul play.'

'Indeed,' said Cedric, looking a little sheepish, obviously regretting his outburst. 'You don't need the likes of me to tell you how to do your job, Constable. Manning will see you out. Good day to you.'

Though they had bid him farewell, the earl and countess showed little inclination, however, to leave the policeman to his own devices. Instead they lingered in the hall, waiting while the constable went to retrieve the glass from the study table and watching as he returned, holding the glass by the stem with the aid of a large white handkerchief, which he had wrapped around the glass like some huge bandage. They stared after him as the constable hurried from the house, holding the wine glass out before him like a torch.

'Well,' said Cedric, watching the policeman's progress down the drive. 'I suppose tomorrow we will know whether we were right. For tomorrow, we will know whether or not Ursula Stapleton was murdered.'

Chapter Eleven

'I've a good mind to telephone Bichester police station,' said Cedric, 'to inquire whether Constable Bright brought them the wine glass to have analysed.'

It was the afternoon of the next day, and he had just returned from a visit to the folly, where he had surveyed the paraphernalia and debris left behind by the thespians, as if to reassure himself that the events of the previous day had actually taken place and were not just figments of his imagination. 'It wouldn't surprise me in the least to learn that he hadn't,' he added.

'I think you're being awfully unfair to the poor constable,' said Rose, descending the main staircase, and coming to stand beside her husband in the hall. 'He might not believe Ursula was murdered, but he did promise us that he would arrange for the glass to be thoroughly examined.'

They had spent something of a restive evening after the policeman's departure, unable to settle at doing anything other than roam the many rooms of Sedgwick Court like two lost souls. For their minds had refused to focus on anything except the indisputable fact that Ursula Stapleton had been murdered, and that they alone seemed to believe this fact. It was true that Constable Bright's obvious scepticism, and the somewhat unexpected discovery that it had been Henry Rewe who had purloined the wine glass, had done a little to dampen their feelings of certainty that a crime had been committed, but still it gnawed away at them like a stubborn headache. Their forced inactivity did little to alleviate the situation, being made to bide their time until the truth was known. And all the while, they were in receipt of the knowledge that a violent death had been committed in their grounds, which was yet to be properly investigated or even acknowledged.

They had barely touched their dinner that night, a fact which had been a cause of some dismay to their cook, Mrs Broughton, who had complained very vocally to anyone who would listen in the servants' hall, that what was the use of her slaving over a hot stove only to have the meals returned to the kitchen untouched. A slight on her cooking, that's what it was and if the master and mistress didn't like her food and were going to turn their noses up at every meal she produced, well, really, she would have to obtain another position where her talents were appreciated. Of course, she wouldn't say it wasn't sad that someone should see fit to die in the folly of all places, but it wasn't as if the woman in question was a particular friend of the master's, or mistress'. Inconsiderate, that's what she called it, someone as good as a stranger dying in the grounds. Why the woman couldn't stay at home and die in her own bed if she had a mind to, she didn't know.

Her flow of words was eventually stemmed by a reproving look from Manning, who did not consider it appropriate that she should speak in such a way in front of the lower servants, whom old Torridge had always instilled in him were particularly impressionable. 'One must lead by example,' he had said sombrely to Manning, who had been the under-butler at the time. 'Such talk, if indeed there needs to be any, is to be reserved to the confines of the housekeeper's sitting room.'

Under Manning's critical eye, Mrs Broughton had brought her tirade to a faltering stop, with cheeks flushing crimson. It was only to herself that she admitted that she was a little worried that there might have been something wrong with the food. Indeed, she had spent a sleepless night tossing and turning in her bed in her little attic bedroom worrying that the piece of beef she had served hadn't looked as fresh as it might have. Meanwhile, the kitchen and scullery maids, who were more often than not the last to go to bed after completing their final daily chores, had, quite unbeknown to the cook, crept into the kitchen to partake of a slice or two of the said meat, giving never a thought to the quality of the beef they chewed, only aware that it filled their stomachs in a delicious fashion. Had Mrs Broughton known the clandestine activities of her staff, she might have been comforted with the knowledge that the maids, at least, had suffered no ill-effects from eating the meat.

The cook had not been the only upper servant to fret. For Mrs Farrier, the housekeeper, had experienced her own share of worries, not helped by being a witness to the footman's rather embellished account of the affair of the poisoned wine glass, as Charlie was wont to call it. Her own concerns, however, focused on the more practical. Would it affect her ability to recruit housemaids, there having been two violent deaths in the grounds in the space of a couple of years? First the maze and now the folly. Really, you would hardly credit it. And everyone knew how difficult it was to get good servants these days, she more than most. She didn't want girls with ghoulish or imaginative natures, who would sneak off to the folly to see if an aura of death still hung about the place, when they should be up to their elbows in household chores, or else timid little mites who'd be forever worked up and jumpy so that they dropped a vase or fainted the minute they heard the wind rustling the leaves in the trees. Still, it did have its compensations she supposed. A housemaid might think twice in future before sneaking out to the folly to meet her young man. That was the trouble with having silly young girls about the place. Mrs Farrier pulled herself up to her full height and pursed her lips. She didn't approve of such goings on. The young these days … And it didn't help having buildings dotted around the grounds that resembled houses and temples. She couldn't see the point of it herself. A waste of good bricks and mortar, if you asked her. It was only encouraging young girls to be led astray …

In the minds of Cedric and Rose, the morning had brought little hope of a speedy resolution to their agitation. The bright clarity of a new day and accompanying sunshine had done little to lift their mood. For the weather seemed only to mock their sense of propriety by suggesting that all was well with the world with its bright, vibrant summer colours, when it so very obviously wasn't. Each felt that the elements should be more reflective of the violent death that had occurred in their midst. If there had been dark clouds followed by a torrent of rain, or if there had been sharp gusts of wind that had pulled at their hats and gloves and numbed their bones, then they might have felt more resigned to wait patiently for the official verdict concerning Ursula Stapleton's death. Instead, the day threatened to be a repeat of the evening before; a frustrating and seemingly endless waiting game.

Even now, they were tempted to loiter in the hall in case anyone should happen to telephone. They had quite sensibly reasoned that it might be a couple of days before the results of either the post-mortem or the analysis of the wine glass were known, particularly if Constable Bright had chosen to drag his feet about the business. There was little doubt that the policeman had advised his superiors of the doctor's view that Ursula Stapleton had died of natural causes. This, in itself, suggested there was little need for urgency unless it was felt prudent to act on the whims of the local aristocracy.

At which point, Cedric imagined the constable's accompanying smirk. He could envisage the policeman's supplemental words: 'See murder wherever they go, do his lordship and her ladyship. 'Course we all know as how they've been involved with more than their fair share of violent deaths and all. But give them a simple case of a poor lady with a weak heart and they see a crime. No one's saying it's not unfortunate that it happened on their land, what with that business with the maze … why, that's the sort of thing that gives a place a bit of a reputation. Death Manor they'll be calling it instead of Sedgwick Court, you mark my words. I'll be surprised if any folk will accept their hospitality.' Cedric imagined him chuckling. 'You wouldn't catch me attending a house party there, I can tell you, not if my life depended on it. Ha, ha.'

'Not as how you'd be invited, Constable,' retorted Cedric forthrightly, though admittedly only in his mind. The young earl took a deep breath and gave himself a severe talking to. It did no good to hold imaginary conversations in one's head, even if it was only to relieve oppressive boredom and frustration. He caught his wife's eye and smiled, aware rather belatedly that she had been watching him closely.

'I've just been giving Constable Bright a piece of my mind,' he said. 'Something along the lines of what I was saying to you earlier. You know, the bit about how well I think he is carrying out his duty.'

'Aloud, or in your head?' enquired Rose.

'Oh, in my head, naturally,' said Cedric, having the grace to blush. 'Not sure I'd have the nerve to tell him to his face.'

'Well, you made a pretty good show of it yesterday,' said his wife, trying not to laugh in spite of herself. In that moment, it all seemed so unreal, as if what they had witnessed yesterday had been no more than a part of the play. Why, Rose half expected Ursula Stapleton to call on them to enquire if there was to be another rehearsal before the actual performance. If the woman were to appear before her now, would she be so very shocked? Would she think she had seen a ghost, as poor Hamlet had done, when instructed by his dead father's spectre to avenge his death? She put a hand to her head and wondered whether she was going to pieces.

It was at that moment that the telephone bell rang out loudly in the hall, the noise seeming to echo and resonate around the room, rebounding off the walls and the black and white tiles of the floor.

In one swift movement, Cedric had sprung to the instrument and picked up the receiver before the butler had an opportunity to answer the telephone extension in his parlour.

'Hello? Yes, it is. I say, would you mind awfully repeating that? Are you quite sure? I take it there's been no mistake? No, I didn't think so. Well, that's splendid. No, I didn't … By that, I mean of course … No, no, poor woman. Awful business. Well, thank you for letting me know. Jolly decent of you. Goodbye.'

'Who was that?' demanded Rose, though she knew the answer as surely as if she had lifted the telephone receiver herself and spoken to the person on the other end. Her husband, meanwhile, was cradling the instrument in his hand, and showed no inclination to replace it on its stand.

'That was someone ringing on behalf of the chief constable; a sergeant, I think, he said he was. I didn't catch his name. He said the chief constable had instructed him to telephone me with the findings from the post-mortem and the analysis of the wine glass …' Cedric passed a hand across his brow and sat down on a convenient chair. A thought struck him and he looked up. 'I say, I've done poor old Constable Bright an awful –'

'What did he say, this sergeant,' Rose asked impatiently. She knelt beside her husband and took his hands in hers. The action caused Cedric to look at her, though there was still something of a glazed look in his eyes. It was a moment before he could bring himself to talk, as if he were slowly recalling himself to the present. When he did at last speak, his sentences came out all in a rush, almost on top of each other, with hardly a gasp for breath between them.

'We were right all along. Ursula Stapleton was murdered. They found traces of potassium cyanide in the wine glass. And the results of the post-mortem showed levels of cyanide in Ursula's blood consistent with her having been poisoned. I …' Cedric faltered. 'I knew she had been poisoned. I could detect the smell of bitter almonds on her breath … the way she died … I knew it … and yet, now it has been confirmed beyond all reasonable doubt, I feel shocked, startled even, as if I weren't expecting …'

'Yes,' said Rose. 'I feel that way too. I suppose it is because it didn't seem real before. It was almost like a game; a jigsaw puzzle. We were trying to find the pieces and make them fit, as if it was all for our own amusement.'

'I say, I don't think we were quite as heartless as that,' protested her husband, recovering some of his equanimity. 'Ursula's death was real all right. We were all shocked and startled by it, but this …' He paused to express a gesture almost of bewilderment. 'The realisation that we actually witnessed the murder. Why, it was played out before us. It's too awful. We watched as Ursula drank the poison and was killed before our very eyes. We should have done something.'

'We thought it was all part of the play,' murmured Rose, almost to herself. 'Indeed, it was. It was a scene from the play. In Hamlet, Gertrude is poisoned in the same way and at the same moment that Ursula was. The murderer took his inspiration from the play. It determined the method by which Ursula was killed.'

'I say, how ghastly. What sort of a person would do that?' pondered Cedric. 'It does mean of course that her death was premeditated. I daresay it would have taken a great deal of planning.'

'Yes, it would.' With a physical effort, Rose roused herself. 'I suppose the police will be here in a few minutes. We had better warn the servants.'

'I suppose they'll send an inspector this time,' said Cedric. 'I wonder who it will be.'

'I hope it isn't Inspector Connor. He'll be accompanied by that awful Sergeant Harris.' Rose shuddered at her recollection of the sergeant. Her cheeks flushed as she remembered how he had looked at her. She had been disguised as a servant at the time and on realising that she was in fact something of an amateur sleuth he had treated her with little courtesy.

'I think I'll telephone to the chief constable,' said Cedric hurriedly, advancing towards his study. 'I'll ask that they assign Inspector Newcombe to the case.'

'Yes, do that, darling,' said Rose though, if truth be told, she had some reservations about Inspector Newcombe investigating Ursula Stapleton's death. The man might be something of a friend of her husband's, playing as he did for the Sedgwick village cricket team, but she felt he also did not fully approve of her sleuthing activities. With some just cause, she admitted to herself, remembering how she had pursued her own investigation surrounding the death that had occurred on Bonfire Night, rather to the initial detriment of the official police inquiry.

'I'll speak to Manning,' Rose told her husband, glad to have something useful to do.

She watched Cedric disappear into his study, while she herself went in pursuit of the butler, who she discovered was on some errand or other. It was therefore a quarter of an hour or so before she spoke with him, conscious all the while that the inspector's arrival was most likely imminent. Indeed, she was half afraid that Inspector Newcombe would arrive before she had had an opportunity to apprise Manning of the situation. The butler, she noticed when she told him, paled visibly at the mention of murder, and she was reminded that generally servants did not like to have the police about the house. It gave the place something of a reputation and added to their heavy workload. While she sympathised with these sentiments, she thought it likely that the inspector would wish to conduct his interviews at Sedgwick Court, due to its proximity to the folly. It would also, she realised with something akin to delight, provide her with an ideal opportunity to speak with the witnesses and suspects in the case herself, as they went to and fro between the interviews. She wondered if they had recovered from the shock of Ursula's death and would be more forthcoming with their answers to her questions. They would naturally be rather shaken to learn that Ursula Stapleton had indeed been murdered and they were all suspects in her death.

Rose was suddenly aware that Manning had asked her a question to which, absorbed in her own thoughts, she had given no answer. The butler was standing before her patiently enough, with something of an expectant look upon his face.

'I believe Detective Inspector Newcombe will be leading the investigation,' she said. 'I realise it will be rather dreadful for you all, but we must make the best of it. Do what you can, Manning, to reassure the staff. I daresay that some of the younger girls will be rather frightened. You must tell them there is nothing to be afraid of.'

It occurred to her then that in her servants' eyes the folly would take on the guise of some sinister edifice, haunted by ghosts and evil spirits. It would no longer bear witness to clandestine meetings between the maids and their beaux, and the knowledge of this filled her with a certain melancholy. For the idea that it would become some monstrous, abandoned construction left to fall into disrepair filled her with a feeling akin to despair. Even if she was to take measures to ensure that it was kept well maintained, there would still be an air of neglect about the place. It was likely to become ill-frequented, even by herself and Cedric. For there was an abundance of follies and eye-catchers scattered in the grounds of Sedgwick Court; they were quite spoilt for choice as to which ones to visit.

They were standing in the butler's pantry. Rose had been keen to speak with Manning as soon as he had returned from his errand, and thus had seen fit to accost him in his lair before he had even had time to remove his hat and coat. A shrill noise rang out and she clutched nervously at the back of a chair.

'What was that?' She enquired, aware that her voice sounded rather high pitched.

'It's one of the bells on the bell board, m'lady,' explained the butler patiently. 'The door bell, if I'm not mistaken. It doesn't sound as loud in the hall.'

'The doorbell? Then it must be the inspector.'

She hurried from the room, determined to be in the hall to greet the inspector as soon as the front door was opened. But, even as she mounted the basement staircase, she realised that she would be too late. One of the footmen had undoubtedly opened the door to him by now, and she would be forced to emerge rather awkwardly from behind the servants' door. Still, it could not be helped, she told herself. It had been necessary to forewarn Manning. The butler needed to be in full possession of the facts so as to be in a position to prepare his staff for the ordeal that lay ahead of them.

It was with a sense of considerable relief, therefore, that she discovered that the inspector and his sergeant had their backs to her as she surfaced from the servants' quarters, their attention focused elsewhere than on the green baize door. Indeed, she was vaguely aware from their murmured comments that they were regarding the old, heavy gilt-framed portraits of Cedric's ancestors that hung on the walls.

It gave her an opportunity to catch her breath and pat her hair and straighten her skirt before they saw her. It was with renewed confidence, therefore, that she prepared to greet them. A moment later and she wished that she had paid less attention to her appearance and more to the silhouettes that stood before her. For if she had, she told herself, she might have realised the assumption she had made so carelessly was false. She felt certain that, had she bothered to give him a second glance, she would have recognised the figure of the tall, dark-haired man, even with his back towards her. As it was, it was only when the two men happened to turn around, that she was aware of her mistake. Involuntarily, she put a hand to her mouth to stifle the exclamation that sprung resolutely from her lips.

For instead of gazing on the forms of Inspector Newcombe and Sergeant Bell, as she had fully expected, she found herself staring up in to the faces of Inspector Deacon and Sergeant Lane.

Chapter Twelve

There was an awkward, desperate moment where each seemed glued to the spot on which they stood; they might have been figures in some strange tableau for all the movement they made. Rose, herself, was aware that she was staring at the policemen rather stupidly, an uncomprehending look upon her face. She had been badly startled, she knew, in that rather confused, dazed way that accompanies shock. Gradually her feelings of disbelief began to subside, and dimly she was conscious of the fact that she must pull herself together. If nothing else, she was rather afraid of what they must think of her, gaping at them so rudely. Only to herself would she admit that she had felt a certain reluctance to catch Inspector Deacon's eye, fearing that the colour would rise vividly to her cheeks.

Meanwhile, she was vaguely aware that Sergeant Lane was regarding her politely and with not a little interest. She could only guess at what was going through his companion's mind concerning her reaction to their unexpected arrival. As the senior of the two policemen, it might have been supposed that, of the two, Inspector Deacon would be the one who stepped forward to address her. Instead, the duty seemed to fall upon his sergeant. A tentative glance at both the countess and his superior had confirmed Sergeant Lane's initial feelings that there was something odd and charged about the atmosphere in which he found himself, which seemed to render the others strangely mute. Certainly, he surmised that neither of his companions were inclined to break the silence, which hung heavily about the hall like some strange mist.

'Miss Simpson.' Sergeant Lane said somewhat shyly, though Rose noticed he looked pleased to see her. 'I knew of course as how you'd be here, your being married to his lordship and all, and this being his estate.' He paused a moment to look about them. 'It don't seem so very long ago since I was last here with Inspector Bramwell.' He turned to his inspector, as if to offer some sort of explanation for his previous visit to Sedgwick Court, though he knew his superior to be familiar with the circumstances. 'We were investigating another murder then too,' explained Sergeant Lane, rather unnecessarily. 'One as happened in the maze.'

Inspector Deacon merely nodded and said: 'Lady Belvedere, how do you do?'

His tone was so formal that it took his two companions quite by surprise. Sergeant Lane reddened perceptibly, conscious that he had committed a *faux pas* in the way he had addressed the countess as Miss Simpson. It also occurred to him that he might have been a little over familiar in the manner in which he had spoken to her. Rather crestfallen, he hastily mumbled an apology of sorts.

By contrast, Rose had stepped back involuntarily and turned slightly pale. She could hardly bring herself to meet the inspector's eye. For she was aware suddenly of how considerably her circumstances had changed since they had last met. Rose was acutely conscious of her newly polished façade, of her fine, expensive clothes, and her hair, expertly arranged, which shone from the vigorous daily brushing given it by her diligent servant. Even the house in which they were standing seemed to proclaim its vast, palatial opulence and wealth. It was all a very far cry from the modest little dress shop in which she had worked as a lowly shop assistant, and in her heightened, agitated state, Rose felt that these variances illustrated only that she was no longer the ordinary young woman she had been.

All this was the realisation of but a moment and, with a stab of dismay, it dawned on her that never had she felt quite so far removed from plain Miss Rose Simpson as she did then, standing rather awkwardly in the main entrance hall with the two policemen, whom she had previously thought of as her friends.

With a tremendous effort, she managed to compose herself sufficiently to muster some sort of greeting.

'Inspector Deacon, Sergeant Lane, how very good to see you both again.' She bestowed on the sergeant a kindly smile. 'You may still call me Miss Simpson if you wish, Sergeant. I shan't be the least bit offended. In fact, I am rather used to it. You see, my lady's maid is forever calling me miss.' A thought seemed to strike her for she added: 'You may remember her? Her name is Edna Jones. She was the scullery maid at Ashgrove House.'

'That little mite,' exclaimed Sergeant Lane. 'I do, indeed. Well I never!'

'I met her again last year at Crossing Manor,' said Rose conversationally, finding, once she had started speaking, it was difficult to

98

stop. 'She occupied the position of kitchen maid. I happened to be there investigating the theft of a diamond necklace.' She continued, more for something to say, than for effect: 'I was disguised as a servant at the time.'

'Were you really, miss?' said Sergeant Lane, sounding impressed, and not a little surprised.

'Yes,' said Rose. 'And I should like very much to give you a hand with this case. If I may, of course.' She hardly dared pause for breath, but hurried on, fearful that the inspector would raise some objection or other. 'Really, it is too awful that there has been another murder here at Sedgwick Court. We are all quite shaken, I can tell you …' She was aware that she was rambling and that her sentiment sounded rather insincere, though she knew herself to be in earnest, affected as she was by Ursula's death. If truth be told, she could not stifle a sob, so overcome was she by emotion, though only a part of it, she acknowledged, was due to the murder.

Sergeant Lane hurriedly produced a handkerchief and, while she dabbed at her tears with the cloth, glad of an opportunity to hide her eyes while she regained her equanimity, she stole a furtive glance at Inspector Deacon, whom she noted was looking a little uncomfortable. He eyed her strangely, and she wondered whether it was with concern or something else.

'I shall be quite all right in a moment,' she mumbled apologetically, feeling she had made rather a fool of herself by going to pieces on their arrival. Certainly, she was conscious that her reaction might be regarded as somewhat extreme and perhaps exaggerated, for she had hardly known Ursula Stapleton in life. Indeed, her knowledge of the woman had been determined largely from what her husband had observed, during the course of the many rehearsals he had been obliged to attend, and which he had subsequently described to her.

It was only now that it struck Rose that she had directed her conversation almost exclusively to the sergeant. She wondered whether her behaviour appeared pointed. Was it apparent, even to the most casual onlooker, that she was all but ignoring the inspector, who stood there like some shadowy presence? She thought it was almost as if he were not there at all, so quietly did he stand in the black and white tiled hall, allowing his sergeant to partake in the idle chatter and reminiscences, while he observed from a distance. With something akin to bitterness, Rose realised that a gulf had sprung up between the two of them, to which poor Sergeant Lane appeared quite oblivious.

She attempted to tell herself that it was because the inspector did not perceive her to be the same person with whom he had been acquainted. Following her marriage, there was now a huge disparity between their social positions. The inspector would be keen to follow etiquette. Whereas Sergeant Lane seemed inclined to treat her as he had always done. To him, she was still Miss Simpson, the amateur sleuth, who would, in all probability, help them with their investigation. The thought restored to her a sense of calm. Meanwhile, she tried to ignore the nagging, persistent little voice in her head which told her that the inspector's reserved manner towards her had little to do with her elevation in society. For it was hardly surprising after their last encounter that they should be a little awkward in each other's company. Her cheeks flushed crimson as she remembered her last conversation with the inspector. They had been standing in the makeshift kitchen-cum-bathroom of Madame Renard's flat. The area had been partitioned off from the main room by a curtain, which had afforded them a little privacy, and as they chattered, washing up the tea things, it had become obvious that Inspector Deacon had been waiting for an excuse to talk to her. He had had something to say to her, and she recalled how she had panicked, knowing that once it was said, it could not be unsaid. She remembered how she had been overcome by a mixture of conflicting emotions, and that before she had had a moment to gather her thoughts or examine her own feelings, Cedric had arrived and told Inspector Deacon of their engagement …

Rose was roused abruptly from her musings. She had returned to the present, yet it was as if history were repeating itself. She might have been back in Madame Renard's kitchen, washing up the cups and saucers while Inspector Deacon dried. Indeed, she almost felt the cup slip from her hands, as it had threatened to do before, as if her recollection was a real, tangible thing, and not just a vivid memory. For the study door had opened, and someone had walked out into the hall behind her. She recognised the tread, and a moment later a familiar figure appeared at her shoulder.

'Hello. I say, it's good to see you again, Deacon,' said Cedric. There was a pause as they shook hands. With a sudden stab of tenderness towards her husband, Rose noted that this courtesy was also extended to Sergeant Lane, who appeared genuinely flattered by the gesture.

'The chief constable has just been telling me how he'd called in Scotland Yard,' continued Cedric. 'I gathered from what he said, or rather from what he didn't say, that he's a trifle embarrassed the case was not investigated properly yesterday. Indeed, if it hadn't been for my wife's quick thinking,' at which point Cedric paused a moment to beam at Rose, 'some vital evidence might have gone astray. Still, no harm done, and I'm jolly glad it's you two who've been assigned to this case. A dreadful business. No doubt, my wife has been telling you all about it.'

He looked at Rose questioningly, and it occurred to her that she had been very amiss in this regard, for she had told the policemen next to nothing regarding the events that had culminated in Ursula's death. Before she had a chance to reply to that effect, Inspector Deacon was hastily explaining that the two policemen had only that very minute arrived, and he would be most grateful if his lordship would do him the honour of regaling them with an account of the proceedings leading up to the murder.

The earl was delighted, and obliged with a very thorough narrative. In the most part, it was a repetition of what he had told Constable Bright, though greatly embellished due to the receptive nature of his audience. Rose was content to remain in the shadows half listening, half absorbed in her own thoughts. She caught snatches of the conversation between her husband and the inspector, and was conscious that Sergeant Lane was giving her the odd worried look, as if he feared she ailed for something. She lowered her gaze so that she saw only the black and white tiles on the floor; they reminded her of a gigantic chess board, and she wondered whether they were all playing some elaborate game.

'Are you all right, miss?' the sergeant inquired, venturing forward in a tentative fashion, as if he feared that he was acting out of turn. The concern was so evident in his voice that Rose felt a lump forming in her throat. 'Only, I hope you don't mind me saying,' he continued, 'but you look a little queer, like.'

'I'm quite all right, thank you,' said Rose, rallying quickly, keen to allay his fears. 'I think it is the shock … Ursula Stapleton's death, I mean.

I can't quite believe that there has been another murder here …' She paused to glance about her. It seemed to the sergeant watching her that her gaze encompassed everything, from the portraits on the wall to the formal gardens that lay beyond the house. It included the woods and the parkland that he knew comprised the grounds, and the lakes and the eye-catchers, and even the tainted maze with its sorry history.

Rose smiled and sighed inwardly. The sergeant's simple act of kindness had helped restore her to her usual self. At last she felt in command of her emotions, and trailed behind the others as they made their way to the ill-fated folly, her husband leading the way. She remembered how, only the day before, she had hurried eagerly to the Greek temple, keen to watch the rehearsal and see the costumes. Now, as she followed the others, she walked more slowly, wondering what lay ahead.

'Miriam. I say, Miriam. Wait a moment, will you?'

The voice appeared from nowhere. It was sufficiently loud, however, to reach the ears of the woman it addressed, even though she was some physical distance from the speaker. Certainly, Miriam Belmore started, arrested in the act of walking, her foot half raised to take her next step. To her, the words had seemed to echo shrilly around the lane in which she stood, bouncing off the tree trunks and the hedges that bordered Lovers' Lane. On another occasion, it might have been all she could do not to cry out in alarm, such was her shock at being hailed in such a dramatic fashion. The voice, however, with its booming tone was familiar to her, and she had no intention of showing any outward sign of surprise or hesitation. Indeed, her first instinct had been either to swing around angrily and confront the speaker, or else to proceed with her walk, as if she were oblivious to his presence. On reflection, however, she had thought better of it, and had reached a compromise. She remained standing in a fixed position, waiting for him to approach, conscious that her senses were heightened. For, with each footstep, she heard the snapping of fallen twigs underfoot, the noise escalating as he came closer, so that she half imagined that it was bones that he was crushing so carelessly with his purposeful stride. And all the while she stood with her back turned resolutely towards him; a detached, cold figure in the sunshine dappled by the shadows cast by the leaves.

When she judged him to be a few feet from her, she turned around and spoke to him in a voice that affected boredom. 'Well, what is it, Algernon?'

It took a moment or two for the man in question to catch his breath, and she looked at him with her usual air of disdain. She took the opportunity of his continued silence to add: 'What were you doing, creeping up on me like that? Were you trying to frighten me?'

'Hardly that, my dear,' retorted Algernon, cheerful despite her tone. 'I called out to you. Didn't you hear me?' She did not answer, but regarded the leaves instead, as if they held a special interest for her. 'But, of course you did. Otherwise you would have continued walking.' He laughed. 'I say, you might have turned around or waved.'

Miriam's response was to lower her gaze. It was a dismissive gesture, almost as if he were beyond her contempt. Certainly, she suggested by such an action that his question did not warrant a reply. However, if Algernon was offended he did not show it. Instead, he laughed heartily again, the noise filling the air about them.

'How very beautiful you look now, my dear,' he said. 'I mean, when you are angry. It brings a sparkle to your eyes.' He lifted a hand to her face. She brushed it aside with an angry gesture, and stared up at him with fierce, challenging eyes. 'I must say that I rather liked it when your hair was wild and tangled,' he continued softly. 'It suited your temperament. You know, you played the part of Ophelia very well.'

'I wish I could say the same about your beard,' Miriam rebutted rather childishly, taken slightly off guard by the intimate sentiment. 'It makes you look quite ridiculous.'

Algernon laughed and, before she could stop him, he bent his head and kissed her full on the lips. It was a moment or two before she pushed him away.

'You beast! How dare you?' Miriam demanded, rather belatedly. She poked him aggressively in the ribs and glared up at him indignantly, the anger she felt flashing in her eyes.

'Very easily,' he replied, studying her closely. He saw a flush of colour appear in her cheeks and grinned. 'I say, I was awfully afraid that you no longer cared for me.'

'I don't care for you at all,' she retorted.

'You little liar! You care for me a great deal, as I do you.'

'Is that why you have ignored me these last few months?' She found it impossible to keep the bitterness from her voice.

'I had my reasons,' mumbled Algernon.

He was at pains not to catch her eye. She noticed too that some of the mirth had gone from his voice. She stared at him, as if transfixed, willing him to speak, and yet half afraid of what he might say. Still, she was determined to take advantage of her companion's obvious discomfort. Taking a deep breath, she said: 'Had it anything to do with Ursula Stapleton?'

It was as if she had struck him, such was his reaction. He took a few steps back and stared at her, half tottering, his face quite pale.

'What do you mean by that?' he demanded.

There was a cold edge to his voice now, which made her recoil from him. She almost wished she had not spoken, certainly not given voice to her suspicions. But it was too late to retreat now, she realised with a dark foreboding.

'I know about your evening visits to her house,' Miriam said, so quietly that Algernon was forced to take a step forward in order to catch her words. 'I suppose you thought you were being very clever, waiting until her maid had retired for the night before you made your … your excursions.' She laughed a sad little laugh. 'Don't you realise that in a village like Sedgwick, everyone knows everyone else's business? You were spotted, darling. Leaving her house on numerous occasions, I mean. Biddy,' she added, referring to the Belmores' housemaid, 'took great delight in telling me all about it. I am sure it formed the gossip in many a servants' hall.'

'Biddy can go to the devil,' said Algernon with such ferocity that Miriam half wished she was somewhere else, or at least that Algernon was not beside her. For it had occurred to her suddenly that they were quite alone in Lovers' Lane. Should she find the need to cry out, there would be nobody to hear her, for the lane skirted the backs of the gardens of some of the larger houses in Sedgwick, and was seldom frequented during the hours of daylight other than by the odd servant dashing to the village for supplies.

Inwardly, she shook herself, and gave herself a stern talking to. This was not the time to go to pieces and become fanciful, to imagine danger where there was none. She had spent too many nights feeling wretched to be afraid. She bit her lip, and stared at the imposing figure before her, aware that it gave her a certain twisted pleasure to see him riled. After all, it served Algernon right. For she remembered how her foes had smirked, and her friends had looked at her in that awful pitying way that had made her blood boil. She had wanted to scream and shout, but convention had dictated that she held her tongue, and kept her emotions in check, bottled up inside her. If she had wept, then she had been her only witness to the fact. To the outside world she had presented a cold exterior, a façade of ice that she had carefully cultivated. Indeed, she had developed something of a reputation for being aloof. Her performance had been so convincing that even she had had difficulty distinguishing which was an act and which was her true self. And all the while she had planned and plotted …

It struck her suddenly that Algernon was strangely quiet. After maligning the housemaid's actions, he had remained silent, though she could sense that he was seething below the surface with a pent-up anger. She gave him a surreptitious glance. He seemed preoccupied, for she had the distinct impression that he did not see her. It was as if his thoughts were elsewhere, focused on something far away beyond the lane. It occurred to her then that this was her opportunity to pry.

'Did you love her?' she blurted out. 'Or was it her money? They say she was very rich.'

'What?' Algernon, recalled to his surroundings, stared at her in bewilderment.

'Did you love Ursula?' repeated Miriam; she might have been speaking to a child, so clearly did she accentuate the words.

'No,' he said loudly and with feeling, almost choking on the word.

'Then it was her money that you were after?'' Miriam said coldly.

Algernon made no reply.

'And now she is dead, you mean to continue where you left off with me?' Miriam continued, her eyes brimming with angry tears. 'How conceited and arrogant you are to suppose that I should want anything to do with you.' She spat out these last words, and was vaguely conscious that her voice had risen until it sounded shrill, even to her own ears. She took a deep breath and added more quietly: 'Do you think I have no pride? Do you think I would lower myself to … to …?' She faltered, struggling to find the words to do justice to her feelings. Failing, she turned away from him abruptly, and the next moment she was walking down the lane at a brisk pace, anxious to be gone.

'Wait,' cried Algernon. In one rapid movement, he was beside her. He grasped her roughly by the shoulders, swung her around, and looked down at her imploringly. 'It's not … it's not what you think.'

Miriam caught her breath and stared back at him. There was an urgency in his voice that caused a shudder to go through her. For the first time, she realised she was truly afraid.

Chapter Thirteen

Rose followed her husband and the policemen as they made their way along the earthen path towards the folly, concealed by its rich canopy of trees. Cedric, eager to be assigned a task, had set off at quite a pace and the inspector and sergeant were doing their best to follow him, while negotiating the roots of the trees that protruded underfoot.

Rose was particularly concerned about Inspector Deacon, who now walked with the aid of a cane, as a result of an injury incurred in the line of duty. When first she had witnessed him hobble, the very act itself had seemed to prematurely age him before her eyes. She had, however, soon become accustomed to it, so that she had become barely conscious of his disability. It was only while she followed him along the path that she was aware of it again, as if she were noticing it for the first time. It tugged at something within her, for she found it difficult to reconcile the image of the limping man before her with the tall, upright figure she had first laid eyes on at Ashgrove House. Yet, as she watched the inspector's progress along the path, it occurred to her that his limp was not as pronounced as it had been at Renard's. For one thing, he no longer walked with a shuffle. Still, she feared he would stumble; though, as she continued to observe him, she noted that he appeared to navigate the various hurdles with relative ease, as if he were familiar with the treacherous path. It was certainly pleasing to note that in the year or so that had elapsed since they had last met, Inspector Deacon had become more agile or better used to disguising his injury. It was the able-bodied Sergeant Lane, in contrast, who seemed to lurch and falter, clinging at the leaves and branches to retain his balance.

They turned a corner abruptly and the side of the Greek temple came sharply in to view. Rose watched the two policemen with an idle curiosity, interested to see their reactions as they spied the folly, which sprung up before them like some monstrous castle, hidden in the depths of an enchanted forest.

'Well, I'll be blowed!' exclaimed the sergeant. 'I can't say as how I thought it would be as big as it is, and all concealed, like. Well, I never!'

'It is certainly very impressive,' said Inspector Deacon, more reserved in his vocal appreciation of the structure than his colleague, but equally impressed. 'Quite a feat of architecture, I'd say. Do you know its history, my lord?'

'I do, indeed,' replied Cedric, delighted to have an interested listener on whom to impart his knowledge of his ancestral estate. 'It was built in 1773 by a student of the architect, Henry Flitcroft. No doubt you've heard of him?' He extended a hand towards the folly and said wistfully: 'As you can see, it would have made a very fine stage for our production. There is something of a palace about it, don't you think? Not that we can go ahead with the performance, of course … no, not now there is no doubt Ursula Stapleton was murdered.'

'I suppose it would be in rather poor taste,' agreed the inspector.

'It's a great pity, 'said Cedric, 'that all our rehearsals will come to naught. The proceeds from the performance were to go to one of our most deserving village charities, you see; for mothers and orphans. I suppose in a year or two when this sorry business is all forgotten …'

'Did this building have any other function?' inquired Inspector Deacon. 'By that I mean, was it used for anything other than as a stage?'

'For family picnics and supper parties, and the like,' said Cedric. 'It even has a heating system, though I don't know when it was last used.'

Rose looked on, wondering what the policemen thought of such indulgence. Her husband's words sounded rather frivolous to her own ears. In her mind's eye, she could visualise the parties. She could see beautiful girls, like her sister-in-law, Lady Lavinia Sedgwick, dressed in frocks made of some sheer, expensive fabric, giggling at young men who were in equally high spirits. She could imagine the champagne flowing and the music playing, the shrieks of laughter becoming louder as the night progressed and the young people indulged in some game or other. It was quite possible, she thought, that one or two of the young men or women would decide, their senses temporarily affected by drink, that it was a fine night for a swim. Or perhaps they might stumble down the bank and fall into the lake, to be rescued by some servant weary of observing the excesses of the monied classes.

She looked up sharply, aware suddenly that Inspector Deacon had been addressing her, and that she had been too absorbed in her own musings to hear his question.

'I'm sorry. I didn't …'

'You were watching the rehearsal,' Inspector Deacon repeated, looking down at a notebook in his hand, which Rose took to be Constable Bright's scribbled notes of the account she had given him of the events leading up to Ursula's murder. Certainly, the inspector spoke as if he were uttering a statement of fact, rather than asking a question; she wondered if she had imagined the note of irritation in his voice.

Rose was aware she had been ideally placed to witness the events as they had unfolded, from the moment Cordelia Quail had snatched the tray rather unceremoniously from the footman and marched up on to the stage with it, to the very moment Ursula Stapleton had slumped to the floor, poisoned.

'Yes,' she said. 'I had a very good view of what happened. I believe I observed the rehearsal pretty closely and gave Constable Bright a fair account of it.' She paused a moment as she remembered that she had given a very comprehensive account indeed. For she had provided certain unnecessary details, the purpose of which had been to allow Manning sufficient time to retrieve the wine glass from the folly.

'Yes,' muttered the inspector, flicking through the pages of the notebook, 'very thorough indeed.'

'Are you familiar with the play of Hamlet, Inspector?' inquired Rose.

'I am. I studied it at school, and have seen it performed once or twice.' Inspector Deacon lifted his head, and for the first time they met each other's gaze and held it for a moment in the shadow cast by the pillars of the Greek temple. It was another brilliant summer's day, and they might have been commenting on the weather, or indeed, as they were seeming to do, on the particulars of Shakespeare's play. To Rose, however, it seemed that the look they exchanged held a deeper meaning. A moment later, and the inspector had returned his gaze to the book in his hand, and Rose was left to contemplate whether she had merely been fanciful in her speculation.

'Do you remember the order of events as they happened?' Inspector Deacon asked.

'Yes. At least, I think so,' said Rose. 'I was watching the rehearsal closely, like I said, and I have been playing it over and over in my mind.'

'Good. I'll refer to the constable's notes as necessary, but first I should like you to tell me in your own words what happened. I think,' he said, pausing in order that he might consult the notebook again, 'we should commence from the moment Miss Quail took the tray of wine glasses from the servant and carried it on to the stage.'

'These wine glasses,' interposed Sergeant Lane, perhaps thinking it was time he contributed to the conversation, 'where were they? That's to say, did Miss Quail bring them with her yesterday afternoon, or had she left them here after the last rehearsal, where anyone might have tampered with them?'

'Oh, she brought them with her,' said Cedric. 'She was rather precious about her wine glasses. I think they were a family heirloom, or some such thing. She brought them with her on each occasion and stood them on the ground beside her. Then she took them away with her at the end of each rehearsal. I remember once that I suggested that she leave them here. I assured her they'd be quite safe, that if she left them in the circular room I would arrange for the door to be locked.'

'The circular room?' queried the inspector.

'Yes. Look, here, I'll show you, Inspector. If you'll follow me.'

With that, the earl set off towards the folly. The others proceeded to follow, the policemen registering, as they did so, the temple's raised porch with its Corinthian columns, which was reached by climbing six wide stone steps.

'It was only this portico, of course,' said Cedric, looking about him and gesturing towards the entrance, 'which formed the stage.'

He led the way through a doorway at the back of the portico, which opened out on to the circular room. The area itself had been left in some disarray, having been hastily searched and abandoned the previous day.

'We stored the props in here,' said Cedric, idly picking up what appeared to be a human skull from a stone bench. Inspector Deacon raised an eyebrow and the young earl grinned. 'You have no need to fear, Inspector. It isn't real. It's made of wax. 'Alas poor Yorick', and all that.'

The policemen wandered round the room, marvelling at its décor and surveying its contents. Various niches, or alcoves, had been cut in to the walls at intervals and housed either statues of Greek gods on marble plinths, or else small stone benches on which one or two persons might sit. The floor was made of a rich pink marble, and bare except for a few old wooden trestle tables and chairs strewn with abandoned garments and boxes of greasepaint. The walls were a shade of deep terracotta, which offset the stark alabaster figures. The overall effect was that of being in a museum and Rose heard Sergeant Lane mutter under his breath: 'Blimey!'

'And when we thespians were not required on stage,' continued Cedric, 'we sat in here and practiced our lines. Well, at least I did. The others were awfully good at remembering theirs.'

'I see,' said the inspector. 'I've read Constable Bright's notes, and my understanding is that Ursula Stapleton died in the same manner as the character she was portraying.'

'That's right,' agreed Cedric. 'And she died at about the same moment that Queen Gertrude dies in the play.' He paused a moment before continuing. 'I say, it's a nasty business this, isn't it?'

'It is a rum affair,' agreed the inspector. 'Someone went to an awful lot of effort. Or perhaps the play suggested to the murderer the deceased's manner of death. Tell, me, did you rehearse the whole play yesterday?'

'Good heavens, no!' exclaimed Cedric. 'It would have taken ages if we had. No, Inspector. We rehearsed only a few scenes. The ones that Miss Quail considered required more practice.'

'I see,' said Inspector Deacon again. He retraced his steps until he stood on the porch, overlooking the lake. 'And all the while Miss Quail had the wine glasses beside her chair on the lawn?' He pointed to an area of grass in front of the folly.

'Yes,' said Cedric. 'They were on a tray.'

Rose ran down the steps and stood before them on the grass.

'She was here, on this spot, Inspector,' she said. 'My mother and I joined her to watch the rehearsal.'

'And at some point during the afternoon Miss Quail gave the tray to the footman to arrange for the wine glass to be filled with water?' continued the inspector, almost as if Rose had not spoken.

'Yes,' said Cedric. 'I think she had quite forgotten about the wine glasses when we started the final scene until Ursula made her usual fuss about the water. At least, I heard Miss Quail calling to one of the footmen and asking him to hurry.'

'Indeed?' Do you know if he arranged for the wine glasses to be washed before filling one with water?'

'I say, Inspector. Are you suggesting that the cyanide was already in the glass before the water was added?' asked Cedric, an excited look upon his face.

'We must consider all possibilities, my lord,' replied the inspector cautiously.

'I've already spoken to the servants, Inspector,' said Rose, in a clear voice that seemed to cut through the summer breeze. She was aware that she had their full attention now and continued hurriedly, lest Inspector Deacon be tempted to comment that she had no right to have done such a thing. 'Charlie, the footman in question, assured me that he washed and dried both glasses before pouring water into one of them. He then carried them out on the tray. I saw him hand the tray to Miss Quail myself. It was not very long after one of the Prentice twins had said something about the arrival of the king and queen. I remember that there were only two other actors on the stage at the time; Hamlet and Horatio.'

'Henry Rewe and Giles Kettering,' Cedric supplied helpfully. 'Kettering's my secretary, don't you know. He's a very able fellow.'

Rose glanced affectionately at her husband and said: 'I can't tell you how relieved I was. You see, darling, I was awfully afraid that I had missed the scene with your fencing match.'

Cedric smiled. 'That wouldn't do. As it happens, we were all huddled in the circular room waiting for our cue.' He looked across at the inspector. 'I say, Deacon, now you mention it, I recall Cordelia bursting in with that damn tray of glasses. She was looking jolly flustered. I remember thinking it really was too bad that Ursula always insisted that her glass be filled with water.'

'Yes,' said the inspector, 'I read that in Constable Bright's notes. I don't suppose, my lord, you remember what Miss Quail did with the tray?'

'She put it down somewhere. On one of the trestle tables, I should imagine.'

The inspector looked rather disappointed with this answer. 'You didn't see where exactly?'

'I'm afraid not,' said Cedric. 'I was rather busy at the time reciting my lines in my head. I daresay one of the others may have noticed.' He gave the inspector a sharp look. 'I suppose you'd like to know if anyone took a particular interest in the glasses, or stood in front of the tray?' Inspector Deacon nodded. 'I say, do you think it possible the cyanide was added to the glass then?'

'Quite possible, I'd say, my lord.'

'The murderer would have had to take an awful risk,' protested Cedric. 'Someone was sure to spot him in the act.'

'Not if the others were absorbed, as you were, with practicing their lines, or applying greasepaint,' said Inspector Deacon, casting a look back towards the circular room. 'It would have been the act of only a few seconds to slip the potassium cyanide into the glass. It would have been in the form of little white crystals. To the naked eye, it would have looked like sugar or table salt. Only a small amount of the compound would have been required. It would have dissolved easily enough in the water and thus released the cyanide.'

'How horrid,' shuddered Rose. 'And to think poor Ursula was probably standing only a few feet from the murderer when he administered the poison.'

'Yes, it was a callous act all right, miss,' agreed Sergeant Lane, feeling again that he should contribute to the conversation. 'Of course, we keep saying our murderer's a 'he', but poison is considered a woman's crime, if ever there was one.'

'Surely you're not suggesting Miriam poisoned Ursula?' protested Cedric. 'She was the woman playing Ophelia,' he added for the policemen's benefit. 'She was the only other woman in the circular room at the time. Come to think of it, there were only two actresses in the play, her and Ursula.'

In his wife's opinion, Miriam Belmore was more than capable of undertaking such a task. For Rose remembered vividly the girl's cool aloofness and lack of empathy. She had appeared a cold, detached figure, standing apart from the others as if she did not share their grief or sense of shock. Certainly, if she had been affected by Ursula's death, she had not shown it. And Rose remembered something else about the girl, something that she had said.

'Miriam asked me whether I thought Ursula Stapleton had been murdered,' said Rose. 'No … that's not quite true. She accused me of suspecting that Mrs Stapleton had been murdered. She said that she supposed that was why Lord Belvedere and I had taken an age to return to the house.'

'Did she, indeed?' said Inspector Deacon, looking distinctly interested by this piece of information.

'But if Miriam had poisoned Ursula she would never have been so foolish as to mention murder,' protested Cedric. 'By all accounts, Ursula Stapleton had a weak heart, and she would have known that. If Miriam had been guilty of Ursula's death, why didn't she suggest that Ursula had died of some heart illness or other?'

'You never can tell with folk, my lord,' said Sergeant Lane. 'Some of them do the daftest things, though in this case perhaps she was being clever.'

'How so?' demanded Cedric.

'Well, perhaps she was bluffing,' suggested the sergeant. 'To put us off the scent, so to speak. And no doubt she is familiar with your reputation, miss …your ladyship; as an amateur sleuth, I mean.'

'Yes, she is,' said Rose. 'At least she referred to it.'

'Miriam didn't do it,' said Cedric stubbornly. 'It's not the sort of thing she'd do.'

The earl sounded so adamant that no one made any further attempts to contradict him. Rose was stung by the unwavering manner in which he defended the girl, whom she had assumed was little more than a vague acquaintance of her husband's. She stared at him anew, conscious only that he was defending a young woman who was not herself. It seemed that the others had registered it too, for an awkward silence filled the air. Rose lowered her gaze and stared at the ground, her cheeks burning. She did not dare raise her head and catch Inspector Deacon's eye. When finally she did look up, she noticed vaguely that Cedric had had the grace to look away, as if he were aware that he had crossed some invisible line.

'Cordelia would have had an opportunity to administer the poison,' Rose said at last. 'When she put the tray down on the table or chair, she could have arranged it so that she had her back to the others. No one would have thought anything amiss if she had stayed a moment or two to arrange the glasses on the tray. She would have had an opportunity then to slip the crystals in to the glass.'

'You are quite right, your ladyship,' agreed Inspector Deacon hurriedly, as if he were as keen as she was to talk of anyone other than Miriam Belmore. 'We certainly cannot rule Miss Quail out as a possible suspect.'

Rose cast a glance at her husband, who was now staring across at the

114

lake, as if it held some infinite attraction. She noted, with a touch of bitterness, that he did not attempt to plead poor Cordelia Quail's innocence.

Chapter Fourteen

'Miss Quail blew a fanfare of sorts on a trumpet,' Rose said, as she proceeded to give the policemen an account of the events leading up to Ursula's death. 'It drew our attention to the stage, and my mother and I moved forward to watch the rehearsal.' She went to stand again on the spot she had previously indicated to the inspector, staring up at the stage which had now taken on rather a sinister air in her mind. 'We stood on either side of Miss Quail,' she continued, remembering how she had marvelled at the folly's architecture. Now, when she looked at it, she was reminded only of a tomb. With an awful feeling of certainty, she knew that if she were to stretch out her hand and feel the cool, smooth stone beneath her fingertips, she would be forced to shudder.

'And quite a ghastly noise she made too,' her husband said, referring to the director. 'The woman must be tone deaf. I don't mind telling you it frightened me half to death. I dropped my script and I remember Walter Drury scrambled on the floor to retrieve it for me, which was really jolly decent of him.' He chuckled. 'Of course, the whole episode caused the Prentice twins to have a fit of the giggles; in stitches they were, and I admit I was rather tempted to join in the merriment myself.' His face suddenly became grave and he gave Inspector Deacon a shrewd look. 'I suppose it would have been the ideal moment for our murderer to strike.'

The inspector nodded. 'It would have been. The murderer probably could not quite believe his luck. For there to be a distraction of sorts the very moment he was contemplating adding the poison to the wine glass was more than he could have hoped for. Yes, the affair with the trumpet was a very fortunate occurrence indeed from his perspective.'

'Of course, said Rose slowly, 'it is quite possible that the poison was not administered in the circular room at all.'

Both Cedric and the sergeant looked at her in bewilderment; only the inspector appeared to grasp her drift.

'Are you suggesting,' he said, clearly interested by Rose's train of thought, 'that the deed could have been done on stage while the scene was being performed?'

'Yes, I suppose I am,' agreed Rose. 'It sounds a little farfetched, I know, and the murderer would have required a very cool head, but I think it could have been done that way.'

'In front of everyone, like?' queried Sergeant Lane. 'But, surely, someone would have noticed? If not anyone on the stage itself, then you or Mrs Simpson or Miss Quail?'

'There was a great deal happening on the stage during the last scene,' explained Rose. 'You see, our attention was drawn primarily to the duel that was taking place between Hamlet and Laertes … Henry Rewe and my husband.'

'We were rather dashing about the stage,' confirmed Cedric. 'At least, I was. Henry was crouching and cowering. The poor fellow looked petrified.' He grinned. 'Frightened I really would stab him with my foil, no doubt. The thing is, I was trying to make the duel look convincing, which is awfully hard when your opponent refuses to fight. And it was jolly nice to have the opportunity to bound about the stage a bit, rather than having to stand on one spot like a stuffed lemon. I daresay you know better than I, Inspector, what Shakespeare's plays are like? There are a great many soliloquies and fine speeches, but very little action to speak of.'

'If I remember correctly, my lord,' said Inspector Deacon, giving a wry smile, 'there is quite a lot of action, as you call it, in that final scene of the play. In addition to the fighting scene, I mean.'

'Oh, yes,' agreed Cedric. 'There's a lot of jolly exciting stuff. For one thing, pretty well everyone gets murdered, often as not as the result of their own treachery.'

'Indeed, my lord?' murmured Sergeant Lane, raising an eyebrow. In less illustrious company, he might have added that he preferred a good Gilbert and Sullivan himself, something that he could tap his feet to. Instead, he contented himself with a study of the foils, particularly the tips.

'They are quite blunt, I assure you, Sergeant,' Cedric said, watching the policeman with interest as he examined the weapons. 'One would be hard-pressed to do much damage with those, I can tell you.' He glanced over at the inspector, who appeared to be perusing a script of the play, which he had found discarded on one of the trestle tables. For some reason, this fact irritated the earl, as if such an act suggested that the policeman was more interested in the intrigues of the play than in catching the murderer.

'Look here, Deacon,' he said. 'I can quite see you would want to have a look at the scene of the crime, as it were, but hadn't you better speak to Henry Rewe? Lord knows, I'm not one to tell a man how to do his job, but it was Henry Rewe who picked up the poisoned glass, don't you know, and brought it to the drawing room. And he would have taken it away with him too, but for the quick thinking of my wife.' He began to pace the portico. 'I wouldn't have had him down as the murderer, myself, but hadn't you better arrest him? I don't doubt the whole village knows by now that Mrs Stapleton was murdered. You don't want to lose your man.'

'All in good time, my lord,' said the inspector pleasantly. 'I'm sure you'll appreciate I have my own way of doing things.'

He spoke politely enough, though Rose thought she detected a slight edge to the inspector's voice which suggested that he had no intention of taking orders on the matter of police procedure from the likes of the gentry.

'Yes, of course, Inspector,' Cedric said, colouring, uncomfortably aware that he had spoken out of turn. 'I wouldn't dream of telling you how to go about your business ...'

'I'd like to get an idea of how things happened on the stage,' Inspector Deacon said. 'To get a picture in my mind of how the action unfolded. Besides, it is of little importance whether we find the wine glass in Rewe's possession or not. We have a witness who saw him take it, which is the thing. And besides, if the lad has any sense he would have disposed of the glass as soon as he left Sedgwick Court.'

'Quite,' muttered Cedric. 'But if he should choose to flee ...'

'Then, we'd find him soon enough,' Inspector Deacon said firmly. He stared at the copy of the script he was holding, as if to indicate there was to be no further discussion on the matter. 'Now, Hamlet and Horatio ... Mr Rewe and Mr Kettering, were on the stage. Miss Quail blows her trumpet, and the rest of you troop on to the stage. Is that right, my lord?'

'Yes, I think so.'

'If I remember rightly, Inspector,' said Rose, 'the king and the queen were the first to emerge from the circular room.'

'Mr Cuffe and the deceased?'

'Yes. Then you appeared, darling,' Rose said glancing over at her husband, who had ceased pacing. 'And Walter Drury too. He was playing Osric. I think he was carrying something. Now … what was it?'

'The small wooden table,' supplied her husband.

'That's right, so it was. Miriam Belmore followed him out on to the stage. She was playing Ophelia –'

'Ophelia?' queried the inspector. 'I didn't think she was in the last scene. Didn't she drown earlier in the play?'

'That's right. But, as she was at the rehearsal, Miss Quail asked her if she wouldn't mind playing a courtier.'

'Which she agreed to do rather grudgingly, I might add,' said Cedric and chuckled.

'Yes,' Rose said, rather coldly. 'She is, I'm afraid Inspector, rather a disagreeable young woman.' She was aware of a sharp intake of breath from her husband and hurried on, lest she lose her nerve. 'She complained dreadfully about the costume she was wearing.' She bit her lip before continuing, horrified at her own spitefulness, her childish show of petulance. 'Then the Prentice twins appeared,' she continued quickly, regaining some of her composure. 'They are playing Rosencrantz and Guildenstern. Of course, their characters are not present in the final scene but, as with Miss Belmore, Miss Quail had enrolled them to play the part of court attendants in the rehearsal.'

'To keep them out of mischief as much as anything,' said Cedric, glancing rather anxiously at his wife, who was rather pointedly not looking at him. Instead, she seemed to be staring out in to the middle distance, as if some object there held her fascination.

'Did Miss Belmore and the Prentice twins know they were to play the part of the courtiers?' asked Inspector Deacon rather sharply. 'By that, I mean was it arranged in advance of yesterday's rehearsal?'

'Why, yes, Inspector,' said Cedric, pleased to have something to distract him from his wife's strange behaviour. 'Miss Quail mentioned it at the rehearsal last week. She intended to recruit some of the villagers to play the parts of the nobles and attendants in the actual performance, but wished to have an idea yesterday of how many would be required to fill the stage.'

'I see.' The inspector turned his attention back to Rose. 'Do you remember, Lady Belvedere, what happened to the table?'

'The table?' Rose looked a little confused, as if she had been brought abruptly back to the present, her thoughts still residing elsewhere. 'The table ... yes, I think Mr Drury set it down at the back of the stage.' She added, almost as an afterthought: 'I do remember that the Prentice twins were carrying the foils and the wine glasses when they entered.'

'Were they, indeed? Do you remember which of the twins was carrying the glasses?'

'No. I don't know. You see, the Prentice brothers are very difficult to tell apart. Not only are they identical in looks, but they were wearing matching costumes ... black and red striped doublets and breeches.'

'Very fetching, I'm sure,' muttered Sergeant Lane grimacing.

'They were certainly very colourful,' said Rose. 'The twin carrying the wine glasses placed them on the table; I do remember that. He then stood behind it and smirked rather unkindly at his brother's misfortune.'

'Oh?' A gleam of interest showed itself in Inspector Deacon's eye. 'What misfortune was that?'

'The poor boy dropped the foils,' explained Rose. 'I suppose he was rather nervous. I remember he looked very worried. Mr Drury rushed forward to help him pick them up.'

'It made an almighty din,' said Cedric, 'the foils clattering on to the stone floor, I mean.'

'And I suppose it caused something of a disturbance?' suggested the inspector.

'Yes, Inspector,' agreed Cedric. 'It was another perfect opportunity for our murderer to slip the poison into the wine glass, if that's what you are getting at.'

Inspector Deacon glanced down at his copy of the script again, while Sergeant Lane shifted rather impatiently from one foot to the other, whistling a tune softly under his breath. Even a casual observer might have commented that he appeared restive, as if he feared his superior were intent on reviewing each line of the final scene of the play in detail. Even Rose, who had watched the rehearsal with a great deal of interest and enthusiasm, sympathised with the sergeant's view. She too felt they were rather wasting their time standing in the folly when there was a whole host of suspects to be interviewed, not least the man who had been spied procuring what he had believed to be the poisoned wine glass.

The inspector looked up from the page he was reading and addressed

Cedric, who was now lounging rather nonchalantly against one of the stone pillars. 'While you and Mr Rewe were leaping about the stage, my lord, what were the courtiers doing?'

'Watching our duel, Inspector. It was quite a spectacle, don't you know. I believe they were supposed to be cheering and clapping, though shuffling and dragging their feet would be a more accurate description. It has to be said they were rather quiet.' He laughed. 'I suppose they were more concerned with ensuring they did not get in our way. Henry was rather lethal with his foil. The poor fellow would insist on waving it around blindly. They were probably afraid he'd have their eyes out.'

'From where I was standing,' Rose said, 'the courtiers appeared to form a crowd around you. I do remember Miss Quail told them at one point to keep to the sides of the stage in order not to obstruct the audience's view of the fight.'

'Yes,' agreed her husband. 'But every time we made a move in their direction, they dispersed.'

'If what you are saying is correct,' said the inspector, 'then there must have been a great deal of activity on the stage. You and Mr Rewe were dashing about –'

'I was,' said Cedric. 'Poor Henry was trying to hide in the corner, waving his foil about in a reckless fashion.'

'And the courtiers were moving to and fro as they watched your duel,' continued the inspector.

'Yes, like I said,' said Cedric, sounding a trifle bored. 'They were doing their best to get out of our way and not be stabbed by Henry. Not a mean feat, I can tell you. They had to be rather quick on their toes.'

'So, in all the confusion, anyone might have had an opportunity to slip the poison into the wine glass. By that, I mean anyone who was on the stage at the time.'

'Yes, I suppose you are right, Inspector. I must say, the thought had not occurred to me,' admitted Cedric.

'And Mr Cuffe, in the guise of King Claudius, picked up the wine glass and dropped in a pearl.'

'I say, Inspector, you're quite right,' Cedric said, looking impressed. 'I'd forgotten that bit in the play. Too busy concentrating on the fight, I suppose. It wasn't a real pearl, of course, just a piece of polished glass.'

'But an opportunity nevertheless for Mr Cuffe to administer the poison, should he be inclined to do so?'

'I'd say!'

'What happened to the wine glass? Did he put it on the table?'

'No. I think Mr Drury took it from him,' said Rose. 'Yes, he did. He was playing Osric. I remember now he looked as if he did not quite know what to do with it. He held it rather awkwardly and looked about him as if he was expecting someone to be standing beside him who wasn't there.'

'The queen, perhaps?' suggested Inspector Deacon, turning a page of the script. 'She had to drink from it. She made a toast to Hamlet.'

'Yes,' said Cedric, all sign of idleness now forgotten. 'The king tells her not to drink from the glass, but she disobeys him.' He paused, as if reliving the moment in his head. 'We all stopped what we were doing and stared at her. I don't know why we did. Henry and I usually continued fighting during the part where she raises her glass to Hamlet. I say, I suppose it is possible that we all had some awful premonition of the disaster that was to follow. How ghastly!'

'Algernon Cuffe sounded very fierce when he told Mrs Stapleton not to drink,' said Rose.

'I say, you're quite right,' exclaimed Cedric. 'He almost shouted the line. It made us all jump, I can tell you.'

'Perhaps he knew the glass was poisoned,' suggested Sergeant Lane, 'or at least suspected it was.'

'Who gave the glass to Mrs Stapleton. Did she take the glass from Mr Drury herself, or did someone pass it to her?' Inspector Deacon asked rather sharply.

'Miss Belmore took the glass and carried it to her,' Rose said slowly, hardly daring to catch her husband's eye. 'Mr Drury looked awfully relieved. I think he thought he would be left holding it.'

Cedric did not plead Miriam's innocence this time as she had feared, but remained resolutely silent on the matter. Instead, he said almost dully: 'I suppose what we are saying is that anyone could have done the crime. We all had an opportunity to slip the poison unseen into Ursula's glass.'

'Yes,' agreed the inspector, 'though I'll wager you, my lord, and Mr Rewe were too preoccupied with your duel to do the deed on the stage, as it were. According to your account, you were darting about the stage and lunging, and Mr Rewe was doing his best to defend himself.'

'Rather ineffectually,' murmured Cedric. His face brightened. 'Look here, Inspector, I daresay you'll want to base your investigation here at Sedgwick Court?' He did not wait for a reply before continuing. 'Sergeant Lane will tell you that I put my study at his disposal when he and Inspector Bramwell investigated the death in the maze.'

'And awfully good of you it was too, my lord, to be sure,' said the sergeant.

'Well, I like to do what I can to assist the police with their duties,' said Cedric. 'My wife and I should consider it an honour if you would do the same, Deacon.' He descended the stone steps. 'Now, if you gentlemen would care to follow me, I'll show you to my study and arrange for some refreshments to be brought to you.'

'That's frightfully kind of you, my lord,' said Inspector Deacon, remaining where he was. His voice sounded artificially loud among the stone pillars, as if he had a mind to project his voice to an unseen audience staring up at him from the lawn below. 'However, it will not be necessary for I've arranged for the use of the private parlour at the Sedgwick Arms for just such a purpose.'

'Oh?' Cedric swung around and fixed on the inspector a look of utter surprise. Even the sergeant, Rose noticed, looked somewhat taken aback by his superior's statement.

'Well, I'll just get Manning to telephone to the Arms to inform them that you have changed your plans,' said the earl.

'There's no need for that, my lord.'

'Oh, but I insist. It's no trouble, I assure you.'

'There's no need for that, my lord, because I shall be conducting the investigation in to the death of Mrs Stapleton from the Sedgwick Arms.'

'Not from Sedgwick Court?'

'No, my lord.'

'I see.' Cedric lowered his gaze, and then, just as abruptly turned to scowl at the inspector. 'Look here, Deacon, I don't see why you have arrived at that decision; I don't see at all. If Inspector Bramwell did not have an issue with –'

'I am not Inspector Bramwell, my lord,' began Inspector Deacon.

'The circumstances were different then,' said Rose slowly, enlightenment suddenly falling on her like a summer shower.

Until those final minutes they had almost appeared to be as one, working together to piece together the fragments from some elaborate jigsaw puzzle. Standing there in the folly, she had almost forgotten the first awkward moments in the hall on the policemen's arrival. But now the gulf between them had returned more vivid than ever, highlighting the disparity between their social positions and professions.

'Those involved were our guests,' she said dully. 'They were staying in our house at the time, whereas –'

'The Sedgwick Players are our social inferiors?' said Cedric, his eyebrows raised, his look incredulous. 'I say, does it matter? We were all in the play together. Why, I took my direction from Miss Quail.'

'That's as may be, my lord,' said Inspector Deacon, 'but I believe the witnesses and suspects will speak more freely if I conduct my interviews in less … imposing surroundings.'

'I wonder what's got in to old Deacon,' Cedric muttered to his wife a few minutes later as they watched the policemen depart.

'He doesn't want me to be present during the interviews,' Rose said, almost bitterly, 'but he's far too polite to say so.'

Cedric shrugged his shoulders and started for the house. It did not occur to him for one moment that Inspector Deacon would be successful in his attempts to thwart his wife's investigation in to Ursula Stapleton's death. Rose lingered a few moments before following her husband's example. It was only when he turned and looked back to see what was keeping her that she quickened her pace.

'I suppose it is quite different now,' she murmured softly to herself, almost under her breath. 'Everything has changed. What a fool I was to think that any of it would be the same.'

Chapter Fifteen

'I've always thought she was a very nice young lady, sir,' said Sergeant Lane, getting up from his chair in the private parlour at the Sedgwick Arms.

He had been busy scribbling notes and, in a pause in the proceedings, had seized the opportunity to pace the room and stretch his legs. He had only to glance down at his notebook to envisage the number of pages he would fill before the day was out; his hand ached already in anticipation of the toil. He sighed, noting as he did so that the inspector had made no comment on his observation.

'Miss Simpson,' he added, for the avoidance of doubt. 'I mean, Lady Belvedere, as I suppose I should call her now, though so grand a title don't seem to suit the young miss nearly as well. Anyway, she looked quite a picture, I thought, what with her fine clothes and her hair styled all elegant, like.'

Inspector Deacon gave his sergeant something of a shrewd look. He did no more, however, than mutter a few words which his subordinate assumed concurred with his own assessment of the young woman.

'She doesn't seem to have any airs and graces about her as you'd expect a young lady to have in her position,' Sergeant Lane continued, 'what with her marriage, and all. Too grand for us, you'd have thought she'd have considered herself now, but no, not at all. Friendly towards us, she was, just like old times, though I thought she looked a little surprised to see us. His lordship, too; he greeted us like we were old friends, he –'

'That'll do, Lane,' said Inspector Deacon abruptly, holding up his hand. 'I am fully aware that you think I erred in declining his lordship's hospitality.'

'Well, sir, it's just that I thought they looked a trifle offended and … well, it did seem a little ungrateful.'

'It couldn't be helped, Lane,' Inspector Deacon said, somewhat brusquely. 'We're undertaking a murder investigation, and I'm afraid the feelings of those involved don't amount for much.'

'But, sir –'

'I don't doubt Lord and Lady Belvedere meant well, but really it wouldn't do for us to be based at Sedgwick Court,' continued the inspector, apparently resigned to the fact that his sergeant required a fuller explanation for his decision. 'For one thing, the parties involved in this affair live in the village. They won't want to have to trudge up to the house to give their statements. And jolly intimidating they'd find it too if they did, being greeted by butlers and footmen and the like. We're not dealing with house party guests this time. Amateur thespians are rather a different kettle of fish. If we were to interview them in Lord Belvedere's study, they'd be on their best behaviour and say as little as possible. As it is, it'll take all our efforts to loosen their tongues. We don't want to put any unnecessary obstacles in the way if we can help it.'

'I suppose so,' said the sergeant, sounding a little unconvinced by his superior's argument. 'Still, it's a shame,' he added, casting a look round their rather modest surroundings. 'You could have sat in a velvet captain's chair behind a large estate desk, sir, and me, I could have sat in a nice comfortable chair to take my notes instead of one of these old rickety dining chairs as has seen better days, to say nothing of that old moth-eaten horsehair sofa.'

'Don't let our landlady hear you saying such things,' the inspector said, shuffling some papers before him on the table. 'She made a point of telling me how she keeps a very respectable house. And most particular, she is, that the place is kept clean and tidy, just as it should be. I wouldn't advise you tell her it's not a patch on Sedgwick Court, not if you want to eat a hearty supper tonight.'

Inspector Deacon rose from his chair and positioned himself with his back against the unlit fireplace. His dark hair gleamed in the late afternoon sunlight that shone through the window of the little parlour. In spite of the cane that he was obliged to use, he still had the appearance of a tall and slightly imposing man. Certainly, there was an authoritative air about him, despite his relative youth. The sergeant, himself a young man, looked at his superior a little apprehensively. He had the odd feeling that he had inadvertently touched a nerve, or strayed on to ground on which he was a trespasser.

'This murder is a rum old business, Lane,' said Inspector Deacon quietly, returning to the particulars of the case. He passed a hand across his sleek, black hair in something of a distrait fashion. 'I don't like it. This affair was premeditated all right, down to the last element. There was something rather spiteful and vindictive about it. Our murderer watched Mrs Stapleton drink the poison and die before his eyes. It takes a certain type of person to do that; watch a woman die, I mean.'

'It sounds to me, sir, as if he hated her,' said Sergeant Lane. 'As if he took a particular pleasure in her suffering, like.'

'Or perhaps we are merely being fanciful,' Inspector Deacon said wearily. 'By that I mean it is possible we are seeing intrigue where there is none. The play suggested to our murderer a method by which Mrs Stapleton might be killed amid a sea of suspects. Talking of which, we had better have a word with this Mr Rewe. If the footman is correct, and we have no reason to suppose he'd lie, Henry Rewe saw fit to steal what he supposed to be the poisoned wine glass from Sedgwick Court.'

'That was quick thinking on her ladyship's part,' said Sergeant Lane, a note of admiration in his voice, 'substituting the poisoned glass with the innocent one, I mean.'

'It was,' conceded the inspector, colour rising to his cheeks unbidden. This fact was not lost on his subordinate, who was determined to play his advantage.

'Quite a lady, like I said. Why, it's quite possible isn't it sir, that we won't need to have our bags unpacked? If this Rewe chap confesses, and there is nothing to say he won't, not with the evidence we have against him. If that happens, we might be boarding the train back to London before you can say Bob's your uncle.'

'I should certainly like to see what this fellow has to say for himself,' replied the inspector, more guardedly, returning to his chair. If truth be told, it seemed to him unlikely that a man who had gone to such considerable effort to construct an elaborate murder would lose his head and go to pieces the moment the police questioned him. If he had been pressed further on the matter, he might also have added that he considered the man's guilt to be a trifle too obvious, yet it was difficult to ignore the fact that the young man had evidently taken the wine glass in the full knowledge that the police were of the view that Ursula Stapleton's death was out of the ordinary.

'Miss Simpson –' began Sergeant Lane, tentatively.

'Lady Belvedere,' corrected the inspector. 'What of her, Lane? She has provided us with a line of inquiry, I admit, but –'

'Knowing her like we do, she'll have her heart set on investigating this murder, sir, like as not, what with it happening in the grounds of her estate, as it were.'

'I don't doubt it.' Inspector Deacon admitted, declining to look up from his papers and catch the sergeant's eye.

To Sergeant Lane, his superior sounded strangely complacent, almost resolved to the fact, as if he had no intention of trying to persuade Lady Belvedere to do otherwise. It was quite possible, of course, that he was aware that such an action would be in vain. Rose Simpson, as the sergeant thought of her still, would not sit by and idly wait for the police to do their job. If they excluded her from participating in their own investigation, as Inspector Deacon appeared minded to do, then she would merely instigate her own inquiries. He knew that absolutely, as if she had stated her intentions to him in the hall. Aloud, he said: 'Wouldn't it be better, sir, if we worked together? Lady Belvedere and us, I mean. She has a flair, she does, for these things. I'll wager she'll discover things they don't want to tell us. She has a knack for it, she does, unearthing people's secrets, and loosening their tongues.'

'She may well have done in the past, I'll give you that, Lane,' said Inspector Deacon. He spoke firmly and decisively, and perhaps also with a little anger in his voice, the precise reason for which his sergeant could not explain. 'But it is quite a different story now since her marriage. She is the Countess of Belvedere. She cannot escape the fact and don the cloak of the amateur sleuth when the fancy takes her. In the villagers' eyes, she'll still be seen as being gentry.' He got up from his chair, and stared out of the window, the view from which was the village green. 'I daresay a village like this is still rather feudal. No one will want to be seen as speaking out of turn to her ladyship, not when it comes to the likes of murder. Lady Belvedere's reputation as a detective won't amount to much in a place like this, you mark my words. They'll see her only as the lady of the manor.'

It was quite an impassioned speech, or at least to Sergeant Lane it appeared so. He sensed there had been much below the surface, which rendered him silent for a moment while he considered how best to respond. He was half tempted to argue that to his knowledge Rose had successfully investigated at least one murder since her marriage; one had only to read the papers to know that. He held his tongue, however, for he had the distinct impression that such an argument would not be well received.

'Then, that is why we are not based at Sedgwick Court?' he said rather feebly, more for something to say than anything else.

'I have already told you it is.' Two bright spots of colour had appeared on the inspector's cheeks giving him a vague resemblance to the painted toy soldier Sergeant Lane had played with as a child.

'Because –'

'It's no use, Lane. Circumstances have changed. Lady Belvedere is not the Miss Simpson you met at Ashgrove House.' There was a strange note to the inspector's voice that his sergeant could not quite place. It was only later that he wondered whether it had been regret.

'But presumably the chief constable requested that Scotland Yard investigate Mrs Stapleton's death,' persisted Sergeant Lane, experiencing an odd reluctance to yield to the inspector's superiority, 'on account of the murder happening on Lord Belvedere's land? That's why we're here. Why, I don't doubt that it was at the behest of his lordship himself,' he added.

'You are quite wrong in your assumption,' said Inspector Deacon rather curtly. 'It had nothing to do with where the murder occurred or Lord Belvedere asserting undue influence, for that matter. It was in fact Mr Cecil Stapleton who requested that Scotland Yard be brought in to investigate this case.'

'Cecil Stapleton?' The sergeant's brow furrowed in rather a comical manner. 'I think I've heard of that name before …'

'I should think you have. An eminent fellow. Moves in high circles. Has his finger in many pies, if what you read about him in the illustrated papers is half true. Government; the City. He even has interests in the coal mines.'

'I see. And he and the deceased had the same surname. Ursula Stapleton … is she by way of being a relative of his?'

'Yes, in a manner of speaking. By that I mean she was his daughter-in-law, though I don't believe he ever met her.'

'His daughter-in-law?' Sergeant Lane looked surprised. He recalled the body he had seen in the morgue. It had not struck him then that the corpse he was looking at had been of high social standing in life, though in truth he found death deprived a body of much that was individual or of character. 'And he never met her, you say?'

'No. There was something of a falling out, I believe. Ursula Stapleton, or Ursula Westbrooke as she was called then, married Stapleton's youngest son, Dudley. On all accounts, he was a rather wild and reckless fellow, couldn't settle at anything. Well, old Mr Stapleton didn't approve of his son's marriage. When the engagement was given out he threatened to disown Dudley if he went ahead with the wedding.'

'Then he didn't favour his son's choice of bride?'

'No. He thought Dudley was marrying beneath him and that the woman was no more than a common fortune hunter.' Inspector Deacon returned to his chair and sat down, propping his elbows on the desk in front of him. 'I daresay the affair would have come to nothing, a youthful infatuation, that's all. It would most probably have died a natural death in the ordinary course of things. But the son was as obdurate as his father. He declared that he was damned if he was going to be told whom he could or could not marry.'

'Dudley Stapleton married Ursula Westbrooke against his father's wishes?'

'Yes. And old Stapleton kept to his word and disinherited his son for his troubles. There was to be no tearful reconciliation.'

'Mr Stapleton never forgave his son for going against him?'

'He was never given the opportunity, Lane.' Inspector Deacon sighed. 'You see, like many other poor devils, Dudley Stapleton was killed in the war less than two years after his fateful marriage.'

'I say, that's pretty rum, sir.'

'It is. By all accounts, Stapleton senior was much affected by his son's death. He held the wife to blame and refused to have anything to do with her. The union had produced no child, so there was no son or heir in which he had to concern himself.'

'You mean, he left poor Mrs Stapleton to provide for herself then, did he, sir?' said Sergeant Lane, a touch bitterly. 'Despite all his wealth and all?'

'I daresay he gave her an allowance of sorts. He'd have put some arrangements in place; had his solicitors draw up some deed or other.'

'And now he wants Scotland Yard to investigate her murder?' Sergeant Lane sounded incredulous.

'I'm afraid it has more to do with the old man's fear of the gossip columns than a wish to avenge his daughter-in-law's death.'

'It seems to me Mrs Stapleton was rather hard done by in life, poor woman,' muttered the sergeant. 'She loses her husband in the war and her husband's family don't want anything to do with her. And then she's murdered. Still a relatively young woman too, she was. It's a crying shame, that's what it is.'

'It is. But then murder's always a sorry business, Lane. All you and I can do is see that her murderer is brought to justice.'

'And Lady Belvedere …' The sergeant allowed his sentence to falter, as if the words had fallen on stony ground.

'Yes?' said the inspector, somewhat impatiently. 'What of Lady Belvedere?'

'Well,' began Sergeant Lane, choosing his words with care. 'I see as how you don't want us to be stationed at Sedgwick Court, as it were, but do you have any objection to my discussing the case with her ladyship?' The inspector frowned, and the sergeant continued hurriedly, thinking that as he was in for a penny he might as well be in for a pound. 'I have every faith in Miss Simpson's detective abilities, countess as she may be now. I'm not saying as how it might not be a bit harder for her, like, but she has a knack, she does, of engendering confidences, as it were. It seems a pity not to discuss the case with her. It would be like missing a trick or cutting our nose off to spite our face, as my dear old mother would say.'

Inspector Deacon stared at his sergeant somewhat dumbfounded. It seemed to him an age since the two of them had investigated a murder together at which Rose Simpson was also present. He had quite forgotten in what high esteem Sergeant Lane held the woman in question. For a moment, in his mind's eye he was back at Ashgrove House …

'Very well, Lane,' he said finally. 'I have no objection to your speaking with her ladyship if you wish.' He sighed. 'I admit it is quite possible that she might make some discoveries which may prove useful to our own investigation.'

'And you, sir,' enquired Sergeant Lane, 'do you intend to speak with Lady Belvedere? If you don't mind my saying, I think she'd appreciate it if you did. It would be a bit like old times, it would. And she was helpful concerning that affair at Renard's, wasn't she? And I read as how she solved that murder on bonfire night, countess though she were, and –'

'I will not be consulting with Lady Belvedere on this case,' said Inspector Deacon.

There was a firmness, coupled with a dangerous edge to the inspector's voice, which was not lost on the sergeant and made him fear he had overstepped the mark. Certainly, it was clear the inspector did not intend to discuss the matter further. As he returned to his chair, the sergeant wondered, not for the first time, what exactly had occurred at Madame Renard's dress shop to cause the awkwardness that seemed to exist between the countess and the inspector like a pervading gloom.

Chapter Sixteen

'An interview with Henry Rewe should clear up this business,' said Cedric. 'I suppose that is where Deacon has gone, to speak to the fellow now?'

He glanced over at his wife, who appeared to be in something of a brown study, for certainly, Rose took a moment or two to respond, and then only to nod her head in an absentminded fashion. By common accord, their return journey to the house had been a rather meandering affair, for they had deviated from the formal paths more than once, and were now standing on the grass in the rose garden, staring at the yellow and pale pink blooms as if they might cast some light on the mystery before them.

'Deacon made it quite clear that he did not wish you to accompany them,' Cedric continued, his face darkening as he remembered the inspector's polite but firm manner. 'Damn the man! He seems to forget that it is thanks to your actions that he has been given a very valuable lead in this case. I say, darling, are you all right? You've hardly said a word. It's rather galling about Deacon, of course, but –'

'Cedric, how well do you know Miss Belmore?' The words sprung from her mouth and were uttered rather more harshly than Rose had intended, and she blushed in spite of herself.

'Miriam? Well, hardly at all.' Her husband glanced at her, and she fancied there was something sheepish in the look he gave her. 'Of course, I've spoken to her a bit during the rehearsals, only polite to do so, what. Passed the time of day, that sort of thing.'

'She is not in the way of being a friend of yours?'

'No. I hardly know the girl at all, as I've said. I've had some dealings in the past with her father in the way of business. He happens to be a partner of an old law firm in Bichester. Not Gribble, Hebborn & Whittaker, I hasten to add,' he added quickly, his thoughts returning for a moment to the events that had occurred on Bonfire Night. 'Rotches, Belmore & Birchen. They are a most respectable law practice; no hint of embezzlement there.'

He attempted a chuckle, but the sound seemed to fall on deaf ears.

Certainly, his wife did not join in the merriment, and Cedric was reminded that perhaps it was no laughing matter. But for the diligent efforts made by a couple of the partners, the law firm in question might lie in ruins, its clients' investments with it, and those whom it employed out on the streets. Feeling rather ashamed of himself, he made a mental note to employ the services of the beleaguered firm in future on small matters of business.

The rose blooms swayed gently in the summer breeze, and the sound of birdsong filled the air. But for the sombre circumstances, it would have produced a lightening in the mood of each of the two young people present. As it was, it seemed to restore to Rose the power of speech, or at least awaken in her the detective's instincts, which had been all but slumbering since the policemen's departure.

'I must go. If Inspector Deacon is intent on excluding me from his investigation, then I ought to try to speak to as many of the suspects as I can.' She paused a moment to glance up at the house, the stately pile dominating the view. 'I only hope that they are more forthcoming than they were yesterday.'

'It's a pity you won't be able to speak with Henry Rewe before they interview him,' said her husband.

It seemed to Rose that the conversation had returned full circle. She smoothed the fabric of her skirt carelessly and said rather flippantly: 'I don't believe he is of much importance in this affair.'

'Oh?' Her husband stared at her in surprise. 'How can you possibly think that? Why, the man stole what he took to be the poisoned wine glass.'

'I am well aware of that fact,' said Rose, in spite of everything, unable to keep the laugher from her voice at the look of bewilderment on her husband's face.

'Yet –'

'In my opinion,' said Rose slowly, aware that she now had Cedric's full attention, 'Henry Rewe is the only one of our suspects who could not possibly have murdered Ursula Stapleton.'

'Why not?'

'As Inspector Deacon said, when the poor man was on the stage he was too preoccupied dodging your blade to focus his attention on doing anything else.' She held up her hand as Cedric made to protest. 'To administer the poison, he would first have needed to locate the wine glass. Then, he would have had to position himself in front of it to obscure his actions from view. Only when he was satisfied that he had done so, would he have been in a position to slip the poison into the glass.' She smiled. 'No, it could not have been done. He did not have the necessary time to do the deed, for he was not able to remain still for one moment.'

'The circular room –' began Cedric.

'Henry Rewe did not go into the circular room. From the moment Miss Quail took the tray from the footman and carried it into the circular room, to the moment Mrs Stapleton drank from the poisoned wine glass, Henry Rewe did not leave the stage.'

Silence filled the air while Cedric digested his wife's words. At length, he said: 'If Henry Rewe is innocent, why did he take the wine glass?'

'That,' said Rose, 'is something we shall have to find out. As it is, I have my own suspicions, but,' she held up her hand again to stall her husband's questions, 'I don't intend to tell you yet. I should like to ascertain first if my theory is correct.'

Before Cedric could protest, Rose was half walking, half running, along the path that skirted the rose garden and proceeded up to the house, and he was left to wonder at his wife's strange mood.

'Edna,' Rose said, walking into her bedroom, and discovering her lady's maid draping one of her gowns across the bed in order that she might study it for faults and creases, 'what can you tell me about Mrs Stapleton?'

'Oh.' Edna put a hand to her mouth and her eyes widened. 'You mean her as died?' Rose nodded, and the girl continued excitedly, the words tumbling from her mouth like a waterfall. 'Murdered, she was, is the talk in the servants' hall on account of the gentlemen arriving from London. They gave Mr Manning their card, they did. A detective inspector from Scotland Yard, it said on it, and anyhow, Mr Manning, he says how he recognised the detective sergeant with him. Same fellow, he says, as came to investigate the murder in the maze.'

'That's quite right. And you'd know them too, Edna,' said Rose hurriedly, trying to stop the flow and get a word in edgeways. 'They are the very same policemen who were sent by Scotland Yard to investigate the … the death at Ashgrove House.'

'Are they really? Well, I never!' exclaimed the lady's maid. 'Ever so handsome we thought they were, and Sergeant Lane, he made me and Bessie giggle with his stories, something rotten.' She paused a moment to laugh at her recollections. 'Even Mrs Palmer, who didn't have a good word to say about anyone but Mr Stafford, why, she was quite taken with the sergeant herself, and gave him great slices of her Victoria sponge cake and had us make him that many cups of tea as you've never seen, you'd think the tea would have come out his ears.'

'Mrs Stapleton?' prompted Rose, though her own thoughts drifted back to the events at Ashgrove House, when she herself had first set eyes on Inspector Deacon and Sergeant Lane.

'A rich widow she was, by all accounts,' said Edna. She had quite abandoned any pretence at studying the dress in front of her, and had perched herself instead on the edge of the bed and was leaning forward with barely concealed excitement. Rose, who was at this stage sitting at her dressing table repairing her face, glanced in the mirror, and gave the girl an encouraging nod.

'She hadn't been here very long, miss, in Sedgwick, I mean. Less than a year, I should say. She was renting Quince Cottage from old Mr Turner, she was, him as sold that bit of woodland to Major Spittlehouse.'

'Did she live alone?' enquired Rose.

'She lived with a maid-companion. At least, Mrs Farrier referred to her as such, and she should know,' said Edna, 'though I never did hear tell of such a position. I suppose it means she did the light work. I know as how they had Tilly Willows come in every day to do the heavy work.'

'The maid-companion, do you happen to know her name, Edna?'

'Prudie Sprat, m'lady.' Edna chuckled. 'It always reminds me of that nursery rhyme, it does. 'Jack Sprat would eat no fat, his wife would eat no lean. Was not that a pretty trick to make the platter clean?' Only Miss Sprat don't look anything like what you'd imagine Jack Sprat's wife to be. All shrivelled up and as thin as a rake, she is, poor woman.' The laughter left Edna's voice abruptly. 'They say she was devoted to her mistress, pour soul.'

'Edna, I should like us to visit this Miss Sprat,' said Rose, turning around in her chair to face her lady's maid. 'Perhaps you could ask Mrs Broughton to prepare a basket for us to take with us? Some of her chicken broth, I think, and a Victoria sponge. Oh, and some eggs. An omelette's awfully good when one doesn't feel much like eating.'

'Very good, m'lady,' said Edna, jumping up from the bed with considerable enthusiasm. For the thought of a journey to the village, away from her daily chores, filled her with delight. Her kind heart was also conscious of the fact that Miss Sprat was most probably feeling friendless and alone in the cottage she had shared with Mrs Stapleton. The girl was certain that, at such a time as this, the woman was in urgent need of companionship.

It was barely twenty minutes later that the Countess of Belvedere and Edna Jones found themselves deposited outside Quince Cottage. Rose, who had been half tempted to stretch her legs and walk the few miles from Sedgwick Court to the cottage had, at Edna's suggestion, relented and resigned herself to being driven there in the Daimler by Adams, her husband's chauffeur. If nothing else, she was aware that they did not have much time. For it was very likely, she thought, as she was donning her hat and gloves, that Inspector Deacon would that very moment be concluding his interview with Henry Rewe. His next move, she felt certain, would be to go to Quince Cottage and make a thorough search of Ursula Stapleton's personal effects and possessions, and she felt a compelling need to talk with Miss Sprat before the full force of the law descended upon her.

Quince Cottage was a house of fair proportions, having originally been three workmen's cottages. The walls were whitewashed and it boasted a thatched roof. Climbing roses grew around the door, and its front garden was an abundance of colour with a multitude of old roses, delphiniums, foxgloves and peonies in overflowing flowerbeds, complete with an old quince tree from which the cottage derived its name.

Miss Sprat herself answered the front door to them for the very simple reason that there was no one else present in the house to do the task. She was a tiny, wizened figure with a wrinkled face that appeared prematurely aged. Certainly, the eyes, though bright and black, were red rimmed and her skin was of an ashen grey. Her funereal garb of a severe black silk gown and a little old-fashioned lace cap which she wore perched on her head and from which tendrils of dull hair protruded in an irregular fashion, did little to dispel the image of sorrow and grief. For a moment, the woman clung to the door knob, her face peering around the door, the eyes staring with suspicion, like a frightened child. For one awful second, it looked indeed as if she might close the door in their faces, had not Edna, a basket clutched firmly in her grasp, put one foot across the threshold.

'Good afternoon, Miss Sprat. Her ladyship and myself, we wanted to pay our respects,' began Edna, in a kindly tone. 'We've brought you a few things, thinking as you wouldn't feel like cooking, and you need to eat and keep up your strength at a time like this.' She thrust the basket forward and the maid-companion shrank back. Indeed, she seemed to recoil almost, for she released her hold on the door knob and soon found herself with her back against the wall of the narrow hallway. Edna, holding the basket before her like a shield, marched past the woman, and Rose, feeling as if she were intruding in the most unforgivable manner on the woman's sorrow, followed her maid's example until the three of them stood huddled and crammed together in the little hall, the front door shut firmly behind them.

Prudie Sprat stared at her unwelcome visitors and blinked hard. She had a handkerchief clasped tightly in one hand, which she had been using to dab at her eyes. With her other hand, she began to pull nervously at the white material, as she might have worried at a spot. 'Your ladyship,' she began and faltered, executing a movement which had a vague resemblance to a curtsey. Rose, full of pity for the unfortunate woman, bit her lip. She wished fervently that they had not seen fit to trespass on this woman's grief. If she could have turned around in the hall and disappeared through the front door without causing offence, she would have done so. Instead, it was left to Edna to take command of the situation. Holding the wicker basket in one hand, with the other she clasped the woman's hand and half steered, half propelled her into a surprisingly spacious sitting room.

Rose followed, her eyes taking a moment or two to adjust to the brightness of the room after the dim, gloomy hall. The sitting room was, she realised, tastefully furnished, if a little unusually decorated for a cottage. Instead of an oak-beamed ceiling and dull plastered walls, the room was painted an ivory colour and the white wooden panelling, which adorned the walls, had a glossy surface that reflected the light, and gave the room something of a bright and airy feel. There was no dark, heavy furniture of simple design. Instead there were tables with mirrored surfaces and armchairs covered in cream and gold-patterned glazed chintz, which seemed to shine in the late afternoon sunlight, as did the pale gold carpet that covered the floor.

'What a beautiful room,' exclaimed Rose.

'My little lamb did it,' said Miss Sprat, her face brightening at praise of her mistress' accomplishments. 'Not that she did the work herself, of course, though I don't doubt she could have if she'd put her mind to it. Employed a carpenter, she did, to make the panelling and mouldings. It was as if she had a vision in front of her. Insisted that it be painted that ivory colour. I was in two minds about it myself and said as much, but she was most insistent, and it was such a dull old room when we first set eyes on this cottage, for it had lain empty that long and was dank and dusty. It had no life about it, but now it shines … while my poor lamb …'

The maid-companion faltered after her long speech and mopped at her eyes with her handkerchief. Rose was aware that the atmosphere in the cottage had changed. It no longer felt so oppressive. Even the hall, when Rose glanced back at it through the open doorway, did not look so dark or uninviting as it had done when they had first entered the cottage unbidden. Certainly, the ice between them had thawed a little, or at least Rose had the impression that their presence was not as undesirable to the inhabitant as it had been. If nothing else, they were an attentive audience. Prudie Sprat desired to speak of her late mistress, and they deigned to listen.

Edna mumbled something about a nice cup of tea and a slice of cake being just the thing to lift one's spirits and provide nourishment, and wasn't it fortunate that Mrs Broughton had seen fit to pack one of her lemon drizzle cakes that fair melted on the tongue? Miss Sprat nodded rather blankly and made as if to go towards the door.

'No. You stay here, Miss Sprat, and keep her ladyship company,' said Edna, firmly. 'Me, I know my way around a kitchen, I do. You wouldn't think it to look at me now, but I was once a scullery maid and I've made that many cups of tea in my time you'd never believe.'

Miss Sprat made no protest. Indeed, she appeared in no fit state to do so. Her little speech seemed to have taken all her strength, for her fingers clung to the top of a convenient bookcase as if for support, her nails denting the pale-coloured surface. As Edna left the room to retire to the kitchen, the maid-companion began to sway slightly. Fearing the woman was about to faint, Rose darted forward and quickly installed her in one of the armchairs amid weak protestations on the part of Miss Sprat who, despite her frailty, evidently did not think it proper that she should sit while her ladyship stood before her. Rose hurriedly pulled up another chair for herself, and positioned it in such a way that the two women were facing each other, with only a little distance between the two chairs.

Thus situated, a casual observer might have assumed that they were ideally placed for a *tête-à-tête*. Rose hesitated, however, wondering how she might start a conversation with the grief-stricken woman. She was half tempted to come to the point and ask Miss Sprat if she was aware of any enemies that her mistress might have had. Looking across at the huddled figure, however, she had just concluded that it might be kinder to approach the subject more gently and begin with the innocuous question of enquiring how long Miss Sprat had been in Mrs Stapleton's employ, when it suddenly occurred to her that her companion might be quite ignorant of the fact that her mistress had not died from natural causes.

Rose wondered afterwards whether it was possible Miss Sprat had read her thoughts. For, as she opened her mouth to speak, and attempted to choose her words with care, Miss Sprat said:

'Constable Bright called on me this afternoon. He said he wanted me to know before it became common knowledge that my poor lamb was … murdered.' The words were uttered in a dull tone, hardly above a whisper, and Rose was obliged to lean forward in her chair to catch what the woman said.

'Who would want to kill my poor lamb?' Miss Sprat continued in rather a sad, pathetic little voice. 'Why, the poor creature had not an enemy in the world.' She paused to stifle a sob. 'Not a bad bone in her body.'

'Had you been with Mrs Stapleton long?' Rose asked gently.

'Nigh on sixteen years, and before that I was her dresser.'

'Her dresser?'

Miss Sprat leaned forward in a conspiratorial fashion. 'You see, she was an actress before her marriage, and a very good one at that, or she would have been if she had made the theatre her profession. I was her dresser, indeed for her and a few of the other young ladies as was in the chorus.'

'Mrs Stapleton was a chorus girl?' Rose said, surprised, thinking of the rather formidable and elegant woman whom she had seen on the stage in the guise of Queen Gertrude.

'She was an actress, like I said,' Miss Sprat said firmly, though there was a pink flush to her cheeks. 'Of course, after she was married, she became a proper lady. But she still sent me the odd letter, what with her being an orphan and me being like a mother to her. Awful fond of her, I was, and she of me, though I say so myself, and shouldn't.'

'She was a widow, wasn't she?'

'Yes. It was awful sad.' Miss Sprat paused to dab at her eyes. 'The poor girl had only been married a couple of years at most. She wrote to me, she did, told me how her husband had been killed in the war like so many other poor souls, and how his family didn't want anything to do with her, seeing how he'd married beneath him. It fair broke her heart, it did, to lose the man she loved and then have his family treat her like that. Wicked, that's what I call it.'

'It does seem very unfair,' said Rose. 'I can well imagine how she must have felt. You see, I rather married above my station. I was a shop girl before I married Lord Belvedere.'

'Was you really? Well, I never!' Her companion stared at her agog, and any remaining barriers between the two women came tumbling down. 'Well, you'll know how my poor lamb felt,' continued Miss Sprat. 'Awful alone in the world, she was, and so was I, come to that. She meets me in a Lyons Corner House, and she says to me: 'Prudie, old thing, how would you like to come and live with me and be my maid-companion? Only light work, mind.' Most particular about that, she was, and kept her word too. Only a little bit of light dusting have I ever been required to do, and the odd alteration of a gown, and perhaps a little cooking though, more often than not, we'd eat in a café or restaurant, except when we came here.' She gave a strange, almost distasteful look around the room.

'You were living in London before you came to Sedgwick?' said Rose, suddenly comprehending the woman's glare.

'Yes,' said Miss Sprat. 'And we should have stayed there, if you ask me. We weren't countryfolk. My poor lamb couldn't abide the quiet, or the fact that everyone knew each other's business. And there's no theatres nor playhouses to speak of. Nothing to do but tennis parties and garden fetes and flower arranging for the church. Begging your pardon, your ladyship,' she added. 'I hope as I'm not speaking out of turn, but, as I said, we should never have come here to Sedgwick, and then my lamb, she'd still be here. And we wouldn't have done, come here, I mean, neither, if …' The end of Miss Sprat's sentence was lost in the confines of her handkerchief as she blew her nose.

'If what, Miss Sprat?' Rose asked, conscious that she was gripping the arms of her chair rather tightly.

'If it hadn't been for that photograph,' muttered Miss Sprat. 'The one as was in the newspaper.'

Chapter Seventeen

Mr Henry Rewe was something of a poet, or at least he informed Inspector Deacon as much when the two policemen appeared at his lodgings, having first inquired of Constable Bright as to where they were likely to find him at that time of day. Mr Rewe's adopted profession may well have explained why, when they found the young man, he was sitting in his shirtsleeves, a rather grubby cream cravat tied carelessly around his neck, in something of a regency style. A fountain pen was in his hand, leaking ink rather badly over his fingers. To complete the portrait of an artist at work, a number of pages had been torn from a notebook, screwed up in to tight balls, and strewn about the room.

On being informed by his landlady of the identity of his guests, Henry Rewe had leapt up from his chair in such haste that he had sent it flying, and had stared at the policemen in something akin to horror. His proprietor, on her part, had first cast her eyes up to the ceiling at the state of the room and her lodger's slovenly attire and then, turning on her heel, banged the door shut behind her, and descended the stairs noisily to return to her own quarters and the nice cup of tea and bit of fruit cake that awaited her.

The inspector and sergeant stared at Henry Rewe with considerable interest. If they had been expecting a tall, imposing figure, then they were to be bitterly disappointed, for the poet was a very slight fellow of below average height. In addition, the manner by which he had sent his chair crashing betrayed him to be in a nervous, agitated state which was not the least becoming. Indeed, he made such an unfavourable impression on Sergeant Lane that on his summing up of the young man later to the inspector he declared with disdain that his hair was almost as long and curly as any girl's, which he took to be in keeping with his occupation and bohemian ways.

'Mr Rewe, how do you do?' said Inspector Deacon, and there followed the perfunctory introductions as he cast his eye around the humble abode to assess its suitability as a room in which to interview the young man. In addition to its rather shambolic state, it was apparent from a cursory glance that the room boasted only one chair.

'I should be very much obliged, sir, if you would accompany us to the Sedgwick Arms, where we have made our headquarters, to answer a few questions concerning Mrs Stapleton's death.'

'Oh? I say, Inspector, is that absolutely necessary?' protested the young man, a worried look passing over his delicate features. 'Can you not put your questions to me here? And dash it all, why should you wish to speak to me at all?' He took a step forward. 'I take it you will be putting the same questions to the others?'

'By others, I take it you mean your fellow thespians? Yes, I shall certainly be speaking with them also,' said the inspector, not quite answering the poet's question. 'As to the other, I am sure you will agree with me, sir, that this room is a little cramped for our purposes, so if you'll just be a good fellow and accompany us to the Arms ...'

The word 'purposes' seemed to alarm the young man for he clung to the edge of the table, his knuckles showing as white as the face which he turned to his visitors. An unruly yellow curl fell over his forehead and he pouted with indecision, showing lips that were surprisingly red and full for a man.

'There'll be no end of gossip if I do,' Henry replied rather sulkily. 'I daresay, coming from London as you do, you have no idea what a country village can be like. It will be common knowledge that you are questioning me before one can say William Shakespeare. Why, my landlady, Mrs Greggs won't like it a bit. She's probably talking with her old man as we speak, arguing that I should be given notice.'

'Mr Rewe,' said Inspector Deacon pleasantly enough, though there was a firm edge to his voice which was not lost on the young man, 'it is a matter of some urgency that we speak with you. If you wish, my sergeant and I will make our way to the Sedgwick Arms now and you may follow us there in a few minutes.' He paused to look at his wristwatch. 'Shall we say that we'll expect you in about a quarter of an hour? I should tell you that if you are late, or choose not to assist us in our inquiries, we shall return here to Grove Row.'

Henry Rewe opened his mouth as if to protest, but evidently thought better of it. Instead, he raked a hand through his hair and merely nodded. To the policemen, he looked a ghastly shade of grey, which had them intrigued.

'And it was he as played the hero in the play, sir?' asked Sergeant

Lane, with a note of incredulity. 'Can't say he'd be my first choice. Rather a feeble little chap, I thought; no backbone to speak of.'

Inspector Deacon laughed. They were retracing their steps back to the Sedgwick Arms to await the young man's arrival, and the inspector had been busy cogitating. His sergeant's words trespassed on his thoughts, and to some degree mirrored his own view of the young man they were intent on questioning.

'Hamlet is rather an indecisive chap, Lane, very keen on shilly-shallying, though he's clever with words and has some very fine soliloquies. No, I'd say young Rewe would make a very splendid Hamlet, and no mistake.'

Sergeant Lane merely raised his eyebrows and let the observation pass. After a while, however, he made reference again to the young man.

'What did you make of him, sir, young Rewe, I mean?'

'Oh, he's frightened all right. He looked as if he wished the earth would open up and swallow him when that landlady of his announced us.'

'My feelings exactly. He's just the sort who'll crumble when we question him. It's like I said, he's got no backbone.'

'I wonder,' mused the inspector. 'Well, here we are, Lane. Let's see if Hamlet keeps his appointment, shall we?'

'He'll be too frightened not to,' muttered the sergeant, as he followed the inspector into the private parlour.

'What photograph was that, Miss Sprat?' enquired Rose, doing her utmost to keep the excitement from her voice. Here, she thought, at last was something tangible, the reason why Ursula Stapleton, a foreigner of sorts, had decided to come to the village of Sedgwick. She herself loved Sedgwick with all its feudal ways, with all her heart, but for someone else, used to the London ways, it might seem slow and sleepy. From what little she knew of Ursula Stapleton, and had seen with her own eyes, she was not a woman ideally suited to village life. Yet, for some reason Ursula Stapleton had resolved to leave London to come and live in Sedgwick.

Miss Sprat, in response to Rose's question, bristled and fidgeted with the fabric of her silk dress. She reminded Rose of a blackbird picking at a crust of bread, for her actions appeared pernickety and rather ineffectual, and all the while her thin pale lips were pursed, as if the mere recollection of the photograph caused her pain.

'T'was a picture in one of those local newspapers. My lamb would never have set eyes on it if we hadn't been sitting in the ladies' waiting room at Paddington. Waiting for a train, we were, and madam was that bored with her magazines and illustrated papers that I thought she was near fit to scream. The newspaper, it was lying discarded on a seat beside her; all creased and dog-eared. But she picked it up anyway and glanced through its pages, barely stopping to read an article, and then she found the photograph.'

'What photograph?' asked Rose again, aware that her voiced sounded rather too keen and eager, even to her own ears.

Miss Sprat gave her something of a shrewd look. A vein throbbed in her temple and she seemed to be contemplating something beyond the sitting room and Quince Cottage. She might have been in Paddington again, watching the steam trains puff and bellow into the station, passengers descending laden with cases and trunks, porters summoned, whistles blowing, and all the while Ursula Stapleton bent over a small photograph in some provincial newspaper. A noise roused her. It may have been the sudden beating of Rose's heart, the ready sound of anticipation. Or perhaps she was just aware that her auditor was not listening to her with mere idle curiosity. What is certain, is that something stirred the theatre in her blood, made her colour and embellish her tale so that it became a story of sorts as it unfolded in the bright little sitting room.

'The photograph, she found it all of a sudden, like. She had been barely glancing at the articles and newspaper columns, reading not a word. It had been something merely to while away the time. And then she came on it.'

'There was something about the photograph that interested her?' prompted Rose.

'Yes, indeed. It was all most peculiar,' replied Miss Sprat. She gave a furtive little glance at the countess, who appeared strangely rapt in what she was relating, and she just a poor simple dresser, with little enough to say, and of no interest to anyone except her poor lamb, who had taken pity on her and her straitened circumstances.

'She turned a page. She was talking to me at the time, I remember, about nothing in particular, and then she stopped all of a sudden, like, in the middle of her sentence. I looked at her and her face, it had gone all white, as if she'd seen a ghost. For the colour, it had gone from her, you see, and she who had that rosy a complexion as you never did see. I remember her hand went to her heart and she uttered a little cry. I thought for one awful moment she might faint, for she looked as if she were about to swoon.

'I asked her what was the matter, did she not feel well. It took her a moment or two to pull herself together and, when she did, she was smiling that broad smile of hers, and a light was dancing in her eyes, as I never did see there before.'

'What did she say? Did she offer some sort of explanation for her strange behaviour?'

'She did. She seemed so happy, poor lamb, like I'd never seen her since her poor husband's death, and she says to me, all sweet, like: 'Prudie, dear, why, if it's not my dear relative, my relative by marriage.' She laughed then, a high, unnatural laugh and two red spots appeared on her cheeks like welts that had me worrying in case she was sickening for something. 'Fancy my seeing a photograph of him in this silly little newspaper of all things.' She gave me the newspaper, then, and pointed to a photograph …' Miss Sprat paused. 'Why, I have it here, for I tore it out of the paper when madam wasn't looking, I was that intrigued. Would you like to see it, my lady?'

Not waiting for a reply, the old woman got up from her chair and went over to the mantelpiece, where she extracted a newspaper clipping from a little, intricately carved wooden box, and proceeded to hand it to Rose, who peered at it as eagerly as Ursula Stapleton had done in the railway station.

It was a photograph of an Elizabethan Pageant that had taken place at Sedgwick a couple of years previously. Rose knew of it vaguely from her sister-in-law, Lavinia, who had taken part in the procession herself, dressed in the guise of Queen Bess. She remembered that the girl had made much of it, giggling as she recalled the event for the simple fact that some admirer or other had laid down his cloak over a muddy puddle so that she might cross without spoiling her gold silk slippers, reminiscent of the act reputedly done by Sir Walter Raleigh for his monarch.

The photograph itself was of a large group of villagers in Elizabethan fancy dress, some of whom Rose recognised by sight, if not to talk to. The Sedgwick Players, she noted, were fairly well represented, for she could just make out Cordelia Quail, complete with headdress and veil, Algernon Cuffe in velvet doublet and breeches, but without the magnificent beard that currently adorned his handsome face, Walter Drury dressed as an Elizabethan peasant, and Miriam Belmore decked out in a fine Tudor costume, her hair flowing freely from an elaborate circlet.

'To whom did Mrs Stapleton refer, Miss Sprat?' asked Rose, the paper gripped tightly in her hands.

The maid-companion came to stand beside her and, with a half trembling hand, jabbed at the photograph with a gnarled finger.

'It was him,' she said. 'It was Mr Drury.'

It was twelve minutes after the policemen had returned to the public house that Henry Rewe presented himself at the Sedgwick Arms. The inspector noted that the young man had taken some steps to tidy his appearance; a tweed jacket had been pulled on over his shirtsleeves, and his hair looked as if it had been brushed. Despite these efforts, however, his fingers still bore the traces of having been stained with ink, though some attempt had been made to scrub them clean; the pigment that remained was muted, giving the appearance of shadow.

Inspector Deacon took a moment to appraise the young man. When he felt he had the measure of the fellow, he said abruptly and without preamble: 'You may feel that it would be advisable to have a solicitor present, Mr Rewe.'

If the policeman's intention had been to shock the young man then he succeeded. For, had he accused him outright of being Ursula Stapleton's murderer, the effect could not have been greater. Henry stumbled backwards, as if he had been shot, and had not Sergeant Lane had the foresight to place a chair behind him it is almost certain that he would have slumped to the ground in a dead faint. As it was, he uttered a cry and half covered his face with his hand. A minute or two later, and the face that emerged was ashen, and the forehead beaded with sweat. Henry half sank, half fell in to the proffered chair and sat there motionless, a frightened, wretched creature.

Inspector Deacon regarded his reaction with interest, while Sergeant Lane seated himself in a chair at a considerable distance from the suspect so that after a while Henry, in his bemused, fuddled state, had all but forgotten that he was there. Certainly, he was oblivious to the fact that the sergeant had produced a notebook in preparation for scribbling down his every word.

'I shall not ask you to give me an account of yesterday's rehearsal or the events leading up to Mrs Stapleton's death,' said Inspector Deacon, deciding that his best course of action in dealing with Henry Rewe was to come straight to the point. Looking at the man before him he felt that, if treated in the correct manner, there was a very strong possibility that the young fellow would go to pieces and confess all. He caught his sergeant's eye and noted that his subordinate was of the same opinion.

'You see,' continued the inspector in a pleasant voice, 'we have an excellent and most reliable witness to the events as they unfolded on the stage.'

Henry raised his head and looked at the inspector. It was obvious that it was on the tip of his tongue to inquire who this witness was, but something held him back for, when he opened his mouth and licked his dry lips, no words came out. Instead, it fell on the inspector to answer his unspoken question.

'Lady Belvedere,' he said. 'A first-rate witness in my opinion. She was watching the rehearsal closely and has provided us with a very detailed narrative of what she saw.'

'On account of her being something of an amateur sleuth,' added Sergeant Lane, much to the annoyance of his superior, who had not intended to divulge such information.

'I say, is she really?' exclaimed Henry, turning around in his seat to regard the sergeant. 'Well I never!'

Inspector Deacon coughed and Henry resumed his position on the chair.

The revelation that Rose was a private detective had brought some colour to his cheeks. On being greeted by the inspector's solemn face and ensuing silence, however, the hue faded, and the young man tapped the arm of his chair with his fingers in something of an agitated fashion. At length, when it became evident that the inspector was in no rush to break the silence that had fallen awkwardly on the room like an enveloping mist, Henry raised his head and asked rather timidly:

'Inspector, I am somewhat surprised by your tone and the fact that Scotland Yard have been called in to investigate Ursula's ... Mrs Stapleton's death. It is all very sad and most unfortunate, of course, but I did not think it was the usual practice for Scotland Yard to be summoned where the circumstances of a case are not suspicious.'

'I was wondering, Mr Rewe,' said Inspector Deacon quietly, 'when you were going to ask me that question. If I may say, I was rather surprised that you didn't put it to me earlier when we came to your lodgings or just now when I suggested you might like to have a solicitor present.' He held up his hand as Henry made to interrupt. 'Well, I have no objection to answering it. Scotland Yard have been called in for the simple fact that Mrs Stapleton did not die from natural causes ...' He paused a moment for dramatic effect before he added in a louder voice: 'Mrs Stapleton was murdered.'

Chapter Eighteen

'Mr Drury?' Rose echoed.

For some reason that she could not fathom, she felt surprised at the revelation and not a little disappointed. She realised that, on seeing the Sedgwick Players gathered there in the photograph, she must have supposed it was Cordelia Quail or Miriam Belmore, or even Algernon Cuffe, to whom Ursula had referred; the thought had certainly not occurred to her that it might be Walter Drury, who had seemed to her in the rehearsal yesterday, and afterwards in the drawing room, rather a quiet and insignificant figure.

'Yes,' muttered Miss Sprat, 'and I was that surprised, because he did not seem very much of a man to me, certainly not one to make your heart leap.'

'But Mrs Stapleton implied that he was a relative of her husband's,' said Rose, somewhat confused by the woman's statement.

'Aye, she did,' agreed Miss Sprat rather grudgingly, 'but you should have seen the look in my lamb's eyes, and 'course we came to Sedgwick all 'cause of him. Awful kind he was to her, when she was married to his cousin, so she told me. He was the only one of that great family that gave her the time of day. You wouldn't think it, would you, to look at him, that she had set her cap at him?'

'Had she?' asked Rose. 'Set her cap at him, I mean?'

'Well, she said as how it would be nice to renew her acquaintance with him,' said Miss Sprat, rather primly. 'Though of course I knew what she meant. You see, she was rather lonely since the death of her dear husband, poor woman, and I wasn't much company for her. Too old and set in my ways. Of course, being not quite forty and still a looker, she wanted a gentleman to look after her, though it'd mean an end to that generous allowance of hers from her husband's family and the freedom that it brought her and —'

A noise in the doorway made them both look up to see Edna struggling with a wooden tea trolley laden with plates of cake and the tea paraphernalia. It dawned on Rose then that the girl had been gone a while, probably intentionally, and her sudden appearance had the effect of bringing Miss Sprat to her senses and reminding her to whom she was speaking. For she sat up very straight on the edge of her chair, her lips pinched firmly together, her words all but dried up in her throat. Her ladyship was sitting before her, and here she was nattering to her about her late mistress as if she were no more than some common village gossip who had nothing better to do, when all the time she was grieving her poor lamb's passing something rotten and wondering how she might last another hour without sobbing her heart out.

There was an awkward silence as Edna distributed the plates of cake and poured out the tea. Miss Sprat, with her downcast eyes, looked as if no morsel of cake would pass her lips, so firmly clamped shut were they. Edna, perhaps realising her mistake in disturbing them, or having perhaps caught some words of their colloquy, handed the maid-companion a cup of tea and said:

'Oh, please, Miss Sprat, you must tell her ladyship everything. We are here to help you, not just by bringing you a bit of food, but helping you to revenge your poor mistress' death.'

Miss Sprat stared at the lady's maid with a look of bewilderment on her face.

'Revenge my poor lamb's death? Pray, what do you mean by that?'

'Her ladyship is a famous detective,' said Edna, not quite truthfully. Indeed, Rose half covered her face with her hand to disguise the fact that she was blushing at such an exaggerated claim. 'She's solved many a case, she has,' continued her maid, quite unabashed. 'Scotland Yard, they defer to her and call her in to solve their most difficult cases, them as has had them tied in knots, being so confusing.' She knelt down beside the old woman and took one of her hands in hers. 'We're here to help you find your poor mistress' murderer. You do want that, don't you?'

Miss Sprat nodded, two enormous tears trickling down her wrinkled cheeks. 'I do, indeed,' she said. 'Wicked, it was, to kill a woman as was so kind to me as my poor lamb. And so full of life, she was. Brightened up any room she walked into. They all turned to look at her, man or woman, they did. She had a certain presence about her. I was always telling her that, when she started fretting about getting old and losing her looks. No one can hold a candle to you, I'd tell her, aye, and I meant it too.'

'You were telling me, Miss Sprat, that you were under the impression that Mrs Stapleton has set her heart on marrying Mr Drury and that is why you came to settle in Sedgwick,' said Rose, mindful that the police might arrive at any minute.

'Did I say that?' Miss Sprat asked, looking a little embarrassed. Some colour had come in to her cheeks, and she picked again at the fabric of her skirt. 'I should never have said such a thing, not to your ladyship. What will you be thinking of me, me who has always kept her thoughts to herself and been proud of it?' She took a deep breath. 'But rather taken with him, she was. As I told you, I didn't think he was anything much to look at myself, and certainly not madam's usual type, but if he had a kind heart –'

'And you came to Sedgwick on account of Mr Drury?' Rose said.

'Madam said as how nice it would be to live in the country for once, for a bit of a change,' said Miss Sprat, in something of a resigned tone. 'Though of course we were town folk and the countryside was not for the likes of us. But she had her heart set on it. She kept saying wouldn't I like to live in a little thatched cottage with roses growing over the door, and a garden stocked with that many flowers as you never did see? I told her how I preferred the town myself. You know where you are with theatres and motor cars and people who speak proper. But of course, she didn't listen to me; she thought she knew best, which is how we came to live here at Quince Cottage, though the ceilings are so low and the hall is that dark that you trip and you stumble. Fair take your life in your hands, you do, every time you go to open the front door.'

The vague reference to death was too much for Miss Sprat, who proceeded to dissolve in to tears. Edna put down her teacup and attended to the woman, speaking to her in soothing tones. At length, Miss Sprat appeared to have recovered sufficiently to continue her tale. Indeed, the tearful outburst seemed to have restored in her the need to speak freely, for the words came tumbling out of her mouth with seldom a prompt required from her listeners.

'Mr Drury, he called on my lamb almost every day without fail,' said Miss Sprat. 'Not much to look at, as I said, but he had very pretty manners, and he made my lamb laugh. And he was always very pleasant to me, I'll say that for him, not like the other one.'

'The other one?' said Rose sharply. 'To whom are you referring, Miss Sprat?'

Miss Sprat's hand flew up to her mouth, as if she had never intended to make mention of another fellow; it was almost as if the words had slipped out of their own accord.

'I don't feel at liberty to talk about him, your ladyship,' she said rather primly. 'My lamb, she wouldn't have wanted me to.' However, despite her fine words, her tongue appeared to think otherwise for, with no prompting from the others, she continued, the colour rising in her cheeks so that she looked as if she had sat a little too long in the sun. 'Ever so mysterious about him she was, and he only visited her after dark when the village was asleep. Not,' she added hastily, 'that there was anything untoward about it, 'cause of course there wasn't,' said Miss Sprat mendaciously, 'my lamb being a proper lady with refined manners and knowing what's right. Still, ever so anxious about it, I was, because you know how people like to gossip, even when there's nothing to gossip about. And it's far worse in a village than it is in a town, because of course everyone knows everyone else's business. Why, you can hardly breathe without everyone knowing about it, and –'

'Miss Sprat …' interrupted Rose, her eye glancing at the clock on the mantelpiece. It may have been only her imagination, but she thought she heard footsteps on the path outside. Certainly, Inspector Deacon and Sergeant Lane would be there any minute, and she desired to be gone before they arrived. For she could too readily imagine the expression on the inspector's face once he realised that she had embarked on her own investigation. It was perfectly possible, she conceded, that he was fully expecting her to follow such a course, but to actually catch her in the act, as it were, would be perhaps a little too much for even him to stomach.

'As I was saying,' Miss Sprat said, 'I didn't hold with it myself, though I knew my lamb to be as blameless as a new-born babe, but folk do talk, what with him walking out with another young lady and everyone expecting their engagement to be given out any day … But my poor lamb … and I'll say this, as perhaps I shouldn't, she did like to be admired and flattered, on account of her growing up in an orphanage where she was all but neglected and ignored … I did say to her: 'My lamb, you cannot have male admirers in the country like what you did in town before you was married. It isn't done in a village, it isn't. Why, everyone will be expecting to hear that you and Mr Drury are engaged. What will they say if they think you are carrying on with *him* … him who has a temper and is that rude to me I could scratch his eyes out.' Well, madam, she just laughs and tells me I am taking on something rotten, that there is no harm in it, and that's just his way to be a little rough-spoken …'

The colour had drained a little from the old woman's face giving her something of an ashen pallor. She mopped at her eyes again with the sodden handkerchief and took a deep breath before she continued, the hand holding the handkerchief visibly shaking.

'Well, I was having none of that, I can tell you. I never stayed in the sitting room when my lamb had her gentlemen to visit, though perhaps I ought to have done, but I've never been one to sit there like a wallflower. They didn't want me there, neither of the gentlemen, or madam come to that, but that doesn't mean that I didn't know … Mr Drury, he spoke to my lamb in that lovely soft voice of his, while the other one seemed to rage and roar. At least there were always raised voices when he came. Why, he had my lamb in tears more than once, and on one occasion he slammed the door so hard it almost came off its hinges and he stormed out into the night and I said to her I really didn't know why she wanted to have anything to do with the likes of him when there was a good, kind man who thought the world of her. And do you know what she did?' Miss Sprat paused and looked up at them, an indignant expression on her face. 'She laughed and told me it was none of my business what she did; I was not her keeper. I'm not ashamed to say that I wept bitterly at being spoken to like that, and my lamb, her face crumpled and she said she was a heartless woman to have spoken to me so harsh and I wasn't to listen to her, and she put her arm around my shoulders and held me ever so tight.'

'Miss Sprat …' Rose said again.

The maid-companion was crying quite openly now at the recollection, the tears trickling down her cheeks and splashing on to her black silk dress.

'I only ever wanted what was best for my lamb,' she said forlornly. 'Lord knows I told her it wouldn't end well her playing one off against the other like she had a mind to. Though there was nothing malicious in it; I knew she did it only for her own amusement for, despite her fine words, she found village life dull and no society to speak of, begging your pardon your ladyship,' Miss Sprat added apologetically, looking across at Rose rather timorously, 'because of course she didn't move in your high circles.

No, there was no real harm in it, but gentlemen, they get jealous, even Mr Drury, and as for the likes of Mr Cuffe –'

'Mr Cuffe?' said Rose, pouncing on the name as a cat might a mouse. 'Was he the other gentleman, the one with the temper?'

Miss Sprat nodded, a sad little movement, as if all the fight had gone out of her. She sank back in her chair, a deflated little creature, her hands cradled in her lap holding the handkerchief between them.

'Aye, it was Mr Algernon Cuffe, and a more unpleasant man you never did meet. Charming he is, I suppose though I never thought it myself, when he walks out with Miss Belmore and all the village can see him. But when he skulked here furtive like in the dark like some wild beast, I saw another side to him. Angry, he was, more often than not, and when I told him once that he had no business coming here and making my lamb cry he accused me of listening at the door, as if I ever would, and I swear he went to strike me, and would have done too if my lamb hadn't clung to his sleeve and begged him not to.' She lifted her head and stared at them. 'He killed her, I know he did. You mark my words. It was him murdered my poor lamb.'

If Henry had been pale before, he was now as white as a sheet. His eyes, which were a very clear blue, widened, so that they appeared a little too large for his face. Even his breathing became rather laboured.

'I say, Inspector, are you quite sure Ursula … Mrs Stapleton was murdered? She had a bad heart, don't you know. We all thought that she died as a result of that.'

'I am afraid, Mr Rewe, that we have absolute proof that there was nothing natural in the manner of Mrs Stapleton's death; she was most definitely murdered.'

'Oh,' Henry said in a small voice. The study of his ink-stained hands suddenly becoming his main preoccupation.

'You don't ask me how Mrs Stapleton was murdered,' continued the inspector, studying the young man closely. 'Most people in your position would, you know.'

'I don't think I want to know how she died,' replied Henry rather petulantly, still regarding his soiled fingers as if they held for him a strange fascination. 'It's too awful; I can hardly take it all in. I suppose it is the shock of it all.'

'Very likely,' agreed Inspector Deacon, 'or perhaps it is because you know how Mrs Stapleton was murdered.'

Henry Rewe's head jerked up. His eyes blazed and his lips quivered. For a moment, it seemed as if he might jump up from his seat.

'That's a damned impertinent thing to say, Inspector. How dare you?'

'However, you do not deny it, Mr Rewe. That you know how Mrs Stapleton was killed, I mean.'

'Well, of course I deny it. I –'

'Mrs Stapleton was poisoned.'

'Poisoned?' Henry gulped hard.

'Yes. The results of the post-mortem showed levels of cyanide in Mrs Stapleton's blood consistent with her having been poisoned.'

'Levels of cyanide?' repeated Henry, pondering over the words. 'Consistent with her having been … Look here, Inspector,' he said suddenly, his face brightening, 'you say it was consistent with Mrs Stapleton having been poisoned. That does not mean that she actually was poisoned, does it?'

'We also found traces of potassium cyanide in the wine glass.'

'You could not have done because I …' Henry's sentence trailed off, and he stared at the inspector for a moment, before lowering his gaze. He now appeared to find a spot on the faded carpet to be of particular interest, for he stared at it, his cheeks flaming, while his fingers fiddled with the knot of his cravat.

Inspector Deacon studied the bowed head before him. Much to his surprise, he felt a touch of pity for the young man.

'We could not have done because you took the incriminating wine glass with you when you left Sedgwick Court?' suggested the inspector. The young man remained resolutely silent and Inspector Deacon raised his voice slightly. 'That is what you were about to say, wasn't it, Mr Rewe?'

'I was not going to say anything of the sort,' said Henry rather sulkily, having regained some of his composure. 'That,' he added, his voice gaining confidence as he looked the inspector full in the face, 'is pure supposition, and I don't think much of it.'

'Pure conjecture on my part, is it? Well, well, we shall soon see about that. It may interest you to know that we have a witness who saw you take the wine glass from where it had been hidden on top of a bookcase in the drawing room at Sedgwick Court. And he'll swear to the fact under oath in a court of law if it comes to it.'

'I see,' said Henry slowly. Inspector Deacon could almost see the young man's brain working frantically, wondering how best to proceed. Henry said finally: 'You are quite right, Inspector. I took a wine glass from the bookcase. But what of it? It does not signify anything. Miss Quail was being very tiresome about those damned wine glasses of hers. Really, she was rather precious about them; she kept reproaching us for not looking after them properly on stage. She was desperately afraid that they would get broken. But, I mean to say, in that case, why give them to us to use as props?'

'That does not explain why you decided to steal one of her wine glasses,' the inspector pointed out.

'Well, I thought it would serve her right,' replied Henry, getting into his stride. 'She'd accused us all of stealing one of her wine glasses, you see; she made a frightful scene about it. And I was rather anxious because I happened to have discovered, a little while earlier, that I had inadvertently picked up one of those damn glasses of hers without thinking when I left the folly. Well, of course, after Miss Quail's outburst I didn't know quite what to do. I had intended handing it to her, but … well, I didn't want to have to endure a lecture, not in front of everyone. I decided that the best thing to do was to put the glass on the bookshelf.' Henry leaned forward and said in something of a confiding manner: 'If I am quite honest with you, Inspector, I have always found Miss Quail rather frightening. Why, I would never have taken a part in this play if Miss Quail had not heard me doing a recital of some of my poems in the village hall and offered me the role of Hamlet. Most particular, she was, that I should play the part, and of course I was flattered.'

Henry sat back in his chair and beamed at the inspector. To his mind, he had come through a horrible ordeal and not been found wanting.

'I see,' said Inspector Deacon. 'But that does not explain why you decided to take the glass with you when you left Sedgwick Court?'

Henry's brain worked quickly. 'I was afraid the glass would get broken or lost if I left it where it was. I thought it best that I take it with me and present it to Miss Quail when she was … in a more reasonable mood.'

'Indeed. And did you do that?'

'Do what, Inspector?' enquired Henry, a blank look on his face.

'Present the glass to Miss Quail?'

'Well … no. That is to say, that I'm afraid I have not had an opportunity to do so, but –'

'If I were to ask you to produce the wine glass now, Mr Rewe, would you be in a position to do so?' Inspector Deacon inquired rather abruptly.

'I … well … no …' said Henry, passing a hand through his hair so that it stuck up in unruly little tufts. 'I'm afraid that I dropped it on my way home and the glass shattered. It was very careless of me, I know, and of course I shall have to apologise to Miss Quail for the damage. But really, Inspector,' he added, looking earnestly at the policeman, 'I do not know what all the fuss is about. If you found traces of potassium cyanide in a wine glass, you are obviously referring to another wine glass, and not the one that I took from the folly.' He sat back in his chair and gave a triumphant little smile.

'There I am afraid I must disappoint you, sir,' said Inspector Deacon, leaning forward in his chair and fixing his gaze on the young man. 'Traces of poison *were* found in the glass that you took from the folly.' He lifted his hand as Henry made to protest. 'You see, when you were in the library being interviewed by Constable Bright, the glass that you had put on the bookcase was replaced by another glass from Miss Quail's set. You do see what this means, Mr Rewe, don't you? The glass that you removed from the drawing room, and which you subsequently broke, was not the same glass that you brought into the drawing room from the folly.'

It took a moment or two for the inspector's words to register. When they did, the colour drained from Henry's face, and the young man sat trembling. With a tremendous effort, he pulled himself together and said: 'I did not poison Mrs Stapleton, Inspector. But of course, you only have my word for that.'

'Why did you take the glass from the folly, Mr Rewe?'

'I have already told you, Inspector.'

'It would be far better for you, Mr Rewe, if you told me the truth.'

'I have no intention,' said Henry, suddenly defiant, 'of telling you anything.'

Chapter Nineteen

'Well, what do you make of our young Hamlet, Lane?' enquired Inspector Deacon as soon as the man in question had left the room, scurrying away like a frightened rabbit.

'He's a rum one and no mistake,' replied Sergeant Lane, closing his notebook. 'I didn't think he had it in him, and that's a fact. Admitting he'd taken that wine glass and then refusing to tell us the real reason he'd taken it, I mean. Not many folk tell us straight to our faces that they have no intention of telling us the truth. It takes some nerve to do that.' He sighed, getting up from his chair. 'Yes, he's an odd sort of a fellow all right. Looks as if he wouldn't say boo to a goose and took quite a turn, by all accounts, when Mrs Stapleton died, and then he's all insolent, like, when you say as how you don't believe a word of what he's saying. Why, he might have thought we were going to arrest him. I daresay we've sufficient grounds.'

'I daresay we have,' replied the inspector, going to stand by the fireplace, 'and yet ... I don't think he's our man. Of course, I may be proved wrong, but I don't think he's got the right temperament to be a murderer, not the sort of murderer we're looking for, in this case. He's just the sort of fellow who might stab a woman in a crime of passion; but a cold, premeditated affair like this? And there is also the question of opportunity. He would have had to administer the poison while he was fighting his duel with Lord Belvedere on the stage. I don't believe it would have been possible for him to halt for a moment to do the deed. By all accounts, he spent all his time dodging his lordship's foil, his lordship being a superior and more energetic swordsman.'

'Aye,' agreed his sergeant, 'there's that, of course.'

'And,' continued Inspector Deacon, continuing with his argument, almost as if his subordinate had not spoken, 'I don't think he'd have the nerve to do it. It's one thing to put a few drops of poison in a glass but quite another to actually watch someone die by your own hand. It takes a certain sort of person to do that.'

'He did come over all queer,' argued Sergeant Lane, not to be beaten. 'Said he was feeling a bit queasy and had to sit down. He might not have realised when he administered the poison that it would be instant, like. Perhaps he thought she'd die at home where he hadn't to watch her.'

Inspector Deacon looked somewhat sceptical. 'Then of course there's his motive for wanting Mrs Stapleton dead. I wonder what that could be?' He moved to the desk and gathered his various papers together and said: 'Well, Lane, I suppose we'd better make our way to Quince Cottage and talk with this maid-companion of Mrs Stapleton's that Constable Bright mentioned.'

'Took it awful bad, she did, her mistress' death, the constable was telling me. Floods of tears and the like when he was obliged to tell her how her mistress had been murdered. He thought the poor woman was about to faint. Apparently, she had known Mrs Stapleton since she was little more than a girl. Very fond of her, she was, fair doted on her, she did.'

'Is that so?' Inspector Deacon looked interested. 'Well, let us hope she can tell us who may have wanted her mistress dead.'

'It's fortunate, sir,' said the sergeant, 'that we only have a few suspects. It could only be one of those who was on the stage who could have done it.'

It being a fine summer's evening, they set off for Quince Cottage on foot in a comfortable silence, for both men were deep in their own thoughts. All of a sudden, just as they approached the cottage, the inspector stopped so abruptly that his subordinate almost walked into him.

'Hello,' said the inspector, 'what have we here?' For he had suddenly spied the chauffeur-driven Daimler, which was almost obstructing their path. 'It would appear Quince Cottage has a visitor. Ah, Lady Belvedere,' he added, as Rose and Edna emerged from the cottage, 'what a pleasure. And what,' he added with barely concealed scorn, 'may I be so bold as to ask, brought you here?'

Rose turned to face him, a rather becoming flush on her cheeks.

'Why, Inspector Deacon, and Sergeant Lane, too!' she exclaimed. 'We were just paying our respects to poor Miss Sprat.'

'And bringing her some nourishment as what Mrs Broughton put together,' piped in Edna, not to be outdone.

If the inspector was surprised that the lady's maid saw fit to contribute to the conversation, he did not show it. Instead, he said: 'Why, if it isn't little Miss Jones. I remember you from that sad business at Ashgrove House.'

Sergeant Lane beamed at the girl. 'Lady's maid, is it, that you are now, Miss Edna? Well, you've come a long way up in the world since we last met, young lady, and no mistake. And most fetching you do look too in your black silk dress with its bit of lace.'

Edna blushed at the compliment, a wide grin appearing on her young face, similar to that of the Cheshire cat's. Sergeant Lane had been something of a favourite of the servants at Ashgrove House and she basked in his praise.

Rose stepped forward so that there was very little distance between herself and the inspector. Indeed, if he had chosen that moment to speak, she would have felt his breath upon her face.

'I am so glad you are here, Inspector,' she murmured, her words little more than a whisper. Inspector Deacon raised his eyebrows quizzically and instinctively Rose's cheeks reddened. 'I am awfully afraid, Inspector, that Miss Sprat may be in danger.'

'From whom?' demanded the inspector, studying her keenly. If he was taken aback by her words, he did not betray it in his look.

'From Mr Cuffe … Mr Algernon Cuffe. He played the part of King Claudius,' replied Rose rather meekly, for it occurred to her that perhaps she was being a little over dramatic. 'I have suggested to Miss Sprat that she might like to stay at Sedgwick Court until this awful business is resolved. She was most agreeable to the suggestion. Quince Cottage holds little attraction for her in the absence of her mistress, and I think the company would do her good.'

'Very well,' said Inspector Deacon, a certain brusqueness creeping into his voice that Rose was at a loss to explain. 'We shall be interviewing Miss Sprat ourselves, of course, and undertaking a thorough search of the cottage and the deceased's personal effects and belongings. Send a servant to call for her in an hour or so by all means. We shall remain with the lady until your servant arrives.'

'You are most kind, Inspector,' muttered Rose, thinking it a little strange that the inspector did not ask her for an explanation regarding her concerns. It occurred to her then that he might be impatient for them to be gone. She watched, feeling rather miserable, as he made his way along the path to Quince Cottage. The sergeant made as if to follow but she apprehended him by clutching at his sleeve.

'Sergeant Lane, did you speak with Mr Rewe?' Rose said quickly, aware that any moment Inspector Deacon might turn to see what was detaining his subordinate. 'Did Mr Rewe admit to taking the wine glass?'

'He could hardly do otherwise, miss … your ladyship, seeing as how he was spotted doing it,' replied the sergeant equally hurriedly, an eye on his superior. 'Though he gave us some cock and bull story as to why he'd taken it. Something about wanting to teach Miss Quail a lesson. The inspector told him as how he didn't believe a word of it, and the young man had the cheek to say as how he had no intention of telling us the truth. Couldn't make head nor tail of it myself. Almost asking to be arrested, he was, though he shook like a leaf.'

It was possible that the sergeant might have said more, had the inspector not turned around at that moment and cast him something of a disapproving look. Instead, Sergeant Lane bid Rose a hasty farewell and hurried to Quince Cottage, just as Inspector Deacon was in the act of raising the brass knocker.

'Henry, old chap, how are you feeling?' said a genial voice. 'No, don't bother to get up on my account,' the man added quickly as Henry Rewe, stretched out full length on his bed in something of a theatrical pose, made to get up. 'I hope you don't mind my just seeing myself up like this, only I didn't much like the look on the face of that landlady of yours.' The man chuckled. 'I don't think she approves of us thespians.'

'She doesn't approve of me,' said Henry gloomily, pushing his fingers though his curls, which had fallen over his face in something of a rakish fashion and all but obscured his view of his guest. 'It hasn't much to do with our theatricals either.' Henry stretched out his hand and caught that of his companion. It is possible that he meant to shake hands, though he clung to the hand so hard that his guest winced. 'I'm so glad you're here, Walter. I could do with a bit of company. I've been lying here thinking until I'm half sick with the worry of it all.'

'I know you are a poet,' replied the older man, retrieving his hand from the young man's grasp, 'but need you always be so dramatic about things? I was quite fond of Ursula myself, as you know, though she could be very trying, but these things happen. It's jolly sad and all that, and ghastly seeing her die like that before our very eyes, but you need to pull yourself together, old chap. You'll be no good to anyone lying here in a darkened room brooding.'

Henry merely grunted. Walter, regarding the young man with something akin to pity and impatience in equal measure, attempted to introduce a lighter note. 'Can't you write a poem about it all to help banish it from your memory, something along the lines of your usual drivel?' He asked, sitting down on the only chair without invitation. If he had hoped his light-hearted insult would generate a response from his companion, he was to be disappointed, for Henry remained lounging on the bed, his face half hidden by an abundance of golden curls.

'Lord knows,' said Walter, trying again to dispel the gloom that filled the room, stifling the air, 'it's affected me too, but I'm not going to pieces about it. Poor Ursula. It was perhaps rather fitting that she died on the stage as she did. It was her first love, you know, the theatre.'

'No, I didn't know,' said Henry, somewhat grumpily. 'And it's all very well for you to speak like that. I don't suppose you've had Scotland Yard banging at your door threatening to arrest you.'

'What are you talking about, Henry?' Walter Drury glanced over at the table on which stood an opened bottle of port and wondered how much of it the young man had consumed that evening. It occurred to him then that he should really have invited Henry to take dinner with him. He glanced at his wristwatch. It was a little after nine o'clock, and he had just finished his own meal. 'Have you eaten anything this evening? You need to keep up your strength, you know, particularly at a time like this. I suppose that old dragon of a landlady of yours does cook you an evening meal?'

'I wasn't very hungry. But, Walter, didn't you hear what I said? Scotland Yard were here, standing where you are sitting now, demanding that I accompany them to their headquarters which they've set up in the private parlour at the Sedgwick Arms. That's why Mrs Greggs is in such a foul mood. She doesn't hold with having the police in the house. She doesn't want her reputation damaged. She's been telling me all afternoon how this is a respectable house.'

Walter cast an eye around the room, dwelling on the dingy carpet and sparse furniture, and the walls with their peeling wallpaper. His gaze fell upon the ink bottle, the top of which was spattered. Aloud, he said:

'What is all this nonsense, Henry? Why should anyone from Scotland

Yard wish to interview you? Next you'll be telling me that you've been funding your poetry writing by stealing the crown jewels.'

'Walter,' Henry said, an urgent note in his voice, which was not lost on his listener. 'Ursula was murdered.'

'Nonsense!' cried the older man, though his face had gone pale. 'She died because of some trouble with her heart. We all know that; I hope you told them as much?'

'They found traces of potassium cyanide in Ursula's wine glass, the one she drank from on stage.'

'What?'

Was it a note of fear that the younger man caught in the older man's voice?

Henry leant forward, grabbed at his companion's arm, and said very quietly: 'She was poisoned, Walter. Who would do such a thing?'

'Let me think,' said Walter, unceremoniously detaching himself from Henry's grasp. He began to pace the room in an agitated fashion. The rather playful mood of a few minutes ago was gone. 'There must be some mistake,' he said at length, though his voice carried little conviction.

'That's what I thought, but if you'd heard the inspector. I tell you, Walter, I was frightened.'

'What reason had you to kill Ursula?' demanded Walter, pausing for a moment to face the young man.

'None that I can think of,' replied Henry, aware that he now had the other man's full attention. He got up from his seat on the bed and poured himself a glass of port. 'Care to join me in a glass to commiserate?'

'I daresay you've had enough,' said Walter, snatching the glass from the young man and draining its contents himself in one gulp. 'Why did Scotland Yard want to interview you, of all people? Why didn't they interview –'

Walter stopped abruptly in mid-sentence and cast a furtive glance at Henry. The young man, however, was busy pouring himself another glass of the port, his attention focused on the task in hand. Inwardly, Walter breathed a sigh of relief and cursed himself for his wayward tongue. He must tread carefully, he thought, until he had decided what to do. Aloud, he said:

'What did Scotland Yard want with you?'

'They wanted to know why I had taken one of Cordelia's wine glasses from Sedgwick Court.'

'Good lord! Not the one that had poison in it?'

'Yes. That's to say it is all rather complicated. Someone set a trap. The glass I took from the bookcase was not the same glass that I had put on it, if that makes any sense?' replied Henry, putting a hand to his head.

'It doesn't,' said Walter. 'You've had too much port, old chap.'

'Do you remember Lady Belvedere asked us to go into the library to be interviewed by Constable Bright?' Walter nodded, interested in spite of himself. 'Well, that was when the deed was done. My glass was replaced with another and, fool that I am, I was spotted taking the wine glass with me when I left Sedgwick Court.'

Walter stared at the young man, his mind working rapidly. It was always so hard to tell with Henry when he was speaking the truth and when he was lost in a world of fantasy. Look at those poems of his. Romantic nonsense, all those flowery words and purple proses. Still, something had frightened Henry all right, and he had just admitted taking a glass which he had believed to contain poison, though if that really were the case, why was he so shocked to learn that Ursula had been murdered? Really, it didn't make any sense at all.

'Why did you take the wine glass, Henry?' Walter asked quietly, almost afraid of the answer that he might hear.

'I was frightened. If you remember, Lady Belvedere came into the drawing room and announced that the constable was dreadfully afraid that Ursula had been murdered. Of course, we just thought Constable Bright was talking his usual nonsense ...' Henry took a large sip of port. 'But ... well, I mean to say, what could I do? I could hardly leave the glass where it was after her ladyship said that, could I? It was no use hoping the servants would wash it up and return it to Miss Quail. Don't you see, Walter? I couldn't take the risk. I had to destroy the evidence, I had –'

'Henry, for goodness sake don't say another word, there's a good chap,' cried Walter. 'You have had too much to drink. I don't think you know what you are saying. Now, have a good night's rest and you'll wake up with a clear head. And whatever you do, don't have any more of this stuff.'

Walter picked up the offending bottle and moved to the door. Henry, he noticed, had followed his instructions and was already asleep, stretched out on his bed fully clothed, one arm flung nonchalantly across his face. Walter paused for a few moments at the door regarding the young man before him, his mind full of indecision. He had demanded that Henry be quiet lest the poor fellow incriminate himself further, though now he wished that he had let the boy speak. Why had he taken that wine glass from the folly? More curious still, why had he taken the glass from Sedgwick Court at the mention of murder?

He, himself, had given little heed to Lady Belvedere's words, knowing as he did that she had something of a reputation for being an amateur detective. To a person like that, every death was likely to be regarded as suspicious. He hadn't believed for one moment that Constable Bright was really of the opinion that Ursula had been murdered. It was a view that had appeared to be justified when that worthy pillar of the law had interviewed them in the library. No, the theory that there had been foul play had originated with the countess, he'd bet his life on it. No doubt, she had been responsible also for the substitution of the wine glass. Henry had referred to a trap, and the poor boy had fallen into it well and truly; if he were not very careful, then the poor fool would get himself hanged.

Walter Drury looked down at the young man indulgently, a frown creasing his brow. In slumber, the cares and worries that stalked the poet during his waking hours showed not a trace on his face, which looked almost unbearably youthful and childlike. Henry Rewe had been the son Walter Drury had never had. Well, he was damned if he would see that poor boy swing due to Henry's own stupidity, not if he could help it.

There was only one course of action open to him and, though in some ways it was no less repulsive to Walter than the potential fate of the young man before him, he was resolved to face it, unpleasant though the task might prove.

Thus resolved, Walter cast one final look at the sleeping form and then turned and closed the door very gently behind him, making hardly a sound. He proceeded down the stairs one at a time, careful not to tread on the stair that always creaked, lest he incurred Mrs Gregg's wrath. He let himself out quietly by the front door and turned up the collar of his coat, though the air was still balmy. He stared out at the deserted street and proceeded out into the night.

'That was an odd sort of tale the old woman had to tell us, and no mistake,' remarked Sergeant Lane to his superior as they made their way back to the Sedgwick Arms, and the rather splendid supper that had been laid on for them by the landlady.

'It was indeed,' agreed the Inspector. He appeared preoccupied with his own thoughts. As they neared the public house, he said: 'I say, Lane, don't you think it rather strange that the deceased decided to reside in this village, of all places, merely on account of seeing that photograph?'

'It sounds to me as if she were a mite too fond of this Mr Drury. Perhaps she was carrying on with him before her husband's death; he scarpered when he got his chance, and she found him and demanded that he make an honest woman of her.'

The inspector laughed in spite of himself. 'What a very vivid imagination you have, Lane. That is one theory, I admit.'

'Well, Mrs Stapleton certainly seems to have had an eye for the gentlemen,' said the sergeant. 'Though I wonder why she decided to play one off against the other. It seems a dangerous sort of a game. I suppose she couldn't make up her mind which of the two gentlemen to wed.'

'We only have her maid-companion's word for it that her intention was to marry one of them. I've made some inquiries regarding that allowance she was receiving from the Stapleton family; apparently it would cease should she decide to remarry.'

'I wonder if Drury and Cuffe were aware of that fact? It strikes me she was just the sort of woman who would have kept such knowledge to herself. I had a bit of a word with the landlady earlier, and she told me Mrs Stapleton was thought to be a rich widow.'

They had reached the Sedgwick Arms, and a few minutes later they were seated at a table, each with a generous plate of roast beef and Yorkshire pudding before them.

'Ah, roast potatoes and gravy,' said the sergeant. 'My favourite. And that's a proper Yorkshire pudding, that is.'

'I am glad that the meal meets with your approval, Lane,' said the inspector, with a smile. 'It seems to me that we should have a word with this fellow, Cuffe, after supper. He sounds a rather nasty piece of work to me. And Drury, we'll need to speak with him. Perhaps we'll learn from him the lay of the land, as it were.'

'And of course, he knew Mrs Stapleton before she came to Sedgwick, when she was married to his cousin,' said Sergeant Lane. 'I daresay he'll have known her character as well as anyone.'

'With the exception of Miss Sprat,' the inspector pointed out, 'though she does seem to have thought her mistress could do no wrong.'

The meal finished, the policemen retired to the private parlour, where the inspector put through a telephone call.

'Well, Lane,' said Inspector Deacon, putting down the receiver, a rather glum expression on his handsome face. 'It seems we are not in luck. I have just been speaking with Mr Cuffe's manservant and it appears his master caught the train to Paddington this morning and is staying at his club tonight; he is not expected back until tomorrow afternoon.'

It was a similar story regarding Walter Drury, in that his manservant informed them that Mr Drury had gone out after dinner and had not yet returned and, no, he did not know where he had gone.

'We could always talk to the director woman,' suggested Sergeant Lane, with little enthusiasm. 'What was her name? Miss Quail?'

However, they were informed by Cordelia's maid that her mistress was staying with her sister after the tragic events of the previous day and would not be returning until the following day.

It was, therefore, with rather heavy hearts that the two policemen decided to call it a day and trudged off to their respective rooms, hoping that the events of the morrow would prove more fruitful to their investigation.

Chapter Twenty

'I say, that's awful queer what you were telling me about old Cuffe last night,' remarked Cedric next morning as he and his wife breakfasted together. 'I always thought he was a decent sort of a chap, not that I knew him very well, of course. I certainly didn't think he was the type to go about shouting at women and making them cry.'

'Yes. I am somewhat surprised,' commented Rose, giving her husband a look, 'that Miss Belmore saw fit to walk out with him.'

'Good heavens, yes!' exclaimed Cedric, tucking in to his bacon and eggs. 'I never knew they were on such intimate terms. Hardly spoke to each other during the rehearsals, as I recall. Not that they would have had much opportunity. Miss Quail was awful strict about us talking in the wings, you know, and I suppose I didn't attend very many rehearsals myself. Still, I can't imagine what a girl like Miriam would see in the likes of a man like Cuffe.'

'Can't you?' said Rose, with a slight edge to her voice. 'I thought he was rather good-looking myself, in a majestic sort of a way, when I saw him on the stage. Is he very rich, do you know?'

'Well, I don't think he's short of a bob or two. He contributed a great deal of money to the repair of the church roof last year. His folk live in the colonies; I remember him telling me once. He made his money mining for diamonds.' The young earl looked up and between mouthfuls said: 'It had always been a wish of his to retire to an English country village, so Miss Quail told me, though he can't be more than forty-five or so, if he's a day. Apparently, the African climate didn't much suit him, not with his fair colouring.'

'Well, I suppose there is nothing to stop Miss Belmore from marrying him now, what with her rival out of the way, so to speak.'

'Rose!' exclaimed Cedric, looking up at his wife sharply. 'What a thing to say! Next, you'll be telling me that you think Miriam poisoned Ursula.'

'Well, she certainly had a motive for wishing her dead,' replied Rose, speaking slowly, her cheeks flaming red.

'Really, darling, I am surprised at you. You seem to have it in for poor

Miss Belmore. What has the poor girl done to offend you?'

'I did not like her manner towards me in the drawing room,' said Rose, rather petulantly. It was on the tip of her tongue to add that she also didn't much like the way her husband had leapt to the woman's defence and pleaded her innocence, but she thought better of it. Instead, she conceded: 'I am afraid I have quite taken against her. It is probably quite unreasonable of me, but I suppose it is just one of those things.'

Cedric merely raised an eyebrow and attacked a sausage.

To Rose, who was acutely aware that she was being not a little jealous and petty, an uncomfortable silence seemed to fill the room. She was only grateful that no servant had been present to hear the exchange between husband and wife. For, fortunately, the footman had taken it upon himself to leave the room at that moment to fetch the kedgeree from the kitchen.

'Darling, how thrilling; a murder in the folly!' exclaimed the speaker on the other end of the telephone. 'Don't you think it is a little like a Greek tragedy, what with it being the Greek Temple too?'

'Lavinia –' began Rose, trying to get a word in edgeways. Her sister-in-law, however, was having none of it.

'I do think it rotten of you not to have telephoned me yesterday and told me all about it. Why, if I hadn't decided to telephone this morning, the first I would have heard of it would have been when I read about it in this morning's papers … For Lady Lavinia Sedgwick was staying at the Belvederes' London house. 'Anyway, you know what Manning is like, he couldn't possibly keep the news to himself, well, that is to say, he couldn't possibly keep it from me. As soon as I had enquired after you and Ceddie, and the servants, he just blurted it out.'

'Fortunately, I do not think it has made the national dailies yet,' said Rose. 'I daresay it will be in them tomorrow, splashed across the front pages. But you see, the police were not certain until yesterday that Mrs Stapleton had actually been murdered.'

'Manning was telling me Scotland Yard have been called in. I say, it's not that frightfully handsome detective, is it?'

'By that, I take it you are referring to Inspector Deacon? He is here, though I thought you didn't much like him because you thought he had been frightfully rude to you during that affair at Dareswick Hall? Now, do be a dear and let me talk,' said Rose quickly, fearing that Lavinia would interrupt. 'I have something very particular to ask you.'

'About the case? How frightfully exciting. You are going to investigate Mrs Stapleton's death, aren't you? There is little use in having an amateur sleuth for a sister-in-law if she does not investigate a murder that occurs on her own doorstep. Though, it is something of a pity that it had to happen in the folly. I don't think I shall feel the same about the dear old place.'

'What can you tell me about Miriam Belmore?'

'Miriam Belmore? That is a name from the past. Her father works for the government, doesn't he? Something quite high up. As to Miss Belmore herself, well, there's not much to say. She's an only child and frightfully spoilt. She gives herself airs and graces, thinks herself frightfully pretty, though of course much of it is due to art.' A vision of Lavinia with her platinum dyed hair sprang to Rose's mind, and she stifled a chuckle in spite of herself. 'Of course,' Lavinia was saying, 'she is quite a few years older than us. Indeed, it wouldn't surprise me at all if she's worried about becoming an old maid.'

'I think you are being awfully unkind,' said Rose, finding herself leaping to Miriam's defence. 'It's just as well that I know you don't mean a word of it, and aren't nearly as awful as you like to make out.'

'Very well. Have it your own way. What would you like me to say?' said Lavinia, sounding slightly contrite. 'She's very beautiful and I can well imagine why Cordelia Quail cast her as Ophelia? Really, you know, you should ask Ceddie about her. He used to know her quite well. In fact, I used to tease him horribly about her. I'm surprised he didn't tell you.'

Inspector Deacon and Sergeant Lane enjoyed a hearty, but hasty, breakfast, before retiring to the private parlour at the Sedgwick Arms to reconvene their investigation.

'We'll go and speak to this Drury fellow first,' said the inspector, glancing through the notes that he had made the day before. 'We'll interview him in his place of work. He's the manager of a bank in Bichester, apparently. We'll see what he can tell us, though I don't mind telling you, Lane, it's this Algernon Cuffe chap that I really want to speak to, but he's not expected back until this afternoon.'

'And Henry Rewe?' enquired the sergeant. 'What about him? We still don't know why he took that wine glass. I reckon he'll go to pieces and tell us everything if we were to go to his lodgings again this morning.'

'All in good time, Lane,' replied his superior. 'I think it will do the young man good to fret a bit. Happen he'll be a bit more forthcoming when we speak to him next without us having to put any questions to him.'

'If you say so, sir,' replied the sergeant, not sounding fully convinced.

Bichester was the nearest large town to Sedgwick, and it was full of the usual tobacconists and dress shops, legal firms and tearooms. The bank in which Mr Drury worked was situated on the main high street. It was fairly modest in appearance, though perfectly respectable, and specialised in offering small saving schemes to its less wealthy customers.

On the production of the inspector's card to one of the bank clerks, Walter Drury himself emerged from a room off the main entrance and came forward to greet them, before ushering them through to his private office.

'It is good of you to see us, sir,' began Inspector Deacon pleasantly, as he took the proffered seat.

He looked across at Walter Drury, sitting behind his large mahogany desk, and studied the man with interest. Miss Sprat had described him as being rather unremarkable in appearance, but with impeccable manners; on first impressions, the inspector was inclined to agree with her assessment. This, he thought, was the fellow who had played both Polonius and Osric, attendants to the king. He could imagine this little man playing the pompous and pernickety Lord Chamberlain of King Claudius' court, but the thought of him portraying the more outlandish and foolish courtier, was more difficult to envisage. Yet, it was in the guise of Osric that Walter Drury had taken the wine glass from Algernon Cuffe, before it had proceeded on its onward and fateful journey to the queen.

'I can't quite believe it, Inspector. That Mrs Stapleton was murdered, I mean,' said Walter, removing his small, gold wire-rimmed spectacles and cleaning them with his handkerchief. 'It is too dreadful. I could hardly take it in when Henry told me the news.'

'You have spoken with Mr Rewe?' inquired the inspector sharply.

'Oh, yes, Inspector. I went to see him yesterday evening. You see, he had taken it rather badly, poor Ursula dying like that in front of us. He is rather a sensitive young man. I wanted to make sure that he was all right.' He glanced up at the inspector and gave him something of a reproving look. 'I found the poor boy in quite a state. If you don't mind my saying, Inspector, you frightened him terribly when you interviewed him yesterday.'

'Are you aware, sir, that Mr Rewe has admitted to taking the wine glass from the folly, the wine glass in which there were found traces of potassium cyanide,' said Inspector Deacon, rather coldly.

'Yes, but –'

'Furthermore,' continued the inspector, disregarding Walter's attempt to protest, 'Mr Rewe was seen by a reliable witness, and indeed has admitted, removing what he believed to be the same glass from the drawing room at Sedgwick Court, where he had temporarily stowed it.'

'How very complicated you make it all sound, Inspector,' said Walter. 'Knowing the young man, as I do, I feel certain that there is an innocent explanation for his behaviour. Tell me, did he admit to knowing that there was potassium cyanide in the glass?'

'Well, no,' said Inspector Deacon, slightly taken aback. 'But to do so would have been foolhardy, for it would have been as good as admitting his guilt.'

'And a trap of sorts was set in which to snare him, was it not?'

'You may call it that.'

'I do. And I think a jury might take a pretty dim view of it. After all, the glass Mr Rewe took from the drawing room did not contain the poison, and you only have Lady Belvedere's word for it that she replaced the wine glass Mr Rewe put on the bookshelf with another one.'

'Mr Drury!'

'Oh, I am not suggesting that Lady Belvedere is lying, Inspector. Far from it. All I am saying is that a good defence barrister could make quite a case out of her ladyship meddling in police affairs.' Walter gave a rueful smile. 'I see I have shocked you. My intention was not to cause offence, Inspector, I assure you, either to yourself or to her ladyship. I just happen to believe in Mr Rewe's innocence, and it will take more than some far-fetched story about a wine glass to convince me otherwise.'

The inspector raised his eyebrows and regarded the bank manager with renewed interest. Walter Drury had delivered what to the inspector had sounded very much like a prepared speech. The man in question stared down at the ink blotter positioned in front of him on the desk. Two large spots of colour had appeared on the little man's cheeks, giving him something of a comical appearance. An awkward silence followed Walter Drury's sermon, which neither man seemed inclined to break. Only the ticking of the old wooden clock on the mantelpiece, and the faint rustle of paper as Sergeant Lane turned a page in his notebook, disturbed the quiet.

'Have you any reason for believing Mr Rewe to be innocent other than your faith in his good character?' Inspector Deacon said at last.

'What do you mean? Is that not enough?'

Was it the policeman's imagination, or was there a trace of fear in the man's eyes? Certainly, to his well-tuned ears, Walter Drury sounded anxious.

'If my understanding of events is correct, you were in the circular room when Miss Quail came in with the tray bearing the wine glasses?'

'I was, as were a number of the others, Inspector.' He had not been mistaken, Walter Drury was on his guard.

'Indeed. Did you happen to see anyone acting in a suspicious manner?'

'Are you asking me, Inspector, if I saw the murderer administer the poison which killed Mrs Stapleton?'

'Yes, if you put it like that. Perhaps you were vaguely aware of someone standing in front of the tray?'

'I am afraid to disappoint you, Inspector, but I didn't witness anything of that kind. You see, I was rather busy with my costume. I was rummaging through the pile of clothes left on one of the chairs to see if Mrs Simpson had finished stitching the cloak I was to wear as Osric. And then, of course, I had to come on to the stage and tell Hamlet that the king and queen requested his presence.'

'At which point,' said the inspector, 'you went back into the circular room and returned to the stage carrying a small table?'

'Yes, indeed, Inspector. You are very well informed.'

'One of the young Prentice boys dropped the foils, didn't he? It created a distraction of sorts. On Miss Quail's instructions, you helped him gather them up. The other Prentice boy was carrying the wine glasses at the time, wasn't he? Would he have had sufficient time to administer the poison, do you think?'

Walter Drury paled under the volley of questions. 'Surely, Inspector, you cannot suspect the Prentice twins of murdering Ursula … Mrs Stapleton?' He looked appalled by the very suggestion. 'They are hardly more than boys.'

'At this very moment, until proved otherwise, I suspect everyone, Mr Drury.'

'I see. Well, in that case, Inspector,' said the bank manager, puckering his lips, 'I should inform you that I had ample opportunity to administer the poison myself, when I took the wine glass from Mr Cuffe after he had held it up to the light and dropped in the pearl.'

There was a sight pause and then the inspector demanded, somewhat abruptly: 'Who took the wine glass from you and handed it to the queen?'

Walter took a deep breath and licked his lips. He remembered all too vividly the words whispered in his ear. 'Let go, Walter, there's a dear.' At the time, he had felt only a sense of relief, because Ursula should have been standing beside him, but she wasn't. He had yielded to panic. The queen would not be in a position to deliver her line, and Cordelia would insist that they do the scene again …

'Miss Belmore,' he said quietly. 'Miriam. She took the glass from me. But she had no reason to wish Mrs Stapleton dead.'

'On the contrary,' said Inspector Deacon, 'it appears to me that she had a very good motive for wishing her harm. For I have it on good authority that the deceased was a rival for Mr Cuffe's affections.'

'Oh?' cried Walter.

To the inspector's astute eye, the little man appeared startled by the revelation, and yet he could not be in ignorance of what he had just been told. It occurred to him then that he had either been a little brusque in his questioning, or that the man thought it was not common knowledge. He decided to change his line of questioning and adopt a less severe tone.

'I understand that you and Mrs Stapleton were great friends?' he said pleasantly.

'Oh?' said Walter again, looking slightly taken aback. 'What makes you think so, Inspector?'

'Well,' said the policeman, suddenly finding the little man's manner rather irritating, not least because his mood seemed to fluctuate between unwavering certainty and total amazement, 'you were a cousin of her late husband's and you made frequent visits to Quince Cottage.'

'Oh, I see what you are getting at, Inspector.' Walter attempted a chuckle. 'Mrs Stapleton and I weren't great friends, as you put it. I just felt rather sorry for her, that's all. The Stapletons, and by that I really mean Cecil Stapleton, Dudley's father, had treated her rather badly. They thought their son had married beneath him and, when he … died, they did not want anything to do with her.' He gave a rueful smile. 'I suppose it would have been different if there had been a child.'

'They gave her a generous allowance,' said the inspector.

'Yes, they did do that. Though in my opinion it was the least they could do.'

'Are you aware, sir, that the reason Mrs Stapleton came to live at Sedgwick was because you were a resident of this village?'

Walter stared at the inspector with a look of genuine surprise. But if he intended to make a comment he was prevented from doing so. For Inspector Deacon had had enough of the little man and his way of making light of the facts. He said:

'You must be aware that Mrs Stapleton chanced on a photograph in one of the provisional newspapers of the Elizabethan Pageant at Sedgwick? She spotted you dressed in Tudor costume, and that was the reason she gave to her maid-companion for wanting to come and live in Sedgwick.'

'Oh, I see,' muttered Walter, looking visibly relieved. 'Mrs Stapleton did say something to me to that effect, now that you come to mention it. But I must admit that I didn't take what she said very seriously. You see, I think she just wanted a change of scene, and she used my being here as a bit of an excuse.' He leant forward and lowered his voice rather unnecessarily. 'I think she felt obliged to give a reason to her maid-companion, whom she knew would be very reluctant to leave London, what with having been born and brought up there, and being a little long in the tooth to up sticks, as it were.'

Inspector Deacon wondered what Miss Sprat would say if she heard Walter Drury speak of her in such a fashion. He remembered how she had spoken of him in very warm terms, referring to his pretty manners and his pleasant disposition. He felt a stab of pity for the old woman, and said rather more harshly than he had intended:

'Then you were not intent on matrimony, Mr Drury?'

'I, marry Mrs Stapleton? Good heavens, no!' exclaimed Walter. 'I admit I am a widower, but … what put that idea into your head, Inspector?'

'Miss Sprat was of the view –'

'Oh, I should have known. Well, I advise you, Inspector, to take anything that Sprat woman says with a large pinch of salt,' Walter said dismissively. 'She has a tendency to believe that every man was in love with her mistress.'

'Including Mr Cuffe? You were aware, were you not, of his rather clandestine visits to Quince Cottage?'

The inspector had the satisfaction of seeing the colour drain from Walter Drury's face.

'Yes, I was. I am afraid they were not very discreet. And before you ask me, Inspector, whether I considered Mr Cuffe a rival for Mrs Stapleton's affections and didn't it make me feel a little jealous, then I suppose my answer is yes. Not,' he added hurriedly, 'that I think Mrs Stapleton wouldn't have come to her senses in time, because I think she would.'

'What an odd little man,' commented Sergeant Lane to his superior, as they made their way back to Sedgwick village some time later.

'Yes. He was certainly that,' agreed the inspector. 'To my mind, he seemed a little erratic in his moods. It did occur to me to wonder if he were frightened.'

'And he contradicted himself repeatedly, sir. About his feelings for Mrs Stapleton, I mean,' said the sergeant. 'I reckon he was in love with her, no matter what he says.'

'You could be right, Lane,' replied Inspector Deacon ruminating.

It was only later that the inspector wished that he had paid rather more attention to the way in which Walter Drury had answered the questions put to him.

Chapter Twenty-one

'Mr Kettering,' said Rose, encountering the young man in the hall. 'I wonder whether I might have a word with you?'

'Of course, your ladyship,' replied the secretary, effecting a bow of sorts. He looked about him rather hesitantly, as if he were uncertain whether the interview should be conducted in the hall under the possible observation of the servants, or in the little room that he used as his office. It was Rose who came to his aid.

'Shall we speak in the library, Mr Kettering?'

Giles Kettering, looking relieved, crossed the hall and held the door of the library open for her. The row upon row of books, filling the bookcases from floor to ceiling, brought something of an official note to the proceedings. Rose, in contemplating how to begin, turned to face her husband's employee and decided to come straight to the point.

'You are aware, of course, Mr Kettering, that Mrs Stapleton was murdered?'

'Yes, indeed, your ladyship,' said Giles, blinking at her from behind a pair of horn-rimmed spectacles, which gave him something of an owlish appearance. 'His lordship informed me yesterday. A most dreadful business.'

'Yes. You played the part of Horatio in the theatricals, didn't you?' Giles nodded. 'You would have been standing with Mr Rewe on the stage when Miss Quail carried the tray with the wine glasses through to the circular room? And all that time you stayed on the stage? During the final scene, I mean?'

'Yes, I did, your ladyship. Miss Quail requested that I remain standing on one corner of the stage, looking on, as it were,' said the secretary, speaking with enthusiasm. 'Miss Quail's idea, I believe, was that I should stand apart from the courtiers and attendants. She thought it would illustrate to the audience that Horatio had little to do with the king's court. It also meant that I could leap forward in a dramatic fashion and kneel beside Hamlet when he was ... dying.'

He had suddenly faltered in saying the last word, as if he thought his enthusiasm for the scene was misplaced given what had happened.

'Yes, indeed,' said Rose, somewhat impatiently. 'It meant, didn't it, that you had a very good view of what was happening on the stage?'

Was it Rose's imagination, or did the young man pause before nodding?

'If the poison was administered on the stage,' she continued, accentuating each word in a deliberate fashion, 'you were more likely than anyone else present to have witnessed the act?'

'Yes.' There was no doubt in Rose's mind now that the word, when it was uttered, was said with obvious reluctance.

'Did you happen to notice anything suspicious, Mr Kettering?'

The secretary took a moment or two to answer, as if he was formulating in his mind exactly what to say. Once or twice he licked dry lips and opened his mouth to speak, then changed his mind.

'I thought I saw something,' he said finally. 'That is to say, it was more an impression that I had ... I should perhaps say that I was not wearing my spectacles at the time, your ladyship. Miss Quail does not wish me to wear them to play Horatio. So you see, it is quite possible I was mistaken ...'

'If you think you may have seen something, you must tell Inspector Deacon,' said Rose, a note of urgency in her voice.

'Begging your pardon, your ladyship, but I cannot do that.' Giles held up his palm in something of an apologetic manner as Rose made to protest. 'You see, I cannot be certain of what I saw. I should never forgive myself if I helped send an innocent man to the gallows.'

There was something very determined and resolute about both the young man's words and posture, which convinced Rose that any attempt to make him change his mind would be futile. No matter how much she was to appeal to his sense of duty, or even command him to do otherwise, he would stand firm. While she felt a somewhat grudging respect for the man's integrity, she felt compelled to try to dissuade him from his chosen course. She was fully aware, however, even before the words had left her lips that her efforts would be in vain.

'I would urge you to reconsider your decision, Mr Kettering. If it were to become known that you were a witness to ... Oh, don't you see?' cried Rose, taking a step forward and instinctively stretching out her hand, as if to grab his arm. 'By not telling the police what you know, you are placing yourself in very grave danger.'

Inspector Deacon stared at the two young men in front of him. It was not usual to interview two witnesses together. Indeed, it was quite unorthodox, and yet the brothers were so very alike in appearance that one might almost be persuaded they were in fact the same person, caught in different poses. One was standing rather nonchalantly with his back to the empty fireplace, his elbow propped on the wooden mantelpiece, while the other, in stark contrast, was sitting very upright on one of the chairs that had been brought forward for them.

So these were the Prentice twins, young Freddie and Gerald, though the inspector was damned if anyone could tell them apart, except possibly their poor widowed mother, for whom, with their various escapades, they were proving quite a handful.

'Will you tell me please, which of you gentlemen is Gerald Prentice, and which of you is Freddie?' began the policeman.

'I'm Gerald,' said the young man lounging against the fireplace. 'Very pleased to make your acquaintance, Inspector.'

'Liar!' cried out the seated brother, jumping up from his chair with indignation. 'Don't listen to him, Inspector. I'm Gerald; he's Freddie.'

Inspector Deacon banged his fists down hard on the desk making the pens and ink well rattle.

'This is a murder investigation, not some childish game of Squeak Piggy Squeak,' he said loudly, his voice barely below a shout. He stared at each twin with eyes that seemed to hold a hidden menace. 'Now, which of you is which, and I want the truth this time mind, or you'll be in a great deal of trouble.'

The two young men looked at the floor rather sheepishly, and it was quickly established that it was Freddie who stood by the fireplace and Gerald who sat on the chair.

Inspector Deacon glanced down at the sheets of paper laid out before him. He made a show of shuffling them until he was aware that he had the brothers' full attention.

'You were playing the parts of Rosencrantz and Guildenstern, weren't you? The inseparable fools.' He looked up from his papers and gave them a measured stare. 'A very good bit of casting, I'd say. And, in the final scene, you were playing the part of the courtiers, for the purpose of determining for Miss Quail how many villagers she would require for the role when the play was performed?'

'That's right,' said Gerald quickly, eager to redeem himself in the inspector's eye. 'We were required to traipse around the stage after the others, which was rather a bore because, of course, we had nothing to say.'

'I can't imagine why the Quail cast Henry Rewe in the part of Hamlet,' said Freddie, rather sulkily, from his position by the fireplace. 'I'd have been much better with the foil, I can tell you. I'd have given Lord Belvedere a run for his money.'

Inspector Deacon ignored this remark. Instead, he said:

'Did you know that you would be rehearsing that final scene?'

'Oh, yes,' replied Gerald. 'Miss Quail had made a point of mentioning it at the previous rehearsal. In her opinion, the fight scene required a great deal of work.'

The inspector nodded thoughtfully. This appeared to confirm the statements that he had read the previous day, written in Constable Bright's laborious hand.

'Will you tell me how it came about that you were cast in the play?'

'Well, it wasn't through our choice, I can tell you,' retorted Freddie.

'Miss Quail approached Mother,' Gerald said. 'Apparently, she was rather taken with the idea that identical twins play the parts of Rosencrantz and Guildenstern, because there is so little difference between the two characters.'

'Where Rosencrantz goes, Guildenstern is certain to follow,' said Freddie. 'A bit like Gerald and me, Inspector.'

'Mother thought it a thrilling idea,' said his brother. 'She thought it would do us good to learn some Shakespeare.'

'It would have been deathly dull if we hadn't come up with the idea of learning each other's lines as well as our own,' said Freddie sardonically. 'I am supposed to be Rosencrantz, but on occasion I play Guildenstern. The Quail never suspected a thing.' He gave a hoot of laughter.

'Is that so?' The inspector eyed both brothers with interest. 'Now, which one of you dropped the foils? And none of your games this time, mind.'

The abruptness of the question and the tone in which it was delivered appeared to take the twins unawares.

'I did,' admitted Gerald nervously. 'I say, is it important?'

'It is if it was used as a device to cause a distraction,' the inspector replied. 'You were sent down from Oxford for a series of pranks, weren't you? Let me see ...' He paused to cast his eyes down the page in front of him. 'Letting the air out of the tyres of a professor's car ... setting fire to the curtains of your college with a Bunsen burner ... putting a chamber pot ... Well, well. It is quite a list. Need I go on?'

'Please don't,' said Gerald quickly. 'It was frightfully childish and stupid of us.'

'Not to say dangerous,' said the inspector. 'Now, I understand the deceased was very particular that there should be water in her glass, made a bit of a fuss about it if it was empty.'

'I should say she did! But what of it?' demanded Freddie.

'Well, looking at this list of your tricks,' said Inspector Deacon, holding up the sheet of paper he had been consulting, 'it occurred to me that the thought might have crossed your minds to put something into Mrs Stapleton's glass.'

'We never meant to poison her,' cried Gerald. 'We –'

'Shut up, or I'll give you what for,' snarled Freddie, abandoning the fireplace and making as if he intended to strike his brother.

'That will do, sir,' said Sergeant Lane, leaping up from his seat with surprising speed and grabbing Freddie's raised arm. 'There'll be no fighting in here.'

'Is that what you were fighting about in the drawing room at Sedgwick Court?' demanded the inspector. 'One of you suspected the other of poisoning Mrs Stapleton?' He studied the two brothers closely. 'You,' he said looking at Gerald, 'by your own admission dropped the foils. Did you,' he added, turning his attention to Freddie, 'take the opportunity to put something into Mrs Stapleton's glass?'

'We never meant to poison her,' reiterated Gerald, sounding close to tears. 'We only meant to put some table salt into her glass to make her splutter.'

'Indeed?' said the inspector gravely. 'Traces of potassium cyanide were found in the wine glass from which the deceased drank. In appearance, it would have looked very like table salt.'

'You damned fool!' cried Freddie, glowering at his brother. 'Why did you have to say anything? Why couldn't you keep your mouth shut?' He turned and glared at the inspector. 'I'll admit we did discuss putting some salt in Mrs Stapleton's glass, but as it happens, at the last minute I decided against it. I was bored of the rehearsal and knew that, if we did play a trick, the Quail would insist that we do the scene again.' He slouched against the fireplace. 'I daresay you don't believe me, Inspector, and I can't say I blame you. But tell me, where is your evidence to show that we purchased potassium cyanide? Wouldn't we have had to sign some sort of poisons sale book?'

'It may interest you to know that potassium cyanide is commonly used as an insecticide, Mr Prentice,' replied Inspector Deacon quietly, fixing Freddie with a cold stare. 'It may also interest you to know that a quantity of it was kept in one of the garden sheds at Sedgwick Court, close to the folly.'

'That does not prove –' began Freddie hotly.

'The under-gardener at Sedgwick Court,' said Inspector Deacon cutting through Freddie's sentence as sharply as if the boy had not spoken, 'a fellow by the name of Hawkins, has advised us that the garden shed in question is always kept locked, and that during working hours he keeps the key on his person. When he isn't working it is kept on a hook in his cottage.'

'Is it missing?' cried Gerald, casting a fearful look at his brother. 'The key, I mean?'

'It is not.'

'Well then –' began Freddie again.

'I requested that Hawkins review his supplies of insecticide, which he did. The lock on the shed door shows signs of having been tampered with, and he has advised me that a small quantity of his potassium cyanide is missing.'

Both twins had turned white. Gerald held his head in his hands and even Freddie looked to be trembling.

'I didn't take it, Inspector,' Freddie muttered. 'I brought some table salt with me from home, I admit. I swear that was all I intended to put in Mrs Stapleton's glass, and at the very last minute, like I told you, I changed my mind. I didn't know this Hawkins chap kept a supply of potassium cyanide. Even if I had done, I'd never have taken any. Gerald, he's got it all wrong. He thought the salt had induced a heart attack.

That's why we were fighting and I gave him a bloody nose. I was afraid he'd tell everyone I'd put salt in her glass, when I hadn't. Though, when she choked, I almost convinced myself I must have done. We'd planned to do it, you see. But I didn't, did I?' he added, brightening a little. 'Because it was cyanide that done for her and I swear I never touched that.'

'That's as may be,' said Inspector Deacon coldly, 'but neither of you are to leave Sedgwick without my permission, do you hear?' The brothers nodded solemnly. 'Now, be off with you.'

Both Prentice twins scuttled to the door. Freddie was the first to depart, his brother following closely on his heels.

'Mr Gerald,' said the inspector, calling him back. 'One moment, if I may.'

Gerald returned, visibly shaking.

'I should like to give you a piece of advice, young man. It is up to you whether you take it or not.'

'Yes?' said Gerald, his voice barely above a whisper, his teeth almost chattering.

'If I were you, the next time your brother suggests some prank or other, I would refuse to take part. If you want to make anything of yourself, go far in the world, as it were, and make your mother proud, you'd do well not to follow your brother blindly.'

Chapter Twenty-two

The door to the private parlour of the Sedgwick Arms was thrown open in one dramatic gesture and a voice wailed: 'Inspector ...'

The two policemen, who had been consulting their notes on the murder investigation, both started and looked up, considerably taken aback by the unwarranted intrusion. For there had been no warning, no courteous tap on the door. Of that Sergeant Lane was quite certain, standing only a few feet away from it as he was. He turned to face the newcomer, a scowl upon his face, quite prepared to take the offender to task for the interruption. The sight that met his eyes, however, had the effect of rendering him temporarily speechless, for it seemed to him that an apparition of sorts had descended upon them. Certainly, there was a theatrical quality about the dress of the woman who sailed into the room like some tidal force, a black silk turban on her head and a full length ebony velvet opera cloak enveloping a body clothed in funereal hues.

'Inspector, I came as soon as I heard the news,' cried Cordelia Quail, throwing her arms up in a dramatic gesture. 'I have just this minute returned from my sister's. Fond of her though I am, she really is rather a tiresome creature; I find I can only suffer her in small doses so I came back earlier than I intended. Well, anyway, I made my excuses as it were and left. I had only just set foot in the door of my cottage when my maid told me. Poor Ursula murdered, and her killer used one of *my* wine glasses ...' She paused a moment, looking indignant. 'The sheer audacity of the fellow! I swear I will never be able to bring myself to drink from it again; it has been tainted beyond repair!' With that, the director collapsed unbidden on to the horsehair sofa, put her head in her hands and arranged her cloak in such a fashion that it was spread out revealing a pale gold silk lining, which she draped rather artistically over one arm of the sofa so that it trailed down on to the floor.

Inspector Deacon was the first to recover. 'Miss Quail, I presume?' he said, indicating the chair that was positioned directly in front of his desk.

Cordelia gathered up her mantle and removed herself and her drapery to the seat indicated. This time, however, she did not arrange her velvet cloak about her; rather, she sat on it and let the ends drop on to the floor.

Her turban, the inspector noted, had been put on at an askew angle so that, despite the gravity of her words, it gave her appearance something of a farcical air. The effect was not alleviated by the woman's liberal use of garish eyeshadow and bright rouge.

'Yes, indeed, Inspector,' Cordelia said, answering the inspector's question rather belatedly. 'This is a quite dreadful business. You will no doubt have heard from everyone how upset I was even when I thought poor Ursula had died a natural death?' Here, Cordelia paused to dab a handkerchief to her eyes, eyes which the inspector noticed were quite dry and surprisingly shrewd. 'When I heard that the poor dear had been murdered, and during one of my rehearsals too, well, I went quite to pieces. Poor Agnes, my maid, almost had to prise me from the floor, for I had fallen on to my knees with the shock of it all. I said to her that someone could have knocked me down with a feather when she told me, and I suppose in a way they did, only of course poor Agnes wasn't actually holding a feather.' She sniffed and removed her handkerchief. With a gallant smile, she said: 'Well, here I am, Inspector. Ask me what you will. I feel I hold some responsibility for what happened. I daresay it is very silly of me, but I was the director, and it was my play.'

'Indeed,' muttered Inspector Deacon, wondering how best to approach the interview. It was not often that those he interviewed were so garrulous, though he knew that more often than not it was a sign of nervousness. Miss Quail, however, struck him as the type of woman who was habitually verbose. He caught his sergeant's eye, and ascertained that he was of a similar opinion. He sighed. There was much to be said for those people who grudgingly gave monosyllabic answers to the questions that he put to them, and remained silent otherwise.

'You were responsible for casting Mrs Stapleton as Queen Gertrude?' began the inspector.

'Well, I was, and I wasn't, Inspector,' replied Cordelia, and the inspector realised too late that he had introduced a subject on which Cordelia Quail could talk a great deal. 'Mrs Stapleton would not have been my first choice or, dare I say it, my second choice. Indeed, I was rather intending to play the role myself. I have played it before, you know, to rather great acclaim. But it is so difficult to direct a play in which one is also acting. Mr Cuffe reminded me of the fact and, really, I had quite forgotten because usually I am either acting in a play or directing it, not both. And then, of course, Algernon was most insistent that I cast Ursula; though naturally I had my reservations as I had not seen her act before.' She lowered her voice. 'And sadly, I was right to have misgivings because poor Ursula had a tendency to over play her part. I suppose she was more used to pantomime. But, as I said, dear Algernon was most adamant that she play the part of the queen, and I did not feel I was in a position to argue the point because I did so want him to play Claudius. Really, there is no one else among the Sedgwick Players who could have played the king; and the ghost, of course, he played that part too.'

'I see,' said the inspector. He would have liked to pursue further the reasons Algernon Cuffe had given Cordelia on why Ursula should play the part of the queen, but he feared this would result in another outpouring of words. Instead, he said: 'Will you tell me about the wine glasses?'

'The wine glasses? Oh, but of course, Inspector. They were my grandmother's and Victorian; a rather nice cranberry colour in fact, which I thought would reflect the light beautifully and be quite visible to the audience. One must think of these things, when one is the director, you know. There are only two remaining from the original set of six; wine glasses, I mean. I suppose it was rather foolish of me, because of course actors do not tend to treat their props very well, but –'

'I understand that you carried them on to the stage and through to the circular room,' said Inspector Deacon quickly, keen to stem the flow. 'Do you remember where you put the tray?'

'On one of the trestle tables, I imagine,' replied Cordelia, rather vaguely. 'I really can't remember quite where. I was feeling a little flustered that I had forgotten them, you see. I had brought them with me to the rehearsal, but it had quite slipped my mind that they were still on the lawn beside my chair. Ursula could be dreadfully tiresome about the wine glasses, you see, always insisting that the one she drank from was filled with fresh water, when it would have been so much easier for everyone if it hadn't been. The audience would not have noticed that it was empty and that she was only pretending to drink, because of the cranberry coloured bowls. But Ursula wouldn't have it, and so it was one more thing for me to worry about, as if I hadn't enough –'

'Did you notice if anyone in the circular room paid particular attention to where you set the tray? Perhaps someone got up from where they were sitting and came to stand beside you?'

'You mean, did I see anyone acting in a suspicious manner?' Cordelia inquired, a gleam of interest in her eye. The inspector nodded. She sighed despondently. 'Unfortunately, I did not. I wasn't paying much attention to anyone in the circular room. I was far too concerned with depositing the tray as quickly as possible so that I could return to my seat on the lawn and direct the scene. I was hoping we would have time to rehearse the scene twice, you see. Henry Rewe, poor boy, alas is no swordsman. I wanted to practice the duelling scene.' She leant forward and lowered her voice. 'Just between ourselves, Inspector, I rather wish Lord Belvedere was not so accomplished at fencing. Poor Henry's performance rather pales in comparison, though,' she brightened unexpectedly, 'on the afternoon in question he was not quite as bad as usual. That's to say, he didn't stand frozen to one spot as happened at last week's rehearsal. It was dreadfully embarrassing for –'

'When did you realise that Mrs Stapleton was ill?'

'Well, I don't think any of us realised at first,' Cordelia said meditatively. 'That is to say, we thought she was merely acting. Ursula had a tendency, as I think I have already mentioned, to rather over act. I had had cause to admonish her for it before, and I thought that was what she was doing. Though one shouldn't speak ill of the dead, she did try to steal each scene she was in, which was most unfair … Ah, I remember now, she looked as if she was about to faint when Walter said his line about looking to the queen. I recall it for the simple reason that she was not supposed to faint until Henry had delivered his line inquiring after the queen.' Cordelia's bottom lip began to tremble and for the first time she looked white beneath the vivid rouge. 'I told her to dab her forehead with her handkerchief if she must. I accused her of intentionally ruining the scene. How very stupid of me. I should have realised she was unwell, but I didn't. She put her hands to her throat and made some awful gasping sound … Oh, dear. It was quite dreadful.'

Cordelia bowed her head and hid her face in her hands. Inspector Deacon regarded her with interest. If he had expected a swish of the cloak or incessant and hysterical wailing, then he was to be disappointed. For, though the woman before him was crying, she was sobbing quietly and without fuss. He gave her a moment or two to compose herself and then said in a voice slightly more gentle than before:

'Are you aware if Mrs Stapleton had any enemies?'

The question seemed to startle Cordelia, for she raised her head immediately and seemed to stare at her questioner with blind, unseeing eyes.

'I suppose that was all poor Ursula had,' she said slowly, 'foes, I mean. A woman of her type does not usually have many friends.'

'What exactly do you mean by that?' demanded the inspector sharply. He was vaguely aware that for the first time Sergeant Lane was showing some interest in the woman's conversation.

'Mrs Stapleton was the sort of woman who took delight in hurting other people, Inspector. In fact, she seemed to wallow in other people's discomfort.'

'Are you speaking of yourself?'

'I … no, of course not,' Cordelia replied, clearly flustered. 'Why would you suppose such a thing? I was thinking of the others. Poor Miriam and poor Walter. I even felt a little sorry for Algernon, though of course he should have known better. But I suppose those types of women are adept at weaving spells, aren't they? They entice a man and when they feel they have him in their grasp, they take a cruel delight in toying with his affections.'

'You believe that was what Mrs Stapleton was doing?'

'I don't doubt it for a moment, Inspector. She was the sort of woman who only regarded her own worth by how many men she had dangling on a string. I even sometimes used to wonder whether she had cast a spell over poor Henry.' Cordelia made a face. 'I don't suppose she had any women friends to speak of except for that maid-companion of hers, who seemed to dote on her. Of course, it was Miriam I felt most sorry for. The girl pretended not to care, but it must have hurt her dreadfully to know how Algernon was carrying on. And then, of course, when Mr Cuffe insisted that Ursula play opposite him in the play … well, she must have suffered awfully, though I'll say this for her, she never showed it except for a bit of sullenness, not that that was out of character, because it wasn't. Rather spoilt, Inspector; I'm sure you know the type? Anyway, I felt dreadful insisting that poor Miriam wear an ill-fitting coarse shrift to play Ophelia when Ursula was dressed in velvet and brocade to play her character. But of course, my duty, as director, was to the play. Still, it –'

'Are you saying that Miss Belmore was aware of Mr Cuffe's visits to Mrs Stapleton?'

'Well, of course, Inspector. Nothing happens in a village like Sedgwick without everyone knowing about it. And it didn't help, of course, that Algernon would insist on visiting her late at night. Ursula, I mean, not Miriam. That sort of thing causes tongues to wag, I can tell you. It suggests a clandestine affair. And everyone knew that he was walking out with Miriam and that the announcement of their engagement was imminent. Really, it was most unfortunate that he should behave in such a way.'

'Yet, it is possible that Miss Belmore was –'

'Miriam knew, Inspector.' There was a firmness to Cordelia's voice that left the detective in little doubt that the woman spoke what she believed to be the truth. 'I saw the way Miriam looked at Ursula when she thought no one was looking,' continued Cordelia. 'And she wouldn't speak to Algernon. She would pointedly ignore him during the rehearsals. And then, of course, Biddy Smith is housemaid at the Belmores', and that girl would take great delight in telling Miriam all she knew. Spiteful, she is. All the family are. The Smiths, I mean, not the Belmores. Why the Belmores ever employed the girl, I can't imagine; she wouldn't know one end of a feather duster from the other and –'

'What you are saying, then, is that Miss Belmore would have had reason to dislike Mrs Stapleton?'

A brief look of fear appeared in Cordelia's eyes. It is possible that she thought she had said too much. Certainly, she suddenly seemed to become conscious of Sergeant Lane seated behind her, scribbling down her every word, for she turned in her chair and glared at him.

'Miss Quail ...'

Cordelia returned her attention to Inspector Deacon. She drew her cloak around her and rearranged her turban on her head. She stared at him, and her bottom lip quivered.

'It seems a dreadful thing to say, Inspector,' she said in a voice barely above a whisper. 'But I think we were all Ursula's enemy in one way or another.'

'I wonder what the old biddy meant by that,' said Sergeant Lane, as soon as Cordelia had departed from the Sedgwick Arms, her cloak flowing behind her in the breeze like a wedding train. 'They were all Mrs Stapleton's enemy in one way or another.'

'I think Miss Quail has a tendency to be over dramatic at the best of times,' replied Inspector Deacon, shuffling his papers.

'A trait she was quick to ascribe to the deceased, did you notice, sir?' said his sergeant with a wry grin. 'She gave the impression that she hadn't much liked Mrs Stapleton.'

'According to Miss Quail,' said the inspector, 'no one liked her, except for that maid-companion of hers.' He selected a sheet from the pile of papers in front of him, on which he had written a few lines. 'While Miss Quail was regaling us with an account of the various difficulties facing a director when producing a play by Shakespeare, I took the liberty of jotting down a few motives for our various suspects.'

'Is that what you were doing, sir?' chuckled Sergeant Lane. 'I thought you seemed awful keen on what she was saying, scribbling down and the like. I daresay she did too. I didn't think the woman would ever stop talking.'

'I suppose directing is a pet subject of hers,' replied the inspector absentmindedly, for his attention was on the page he held in his hand.

'I should say it is!'

'Let us begin with the Prentice twins,' said Inspector Deacon, returning to the business in hand. 'Freddie Prentice has admitted that he and his brother intended to play a silly practical joke on Mrs Stapleton. Not with cyanide, I admit, but we only have his word for it that they planned to use table salt.'

'Or that he changed his mind at the last minute,' piped Sergeant Lane, 'about putting it in her glass. Gerald Prentice thought he had done, if you remember, sir? That was the reason for the fight.'

'Indeed,' said the inspector. 'There is a nasty streak to Freddie Prentice, all right. Some of the foolish pranks they played at Oxford, for which they were sent down, were downright dangerous. We will not rule them out just yet.' He glanced at his sheet of paper. 'The next person I have on my list is Miriam Belmore. We shall need to speak with her. If what Miss Quail says is true, she would have had a very good motive for wishing Mrs Stapleton dead.'

'Because she was walking out with Mr Cuffe, you mean?' There was a look of interest in the sergeant's eye. 'She's quite a looker, by all accounts, and this Cuffe chap was pretty fond of her. But this business with Mrs Stapleton … well, I suppose Miss Belmore might have had a motive if she felt she had a rival for his affections, but to kill the woman …' He shrugged.

'That brings us on to Algernon Cuffe himself,' said his superior, getting up from his chair and beginning to pace the room, the sheet of paper still in his hand, 'If the picture we have put together of Mrs Stapleton is correct, it would appear she was just the sort of woman who would have cultivated the idea that she was rich.'

'Wasn't she, sir? Rich, I mean? After all, we know as how she received a generous allowance from her dead husband's family.'

'Yes, Lane. But we also know that, if she remarried, her allowance ceased.'

'You mean Mr Cuffe might have thought her a rich widow when she wasn't one?' said Sergeant Lane, looking somewhat confused.

'Yes. And in a fit of passion he might have killed her on discovering the truth.' The inspector looked a little sheepish as his subordinate gave him something of a sceptical look. 'Yes, I know, Lane. For a motive, it seems pretty weak.'

'Particularly as we know it was premeditated. Her killing, I mean, with the cyanide and all.'

'Yes. But we do know her finances were in an unsatisfactory state. I sent one of our local chaps to meet with her bank manager yesterday. He telephoned to me earlier. It appears that Mrs Stapleton did not save any of her allowance, and was extravagant in her spending habits.'

'Even so, sir, I can't see as how he would have killed her just because she lied to him about her circumstances.'

'Ah, but I have a far better motive for this Cuffe fellow than that, Lane,' said Inspector Deacon, leaning against the empty fireplace, his elbow on the wooden mantelpiece. 'Suppose Cuffe believed Miss Belmore knew nothing about his evening visits to Mrs Stapleton.'

'And Mrs Stapleton threatened to tell her if he didn't agree to continue the affair? I say, sir, that's rather weak too for a motive.'

'I daresay you're right, Lane, but it's the best I've come up with. Now, who do we have next on our list? Henry Rewe. We don't know of any reason yet why he might have wanted to murder Mrs Stapleton, do we?'

'He's admitted to taking the wine glass. And Miss Quail hinted that she thought he might be a little sweet on the deceased. Perhaps he killed her because he was jealous that she'd marry Cuffe or that Drury fellow.'

'H'm. Mrs Stapleton had been toying with the poor boy's affections and he killed her in a rage, huh? No, Lane. That won't do, and for the same reason it won't do for Mr Cuffe. This death was very carefully planned.'

'Perhaps Mrs Stapleton killed herself, sir,' said Sergeant Lane flippantly. 'You never can tell with these thespian types. Perhaps she wanted a dramatic death that was in keeping with her character, as it were.'

'If that were the case, Lane, Mrs Stapleton would have killed herself on the night of the performance itself, not at a rehearsal, though that idea of yours is rather intriguing. But, no, she was murdered all right. Now, who do we have left?'

'Miss Quail, sir. Now, she was an odd sort of lady if ever there was one. Passionate about her play, she was. I wouldn't put it past her to bump off Mrs Stapleton so that she could play the part of the queen herself opposite Mr Cuffe's king. A bit sweet on him too, I thought she was.'

'That is your idea, then, is it, Lane? All the women were in love with this Cuffe chap? Well, I, for one, can't wait to meet the fellow.' His face darkened and his manner became more serious. 'Joking aside, Lane, I can't see a decent motive for any one of them wishing Mrs Stapleton dead.'

'What about Mr Drury, sir? We've forgotten about him.'

'We have. But if Drury were to murder anyone my money would have been on him killing Cuffe, his rival for Mrs Stapleton's affections, not the woman herself.'

'And if he were to murder Mrs Stapleton, it would have been in a fit of passion.'

'Yes, and we've agreed that this is not that type of murder.'

'So, what are we saying, sir?'

'No one particularly liked Mrs Stapleton,' said the inspector somewhat exasperated, 'but no one had an adequate motive for wishing the poor woman dead.'

Chapter Twenty-three

'Begging your pardon, your ladyship,' said Manning, 'but Miss Belmore is here to see you. Most urgent she said it was.'

Rose had remained in the library after Giles Kettering's departure, ostensibly to gather her thoughts, but also because she did not know whom to speak to next without stepping on the policemen's toes. Her mind had at length drifted to contemplation of other matters, before she returned to the task in hand. She was seated behind the carved oak, octagonal library table, as favoured by Constable Bright, when the butler appeared to inform her of her visitor. She cast her eyes down at the sheets of notepaper in front of her, on which she had written a summary of the events leading up to Ursula Stapleton's death, as well as the salient points gleaned from her interviews with Prudie Sprat and her husband's secretary. She had just finished scribbling a note on the policemen's interview with Henry Rewe, as told her by Sergeant Lane, when the servant appeared beside her like a shadow. It was with a sense of relief that she set aside her fountain pen, for the task she had set herself had proved rather laborious, and she welcomed the interruption.

'Very good, Manning,' she said, gathering her papers together. She got up from her chair and surveyed the room. 'Show Miss Belmore in here, if you will.'

She had been tempted to suggest the drawing room, but, on reflection, had changed her mind. For the room brought back to her memories of the immediate aftermath of Ursula's death when the Sedgwick Players had stood dejectedly in the corners of the room, or perched despondently on the upholstered stools, all inclined to hold their tongues and brood. Certainly, none of them had been very forthcoming when she had attempted to ask them questions. The library, which was smaller in dimensions and, despite the vast array of books and bookcases which lined the walls, had a more intimate feel to it, might serve to loosen Miriam Belmore's tongue.

'Is it true what people are saying?' demanded Miriam without preamble, as she entered the room.

Rose was rather taken aback by the lack of pleasantries, and also by the girl's rather unkempt appearance. For it was obvious, even to the most casual observer, that the girl had taken little trouble over her toilet. Her blouse was creased, and her hair appeared not to be brushed, falling in a mass of tangled waves to her shoulders. Even her face looked as if it had not been washed, accentuated perhaps by its unnatural pallor. For there was no trace of rouge, and the fine lines around her eyes, which had not been very noticeable on the previous occasion when Rose had seen the woman, were now clearly visible. The effect was to age Miriam by some ten years or so. She was also clearly in an agitated mood, a stark contrast with the cold, almost haughty manner of the woman who had appeared to take Ursula Stapleton's untimely death in her stride. The woman's transformation brought to Rose's mind Ophelia, as she was portrayed in the height of her madness.

'Is what true?' Rose enquired, though she knew full well to what Miriam referred.

'That Ursula was murdered, of course. They are saying she was poisoned.'

'I'm afraid it's true. Someone put potassium cyanide in Mrs Stapleton's wine glass.'

'Not the one she drank from on stage?' said Miriam, her voice hardly above a whisper.

'Yes.'

'Then it is true … it must have been one of us. I was hoping …'

'If by that you mean one of the Sedgwick Players, then yes, I don't see how it could have been anyone else.'

It was almost as if Miriam's worst fears had been realised and she found herself rooted to the spot. She put a hand to her head and stared at a corner of the rug, as if she had a sudden need to focus on something that was mundane and tangible in equal measure. Rose studied her closely and, for a moment, neither woman spoke.

'You sound as if you are surprised,' said Rose at last. 'Yet it was you who asked me whether I thought Ursula Stapleton had been murdered. Do you remember?'

'Yes, yes,' Miriam replied irritably, gesturing with her hand as if she were brushing away Rose's observation. 'I said it merely for something to say. You are a sort of private detective, aren't you?' Rose nodded. 'Well then, you must regard every death as suspicious.'

'I told you at the time that Constable Bright was also of the opinion that Mrs Stapleton had been murdered,' countered Rose, though she had the grace to blush, knowing that when she had uttered the statement she had spoken mendaciously.

'Only because you told him she had been, you and his lordship,' cried Miriam, as if she could read the girl's thoughts, splashes of colour appearing on her cheeks for the first time. 'He would never have thought of it himself.' She bit her lip and added rather spitefully: 'He doesn't live up to his name, you know; Constable Dim would be a far better name for him.' She gave a mirthless laugh.

'How very unkind you are,' said Rose, still reeling from the woman's abrupt manner. 'I daresay it's the shock, but I really think you should leave. I'll ring for Manning and he can show you out.'

'No, please!' cried Miriam springing forward with surprising speed and clinging at Rose's sleeve before the countess could summon her servant. 'I … I … I am afraid, that is all.'

'That Henry Rewe killed Mrs Stapleton?'

'Henry?' Miriam gave her companion a look of utter amazement. Rose, watching her closely, wondered whether it was merely an act, though the woman's reaction appeared genuine.

'Mr Rewe has admitted to taking the wine glass from the folly.'

'Why would Henry do that?'

'Admit to taking it, or actually taking it?'

'I don't know what you mean. You are talking in riddles,' cried Miriam, wringing her hands. 'There was a pause and then she added rather grudgingly: 'Your ladyship.'

'He told the inspector that he wanted to teach Miss Quail a lesson,' said Rose. She was aware that her manner towards the girl was rather cold.

'Why would he want to do that?' Miriam looked bewildered.

'I cannot imagine. When the inspector informed him that he did not believe a word of it, Mr Rewe told him he had no intention of telling him the truth.'

'Henry said that?' Miriam looked incredulous. 'What utter madness.'

'Yes.'

'But why would he say something like that?' persisted Miriam. 'He's talking nonsense. You do know that, don't you, your ladyship? Henry wouldn't hurt a fly.'

'Yes,' Rose replied, and she saw the look of relief appear on the girl's face, reducing the fine lines and bringing back her youth. 'I do not believe he was telling the truth. By that, I mean I do not think he took the wine glass from the folly. He was speaking the truth, however, when he said he took it from this house. He was spotted removing the wine glass, or should I say what he believed to be the wine glass, from the drawing room.'

'But why? What made him do it, do you think?' cried Miriam.

'I fancy,' Rose said slowly, articulating every word, 'that Mr Rewe thought he was protecting you.'

'Good heavens!' cried Sergeant Lane, marching to the door. 'Is that someone else coming?'

Inspector Deacon paused in what he was doing, and the two men waited silently, craning their necks. Their efforts were rewarded by the sound of a man's long strides, which could be heard distinctly on the landing outside. This was followed by a hurried rap on the door, which was opened before the sergeant had an opportunity to answer it.

'Inspector Deacon, I presume?' said the man hurriedly, striding into the room and grasping the inspector's hand. 'Algernon Cuffe. I came as soon as I could. My man called me at my club last night and told me about poor Ursula. Didn't sleep a wink all night for thinking about it. I decided to take an earlier train. It shook me, I don't mind telling you, hearing she'd been murdered. We thought it was her dicky heart.' He gave the inspector a penetrating gaze. 'I don't suppose there is any chance you're making some dreadful mistake?'

'No, I'm afraid not.'

Inspector Deacon stared at the figure before him. This, then, was the man who had by all accounts set the hearts of the women of Sedgwick aglow. Well, there was a certain vitality about the fellow, he wouldn't deny it. There was an energy and strength that radiated from him, and which the policeman could feel even in his handshake. In appearance, he cut a fine figure of a man with his broad shoulders and above average height. There was also something in his bearing which suggested a military man, for he held himself very upright, which gave the impression that he was even taller than he was. The auburn hair suited him too, the inspector decided, even the full beard in its striking shade of red. He could well imagine this man playing King Claudius, for there was the hint of ruthlessness about his character ...

'Poor Ursula,' Algernon continued pensively. All the liveliness seemed to go out of him suddenly and he took the chair offered, though, if he had a mind to slump in it, he did not do so. Instead, he sat perfectly upright. Some of the energy had left him, it was true, but he was still alert. The inspector had the odd feeling that he was ready to pounce should the need arise.

'Traces of potassium cyanide were found in the wine glass from which Mrs Stapleton drank on stage,' said Inspector Deacon. 'The results of the post-mortem showed levels of cyanide in the deceased's blood which were consistent with her having been poisoned.'

'Yes, I am aware of that, Inspector,' said Algernon, rather brusquely. 'My man told me as much when he telephoned me at my club. What I want to know from you,' he said, leaning forward and thumping the desk, 'is who did it?'

'That is what we are trying to find out, sir,' said the inspector equably. 'Now, I understand that you and Mrs Stapleton were intimate friends.'

'Oh?' Algernon looked surprised. 'Who told you that?' His face clouded. 'I suppose it was that Sprat woman. Inquisitive old busybody, that's what she is. I wouldn't listen to what she has to say, if I were you. I caught her once or twice listening at the door. Can't abide eavesdroppers myself. Still, I suppose her own life is so uneventful that she –'

'Miss Sprat was particularly fond of her mistress,' said Inspector Deacon rather coldly, for he found the man's manner riled him. 'Naturally she is anxious that Mrs Stapleton's murderer is apprehended and brought to justice.'

'As are we all,' cried Algernon. 'Damn it man, do you –'

'You were in the habit of visiting Mrs Stapleton at a late hour,' continued the inspector cutting through the man's sentence as cleanly as a knife through butter.

'What of it?' demanded Algernon. 'There's no law against it, is there? And as to the lateness of the hour, well, that Sprat woman would think anything past seven o'clock was late. Mrs Stapleton kept late hours, that was all. It's not so unusual in town you know. It is only in a sleepy little place like this that the denizens are in bed by ten o'clock.'

'It had nothing to do, then, with a wish to keep your visits to Mrs Stapleton a secret?' Inspector Deacon held up his hand as Algernon made to interrupt. 'By that, I mean, perhaps you did not wish news of them to reach the ears of Miss Belmore … or Mr Drury, for that matter.'

'Walter?' For a moment Algernon looked bewildered. 'What had my visits to Ursula to do with him?'

'You were not aware, then, that Mr Drury was a regular visitor to Quince Cottage?'

'Well, of course I was,' Algernon blustered. 'He was a relative of Ursula's late husband, wasn't he? I remember him mentioning it to me once. He visited her out of common courtesy. Well, what of it? Why should he mind my visiting Ursula?'

'You were not aware, then, that Mr Drury had a mind to marry Mrs Stapleton and was jealous because he considered you a rival for that lady's affections?'

'Who told you that?'

'Mr Drury himself.'

'Good lord!' cried Algernon. 'Did Walter really say all that?'

'He did,' admitted Inspector Deacon, instantly regretting that he had mentioned Walter Drury, for he felt that he had said too much and betrayed a confidence, which he was aware had been very grudgingly given. He looked up, caught Sergeant Lane's eye, and groaned inwardly. For it was obvious that his sergeant had been surprised by his disclosure.

'I say, I didn't think the little man had it in him,' chuckled Algernon. 'To set his cap at Ursula of all people. Ha, ha.'

'I am pleased you consider it to be so amusing, Mr Cuffe,' said Inspector Deacon, rather more coldly than he had intended. 'May I remind you that a woman has been murdered and –'

'Look here, Inspector,' said Algernon hurriedly, 'you've got me all wrong. I was surprised, that's all. I knew Walter was fond of Ursula because she was a relative of sorts and he felt he had a duty towards her, but I didn't know he had any intention of making her his wife.'

'You didn't consider him to be a rival for Mrs Stapleton's affections, then?'

'Certainly not. To be quite frank, I don't mind telling you I'm dreadfully cut up over this business, whatever you may think. I was awfully fond of Ursula, and for her to die in the prime of her life like that, well, it's wicked, that's what it is.'

'What were your intentions towards Mrs Stapleton, Mr Cuffe?'

'My intentions? What do you mean, Inspector?' Was it the inspector's fancy, or did a look of fear come into the man's eyes?

'I would have thought it pretty obvious what I meant, Mr Cuffe. But if you wish me to spell it out … Were you hoping to marry Mrs Stapleton yourself?'

'I …' Algernon Cuffe paused, and half covered his face with his hand. It occurred to the inspector that the man was desperately trying to decide what to say. Certainly, it was clear that he was trying to compose himself, not just to gather his thoughts. He raised his head and said: 'I honestly don't know, Inspector. I enjoyed her company, that was all. And she was a fine figure of a woman, carried herself well. I … I … don't know. I suppose, if I am to be perfectly honest, the thought had occurred to me but –'

'There was Miss Belmore to consider?'

'Yes.' Algernon lifted his head and, though colour had risen to his cheeks, it seemed to Inspector Deacon that the man had recovered some of his equanimity. Certainly, some of the old vitality had returned to him. He stuck out his chin in something of a defiant manner and said:

'I don't doubt that you consider me to be something of a cad, Inspector, and I can't say I blame you. Well, I'll put my cards on the table and you can judge. You are quite right to suppose that I wanted to keep my visits to Mrs Stapleton a secret. The lady herself used to enjoy the clandestine nature of them, and I wanted to keep knowledge of them from Miss Belmore until … well, until I had quite made up my mind what to do.'

'By that you mean whether to marry Mrs Stapleton or Miss Belmore?'

'That's it, Inspector, though it sounds rather awful when you put it like that. I was all set to ask Miss Belmore to be my wife and then Mrs Stapleton arrived in Sedgwick and … well, she quite took my breath away.' He chuckled, as if at some fond recollection or private joke.

'Miss Sprat told us you and Mrs Stapleton often argued. Indeed, on several occasions you reduced her to tears, and once you slammed the door behind you so hard it almost came off its hinges.'

'Damn that woman. Miss Sprat can go to the devil!' boomed Algernon with considerable feeling.

'She also mentioned you were rough-spoken and had a temper,' Inspector Deacon said calmly, apparently unruffled by the man's outburst. 'I see she spoke the truth.'

'Now, look here, Inspector, I –'

'No, you look here, Mr Cuffe.' There was a cold edge to the inspector's voice now and, though Algernon opened his mouth as if to protest, he obviously thought better of it. 'A woman has been murdered,' continued the inspector. 'A woman, I might add, whom it is known you argued with on a regular basis during the course of a series of clandestine meetings. Why, it seems to me that I do not need to look any further for our murderer than this very room; he is sitting in front of me!'

Algernon visibly flinched and paled at such words, but did not speak. It occurred to the inspector that the man did not know quite what to say, and thought it best to keep quiet. It also struck him that Algernon Cuffe might be too proud to protest his innocence for fear of appearing weak. Instead, he sat on his chair looking rather sulky, and bestowed on the inspector the odd contemptuous look.

'Why did you and Mrs Stapleton argue?' Inspector Deacon said finally.

Algernon sighed. 'She had grown bored with the illicit nature of our meetings,' he said. 'She wanted me to throw over Miss Belmore and announce our engagement.'

'And you did not want to do that?'

'I have already told you, Inspector. I had not quite made up my mind what to do. I argued with Mrs Stapleton because I did not like being forced into a corner, as it were. I wished it to be my decision whether I married Mrs Stapleton or not.'

'I see. Did Mrs Stapleton threaten to tell Miss Belmore about your … meetings?'

'Tell Miriam?' A look of fear came into Algernon's eyes, which was quickly replaced by one of relief. 'I suppose she did. Not that it would have mattered much because Miriam already knew about them. It is difficult to keep anything a secret in a village like this, though of course it would have been jolly unpleasant for the poor girl if Ursula had spoken to her.'

Inspector Deacon looked at him sharply. 'How do you know that Miss Belmore knew? Did she tell you?'

'Good lord, no. But she did not need to, Inspector. I saw it in the way she behaved towards me. To put it bluntly, she ignored me when I passed her in the street and refused to see me when I called. She instructed the servants to tell me she was not at home. I won't tell you how awkward it has been during the rehearsals, with Miriam refusing to have anything to do with me.'

'Particularly as you had arranged with Miss Quail that Mrs Stapleton be cast as Queen Gertrude opposite your King Claudius. Not a very wise move, I'd have thought. Now why, I wonder,' mused Inspector Deacon aloud, 'did you do that?'

Chapter Twenty-four

'Protect me?' said Miriam, looking startled.

To Rose, the woman's bewilderment appeared genuine, though she reminded herself that Miriam was a skilled actress. Indeed, had Cedric not declared as much when they had been discussing the production? She recalled the colloquy, during which he had stated that the woman's portrayal of Ophelia in her madness was most convincing.

'Why would Henry wish to shield me?' demanded Miriam.

'Presumably because he thought you guilty of Mrs Stapleton's murder, and being rather fond of you he did not wish you to be found out.'

'Henry fond of *me*?' Miriam gave a high-pitched little laugh, which seemed to Rose's ear to lack sincerity. Indeed, it had something of a mocking element to it, which increased the countess' distaste towards the girl. 'Surely you must be mistaken?'

Rose thought it rather strange that Miriam's first inclination had been to pounce on the suggestion that Henry Rewe had feelings for her, rather than to protest her innocence in respect of Ursula's death.

'Yes. I believe Mr Rewe to be fond of you,' Rose said, 'which would explain why he has placed himself in some jeopardy. I wonder,' she added, as Miriam threatened to laugh again, 'whether Mr Cuffe would have been so obliging.'

Colour flowed into Miriam's face and her eyes flashed with anger.

'I'm sorry,' said Rose, hastily, 'that was rather beastly of me. 'But I wonder why Mr Rewe thought you were implicated in Mrs Stapleton's … death. There must be a reason.'

In reply, Miriam got up from her seat and began to pace the library, somewhat hindered in her progress by the array of leather chesterfields, writing desks and wooden writing steps which adorned the room. She clenched and unclenched her fists, and there was a look of indecision on her face. Rose watched her eagerly, for she felt that with a little encouragement Miriam was on the point of revealing a confidence. Certainly, the girl was clearly agitated, as if she was summoning up the courage to say something of importance.

Rose was conscious that she must remain silent and contain her excitement. Any outward sign of curiosity was likely to have a detrimental effect. Just as she thought she could not stay still nor impassive a moment longer, Miriam walked over to the empty fireplace and turned to face her hostess. She stood erect, her shoulders thrown back, her head held high, her hair falling to her shoulders in a mass of dark tangled curls.

'I suppose,' Miriam said finally, her voice clear and loud, as if she were projecting from a stage and Rose was her audience, 'the reason was, he knew how much I hated her.'

If Rose was shocked by the girl's statement, she did not show it, though the words were spoken with such ferocity that they seemed to echo around the room. Outwardly, at least, Rose appeared unruffled. She said calmly:

'You were aware then, of Mr Cuffe's evening visits to Mrs Stapleton?'

'Of course, I was, along with half the village,' snapped Miriam, somewhat irritably. 'How stupid men are to think they can keep matters of that nature a secret.' She gave a contemptuous look.

'It must have been very upsetting for you,' Rose said gently.

'It was the pity that I despised most, or being laughed at, depending on what people thought of me.'

'Indeed? Yet Mr Cuffe's behaviour must have hurt you dreadfully.'

'It was not Algernon's fault,' Miriam said, somewhat defensively. 'I fancy they do things differently in the colonies, and that woman … well, despite her money she had no breeding. She was very common, and I daresay she did not know how to behave. She probably thought there was nothing very amiss with her conduct.' Miriam made a face. 'She was horrid and spiteful. She set her cap at him, but she didn't want him, not really. She regarded it all as some sort of wretched game. And Algernon … well, he is like most men. He's weak. He was tempted by her charm and by her money. What man wouldn't be?' She paused a moment, and then added bitterly: 'They say she owned a great house in London, and a villa on the Riviera.'

All the while Miriam had been delivering this tirade, her voice had risen, fuelled by repressed fury, and Rose, glancing nervously at the door, was half afraid that her words had carried out into the hall, to be overheard by any servants who happened to be there.

'And now Mrs Stapleton is dead ...' said Rose quietly, hoping the girl would follow her example with regard to volume. She let the sentence drift unfinished into the charged atmosphere.

'Yes,' snapped Miriam, 'but it was not by my hand.'

'But you –'

'Did I have a satisfactory motive for wishing Ursula dead?' said Miriam, an edge of danger creeping into her voice. 'That is what you want to know, isn't it? Well, I shall tell you what you want to hear. I hated her. There, I have said it again. I hated her like ... like poison,' the girl spat out the words. 'With her dead, I thought Algernon would come crawling back to me. And I was right because he's renewing his affections to me, and yet ...' said Miriam, lowering her head, her voice now barely above a whisper, 'I did not do it. I wanted to, but I did not do it.'

'But that does not explain why Mr Rewe was so sure that you were guilty of causing Mrs Stapleton's death. By that, I mean he was sufficiently certain as to tamper with the evidence,' said Rose, half wondering if the girl's performance was merely an act, for she remembered the cold and aloof woman at the rehearsal and the drawing room, who had seemed to lacked empathy or any other type of feeling come to that.

'Well, there is nothing else I can tell you. I didn't do it,' Miriam said impatiently, before giving her hostess a wry smile. 'Of course, you only have my word for that.'

'You had an opportunity to administer the poison,' Rose said quietly, almost as if her companion had not spoken.

'No more than anyone else,' cried Miriam.

'You took the wine glass from Mr Drury and handed it to Mrs Stapleton only a few minutes before she drank from it,' Rose pointed out. 'You weren't supposed to take the glass. What made you do that, Miss Belmore? It should have been Mr Drury who handed the glass to Mrs Stapleton.'

'Ursula was not standing where she was supposed to be,' Miriam said hurriedly. 'Walter ... well, he was flustered. He is not very good at improvising at the best of times, and ... well, I was afraid Cordelia would make us do the scene again from the very beginning if the glass was not passed to Ursula in time for her to raise it to her lips and deliver her line. As it was, it was dreadfully late. If only I had known what I was doing ...'

Miriam paused and put her hand to her face. 'How I wish I had never handled that wretched glass.'

'Do you remember what happened to the glass after Ursula drank from it?'

'Yes. It slipped off her lap and dropped on to the floor. I remember thinking it was dreadfully clumsy of her, and that Cordelia was certain to comment on it. I mean to say, it might have broken, and you know how precious Miss Quail was about those wine glasses of hers.' Miriam went deathly pale. 'Of course, I didn't realise at the time she had been poisoned …'

'I wonder what happened to it after it fell on to the floor,' pondered Rose, more to herself than as a question to be answered.

'I picked it up and put it on the table,' said Miriam.

'Did you?' The two women stared at each other.

'Do you think that is what Henry saw?' said Miriam. 'Me pick the glass up and put it on the table?'

'I don't think that would explain his actions,' said Rose. 'There is nothing very odd about your picking up the glass from the floor. Anyone might have done the same. There must be something else that Mr Rewe saw you do which made him suspect that you might have killed Mrs Stapleton.'

'I don't know what you mean,' retorted Miriam, some of the colour returning to her cheeks in her indignation. 'There is nothing else.'

'There must be something else to explain his actions,' reiterated Rose firmly. A sudden thought occurred to her. 'I have already told you that I do not think Mr Rewe was telling the truth when he told the policemen that he took the wine glass from the folly.' She paused slightly for effect. 'I think it far more likely that he saw *you* take the glass.'

'What utter nonsense! I put the glass on the table, that is all. I don't know what happened to it after that.' Miriam glared at her hostess. 'Why are you so certain, anyway, that it is me Henry is protecting? It could be Walter, you know. He regards the man as some sort of father figure.'

'Because of the look he gave you,' said Rose slowly. 'It was when I told Miss Quail that one of her wine glasses was missing and she demanded to know which one of you had taken it. If you remember, she made quite a scene.'

'I do, now you come to mention it, but what has that to do with me?'

'There was an exchange of looks between you and Mr Rewe. It struck me at the time as rather odd because afterwards you appeared to be staring at anything but each other. Indeed, there seemed to me something rather furtive in your manner.

'How fanciful you are, your ladyship,' said Miriam. To Rose's surprise the girl looked relieved. 'I remember the incident you are describing very clearly. I heard Henry gasp, that is all, and so I turned towards him and caught his eye.' She laughed, and this time the action appeared genuine. 'I daresay the poor boy was embarrassed that his gasp had been overheard. He went awfully red and stared at the carpet and, if you must know, I thought he had been rather silly, so I stared rather pointedly in the other direction.'

'Did you happen to see what Mr Rewe was looking at when you heard him gasp?' Rose asked, having some difficulty in keeping the excitement from her voice.

'I don't know what you are getting at.' Miriam gave her a sharp look and then closed her eyes, as if in concentration. 'Now you come to mention it,' she said slowly, 'I think he was regarding a waste-paper basket.' She opened her eyes and looked puzzled. 'How very strange. Why would Henry be staring at a waste-paper basket of all things?'

'Mrs Stapleton took a fancy to playing Gertrude,' said Algernon. 'She had once been something of an actress, don't you know, and I think she was eager to tread the boards again. I wasn't keen, of course, because of Miss Belmore playing Ophelia, but Ursula was most insistent, and really anything was better than Miss Quail playing the role, what with her also directing the play. It would have led to disaster.'

'I see,' muttered Inspector Deacon.

In truth, however, he found Algernon's explanation unsatisfactory. The man had gone to considerable lengths to keep his relationship with Ursula Stapleton a secret from Miriam Belmore, albeit unsuccessfully; it therefore made little sense for him to have created a situation whereby he brought both women together. The notion then occurred to him that Algernon's intention might have been to make both women jealous, though it seemed to the inspector to be such a risky and foolhardy strategy that he instantly dismissed the idea. He decided, however, that little would be achieved by pursuing the matter further. Instead, he focused on another point to which Algernon had made a reference.

'Mrs Stapleton mentioned to you that she had once been an actress, you say?'

'Yes,' said Algernon, adjusting his tie. 'It was before her marriage, of course. Between you and me, Inspector,' he said, leaning forward and becoming confidential, 'Mrs Stapleton came from rather humble beginnings.'

'Indeed? You are very well informed, sir. Miss Sprat told us that her mistress went to great pains to keep that fact a secret.'

'Is that so?'

Was it the inspector's fancy, or did the man look a little anxious? Certainly, he shifted his position on the chair, as if he suddenly found it uncomfortable.

'Yes,' replied Inspector Deacon, watching him closely.

'Well, I daresay you're right.' Algernon chuckled. 'One can't be too careful in a place like this. A little too much emphasis is placed on one's social position, if you ask me. Sedgwick is rather old-fashioned that way. Things are different in the colonies, I can tell you. Mrs Stapleton realised as much and had a habit of confiding in me.'

'Did she, indeed? I don't suppose,' said the inspector rather sharply, 'that she confided in you who might have wished her harm?'

'Well … no, she didn't.' Algernon Cuffe said, looking distinctly taken aback by the question. 'Don't you think I'd have told you if she had, Inspector? The poor woman didn't have an enemy in the world.'

'Well, obviously she did,' countered the inspector curtly, 'or she would not have been murdered. Come, sir, did she not mention anyone with whom she had a grievance?'

'She did not,' Algernon snapped, clearly irritated by the inspector's manner towards him.

'Miss Belmore, perhaps?'

'Now look here, Inspector, you keep Miss Belmore's name out of this, do you hear?' Algernon's voice had risen to a dangerous level, and he made as if to rise from his chair. 'Miriam had nothing to do with Mrs Stapleton's death.'

'You cannot possibly know that for certain, Mr Cuffe; unless, of course, you yourself are the murderer.'

Inspector Deacon caught his subordinate's eye. Sergeant Lane was looking a trifle surprised at his superior's outspokenness. The truth of the matter was that Algernon Cuffe had vexed the inspector, who rather resented the man's pompous attitude and the temper that lurked beneath the surface. Nevertheless, inwardly he cursed himself for being riled, and braced himself for another verbal onslaught. Algernon Cuffe, however, sat back in his chair gaping rather stupidly at the inspector, apparently at a loss for words. It was almost as if he could hardly believe his ears.

'Now, let us get back to the business in hand,' Inspector Deacon said quickly, taking advantage of the man's temporary muteness. 'We are determining which members of the Sedgwick Players had an opportunity to administer the poison.'

'I believe you said traces of potassium cyanide were found in the wine glass?' said Algernon, having recovered the use of his voice.

Inspector Deacon nodded. 'I did.'

'The wine glass, it was left in the folly, I suppose?' said Algernon, stroking his beard.

'It was not,' the inspector said. 'It was discovered in the drawing room at Sedgwick Court.'

'Oh? Might I ask where exactly it was found?'

'On a bookcase. An attempt had been made to conceal it behind a vase.'

'Oh?' Algernon looked slightly perplexed, and then: 'I see.'

'What do you see, Mr Cuffe?' asked the inspector, giving him a sharp look.

'Nothing,' said Algernon quickly. It is quite probable that he had not intended to expand on his answer, but a quick look at the inspector informed him that more was expected of him. 'Really, it's nothing, Inspector. It is only that I was thinking how stupid or careless the murderer must have been to leave the wine glass in the house to be discovered.'

Inspector Deacon refrained from comment, being of the opinion that this was not in fact what had made such an impression on his companion. Really, the fellow was being as vague and elusive in his answers as Henry Rewe, which was saying something. However, even if he were to press the man further, he thought it unlikely that Algernon Cuffe would speak truthfully or elaborate. Instead, he decided to revert to the question of opportunity. On this matter Algernon proved surprisingly obliging, for he said without prompting:

'I think we all had an opportunity to administer the poison, Inspector. All except, perhaps, for Giles Kettering.' He gave a wry smile. 'I should perhaps mention that I had a perfect opportunity to dispense the dose myself. You see, I had to hold up the wine glass and wave it out to the audience. What is more, I had to slip an artificial pearl into the glass. With a quick sleight of hand, I daresay I could have administered the poison without being observed.'

'I am certain of it,' agreed the inspector gravely.

Algernon Cuffe looked at him somewhat apprehensively, but did not speak.

'Is there anything else that you wish to tell me, Mr Cuffe?' inquired the inspector, becoming a little bored with the interview, 'anything that you think might help us with our investigation?'

'I cannot think of anything, Inspector,' said Algernon, rising from his chair to leave. 'But I'll do my best to rack my brains to see if I can think of something.'

He crossed the room purposefully and Sergeant Lane sprang up from his seat and opened the door for him. On the act of leaving, however, Algernon wavered for a moment and looked back, as if undecided. After a moment's hesitation, he strode back to the inspector and said:

'One thing I do know for certain, Inspector, is that Miss Belmore didn't do it.'

With that, he left the room and Inspector Deacon and Sergeant Lane were left to look out of the window at the retreating figure.

'My money is on him,' said the sergeant. 'He's got the right temperament for murder, I'd say. I certainly wouldn't want to get on the wrong side of him. A nasty temper, he's got, and no mistake.'

If he had expected to receive a comment on this observation, Sergeant Lane was to be disappointed, for the inspector remained resolutely silent. The sergeant gave him a sideward glance and Inspector Deacon, who had been busy meditating, gave him a rueful smile.

'I was just wondering, Lane, whether the man doth protest too much with regard to Miss Belmore's innocence,' he said.

Chapter Twenty-five

'Well, we've learned little that we didn't know already,' muttered Cedric to his wife as they emerged from the village hall the next morning. 'Not that I thought for one moment we would find out anything new.'

They had just attended the inquest in to Ursula Stapleton's death, which had opened that day. The inquest itself, perhaps out of necessity, had been a very brief affair. It had begun with Algernon Cuffe and Cordelia Quail being called to give witness accounts of Ursula's death. This had then been followed by the medical evidence, which had been provided by both the old village doctor and the police surgeon. The doctor had admitted, in rather an embarrassed tone, that he had misdiagnosed the cause of death due to the close resemblance of the body to that of a person who had died from heart disease, while the police surgeon stated that the results of the post-mortem had revealed levels of cyanide in the deceased's blood consistent with Mrs Stapleton having been poisoned.

This discrepancy between the two pieces of medical evidence had caused a titter from the public spectators, with many feeling it was high time the village doctor retired from his profession, while the man in question hobbled from the building as fast as his old legs would carry him, his habitual rather grey cheeks now a vivid scarlet. A few minutes later, and the coroner had adjourned the inquest for a week to enable the police to pursue their inquiries.

While it had been determined in advance that only Cordelia and Algernon of those present at Ursula's death would be called upon to give evidence, Rose was somewhat surprised that none of the other Sedgwick Players had seen fit to attend the proceedings, if only in the capacity of interested onlookers. She concluded that, having considered it unlikely they would learn anything new regarding the events in the folly, they had determined to stay away from the inevitable attention and gossip that the inquest had generated. Rather guiltily she acknowledged that, while she had been effectively cocooned from the village tittle tattle at Sedgwick Court, the others had no doubt been less fortunate; she could imagine only too well the whispers and pointed fingers that haunted them during the course of their daily business.

Rose looked around for Miss Sprat, who had accompanied them to the inquest. She remembered how the maid-companion had listened to the evidence surrounding her mistress' death quietly and with a certain dignity, sitting very upright in her seat, her hands folded neatly in her lap. She had made no display of emotion except for the odd tear, which she had dabbed at quickly with a handkerchief lest it trickle down her cheek and become noticeable. Rose had felt a pang of pity for the woman, and thought how unbearable it must have been for her to hear her mistress referred to in such official and dispassionate tones, particularly when in life Ursula Stapleton had radiated a presence which had set the village tongues alight.

After a quick survey of the crowd that spilled out of the hall and on to the pavement, Rose located Miss Sprat almost cowering against the wall of the village hall, looking for all the world as if she wished she were invisible, or that the earth would open up and swallow her. The cause of her distress was quickly apparent, for the maid-companion was being stared at with considerable interest by those members of the public who had taken to loitering outside the building for a gossip and recognised her as having been in the employ of the deceased.

'Take Miss Sprat back into the hall, darling,' said Cedric, quickly surmising the situation. 'I'll get Adams to drive round to the back of the building. There's a door there, which leads off from the kitchen. It won't be very grand, I'm afraid, but at least Miss Sprat won't be gawped at by the denizens or pestered by the newspaper men whom I'm assuming are lurking somewhere around here eager to get a scoop.'

Rose followed her husband's suggestion and, supporting the maid-companion by her elbow, ushered Miss Sprat back into the hall. Prudie Sprat muttered her thanks and Rose could feel the tremble of the woman's frail body beneath the thin fabric of her funereal garb. Rose felt desperately sorry for her, and was pleased that she had gone to the trouble of visiting Miss Sprat in the servants' quarters the night before to ensure that she was suitably settled in her temporary abode. The countess had suggested tactfully that she might prefer one of the guest chambers to a servant's bedroom in the attic. Miss Sprat's had appeared quite vexed at the suggestion.

'I like to earn my own keep, your ladyship. Always have done and always will. I can't abide charity, not when it's not deserving, and not while I've still got the use of my arms and legs and a bit of a brain in my head; not that I'm not grateful for your ladyship's kindness, because I am, but I shouldn't want you to treat me like I was one of your grand guests and have your servants wait on me.'

They were sitting in the housekeeper's sitting room. Miss Sprat had a delicate lace collar stretched out on her lap, which she had evidently been in the process of repairing, unaware that she would shortly be receiving company. Indeed, the maid-companion had been somewhat taken aback by Rose's sudden appearance in the servants' quarters and had hastily put aside her sewing, but not before Rose had noticed the quality of her companion's needlework and commented on it.

'I've mended many a garment in my time as a dresser,' Miss Sprat said, obviously flattered by the praise. 'There's not much in the sewing line that I can't turn my hand to. I asked Mrs Farrier if there wasn't a bit of work that she could give me because I couldn't just sit here and be given my food and board, like; it isn't in my nature to be idle. Besides, it helps take my mind off … oh, my poor lamb.' The woman stifled a sob.

'I didn't mean to upset you, Miss Sprat,' Rose said, with genuine concern. She looked about her for a chair to draw up to the fireplace, and then stretched out a hand to comfort the maid-companion. I didn't mean to disturb you. I only wanted to see if you were all right and had everything you required.'

'That's very kind of you, your ladyship, and I'm sure I couldn't ask for more,' mumbled Miss Sprat. 'You have been very good to me, as have your servants. I … oh, where are my manners?' she cried, jumping up from her seat and doing an old-fashioned curtsey. 'And making you get your own chair, too. What must you think of me, your ladyship?'

'Never mind that,' Rose said quickly. 'I came to see how you were, not to be waited on.'

'Well, that's nice of you to say so, your ladyship,' muttered Miss Sprat. 'I have my good moments and I have my bad moments, as you might say. There are hours when I can do nothing but cry remembering how my poor lamb died, and hours when I think only of the good times. Reminiscing is what I call it, remembering how happy and full of life she was, when she had the theatre at her feet, as you might say. She would have made a very fine actress. Gave it all up for a love, she did, and such a short love it was too. Cruel it was, Mr Stapleton dying like that in the war, and not even a child to lesson her grief.' She fumbled in the pocket of her apron and produced a very creased photograph, which she handed to Rose. 'I found this when I was going through her things. Happy, she was there. Why, you can see the joy in her face, shining out, like.'

Rose studied the photograph closely. It was of a couple standing in a traditional wedding pose. The man was tall and handsome and wore a waxed moustache. The woman, who was dressed in a simple Edwardian tea dress offset by a silk satin cummerbund, she recognised immediately as a younger and prettier version of the Ursula Stapleton she had seen parading on the stage. This, then, was a picture of the Stapletons on their wedding day, before disaster had struck. That Ursula had been happy on that day, there was little doubt, for the contentment on her face seemed to radiate from the paper as if it were a real, living thing. Rose felt a sudden pang of sadness, for it occurred to her that the photograph was now no more than a record of a young couple who had both been killed before their time in cruel acts of violence.

'I've looked at that photograph that many times since she died,' confided Miss Sprat. 'I want to remember my lamb as she was on the happiest day of her life. I carry it around with me in my apron so that if I feel like I might weep, I can take it out and look at it. To know she was happy …' The old woman faltered as she retrieved the photograph and restored it to the safety of her apron pocket.

'What will you do now?' enquired Rose, 'once the murderer has been brought to justice, I mean?'

'Well, I've a little put by,' said Miss Sprat, recovering some of her composure. 'I've always been frugal in my ways and my lamb was very generous. I don't doubt she's left me a small legacy; she always said as she would, though of course we thought how it would be me as would go first. Not that it matters much because I've made up my mind to go back to the theatre. A dresser is my profession and the theatre is where I belong.'

It was some fifteen minutes after they had first emerged from the village hall that Rose found herself seated beside her husband in the Daimler. The rescued Miss Sprat was installed beside the chauffeur in the front, gazing absentmindedly at the view from the window as the motor car negotiated the country lanes on its way back to Sedgwick Court.

Settling down against the car's leather upholstery, Rose's thoughts drifted again to the previous day and, in particular, to Miriam's visit. Both women had felt disposed to interview Henry Rewe regarding his strange behaviour on the day of the murder. With certain misgivings on Rose's part, they had agreed to go to his lodgings together. Their visit, however, had proved to be in vain. For Mrs Greggs informed them on opening the door that the poet was not at home. Her manner had been offhand to begin with, her words spoken brusquely. Indeed, she had almost closed the door in their faces, so keen was she to be rid of them. It was only when Rose had given the landlady her calling card that she had realised the identity of her visitor. Then, she had been almost beside herself, fawning and grovelling at the countess' feet to such an embarrassing extent that Rose almost wished they had not taken it upon themselves to visit the poet's lodgings. Had Henry Rewe been watching the spectacle, he would have been amazed at how polite and accommodating his landlady could be, for it was a side of her of which he was ignorant. The only Mrs Greggs he ever saw was a grumbling one who bestowed on him the sharp edge of her tongue when he was late with the money for his lodgings.

'Mr Rewe was it you were wanting, your ladyship?' the landlady had inquired. 'A nice young gentleman is Mr Rewe. Educated, he is; full to the brim with learning. Usually you'd find him scribbling away upstairs in his rooms, but not today. Gone wandering about in the fields and the meadows looking for inspiration for his poetry, least that's what he said. Not to delay supper, that's what he told me, as if I would.' Mrs Greggs had bent forward at this point to inform her visitors that she prepared supper for all her gentlemen lodgers, but that Mr Rewe had told her that he was dining out that evening and that she shouldn't expect him back until late. She had insisted that he take his key so that he wouldn't wake up the whole house when he returned full of drink as likely as not.

Disappointed though Rose had been at this news, she had not felt too despondent having resolved to waylay the young man after the inquest. To find, then, that Henry Rewe had not deemed it worthwhile to attend the hearing was particularly galling. She was just pondering whether it was too late to invite the poet to join them for luncheon when Cedric roused her abruptly from her deliberations with the following words:

'I say, I wonder what was in that note that was passed to Deacon?'

'What note?'

'Didn't you see?' Cedric turned to face his wife, hardly able to keep the excitement from his voice, though he spoke in a low tone so as not to be overheard by Miss Sprat. 'It must have been when you were helping Miss Sprat to find a seat. A man hurried into the hall and gave the inspector a note. I suppose he must have been a policeman. Well, you should have seen the expression on old Deacon's face when he unfolded the paper and read what was inside.'

'Oh?' Rose was intrigued. 'Did he look surprised?

'I should say! Shocked more like. I thought he looked fit to burst.' Aware that he now had his wife's full attention, he clasped her hands in his and said earnestly: 'It must have been dashed important anyway, because Deacon and the sergeant made their apologies to the coroner and fled from the hall.'

'Before the inquest began?' Cedric nodded. 'I didn't see them go,' murmured Rose. 'It must have been while I was arranging for a glass of water to be brought to Miss Sprat. I was awfully afraid she was about to faint. Now you come to mention it, I wondered at the time why they weren't there.' Rose stared at her husband. 'What could have been of such importance that they couldn't stay for the inquest? They must have known that it wouldn't last long, what with it being adjourned.'

'Yes, it's dashed odd. I say,' said Cedric, a thought having struck him, 'you don't think someone has confessed to Ursula's murder, do you?'

'I shouldn't think so,' muttered Rose, though she was far from certain. For what else could explain the inspector's rather hasty departure?

On their arrival at Sedgwick Court, claiming a headache and a wish for solitude, Miss Sprat had returned to her little room in the servants' quarters. Rose had stood for a moment watching her go, reflecting that the woman made a forlorn little figure as she disappeared behind the green baize door; it struck her then that the maid-companion had aged considerably in the last few hours.

Before she could dwell any further on the fact that Ursula Stapleton's death had taken its toll, Manning appeared in the hall. One look at the butler's face told the earl and countess that something was the matter. However, before they had even opened their mouths to speak, Manning said hurriedly:

'That was the chief constable on the telephone, your lordship. He wants you to telephone him immediately.'

'Righto,' said Cedric, in an attempt to sound light-hearted. 'I'll use the telephone in my study.' He looked inquiringly at Rose. 'Will you join me, darling?'

Looking back on the events afterwards, it seemed to Rose that she had followed her husband into the room in something of a daze. For she was barely conscious of the fact that Cedric had even lifted the telephone receiver to his ear before she was surprised to realise that he was speaking. Her brain in its muddled state could hardly distinguish the words uttered, though the detective in her studied her husband's face for clues. Vaguely she was aware that the earl's brow had become furrowed, and that he was passing a hand through his hair in an agitated fashion. His face, when she studied it closely, had gone quite pale.

'What's the matter?' she cried, as soon as he had replaced the telephone receiver.

Cedric took a moment or two to answer, and Rose found herself clinging to his sleeve like a frightened child. He looked down at her in a distracted manner, as if he hardly recognised who she was, or what she was asking. At last he said in a voice so quiet that she had to stand on tiptoe to catch his words:

'There has been another murder.'

Chapter Twenty-six

'Who found the body?' demanded Inspector Deacon, as soon as they entered the house.

'The manservant, sir,' replied Constable Bright, coming forward and greeting them. 'Brown is his name. He's taken it awful bad. He's through there in the drawing room if you want to see him,' he added, pointing to one of the doors leading off the hall. 'I took the liberty of giving him a bit of brandy, else I doubt you'd have got a word out of him.'

The inspector drew the constable aside out of earshot of the servant.

'The doctor said he thought the poor devil had been killed around midnight, didn't he?' Inspector Deacon looked down at the note that had been passed to him at the inquest, which he still held clutched in his hand. 'Yes, I was right. Between midnight and two o'clock in the morning was the doctor's rough estimate. How is it then that this fellow,' he said, indicating the domestic, 'only found his master an hour or so ago?'

'He's only just returned, sir. He spent the night at his sister's, on account of her having been taken bad a few days ago.' Constable Bright consulted his notes. 'Brown left Sedgwick yesterday afternoon,' he said. 'According to him he left at about two o'clock, give or take the odd minute. Went as soon as he had finished his daily chores, he said. His master usually dined in Bichester during the week, you see, what with him working as manager in a bank there.'

'It makes you wonder why he went to the expense of employing a manservant if he was out all day,' commented Sergeant Lane. 'I would have thought a widower like him could have made do with a daily charwoman.'

'Brown is something of an old family retainer,' answered the constable. 'He was just after telling me how he's been with the Drury family for years. Worked for Mr Drury's parents before he worked for the deceased. Long gone, they are, and their money with them. He came to work for Mr Walter Drury after the death of his wife, so he's known his master since Mr Drury was a nipper. That's why he's awful cut up by what's happened.'

'It's never very pleasant to discover a dead body,' muttered the inspector, 'particularly if one is not used to it. What's in here?' He opened one of the doors off the hall which revealed a study of sorts. 'Ah, good. In you go, Lane. I'd like a quick word with you before we view the body and interview this Brown fellow.'

Constable Bright made as if to follow and then obviously thought better of it, remaining in the hall, as if to guard the door.

'This is a rum old business and no mistake, Lane,' said Inspector Deacon, as soon as the sergeant had closed the door behind them. 'A murder happening under our noses like this and us no further forward in our inquiries than we were when we started.'

'Our murderer has some nerve, I'll say that for him,' said the sergeant, 'what with a couple of Scotland Yard detectives being in the village at the time.'

'He has some audacity, all right,' agreed his superior, 'or else we have him rattled.' He sighed and struck the side of the mantelpiece with his fist. 'I blame myself for what has happened. I should have pressed Drury when we interviewed him. He knew something, I'm certain of it. I thought at the time his behaviour was odd.'

'Yes, a strange little man,' agreed the sergeant. 'He contradicted himself repeatedly, if you remember, sir?'

'I do indeed, Lane. I wonder if the poor chap was frightened? Hello?' said the inspector breaking off from what he was saying, following a tap on the door. 'Who is this?'

'The police surgeon is keen to move the corpse to the mortuary, sir,' said Constable Bright, entering the room rather timidly. 'He's finished his examination of the body and says if you want to see it in situ you'd better hurry.'

The policemen found Walter Drury's corpse in the back garden of the property, stretched out full length on the lawn not far from the garden gate which led on to Lovers' Lane. He was lying half on his front, as if he had rolled over in sleep. The cause of death was obvious, even to the most casual of onlookers, of which the inspector and sergeant were definitely not.

'He was killed by a blunt object to the back of the head,' observed Sergeant Lane.

'Yes. The poor devil didn't have much of a chance to put up a fight,' agreed the inspector, crouching down beside the body. 'Still, at least it was quick. He may never have known the identity of his murderer or the fact that he was being attacked, come to that.'

'If he was caught off guard, as it were,' mused his subordinate, 'it could just as easily have been a woman who did it, as a man.'

'You're quite right,' concurred the inspector, standing up to survey the garden. 'The same thought had crossed my mind, Lane. And it is too much of a coincidence not to be connected with Mrs Stapleton's death.'

'I don't reckon this murder was premeditated though, do you, sir?' said the sergeant. 'It's nothing like the other one, where he slipped some poison into her glass. That would have required some planning. This one looks as if it might have been done sudden like, in a fit of anger.'

With which observation, they returned to the house and entered the drawing room, where Brown, the manservant, was sitting on a chair nursing a half empty glass of brandy, which he hastily put down on a table beside him.

'No, don't get up, Brown,' Inspector Deacon said quickly, as the man made as if to stand. 'You've had the most awful shock; much better to remain seated. This is a dreadful business, I know, but I'm sure you understand that we need to ask you a few questions. We won't keep you any longer than necessary.'

'Yes, sir,' mumbled the unfortunate servant.

The inspector studied him closely. The poor man, with his ashen face and thinning hair, looked close to tears. The inspector wondered idly what would happen to him with his master dead, and hoped he had sufficient savings to enable him to retire from service for, to his mind, the man did not look well or a day under seventy. He comforted himself with the thought that Walter Drury, with his prudent, financial brain and no kin that he was aware of, had no doubt left his faithful old domestic well provided for in the form of a decent legacy.

'When did you last see your master?' the inspector inquired.

'Yesterday morning, sir, just before Mr Drury left for work. I ... I didn't see him again.' There was a break in the old servant's voice.

It occurred to the inspector that it would be as well to get straight to the point. In an ideal situation, he would have liked to ask Brown a number of questions concerning his employer, but it was obvious that the poor man was not up to being interviewed for any length. To that purpose, the inspector said:

'According to the medical evidence, your master was killed between midnight and two o'clock in the morning.' The old servant shuddered, and the inspector cursed himself for not having phrased his sentence more tactfully. 'Do you know what he might have been doing out in the garden at that time of night?'

'He always took a walk around the garden before he turned in,' replied the manservant. 'It was a habit of his. He used to say the night air cleared his head and helped him to sleep.'

'I see. And was this fact common knowledge, do you know?'

'Among his acquaintances, it would have been, sir. The time he took his constitutional varied, of course, because sometimes he retired early, and sometimes he retired late. But whatever the time, he always took a walk around the garden. I never knew him not to.'

Inspector Deacon caught Sergeant Lane's eye. It was apparent they were having the same thought. Whoever had killed Walter Drury had lain in wait for him in the garden, aware of his evening ritual.

'Is the garden gate kept locked,' inquired the inspector, 'the one that leads out in to Lovers' Lane?'

'No, sir, not as a rule,' admitted the servant. 'The master didn't see the need.'

So, anyone, thought the inspector, could have crept into the garden to await their prey. He had already noted that the garden was a very fair size for such a property and contained a great deal of dense shrubbery and bushes, not to mention trees, behind which the murderer might have hidden. A thought struck him, and he said:

'It was rather late for Mr Drury to be doing a round of his garden, wasn't it? Midnight, or even a couple of hours later. Very late, what with him having to go to work the next day, I mean?'

'I suppose it was,' admitted the manservant, 'though the master tended to keep late hours, and of course,' he added, almost as if it were an afterthought, 'he was entertaining last night.'

'Entertaining?' inquired the inspector, his ears pricked. 'Why didn't you say anything before? Do you mean to tell me Mr Drury was expecting a visitor last night?'

'Why, yes, sir. As I've mentioned, Mr Drury always dined in Bichester during the week. He normally had only a cold supper in the evening, which I laid out for him on a tray, and which he ate in his study. He seldom used the dining room except for entertaining. And more often than not, he took his breakfast with me in the kitchen.'

'I see,' muttered the inspector, somewhat surprised by these domestic arrangements. 'But yesterday it was different, you say?'

'Yes, indeed, sir. My master advised me that he was expecting a visitor and could I leave him something laid out on a tray which was enough for two and which he could heat up later in the stove.' He leant forward and said quietly. 'He knew as how I meant to visit my sick sister yesterday. He didn't want to put me out; awful considerate that way, he was. Of course, I offered to remain and wait on him and his guest but he said there was no need.' The manservant hung his head dejectedly. 'If only I'd stayed, I might have been able to save him.'

'It won't do thinking like that,' said the inspector, rather brusquely, afraid that the man was on the verge of becoming melancholy. 'It doesn't do any good. Tell me, the meal you left out, was it eaten?'

'Yes, it was; every last crumb of it. It was a steak and ale pie with some boiled potatoes and vegetables. He liked a proper pie with a thick crust on it, did my master. It was a great favourite of his, though I say it myself.' The manservant paused to stare at his hands, and the inspector wondered whether he was recalling making the pastry for the pie. 'I put out a board of cheeses as well,' continued Brown. 'I thought as how it would go well with the gentlemen's port.'

Inspector Deacon's head shot up in one swift movement.

'Gentlemen's port, you say? Your master was expecting a gentleman visitor?'

'Yes, sir. He wasn't much of a ladies' man, as you might say, except for the late Mrs Drury, that is; he was devoted to her.'

'I don't suppose,' hazarded Inspector Deacon, 'that you are aware of the identity of Mr Drury's guest?'

'But of course, sir,' answered the manservant, looking surprised. 'It was Mr Rewe.'

'Rewe,' exclaimed Sergeant Lane, as soon as the butler had departed. 'Didn't Mr Drury visit him on the evening that it became known that Mrs Stapleton had been poisoned?'

'Yes. It was also the day that we interviewed Mr Rewe,' said the inspector, grimly.

'During which he admitted taking the wine glass,' said Sergeant Lane excitedly, 'and gave us some cock and bull story about wanting to teach Miss Quail a lesson?'

'The very same,' replied his superior. 'He also told us, if you remember, that he had no intention of telling us the truth.' Inspector Deacon gathered his papers together. 'Grab your hat, Lane. Let's see what our young poet has to say for himself this time.'

'Mr Drury, dead?' muttered Rose, stretching a hand out to grab the arm of a chair lest she fall. 'What can it mean?'

'That someone is intent on killing off the Sedgwick Players,' replied her husband, 'that's what. No,' he said, holding up his hand as his wife made to protest, 'I don't mean to be flippant, darling. I can't quite take it all in, that's all. I mean to say, what could anyone have had against poor old Walter? He was such a harmless little man, and as straight as they come. Why, I can't imagine him in any other profession than as the manager of a bank. One knew one's money was safe with Walter, which is saying something given the current times.'

'He must have known something,' said Rose, 'or at least had a suspicion regarding the identity of the murderer. The more I think about it, the more I am inclined to believe that it must have had something to do with Mrs Stapleton's –'

'Begging your pardon, your lordship, your ladyship,' said Manning, who had entered the study unobserved. 'Mr Rewe and Miss Belmore are here to see you; something about a wine glass, they said.'

'Very well, show them in to the drawing room,' said Cedric. 'We'll be along in a minute.' He waited until the butler had disappeared, before turning to his wife.

'Do we tell them about poor Walter? I daresay it isn't common knowledge yet. The chief constable telephoned me as a sort of courtesy. It was jolly decent of him, but I'm not sure old Deacon would have approved.'

'I don't think we should say anything,' said Rose, after deliberating. 'One or other of them might let something slip.'

'Surely you don't think either of them had anything to do with Walter's murder?' exclaimed Cedric, clearly horrified by the suggestion.

'I think it quite likely,' said Rose, 'that one of them is the murderer.'

'Not Miriam,' Cedric exclaimed, before catching his wife's eye. 'And surely not Henry; he and Walter were the best of friends, don't you know.'

'What I do know,' said Rose quietly, 'is that one of the Sedgwick Players is a murderer; not once, but twice, and we must do our utmost to ensure they are not put on their guard.'

Despite her fine words, Rose experienced some pangs of conscience when Miriam and Henry entered the drawing room and the latter made some casual reference to the bank manager. These soon passed, however, as both the young people appeared determined to come to the point regarding the purpose of their visit.

'I've told Henry … Mr Rewe, the conclusion we reached regarding the wine glass,' began Miriam, without preamble. On this occasion, the girl appeared in full command of her emotions, for the cold aloofness had returned. It was with a sense of considerable unease that Rose noticed that Miriam and Cedric appeared at pains not to catch the other's eye.

'Well, what have you to say on the matter?' Rose said, a little more brusquely than she had intended. Her remark had been directly primarily at Miriam, but now she turned her attention to Henry Rewe. 'You found the wine glass hidden in the waste-paper basket, didn't you?' Henry nodded, though the expression on his face was one of almost disbelief. 'At the very same moment you made your discovery,' Rose continued, less harshly, 'you happened to catch Miss Belmore's eye. You remembered then that you had seen her pick the wine glass off the floor where Ursula had dropped it.' Rose crossed the room and stood before the fireplace, her back against the marble. 'A little while afterwards, you heard Miss Belmore say that she thought I believed Mrs Stapleton to have been murdered.' Rose turned her attention to Miriam. 'I remember at the time I was rather afraid your voice had carried and that the others had heard you mention the word 'murder'.'

'You are quite right, your ladyship,' affirmed Henry enthusiastically, 'though for the life of me I don't know how you did it. Made a guess like that, I mean. I daresay it was rather foolish of me, but I was worried what your servants would think if they discovered the wine glass in the basket like that. I thought it would be much better if they found it on the bookcase.'

'What was foolish of you, Henry, was to think I could be guilty of Ursula's murder,' said Miriam. Though her words were scornful, there was some warmth in her tone. 'I suppose I should feel grateful that you should do such a thing for me, but …' She faltered, as if she did not know quite how to finish her sentence.

'But it is Algernon you love?' Henry said. He sounded wretched.

Miriam hesitated a moment before she said: 'Yes.'

A silence filled the room. Rose hardly dared glance at her husband for fear of the expression she would discover on his face. Instead, she decided to steer the conversation back to the matter in hand.

'And then when I announced that the constable was of the view that Mrs Stapleton had been murdered …' she said.

'I was dreadfully afraid,' said Henry. 'It was stupid of me to take the glass, I know, but –'

'You didn't know how else to shield Miss Belmore?' finished Rose.

'Yes.' Henry hung his head, as if he were aware that it had proved a useless gesture.

'I don't suppose,' said Cedric, contributing to the conversation for the first time, 'we are any the wiser in knowing who took the wine glass from the folly and brought it to the house?'

'No,' said Rose. 'When we know that, we will know the identity of our murderer.'

'Hello?' said Cedric. 'What's that noise?'

For a kerfuffle of sorts appeared to have broken out in the hall. Certainly, Rose thought she heard the sound of hurrying feet and Manning protesting in vain. A moment later, and the door of the drawing room was burst open unceremoniously.

'I say, what's the meaning –' began Cedric.

'I tried to stop them, your lordship,' said the butler. 'But they weren't having any of it.'

'Please accept my humblest apologies, your lordship.' Inspector Deacon stood in the doorway, Sergeant Lane at his shoulder. He quickly surveyed the room and his glance fixed on Henry Rewe. 'I was afraid our bird might have flown, but I see he is here.'

'I have already told you,' said Henry sulkily. 'Walter was alive when I left him. I had no reason to kill him.' He was seated in front of Cedric's octagonal table in the library at Sedgwick Court. He leant his elbows on the desk and held his head in his hands, making rather a dejected figure. 'We were by way of being friends, Inspector,' he mumbled. 'He meant more to me than my own father.'

Rose caught Inspector Deacon's eye and dropped her gaze. Henry Rewe had insisted that she be present during the interview, for it appeared that, after the business with the wine glass, he thought her in possession of some divine power. So far, however, she had made a pretty poor showing, merely listening to what Henry had to say for himself. The evidence against him, though mostly circumstantial, she considered rather damning.

'Did Mr Drury mention anything?' she inquired, aware that Inspector Deacon's eyes were on her. 'By that, I mean he must have made some reference to Mrs Stapleton's murder?'

'He said only that it would be all right, and I had nothing to fear. You see,' Henry lifted his head to glare at the inspector, 'I was dreadfully worried the police were going to arrest me for Ursula's murder.'

'You were very foolish to tamper with the evidence, Mr Rewe,' replied the inspector reproachfully.

Henry pointedly ignored the policeman by turning in his chair to address Rose.

'He seemed awfully distracted, Walter that is. He had invited me to dinner, but I had the distinct impression that he rather regretted his decision and wanted me gone.'

'What do you mean by that?' demanded Inspector Deacon.

'Well, if you must know, Inspector,' said Henry, glancing at him over his shoulder, 'he kept looking at his watch. I also caught him gazing at the clock on the mantelpiece. It was not like him at all.' Henry scowled. 'Really, he seemed irritated by my presence. The previous evening –'

'The previous evening? You spoke to him then?' asked Rose, for whom this was news.

'Yes. It was then that I told him about the wine glass. He wanted to know why anyone from Scotland Yard should wish to interview me. He hadn't heard that Ursula had been poisoned, you see; it was a dreadful shock for him, as it is for me now to know that someone has killed him.' He glanced up at the inspector, a hopeful look on his face. 'There hasn't been some sort of ghastly mistake, has there? I can't quite bring myself to believe he is dead. Perhaps it was his manservant, Brown, that you found in the garden?'

'I'm afraid not, Mr Rewe,' said Inspector Deacon, feeling he was doing the servant in question a slight disservice. 'It was Mr Drury that was discovered in the garden all right; his manservant has identified the body.'

'Perhaps Mr Drury said something to you that evening that struck you as strange?' suggested Rose.

Henry paused a moment to deliberate and then said: 'I think he was about to say something and then changed his mind.'

'What do you mean?'

'He was surprised that the police wanted to interview me, like I said. He said, 'why didn't they interview', and then stopped abruptly, as if he thought he'd said too much.'

'I wonder to whom he was referring?' said the inspector.

'He might have been referring to himself,' suggested Rose. 'He was a great friend of Mrs Stapleton's, after all. It stands to reason, therefore, that he might have expected you would want to speak with him before you interviewed Mr Rewe.'

'Walter couldn't stand the woman,' said Henry. 'He just felt sorry for her, that was all.'

'He told us when we interviewed him that he was interested in marrying Mrs Stapleton,' said the inspector, not quite truthfully. 'That is why he visited her regularly.'

'Well, I don't believe that for one minute,' said Henry rather insolently. 'He was having you on, Inspector.'

'Do you remember nothing of the events of last night which might help us, sir?' asked Inspector Deacon wearily, rather tiring of his interview with the young man.

'Now that I come to think of it, there was one thing,' admitted the poet. 'It may have been just my fancy, but I thought I caught sight of someone in the garden. I told Walter, and he said I was just imagining it. He said it was too dark to see anything, and it was probably just a shadow.'

'Indeed?' For the first time during the interview, the inspector appeared interested. 'Why didn't you tell us this before? How did Mr Drury seem when you told him? Did he appear nervous or agitated?'

'Well, that's the odd thing, Inspector,' said Henry. 'He seemed rather pleased, as if all the time he had been waiting for that person to arrive.'

Chapter Twenty-seven

It had been an odd sort of day, Rose reflected. Henry's suspicion that Walter Drury had been anxious to meet the person, who in all likelihood was his murderer, had them greatly mystified. Inspector Deacon had viewed Henry's story with a great deal of scepticism, but there was little evidence on which to detain the young man other than the probability that he had been the last person to see the bank manager alive. It was with some reluctance and misgivings that the inspector had watched the poet depart, but not before giving him strict instructions to remain in the village in case he should be required to help the police with their inquiries.

The inspector and sergeant had stayed only a little while longer before they too had taken their leave. Rose had caught Inspector Deacon's eye and seen the look of bewilderment which clouded his face, and which mirrored her own feelings of confusion. Certainly, she sympathised with his predicament. Events seemed to have escalated at an alarming rate and yet neither she nor the inspector felt any the nearer to ascertaining the identity of the murderer, whose very presence seemed to loom over the village like some ominous force.

Rose had spent the rest of the day walking in the grounds, initially rather listlessly. It occurred to her that she might call on the other Sedgwick Players, for there was always the possibility that she might obtain some additional information which would prove useful to her investigation. However, she found herself oddly reluctant to do so. It was not because she feared for her own safety, but rather that she felt a certain unwillingness to engage with the characters involved. For it seemed to her that she had lived and breathed nothing but the Sedgwick Players and their theatricals, and a longing for her ordinary, commonplace existence overwhelmed her.

It was another fine summer's day and, after a while of aimless wandering, the sunshine and fresh air seemed to revive her and liven her spirits. While her steps were without purpose, her mind seemed to gradually awaken, and though her intention had been to avoid dwelling on the events of the past few days, her perseverance was weak. Indeed, the longer she thought about it, the more she had the growing feeling that she held all the necessary pieces of the puzzle in her hand. She had only to arrange them in some semblance of order to enable her to piece them together and solve the mystery that had so far eluded her.

Of course, it was all very well to believe that she was in a position to identify the murderer if she so chose, quite another thing entirely to assemble the pieces and prove her theory correct. She spent the rest of the day with the odd sensation that the solution to the problem lay just out of reach. Indeed, she felt that she could almost see it out of the corner of her eye, and that if she were to stretch out her hand she could touch it with her fingers. If only she could grasp hold of it and pull it towards her!

That night she slept fitfully, and when morning came her head ached and felt heavy, as if she had not slept at all. As she dragged herself through the day, her eyelids drooped and every movement became more arduous and each chore more onerous than the last. At length, she yielded to the demands of her body and retired to the library, where she curled up in one of the armchairs and gave herself up to sleep.

A little while later she awoke feeling refreshed both in spirit and body, and it was with a certain relish that she indulged in her afternoon tea. Manning had informed her that Lord Belvedere had sent his apologies for he was delayed with estate work and would not be joining her. Therefore, she ate alone, in quiet solitude. It was only then that her mind seemed to come alive and work almost unbidden, turning over the pieces of the jigsaw puzzle and arranging them in such a way that after a while she grabbed at the arm of her chair as if to steady herself. The next moment she was frozen to the spot, the piece of fruit cake she was eating still clutched in her hand. The tea plate she was holding in her other hand slipped from her grasp and clattered on to the floor. Of all this, however, she was barely conscious. For a sudden realisation had crept up upon her. The last piece of the jigsaw was in place. She knew the identity of the murderer, that shadowy figure that had haunted the stage and pranced in the wings.

Rose stood on the threshold of the drawing room, deliberating whether or not to enter the room immediately and let her presence be known, or to linger for a moment in the doorway and survey its occupants. She chose the latter course and thought, not for the first time, what an odd collection of people the Sedgwick Players were. Coming hot on the heels of this observation came a memory of the day of Ursula Stapleton's murder, when she had entered this very same room and been greeted by a similar tableau of thespians. Then, they had been dressed in a strange assortment of Tudor costumes and contemporary dress, and some of their faces had been smeared crudely with greasepaint. She could see the same faces now, though they looked rather pale and insipid in comparison with the previous occasion. Even Cordelia's complexion looked sallow under its liberal application of rouge.

Their clothes today were a strange mixture due to the lateness of the hour, with some having opted to wear evening dress, while others still wore their daytime tweeds. It was obvious to Rose that the confusion had arisen from the fact that, while their presence had been requested at Sedgwick Court, the invitation, ostensibly from Cedric, had not made it clear whether they were being invited for dinner or cocktails, or merely for a discussion on the fate of the theatricals.

The Sedgwick Players had positioned themselves about the room in a variety of poses, some seated, some standing, as they awaited the arrival of their host and hostess, and Rose caught the murmured conversations of one or two, inquiring of the others if they knew why they had been summoned.

They were all there, Rose noticed, as she reeled off their names in her head. Freddie and Gerald Prentice were standing rather pointedly at opposite ends of the room like two bookends, looking for all the world as if they could not bear each other's company. Giles, in his tweed office attire, was standing over Cordelia Quail, who was reclining on a sofa, her head adorned by an elaborate headdress of black ostrich feathers and beads. Miriam, in an evening gown of black silk satin, which seemed to accentuate the very paleness of her skin and her mass of raven hair, stood with her back to the wall. Her face was half turned towards Algernon Cuffe, who was regaling her with some tale or other. Rose realised with a start that it was the first time that she had seen Miriam smile. Her companion, with his commanding presence was in full evening dress and looked rather dashing with his vivid red beard. Instinctively, Rose sought out Henry Rewe, who she discovered crouched on a chair in a corner of the room, looking alternately, enviously at his rival and forlornly at

Miriam.

The only other occupant in the room was Miss Sprat, who had adopted her habitual pose of sitting very upright in her chair, her hands folded neatly in her lap. She appeared to be deep in her own thoughts, quite oblivious to both her surroundings and to the company. The Sedgwick Players, for their part, cast the odd embarrassed or concerned glance in her direction, though it was only Giles who went as far as to enquire after her health and how she was holding up after the tragedy.

There was a slight movement behind her and Rose turned her head. Cedric had appeared at her shoulder.

'They're here,' he whispered. 'There was some trouble with the car, I believe.'

'Thank goodness,' said Rose, sounding relieved. 'I was afraid that we would have to start the proceedings without them and pretend that we were hosting a party of sorts, and they were our guests.'

'God forbid,' said her husband, with feeling. 'That would be dashed awkward.' He turned his attention to the two men waiting behind him patiently in the hall. 'Are you ready?' he enquired. 'I, for one, would like to get this over with.'

Cedric and Rose proceeded into the room, supposedly to greet their guests. Rose was reminded again of a tableau. It seemed to her almost as if the day of Ursula's murder was being repeated, for the chatter had ceased and the room's occupants were once again arrested in their various activities, eyeing the earl and countess with curiosity. Indeed, they were so still they might have been statues, or portraits, like the many which adorned the walls and alcoves of the house.

In the end, it was Cordelia who was the first to step forward. She had risen from her sofa fully prepared to exchange pleasantries with her host and hostess, when she suddenly spied the two men standing behind them in the doorway, barring the way to the hall.

'Inspector Deacon!' she exclaimed in a voice that carried across the room.

All eyes flew to the door, and the apprehension that had been bubbling steadily beneath the surface came charging to the fore, pervading the atmosphere, and lurking like a shadow in the room. Rose, aware of the heightened tension, was conscious also of the presence of a stronger emotion; it took her a moment to realise that it was fear.

'I should like to thank you all for coming,' said Inspector Deacon, closing the door and immediately assuming command of the situation. He crossed the room to take up a position on the hearthrug, his back against the fireplace; Sergeant Lane, Rose noted, remained standing in front of the door, effectively blocking it as a possible means of escape.

'Look here,' said Algernon, taking a step forward and glaring at the detective, 'what's the meaning of all this? It seems to me that you have assembled us here under false pretences. I've a good mind to –'

'Stay where you are, Mr Cuffe, if you please,' said the inspector quickly, forestalling the end of Algernon's sentence.

The inspector's tone was pleasant but firm, and for a moment Algernon looked as if he were about to protest further, but on reflection evidently thought better of it. Instead, he contented himself with scowling and muttering a few words under his breath.

'Why did you summon us here, Inspector?' enquired Miriam. Her voice sounded bored, though her eyes, Rose noticed, were keen and alert. 'Do you wish to make some sort of announcement?'

'You are quite right, Miss Belmore, I do,' the inspector affirmed. He glanced around the room, and when he spoke next it was slowly, each word carefully articulated. 'I have gathered you together this evening as I wish to make an arrest.'

'An arrest?' said Cordelia, looking a little confused. 'An arrest for what?'

'An arrest for the murders of Ursula and Walter, of course,' snapped Freddie. 'That's right, isn't it, Inspector?'

'Good lord!' exclaimed Algernon. 'Have you gone quite mad, Inspector, or do you mean to tell us that you know the identity of the murderer?'

'I believe I am perfectly sane, Mr Cuffe,' Inspector Deacon replied, a touch coldly. 'But, yes, I know who murdered Mrs Stapleton and Mr Drury, and I intend to make an arrest.'

There was the sound of sharp intakes of breath and the shuffling of feet. Inspector Deacon looked at the faces turned towards him and noted that, without exception, they were deathly pale. A real, tangible fear stalked the room and all of them, he hazarded, were feeling wretched, though for all but one there was the possibility of salvation at the end of the tunnel. A ridding of the burden of fear and uncertainty that they had carried like a heavy load. Even Algernon appeared genuinely dumbfounded. Miriam had lost some of her icy aloofness, and Freddie looked truly solemn.

'Oh, do tell us,' cried Cordelia at last, dabbing at her forehead with her handkerchief. 'I, for one, cannot bear this feeling of suspense.'

'I am not the best person to tell you,' answered Inspector Deacon, rather unexpectedly.

He looked over at Rose. Despite the sombre circumstances, there was something akin to a twinkle in his eye, and the girl visibly started, realising that he meant for her to make the *dénouement*. Cedric squeezed her hand and smiled at her encouragingly.

'It is Lady Belvedere we have to thank for solving this case,' admitted Inspector Deacon.

With that, he made way for her to stand beside him at the fireplace. It was with some trepidation that Rose crossed the room to take up her position, for she was aware that all eyes were now focused upon her. She took a deep breath, but before she could open her mouth to speak, or to consider where exactly in her tale to begin, Cordelia Quail ran forward, wringing her hands, her turban slanted at its usual ridiculous angle.

'Lady Belvedere, may I beseech you to come straight to the point and tell us who did it? I am sure that I speak for everyone present when I say we are all on tenterhooks?' She glanced around the room and was gratified to see some nodding of heads. 'I daresay it is the common practice to point to each of us in turn and assign a reason as to why each of us should have wished Ursula dead, but I'd rather you didn't prevaricate and prolong this dreadful ordeal. I fancy we all had a motive for wishing Ursula harm. I know I did. Really, she was the most trying of women.'

'Cordelia!' cried Algernon, clearly shocked.

'It's no use your looking at me like that, Algernon,' said Cordelia, making a face. 'I am only saying what we all thought.'

'I didn't have a motive for wishing her dead,' said Henry, rather sulkily from his place in the corner. 'In fact,' he added, looking pointedly at Miriam and Algernon, 'it would have suited my purposes much better if she hadn't died.'

'It wouldn't have done any good if she hadn't, you silly boy,' said Cordelia, rather dismissively. 'Any fool could tell you that you are just not Miriam's type.'

'I say,' objected Henry hotly, 'there's no call to be so unkind.'

'Very well, I will do as you ask, Miss Quail, and not beat about the bush,' said Rose hurriedly, fearing that the situation might escalate into something of a riot. She was also keen to relinquish her position in front of the fireplace. Taking one last look around the room, noting the faces that were now staring at her intently, she said: 'The person who killed Mrs Stapleton and Mr Drury was Dudley Stapleton.'

There was a stunned silence, and then Cordelia said:

'Dudley Stapleton? Never heard of the fellow. Was he some sort of relative of Ursula's?'

A cry rang out through the room; it was something akin to the high-pitched shriek of an animal in pain and had the effect of rendering everyone else silent. They all turned as one to face Miss Sprat, who sat huddled in her chair, rocking to and fro, her head clutched in her hands.

'Oh, your ladyship, how could you be so heartless and cruel?' The old woman spluttered. She lifted her head and gave Rose an imploring look. 'How could you say as it was my poor lamb's dead husband that killed her? Him as has lain in the ground these last sixteen or seventeen odd years and died for his country. Begging your pardon, I'm sure, but it's wicked for you to say such things. Devoted to him she was.'

Rose moved forward and, crouching down beside the woman, put an arm around her shoulders, which she noticed were shivering.

'I didn't mean to be unkind, Miss Sprat,' she said gently. 'I wouldn't upset you for the world. But I am afraid that what I said just now is quite true. Mr Stapleton killed his wife, and Mr Drury, too.'

'But that can't be right,' protested the maid-companion between sobs. 'He's dead.'

'I assure you that he is very much alive,' said Rose firmly. 'And what is more, he is here in this room.'

A shocked silence filled the drawing room, broken only by the maid-companion's protests.

'I don't believe you, your ladyship,' cried Miss Sprat, 'Why do you persist in saying such dreadful lies?'

'They are not lies, Miss Sprat,' said a voice. 'May God forgive me, but

… I am Dudley Stapleton.'

All those present turned to face the direction from which the voice had come, eager to ascertain who had spoken. With varying degrees of amazement, they watched as the owner of the voice stepped forward. It was Algernon Cuffe.

Chapter Twenty-eight

Later, Rose remembered only the shocked expressions, and looks of utter confusion and bewilderment that had shown themselves on the faces of the Sedgwick Players following Algernon's startling revelation. She had paid particular attention to Miss Sprat's reaction to the news, fearing the woman might faint from the shock. The old woman had maintained her composure, however; the only outward sign she had given that she was in any way perturbed was that she had stared at Algernon so intently that Rose was half surprised that the man did not buckle under her gaze. Instead, he stood motionless, though she thought she detected a slight sagging of his shoulders, as if he had been carrying a great burden on his back, which had now evaporated.

'You ... you were Ursula's husband?' Miriam said, staring at Algernon in disbelief.

It struck Rose as rather odd that it should be this fact on which she pounced, and not Rose's accusation that her lover was a murderer. The reason for this was explained a moment later when Miriam's hand shot to her mouth and her eyes widened. For it was only now that the girl fully comprehended the dreadful truth.

'You murdered Ursula ... and Walter?'' she muttered. Even then, every bone in her body seemed to protest his innocence. 'No! I don't believe it. Algernon,' she said, grabbing wildly at the sleeve of his jacket, 'you must tell them it is not true.' She abruptly loosened her grip on his arm and turned to glare at Rose. 'You have it all wrong, Lady Belvedere. I don't think you are much of a detective if you go about accusing perfectly innocent people of the most appalling crimes. Why, I –'

'Miriam,' said Algernon, in a firm voice, which was also filled with tenderness. He took a step forward and took the girl gently by the shoulders, holding her until he was certain he had her undivided attention. 'It's no good, my dear. I've been fairly caught, and I don't know that I'm not glad of it. I never meant to kill Walter, you see. You don't know how wretched I have felt about it. And really, I'm no good. You deserve a much better man than I will ever be.'

Miriam made to protest but he silenced her with a look of such intensity that she half recoiled from him, her eyes not leaving his face. Algernon's voice had threatened to break with emotion; now there was something of a detached note to it.

'You will look back on this and think what a very fortunate escape you had, my dear,' he added, glancing around the room until he spied the policemen. 'I am ready to go with you to the police station, Inspector,' he said calmly. He looked at the staring, incredulous faces of his companions. He appeared about to say something, but on reflection seemed to change his mind. Instead, he looked towards Cordelia and said: 'Look after Miriam for me, there's a dear.'

There had been something so theatrical and dramatic about the performance that it took a moment or two before anyone stirred, so enthralled had they been by the spectacle. Indeed, one or two of the Sedgwick Players had been half tempted to applaud, unsure whether or not it was some elaborate display of fiction, albeit in rather poor taste. Even the policemen had been somewhat taken aback by the frankness of Algernon's admission, and it was only now that Inspector Deacon stepped forward to arrest the man he knew to be the murderer and to give him the official warning, which seemed to fall on deaf ears.

As the man they had all known as Algernon Cuffe was led away, he paused for a moment in the doorway to look back and catch one last glimpse of the woman he had loved, and for whom he had committed murder. However, if he had hoped to receive some sign from her that, in spite of everything, she forgave him his crimes and returned his affections, he was to be disappointed, for, at that very moment, Miriam Belmore was standing with her back to the room in her habitual pose of a seemingly cold and aloof figure. He was not to know, of course, that she had turned away purposefully to conceal the tears that were now streaming down her face, nor was he close enough to hear her whisper his name.

'I should like to make a clean breast of it,' Algernon began, lowering himself wearily into a chair. There was only a vague remnant of the military man about his posture now for, all of a sudden, he looked deflated, as if the air had left his body. It would not be long before all that remained of him was the shell of the man he had once been.

On reflection, Algernon had asked that he be allowed to make his confession in the library at Sedgwick Court, rather than at the police station. It is possible that he was deferring the inevitable, and Inspector Deacon had deliberated for a moment, before acquiescing to his request.

'I do not need a solicitor to be present,' Algernon had continued in a weary tone. 'I intend to plead guilty. I do not ask for mercy, for the truth is, I don't deserve it.'

Inspector Deacon looked at him somewhat cynically. While the fellow looked dejected enough and had evidently been living under a great strain, to the inspector's ears, the little speech he had given Miriam had sounded contrived, though it had obviously cost him dear. The policeman could not rid himself of the feeling that the thespian was still playing a part, and was likely to do so up to the very end.

'I should like to tell you how it came about,' said Algernon. 'You will think me a wicked man, and perhaps I am, but I should like someone to know the truth.' He turned to regard Rose. 'I am curious to know how you pieced it all together, Lady Belvedere. I heard you were by way of being an amateur sleuth, but … well, I never … I thought I had covered my tracks too well…'

'I should like to know how it happened that you assumed the identity of Algernon Cuffe, Mr Stapleton,' Inspector Deacon said, rather brusquely.

'To tell you that,' said Algernon, 'I shall have to start at the very beginning. Oh, you needn't worry, Inspector,' he added quickly, as the policeman shifted in his chair, 'it is not a long story; I can tell it in a few words. You will have heard of my father, of course, he is something of a rich tycoon. What is less well known is that he is also a tyrant. He did not approve of me, and I thoroughly despised him. To infuriate him as much as anything else, I chose to marry a woman he considered beneath me.'

'Ursula Stapleton?' said the inspector.

'Yes, or Ursula Westbrooke as she was called then; a young actress, as she referred to herself, though she spent most of her time in the chorus. My father threatened to disown me if I went ahead with the marriage. I knew he'd keep to his word, but it did not worry me as I intended to make my own way in the world.'

'Very noble of you, sir,' muttered Sergeant Lane, who was seated a little behind Algernon, taking down his words in his notebook.

'You might think so, Sergeant,' said Algernon, turning his head to glance at him. 'Unfortunately, my wife thought otherwise. I had assumed, wrongly, that she and I would rub along all right, but I soon came to realise that she had married me only for the money she thought I'd inherit. She did not know my father's character as I did, you see, and fully expected that in time he would change his mind about disinheriting me. When it became obvious that he would not, she took against me and we had no end of arguments and rows. How it would all have ended, I don't know, but then war broke out.' Algernon sighed. 'Fool that I was, I almost welcomed it as a respite from the quarrels that faced me at home. How very young and unsophisticated I was. If I had only known then that I was exchanging one hell for another ... but I digress. I shall get to the point. I became great pals with a fellow named Algernon Cuffe. He was an orphan of sorts, in that his immediate family were dead. But he had some distant relatives in the colonies, and he used to regale me with tales of how he intended to join them after the war and make his fortune.'

'This chap, Cuffe, what happened to him?' asked Inspector Deacon curiously. 'I take it he was killed in the war?'

'Yes,' said Algernon quietly. 'He was the nicest fellow you could hope to meet, was Algernon. He had his whole future mapped out before him, and then ... then an artillery shell fell on the trench we were stationed in ... and did for him. I thought how unfair it was. There was I, who'd had a privileged childhood, trying to leave my life behind and not caring too much what happened to me, and there was Algernon who'd grown up in an orphanage, and was eager to improve his lot ... I couldn't help thinking what a waste it was, his dying like that when he had everything to live for. And I got to thinking, by rights it should have been me who'd died, and it would have been too if Algernon had been asked to run an errand instead of me moments before the shell fell. And then the thought came to me. Why couldn't it have been me that died, not Algernon? What was to stop me assuming his identity and leading the life he had planned? If Dudley Stapleton returned to England, Ursula and I would only make each other miserable. And I knew that, in the event of my death, my father would consider it his duty to provide for my widow; I wouldn't be leaving Ursula destitute. The more I thought about it, the more the idea took hold of me. Algernon and I were about the same age. His distant relatives had never set eyes on him, and there was no one at home in England who would mourn his death. I could see no obvious flaw to my plan. Indeed, I became convinced that it was the right and proper thing to do; it was almost as if fate had decreed it.'

Some of the colour had gone from his face, and Rose wondered whether he was remembering again the sound of the artillery shells, and the smell and the mud of the trenches.

'I suppose I was half mad with the horror of it all; the war, I mean,' continued Algernon. 'I'd just recovered from a bout of trench fever, and the shock of the artillery shell … If I'd been in my right mind, I daresay I wouldn't have gone through with it.'

'You went to the colonies after the war and made your fortune,' said Inspector Deacon, eager to deal with the matter of the murders. 'That's what you did, isn't it? Algernon nodded. 'What made you come back to England?'

'The heat didn't agree with me and, somewhat to my surprise, I found that I rather missed old Blighty,' said Algernon, with a rueful smile. 'It occurred to me that enough time had elapsed whereby I might settle down in a quiet little spot and no one would be any the wiser.'

'The mistake you made was to look up Mr Drury,' said Rose gently, contributing to the conversation for the first time.

'Yes', agreed Algernon, his voice breaking. 'You are quite right, your ladyship. Walter and I had played together as boys and had been great friends in our youth. He was a distant cousin, but I looked on him almost as a brother, I ...' He faltered and stared into the middle distance, as if conjuring up memories of long ago. 'If only I had stayed in the colonies,' he said, his voice hardly above a whisper, but with such feeling that even the policemen were moved. 'Then all this,' he threw his hands in the air in one final desolate gesture, 'would never have happened.'

'I still don't understand why he murdered Ursula Stapleton and Walter Drury, or how you managed to piece it all together,' Cedric said, sitting back in his armchair and stretching out his legs in something of a relaxed fashion.

He was addressing his wife, who was seated on a sofa opposite. It was a few hours since Algernon and the remaining Sedgwick Players had departed, and they were sitting in the now all but deserted drawing room, all thoughts of dinner quite forgotten in the excitement of the events of the evening.

'Begging your pardon, my lord, but Mrs Broughton thought you and her ladyship might like some sandwiches, what with you missing dinner,' said the butler, gliding effortlessly into the room.

'Good old Mrs Broughton,' replied Cedric heartily, 'that's a splendid idea. We'll eat in here, I think. Ask Mrs Broughton to make plenty. We're expecting Inspector Deacon and Sergeant Lane any minute. There's no sign of them yet, I suppose?'

'We're here my lord,' replied the inspector, entering the room, the sergeant just behind him. 'Mr Cuffe is safely in custody.'

'Splendid,' cried the earl. 'Pull up some chairs. My wife was just about to explain to me how she did it; solve the case, I mean.'

Rose glanced rather anxiously at Inspector Deacon, wondering if he would consider her husband's words rather tactless. The inspector, however, smiled at her graciously, as did Sergeant Lane, who said:

'Do tell, miss …your ladyship. How did you know it was all to do with the lady's past?'

'Well, there was the photograph of the Elizabethan Pageant, of course,' said Rose. 'That was the first real clue. It was the photograph Mrs Stapleton found by chance in a provincial newspaper. It was the reason she came to live in Sedgwick. I have the cutting here,' Rose added, producing the article, 'I borrowed it from Miss Sprat.'

Cedric, being the only one of them not to have seen the photograph before, took it from his wife and studied it closely.

'Cordelia, Miriam, Walter and Algernon. He looks rather different without his beard. I say, I suppose it was Algernon she recognised?'

'She recognised them both,' said Rose. 'Algernon and Walter, though of course it was seeing Algernon in the photograph that made her start. Miss Sprat said Mrs Stapleton went awfully white, as if she had seen a ghost. And, of course she had in a way, because she thought her husband was dead.' Rose produced another photograph from her pocket, this time the one taken of Ursula and her husband on their wedding day. 'It occurred to me this morning to compare the two photographs. I suppose I must have noticed a resemblance. When I studied them together, I knew I was right about Algernon Cuffe being Dudley Stapleton.'

'It must have been an awful shock to Mrs Stapleton to see a picture of her husband in the newspaper like that,' agreed Sergeant Lane. 'I wonder she didn't blurt it all out to Miss Sprat.'

'She did in a way,' said Rose. 'She told Miss Sprat that she had spotted a relative by marriage, which of course was true, for it applied as much to Mr Cuffe as to Mr Drury. In fact, it was rather a good pun.'

'Why didn't she tell her maid-companion the truth?' queried Cedric.

'It is only conjecture on my part,' said Rose, 'but I rather fancy that she wished to know the lay of the land before she said anything. She had led Miss Sprat to believe that she and her husband had been a devoted couple. It would have been difficult, therefore, to explain why her husband should have chosen to abandon her and fake his own death.'

'And Walter's role in all this,' said Cedric. 'Was it to plead Algernon's case?'

'Yes,' said Rose. 'It was a frightful shock to Algernon when Ursula appeared in Sedgwick, and I believe Mr Drury did his best to persuade her to leave. That is why he visited her so often. I don't think he had much luck, though, which is why Algernon took to visiting her. He had something of a temper, which explains why Miss Sprat often overheard raised voices.'

'But why did Algernon kill Ursula?' asked Cedric. 'Was she blackmailing him?'

'He killed Mrs Stapleton because he was in love with Miriam Belmore and wanted to marry her,' said Rose, stealing a glance at her husband at mention of the girl's name. 'From what little I have learnt, Ursula Stapleton was rather a vindictive woman. She did not wish to resume her marriage to Algernon and relinquish the allowance she was receiving from the Stapleton family, but neither did she wish to see him settled with a new wife, particularly one who was considerably younger and prettier than herself. She had a hold over Algernon and I think she enjoyed exploiting it.'

'She sounds a thoroughly unpleasant woman,' said Cedric, 'and yet, on the occasions I met her, she seemed perfectly charming.'

Rose suppressed a smile, for it occurred to her that Ursula was the type of woman whose primary aim in life had been to charm every man she met. Aloud, she said:

'Mr Cuffe had intended that his visits to Ursula remain a secret. It is perhaps unfortunate that he chose to visit her in the evenings when he thought there were less people abroad, because it had the opposite effect. The visits soon became the subject of village gossip and news of them reached Miriam's ears. Algernon was faced with the very real possibility that Miriam would throw him over unless he got rid of Ursula.'

'And he decided to poison her?' said Cedric. 'And during the rehearsals as well. I suppose he thought it would be too much of a risk to poison her during one of his visits?'

'Yes. He needed to ensure that a few suspects were present, in the event that it was discovered she had been poisoned. Of course, he hoped that it would be assumed she had died of natural causes.'

'I say,' exclaimed Cedric, 'the poor fellow must have had second thoughts about poisoning her. Do you remember, darling, how he delivered that line telling Ursula not to drink? He spoke so loudly that we all stopped what we were doing and stared at him.' He paused for a moment, evidently remembering the scene. 'I suppose he must have administered the poison at the same time he dropped the pearl into the glass?'

'Yes,' said Rose. 'Giles Kettering saw him do it, or at least he thought he did, but he couldn't be certain.'

'If only he'd said something at the time,' Inspector Deacon said gravely, 'Walter Drury might still be alive.'

There was an awkward silence, and Rose was relieved that the secretary was not present to hear his actions condemned. She could only imagine how wretched he must be feeling over Walter's death.

'What about the business with the wine glass?' enquired Cedric, keen to break the silence. 'Was it Algernon who brought the wine glass from the folly to the house?'

'Yes. He hid it in the waste-paper basket as a temporary measure. His intention was to take it with him when he left the house. Unfortunately for him, Henry Rewe spotted it and, thinking Miriam had put it there, moved it to the bookcase. Algernon must have had a dreadful fright when he couldn't find it, particularly when I announced that Constable Bright was of the opinion that Ursula had been murdered.'

'I suppose,' said Cedric, rather sadly, 'that once it became common knowledge that Ursula had been murdered, Algernon had to kill Walter to prevent him from going to the police. He would have realised Algernon was guilty of the crime.'

'I think he suspected Algernon, but did not know for certain.' Rose said slowly. 'He wished to give him the benefit of the doubt, and did not intend to say anything to the police until he had spoken with him. However, the day it was revealed that Ursula had been murdered, he discovered Algernon had gone to London and was staying the night at his club. Meanwhile, Henry told Walter about his interview with the police and that they suspected him of Ursula's murder because of the business with the wine glass.'

'It helps explain Mr Drury's rather erratic behaviour when we questioned him,' said Inspector Deacon. 'He must have been very worried and on edge. He kept protesting everyone's innocence.'

'Everyone except Mr Cuffe, that is,' said Sergeant Lane.

'The figure Henry saw in Walter Drury's garden last night was Algernon, of course,' said Rose. 'Mr Cuffe confessed as much. He knew at all costs he must speak with his cousin. Mr Drury had spent the evening with Henry, during which the young man had done nothing but say how frightened he was that he would be arrested for Ursula's murder. Walter demanded that Algernon tell him the truth. Initially Algernon claimed he was innocent, but Walter did not believe him. He threatened to ring up the police. Algernon pleaded with him and there was an argument. Rather foolishly, given Algernon's character, Walter turned his back on him and was killed for his efforts.'

'I feel I rather misjudged Mr Drury,' said Inspector Deacon. 'I thought him quite an odd little man. But, in his own way, he was quite remarkable.'

'Do you think it was Walter's death that made Algernon confess?' mused Cedric.

'Yes,' said Inspector Deacon. 'The fellow was full of bluster, but one could tell the fight had gone out of him. Walter Drury was his greatest friend, and the only person who knew his real identity. I am quite certain he never set out to kill him. Besides, as to confessing, once he realised we knew he was Dudley Stapleton, he appreciated the game was up.'

Chapter Twenty-nine

Rose entered the study the next morning at the very moment Cedric put down the telephone receiver. There was nothing very strange in this fact, and she would no doubt have thought nothing of it, had it not been for the rather furtive manner in which her husband had swung round to face her, or his somewhat guilty expression, which suggested that he had been engaged in no ordinary colloquy. It was distinctly odd and, for the first time during their marriage, Rose had the uncomfortable sensation that she had disturbed something of an illicit nature.

'To whom were you speaking?' she demanded primly.

Cedric looked rather taken aback by the question, and was obviously at something of a loss as to what to say. There followed an awkward silence.

'Won't you tell me?' Rose said at last, trying to keep the emotion and suspicion from her voice.

'If I do,' said Cedric quietly, as if he were picking his words with care, 'I will upset you, and I do not wish to do that.' He passed a hand through his hair. 'For some reason, you seem to have quite taken against her.'

'Miriam! You were speaking to Miriam Belmore?'

'What if I was?'

'I see.'

'Rose, I didn't mean that, I –'

But it was too late for apologies and explanations, because Rose had turned tail and fled the room, pulling the door to noisily behind her. It had been an instinctive reaction but, as soon as she walked into the hall, she regretted it, for it occurred to her that she had acted rather foolishly, unwisely even, and that it would be far better to return to the study and have the matter out with her husband. There was no doubt some perfectly innocent explanation for his odd behaviour.

She might well have done just that had she not remembered, in that instant, the look of mortification on Cedric's face at being discovered about his task. With her heart pounding, she leant against the wall, her hand on her chest, as she attempted to regain her composure, grateful that the hall was unusually empty of servants. She heard the sound of a door opening and instinctively looked at the door from which she had emerged, wondering if Cedric had decided after all to come after her. It was not that door that was being opened, however, but the green baize door that led to the servants' quarters. Not wishing the servants to observe her troubled state, and without giving it much thought, she darted into the nearest room, which happened to be the library.

She was brought up short, however, by the sudden realisation that the room was not empty as she had first supposed. For, in front of the fireplace, regarding the picture hung on the wall above it, was a familiar figure of above average height. Rose gave a startled exclamation and the figure turned around.

'Inspector Deacon,' said Rose. 'I thought you had gone.'

'I had, your ladyship, but then I remembered that I had left some of my papers on the desk. It was when I was interviewing Mr Cuffe. I jotted down some notes and I thought it as well to pick them up and have them with me.'

'Oh. Where is Sergeant Lane? Isn't he with you?'

'He took the opportunity to visit your servants. I believe he has made rather an impression on your cook; she has promised him a copy of the recipe for her spiced apple cake for him to give to his mother.'

'I see,' said Rose. She put a hand to her head and the inspector took a step forward.

'I say, are you all right, your ladyship? You look a little queer, if you don't mind my saying so.'

'I didn't expect to find you here, that's all.'

Later, Rose wondered whether she would have spoken as she did next, had she not been in such a confused and agitated state. Had she not surprised Cedric, she most probably would have left the inspector to his task, and bid him a hasty farewell due to the lateness of the hour. Instead, before she could stop herself, she found herself alluding to the last time she had seen him at Madame Renard's flat.

'We were in that little makeshift kitchen, do you remember? We were washing up the tea things. You were going to say something to me; ask me a question, I think. I have often wondered what you meant to say. Of course, it was a long time ago and I daresay you can't remember, I ...'

She allowed her sentence to falter, rather alarmed by the expression that had appeared on Inspector Deacon's face. For it was clear that he was rather taken aback by her question; he had suddenly averted his gaze to stare at the floor, two bright spots of colour appearing on his cheeks. A silence followed and Rose, aware that she had made some awful *faux pas* by alluding to a delicate matter, cursed herself, fervently wishing she could take back the words she had so foolishly uttered, realising that she should never have given them voice.

'I'm sorry, I shouldn't have asked you,' she said miserably, mortified by her own actions. She turned and made as if to leave. 'If you will excuse me, I –'

'Rose,' Inspector Deacon said.

The intimacy implied by the use of her Christian name arrested Rose in the act of leaving, her hand on the door knob. He had her attention now, but she was aware, as soon as she turned back, that he could not bring himself to look her in the eye. The colour had risen rapidly to his cheeks.

'I think you know what I was going to ask you,' he said quietly. 'I cannot repeat it now, for both our circumstances have altered. If I could, I –'

'Are you there, sir?'

Rose felt the door move sharply against her hand, the force propelling her slightly towards the wall. A moment later Sergeant Lane appeared, a hand-written recipe in his hand. 'I beg your pardon, your ladyship, I did not see you there.' He gave her a curious look.

'I was just telling her ladyship that we must be leaving,' Inspector Deacon said quickly. 'All my notes were there,' he said, gathering together his papers. 'They were just where you said they'd be, your ladyship, in the desk where your servant had put them for safekeeping. Well, Lane, I think that is everything. We had better get going.'

'Yes,' replied his subordinate. 'We mustn't be late, sir, not with your wedding tomorrow; the future Mrs Deacon would never forgive me.'

'You are getting married tomorrow, Inspector?' Rose was amazed that her voice sounded like its usual self.

'Yes, he is, miss …your ladyship,' answered Sergeant Lane. For he had noticed that for some reason the inspector was experiencing some difficulty in finding his voice; he had opened his mouth to speak, but no words had come out. 'Of course,' Sergeant Lane continued, conversationally,' it won't be such a grand affair as your own wedding. There won't be pictures of it in the society pages. But everyone at the station is looking forward to it all the same.'

It was only on the point of leaving that Inspector Deacon seemed to find his voice.

'Until we meet again, Lady Belvedere.'

'Will we?' asked Rose, rather doubtfully, though she held his gaze.

'Oh, we're certain to, miss,' said Sergeant Lane. 'You have a knack, if you don't mind my saying, for being where there's a murder, and we're employed to deal with them. I don't doubt we'll meet again under similar circumstances.'

'I hope so,' muttered Rose, as she watched them leave. 'That we meet again,' she clarified, 'not that there will be another murder.'

With that, she turned back into the hall, somewhat deep in thought, wondering what the future would bring.

BIBLIOGRAPHY

Harkup, Kathryn, *A is For Arsenic*, Bloomsbury Sigma, 2015

Shakespeare William, *Hamlet, Prince of Denmark*

AUTHOR'S NOTE

The folly at Sedgwick Court is loosely based on the Pantheon and Temple of Flora follies located in the grounds of Stourhead in Wiltshire, England, owned by the National Trust.

25141536R00150

Printed in Poland
by Amazon Fulfillment
Poland Sp. z o.o., Wrocław